'1

NEL

THE UNCHANGING HEART

THE UNCHANGING HEART

Maggie Bennett

This first world edition published in Great Britain 2007 by
SEVERN HOUSE PUBLISHERS LTD of
9–15 High Street, Sutton, Surrey SM1 1DF.
This first world edition published in the USA 2007 by
SEVERN HOUSE PUBLISHERS INC of
595 Madison Avenue, New York, N.Y. 10022.

British Library Cataloguing in Publication Data

Bennett, Maggie
     The Unchanging Heart
     1. Social classes - England - Fiction 2. London (England) -
     Social conditions - 18th century - Fiction 3. Love stories
     I. Title
     823.9'2[F]

ISBN-13: 978-0-7278-6519-9   (cased)
ISBN-13: 978-1-84751-021-1   (trade paper)

All Severn House titles are printed on acid-free paper.

Typeset by Palimpsest Book Production Ltd.,
Grangemouth, Stirlingshire, Scotland.
Printed and bound in Great Britain by
MPG Books Ltd., Bodmin, Cornwall.

ACKNOWLEDGEMENTS

My grateful thanks are due to:

My friend Chris Wainwright for introducing me to Masefield's *Reynard the Fox*.

The hunting diarists for guidance regarding the history of fox-hunting.

And as always, my agent Judith Murdoch.

Prologue

On the Common

1770

The boy stretched himself out in the long grass of Cove Common, and closed his eyes. The low humming of myriad winged insects was more soothing to his spirits than any human sound, and far above him a lark poured out her lovely song. It must be like this in heaven, he thought, breathing a long sigh of sheer contentment. In his twelfth year, Billy Siggery was strong and wiry and had spent the morning digging in his mother's vegetable patch where he grew potatoes, onions, carrots and beans. Widow Siggery had gathered enough gooseberries to make half a dozen pies and tarts, far above her own needs. The extra few shillings they would add to her earnings as washerwoman at Oak Hall would be handy. She turned and smiled fondly upon her young son, and then, as always, a shadow fell across her face. She sighed resignedly.

Billy's wide grey eyes gazed up at the arching July sky, where a few high, wispy clouds signified that the sunny spell would continue. His feet were bare, but the coarse fustian breeches he wore were uncomfortably hot. He kept his sweat-stained shirt unbuttoned to the waist. His face, browned by the sun and framed by a mop of thick brown hair, held some curious scars on his forehead, one which had split his right eyebrow in half, but aside from these healed blemishes, he seemed to be a typical healthy country boy.

Until he stood up to walk and his awkward gait showed the deformity of his left foot. When he opened his mouth to speak, he was also hindered by a severe stammer that made it almost impossible to understand him, no matter how hard he struggled to overcome it. And so Billy's destiny was to become the village fool in Wollaston, set apart from the other boys.

On the breeze his sharp ears caught the sound of girls' voices. He sat up quickly, immediately recognizing three girls, a year or two younger than he, who had also come up to the Common that afternoon. One was Elizabeth Pond, the poor parson's daughter, and another her close friend Meg Venn from the tumbledown cottage on the other side of the Common. It had been built in the last century on a half-acre of land where Zack Venn also grazed his pig, goat and half a dozen chickens. The third girl was Sally Partridge. Elizabeth and Meg wore similar plain gowns of unbleached calico, whereas their little friend Sally was more daintily dressed. Elizabeth's fair head was protected by a sun bonnet; Meg wore a large, very old straw hat of her mother's, tied round with a stringy ribbon to keep it on over her dark curls, and pretty little Sally wore a hat of fine straw, decorated with silk ribbons. They chatted eagerly as they gathered dandelions and sow thistle, whatever they could find for the Venn's ever-hungry pig.

'Did you see that rabbit run across to the copse?' asked Elizabeth. 'Look over there, maybe he'll show himself again.'

'Never mind the rabbit, Lizzie, we sees plenty o' those, an' Pa traps a few of 'em,' answered Meg. 'D'ye see what I see, over there? Silly Billy Siggery sittin' up an' lookin' at us. My ma says he shouldn't be allowed out on the Common, follerin' folks an' makin' them noises. She's told me to keep well away from 'im.'

Little Sally stared at Meg in horror, but Elizabeth tut-tutted.

'Oh, go away with you, Meg, there's no harm in poor Billy. Father reckons he sees more than folks give him credit for. You know Father's teaching him to read, and says he's quicker even than young Adam Horrocks, and twice as good as those three ploughboys who come each week to fidget and laugh and play the fool 'til Father can't stand it any longer and turns them out. It is what they've been wanting all along – the great numbskulls!'

'And does Mr Pond – I mean does your father teach Billy then, after they've gone?' asked Sally, looking slightly askance at the boy who had got up and was slowly coming towards them, dragging his club foot.

Elizabeth hesitated, turning down the corners of her mouth, for the parson's attempts to educate Billy Siggery was a sore point at home. 'Well, yes, Father can teach him well enough in this fine weather, but if it's wet they go into the toolshed.'

'Why? Can't Mr Pond teach him indoors, like the others?' questioned Sally.

'My mother won't have Billy in the house,' replied Elizabeth with a shrug.

'Huh! No more would *my* ma,' said Meg with a nod in the direction of the boy. 'Everybody knows 'e ain't right in the 'ead, an' sometimes 'e falls down in a fit, like in the gospel stories when Jesus cast devils out o' folks.'

'Billy's got no devil,' said the parson's daughter indignantly. 'And he's had no fits since he was little. If the Lord Jesus was here this afternoon, He might mend Billy's twisted foot, but there's no devil to be cast out! Don't let her frighten you, Sally.'

'I ain't so sure, Lizzie,' said Meg. 'There was dumb spirits that got into folks and stopped 'em talkin'. Maybe 'e's got one o' 'em.'

'Sssh, be quiet, Meg. He'll hear us,' Sally said, creeping closer to Elizabeth and hiding behind her skirt.

'Well, I ain't goin' to speak to 'im,' said Meg, turning her back and walking a little distance away. 'You just watch out, Lizzie Pond!'

The boy approached the parson's daughter with a smile of greeting. He pointed to the basket she was carrying. 'P–p–pig,' he managed to say. 'F–f–f . . . the p–p–pig.'

'That's right, Billy,' answered Elizabeth. 'Meg and Sally and me, we're gathering stuff for the Venns' pig. What he likes best is snails, only there aren't many of them up here on the Common.'

'Ah,' said Billy, nodding and pointing up to the sky. 'N–n–n–no r–r–r–r—'

'That's it, Billy, no rain. When it rains the snails come out, and then ye can go out with a pail and pick them off the hedgerows.'

Meg Venn watched from a short distance at her friend talking so easily and naturally to poor Billy. She knew that *her* parents would be cross if they caught her talking to him –

Pa might even shout and give her a slap around her ears. While she was wishing he would go away, she heard her young brother Sam calling to her, and in a moment he was at her side, accompanied by a ploughboy known as Chopper, who was always grinning and getting up to mischief.

'Hey, Siggery, don't ye say nothin' to them girls!' yelled Sam Venn, who was a stocky child as big as his sister although he was almost a year younger.

A wary look came into Billy's eyes and he glanced at Elizabeth.

'Shut up, you little monkey!' Elizabeth said to Sam, who continued to insult Billy. 'Be off with you!'

'That's right, go away!' cried Sally Partridge, emboldened by Elizabeth's stance, but Chopper only grinned. This looked like good sport to him. Bending down, he picked up a small, sharp stone and threw it at Billy's head. It caught him above the left ear and he cried out in pain. Sam Venn picked up another stone.

'Watch me score with ev'ry throw,' he said gleefully. As the stone hit the back of Billy's head, the boy tried to shield himself with his arms, and Sally Partridge screamed.

'Another! Here's another!' shouted Chopper, throwing a much larger stone at the boy. 'Crack 'is skull open, Sam.'

The girls had been staring in dismay, but Elizabeth now found her voice. 'Stop it, you great louts, *stop it*! He's cleverer than either of you – *stop it!*'

As Chopper bent down to pick up another stone, he was suddenly kicked so hard in the buttocks that he lost his balance and fell forward, hitting his head on a stony bit of ground. Sam Venn found himself attacked by what seemed like a wild animal, a fury of screaming, kicking calico with flailing arms. Sally stared in astonishment, then ran off to take refuge with Meg.

'You thieves, liars, extortioners, scribes, hypocrites!' shrieked the parson's daughter who knew her Bible well. 'You whited sepulchres, full of dead men's bones!'

A fist flew into Sam's right eye and he staggered backwards. A kick caught him on the shin. Chopper had got to his feet, gaping at the girl's fury. Billy turned round and began to return to the group, for he was ashamed to leave the girls to defend themselves.

'No, Billy, *no!*' cried Elizabeth. 'Go along, get yourself indoors as quick as you can! Go on!'

She was not to be disobeyed, and Billy did as she bid him, limping his way down the hill to his mother's. The girl then threw herself at Chopper.

'Get orf me, ye little devil!' he roared, beating off her fists before she could deliver a blow to his eye. 'Leave orf, I tell yer!'

The words she used were almost more humiliating than the blows. 'You great idiot, you dunce, half-wit, numbskull! Billy's got more sense than you were ever born with.'

Sam Venn stood holding his hand to his eye. Blood trickled down his cheek alarmingly, and Meg decided it was time for her to intervene. 'Get yeself off 'ome, Sam, an' let Ma see to that eye. Don't say a word about Lizzie Pond, and I won't tell 'em 'ow you an' Chopper was beaten by a girl for throwin' stones at poor Billy.'

Sam whimpered, his hand still over his eye. 'Come on, Chopper, let's go. Gimme a hand – I can't see out o' this eye.'

'Parson's daughter, eh?' growled Chopper. 'More like a cat out o' hell. Takes after 'er ma, that one.'

He took Sam's arm, and they disappeared off in the direction from which they had come.

Elizabeth picked up her sun bonnet, shook the dust from it, and adjusted her gown, which had become twisted round her sturdy body. She stared after Billy's retreating figure; he was safely on his way home, and by common consent, the three girls also made for Wollaston, little Sally thinking what a tale she would have to tell when she got home.

Elizabeth felt that she should say something about her treatment of Meg's young brother.

'I'm not sorry for clouting him, Meg. He deserved it.'

'I can see ye're not sorry, Lizzie. It's true 'e asked for what 'e got, but . . . well, I never knew ye was as strong as that or as wild. Ye could've blinded him.'

The incident had clearly astonished Meg, who eyed her best friend with a new and wary respect. They parted where the road forked; Elizabeth and Sally going into the village and Meg toiling up towards the dilapidated dwelling where Zack and Mary Venn lived with her and her two brothers.

'Ah, good girl – ye've picked a deal o' greenstuff for the

ol' man,' said Mary, referring not to her husband but their much-prized pig. 'Ye ought to see the state young Sam's come 'ome in – been in a fight somewhere. 'Is nose is bleedin' an' 'e'll have a great black eye. I *told* 'im to keep away from that Chopper, there's always trouble when 'e's around. Anyway, Sam's 'ad a good beatin' from a lad 'e said 'e didn't know. Less said to yer pa the better, Meg. D'ye 'ear? 'E's been surlier than ever lately.'

Meg Venn kept her own counsel, and said nothing about her brother's encounter. She knew that her father wore himself out trying to scratch a living from his strip of common land and her mother was often hard pressed to put food on the table. The elder boy, Joshua, would soon be leaving home to work as a farm labourer for Squire Horrocks, though he was scarcely twelve years old. 'If Silly Billy Siggery can dig, so can Josh,' Zack had said. 'It's only right 'e should earn 'is own bread.'

Mary Venn sighed at the thought of parting with her first-born, but saw the wisdom of turning him out to make his own living. Meg too would have to find a place as a maid-servant in another year or two. Mary Venn silently hoped that none of her children would know the back-breaking poverty that had turned Zack into a dour, embittered man and herself into a woman old before her time, worn down by the daily grind. She was always tired these days and that made her cross when she would much rather have been patient with her children.

In fact Meg understood that her parents cared for each other in their way and wanted the best for their sons and daughter. In spite of Zack's rough manner and Mary's weary sighings, Meg would not have changed places with her friend Lizzie Pond: for there was precious little goodwill at the parson's house.

Elizabeth saw Sally safely home, and then made for the row of cottages facing the green, their front gardens brilliant with summer blooms. Her heartbeat had slowed down and her face was reasonably composed as she passed the cottages. Her parents lived in the end one, a humble dwelling sometimes called the parsonage, though there were few visitors to it. Mrs Pond was not known for her hospitality and even on warm summer days the front door was always firmly shut. Elizabeth went round to the back, where her father was hoeing the earth. When he saw her he stood up, straightening his back, and smiled fondly upon his only child.

'Ah, 'tis our Lizzie! Have you had a pleasant walk with your friends, dear? Isn't it hot?'

'And about time too!' came Mrs Pond's voice as she appeared at the kitchen door, hands on her hips, regarding her daughter disapprovingly. 'A fine lot o' help you've been to *me*, miss, gaddin' about all over the place while I'm busy workin'! I hope you ain't been up on Cove Common – there's all sorts go there and get up to no good. Well, have you?'

'We went a little way up there, Mother, to gather greenstuff for the Venns' pig.'

'The bare-faced cheek o' them Venns, gettin' other people to do their work! It'd be more to Mary Venn's credit to keep an eye on her youngest – always consortin' with that Chopper. He'll end up bein' hanged one o' these days. An' did you see anythin' o' that idiot boy yer father brings round here?'

Father and daughter exchanged a glance. It was no use trying to stem the vicious flow from the parson's wife. They had to wait until she had finished before they would be able to talk with each other. To Herbert Pond his golden-haired girl was ample compensation for his wife's habitual ill-humour, and Elizabeth adored her father. She was not the only one to realize his true goodness, his everyday practice of true Christianity.

The real parsonage had been let to a pair of virtuous sisters who jointly ran a small school for village girls. Dr Webb, the incumbent of the Suffolk parish of St Bede's, lived in Ipswich for most of the year, and Mr Pond was paid a miserly sum for discharging the rector's official duties. It was well known that he far exceeded what was expected of him for in addition to taking services, christening, marrying and burying as required, he was also a regular visitor to most of the village homes. He knew every family, visited the sick and admonished wrongdoers, he had even been known to kneel down and pray with them so that they might see the error of their ways and repent. He settled arguments, acting as an unofficial magistrate, the actual Justice of the Peace being Squire Horrocks.

Herbert Pond eked out his meagre income by teaching a class of boys to read; they came twice-weekly to his house and sat in his study for the lessons, much to Mrs Pond's indignation at this invasion. She frequently shouted angrily at Mr Pond, to the amusement of his pupils, who reported her harsh words to their families, amidst laughter and pity for the poor parson who was married to such a scold. Those who had learned his worth through his kindness to them in times of trouble saw him as a suffering saint, an example to all, but to others he was a figure of fun, the classic henpecked husband.

'Young Adam never fails to set us laughing when he comes home from his lessons with the latest tale of poor Pond,' chuckled Squire Horrocks to Sir John de Boville. They had been to look at Horrocks's prize bull, a formidable beast of which his owner was extremely proud.

'That bull stands no nonsense from the cows, sir,' the squire said. 'When he would mount one, he rears up and will serve her, no matter how contrary she may be! Oh, he is the best type, and will breed a good herd of cattle for years to come.'

Sir John gave him a sideways glance. 'Would that Parson Pond would imitate him and get his wife with child again, Horrocks!'

'Either that or put a scold's bridle on her,' rejoined the squire. ''Tis a pity we have no ducking stool in Wollaston.'

'It would be a different story if she belonged to me!' said the baronet laughing. 'But I doubt if Pond ever dares to assert his power over her. They have only one daughter – she seems to be a little beauty in the making – but every man should have at least one son for the sake of the family name.'

The squire was following his train of thought. 'She has probably banished him from her bed to avoid another child. Their girl has lived a half-score of years without siblings.' He smiled, hesitated and then asked, 'Tell me, sir, what age would you take Pond to be?'

'Hmm, I don't know. He walks for miles and has a good head of hair. Forty?'

'He is just thirty, sir. She's a few years older than he.'

'Good heavens, she *has* worn him down, the shrew!' The baronet gave an amused guffaw, then noticed the squire's meaningful look: he too became thoughtful.

'Aha, I see where you're leading, Horrocks. If the daughter be indeed ten years old or thereabouts, and Pond is only thirty, it follows that he bedded the woman when he was scarcely twenty. What a fatal pairing, then, that tumbled him into marriage. Oh, foolish youth! And she has punished him by locking her door ever since. That is the most comical thing I've heard this week, Horrocks! Say, do you think he had drunk too much strong ale when he . . . God knows, *she* can never have been a tasty dish!'

Both men laughed heartily as they returned from the field, making many bawdy jokes at the parson's expense, until they were met by Lady de Boville at the door of Oak Hall. She was frowning.

'Do you know, Sir John, young Richard has been out on his new horse for a gallop and he was pulled up short by that disagreeable fellow – what's his name? The one who lives in that wretched cottage on Cove Common. The brute had the effrontery to tell Richard not to ride over his grazing land, scaring the chickens. Imagine that, Sir John – our son forbidden to ride on common property!'

The baronet, Master of the Wollaston Hunt, shook his head in irritation. ''Tis that sullen oaf Isaac Venn – never shows any respect for his betters. His sons had better not come to me for work because I won't have them.'

'Neither will I take on the daughter,' replied the lady. 'The whole family should be driven out of Wollaston and go on poor relief.'

Squire Horrocks said nothing, remembering that he had agreed to take on Joshua Venn at harvest time. He had felt sorry for Mary Venn, a poor woman who had lost her health and looks in the daily struggle to make ends meet.

'It might come to that one day, my love,' said Sir John. 'I may have to claim their land. With these new seed drills and harrows that can be drawn by horses, there's going to be a demand for more land to cultivate. The rising population in the towns will be wanting more food. Common grazing land for mere peasants is a waste of available acres. We're going to need bigger farms – eh, Horrocks?'

The squire nodded. He had not taken to the new agricultural methods at first and had opposed the ideas of men like Jethro Tull and Lord 'Turnip' Townshend, but he now saw the sound economy of crop rotation and the growing of winter feed. He was also sorry to hear of the bitter hardship endured by poor peasants who had lost their livings due to the enforced enclosures. However, it would not do to go against the de Bovilles. Horrocks had only earned his honorary title of squire through his prosperity as a farmer, and his standing in Wollaston depended on keeping in with the landowners at Oak Hall who could, it was said, trace their ancestry back to William the Conqueror.

So he merely smiled and accepted a glass of Sir John's excellent Madeira wine; they lit their pipes and continued to talk of farming methods until the summer dusk fell, when Horrocks took his leave. As he arrived at his own comfortable farmhouse, he was greeted by his loudly barking dog and his wife Annie, who gave him a kiss.

'I don't like you spending a whole evening up at Oak Hall,' she reproached him. 'Lady de Boville doesn't bother herself with visiting *us* and neither do her haughty daughters!'

'Don't fret, Annie,' he replied. ''Tis better for me to stay in his good books. And besides, it might not be wise for the de Bovilles to come here and see our servants – the kind of people they won't have in their own homes.'

'Well, as long as you don't take on that poor idiot Siggery out of pity,' she told him.

That night Billy Siggery lay on his straw mattress and looked out of the window at the night sky, thick with stars. His mother had been angry and upset when she saw his new crop of cuts and bruises and had bathed his face with spring water.

'Them great oafs, they be nothin' but cowards,' she muttered. 'My poor boy, ye've got twice the sense o' any o' them – Parson Pond says so!'

But the truth was that Billy had been even more shaken by Elizabeth Pond's furious defence of him than by the stone throwing. And when he thought of her it was not as a furious girl kicking and punching the two astonished boys; he saw her smiling, her sun bonnet over her golden hair. Smiling and talking and not afraid of him.

One

Departures

March, 1777

The vicarage school was closed for the day out of respect for the bereaved Partridge family, but the young pupil-teacher was asked by Miss Buxton to stay at the school for the afternoon.

'We'd like you to take the needlework class, Miss Pond. My sister and I need to attend poor Sally's funeral and serve refreshments to the mourners afterwards.'

'Very well, Miss Buxton,' replied Miss Pond, knowing that her father had a painful afternoon ahead, conducting the funeral service and burial of the young woman who had been her childhood playmate. Pretty little Sally had fallen into a consumptive decline and rapidly weakened in spite of all the tender care and herbal remedies that her sorrowing parents had tried. Many Wollaston folk would follow her coffin into the church and from there to the graveside on this blowy March day.

Both the younger and elder Miss Buxtons would be in attendance wearing their sombre dark gowns and capes, silently following the mournful procession, both supporting the relatives and discreetly keeping order. Parson Pond greatly appreciated their unofficial help at such events and was proud that his Elizabeth could safely be left in charge at the school. She mostly assisted with the younger girls who found it hard to follow the elder Miss Buxton's reading and writing classes and Miss Letty Buxton's instructions in simple arithmetic. Both sisters shared the daily scripture lesson, one telling Biblical stories from both the Old and New Testaments, the other teaching them prayers, hymns and simple songs about country life and how good children should behave towards the wild creatures that God had placed on the earth. The sisters played the piano and allowed Miss Pond to practise on the instrument after classes were ended, for she was seldom encouraged to practise at home. Her mother often declared that there were better things to do than 'tinkle away at that thing', though her father loved to hear her playing when Mrs Pond was out of the house. He smiled fondly at her hesitant progress and did not hear when she struck a wrong note. He regularly declared that her playing was greatly improved.

Dear Papa! She had remained his only child and dearest treasure, for Mrs Pond's ill-temper and sharp tongue had only served to bring father and daughter closer together. It was he who had approached the Miss Buxtons on her behalf, to be taken on as an assistant, when she was fifteen. They had been reluctant but sympathetic, and had settled for a month's trial at sixpence a week, for they were not wealthy. Three years later they sometimes wondered how they had managed without her; she was now paid a shilling a week, with the promise of a further sixpence the following year.

She knew that Sally's burial would be a desperately sorrowful occasion and was almost thankful to have an excuse not to attend. Mr Pond had regularly visited the home of the dying girl for some weeks, bringing her the Blessed Sacrament of Holy Communion and endeavouring to prepare her family for the end. It pained him deeply to discourage the mother's desperate hopes of a recovery and instead to direct her to pray for the strength to accept the inevitable. Elizabeth had seen his grief for the family when Sally drew her last breath and lay still and peaceful. He was unable to confide in Mrs Pond, and did not care to burden his beloved Lizzie; even so, she comforted him with her loving glances and her habit of sitting quietly beside him with her embroidery while he composed his sermons and attended to parish business. After an hour she would usually rise and brew a pot of tea for them both, though she was frequently rebuked by her mother for not consulting her first.

'D'you know how much I have to pay for them tea leaves? It costs money to bring luxuries across the sea, miss.' Whereupon Elizabeth would always nod silently but she would never apologize, knowing that if she asked permission, it would never be granted. Once a pot was brewed, however, all three of them would partake of it, and Mr Pond and Elizabeth would exchange satisfied looks. When he had finished his book work he would go to his little library and take down Chaucer's *Canterbury Tales* or one of the works of Shakespeare or a favourite metaphysical poet to read and discuss with Elizabeth. These were happy hours for them both.

At eighteen Elizabeth Pond was an undoubted beauty, with deep blue eyes and abundant corn-coloured hair; she already had a few tentative admirers in Wollaston. Ploughboys nudged each other and grinned as she walked past them and older men sighed and dreamed of their youth. The only possible candidate in Mr Pond's eyes – and he prayed that he might not lose his darling for a few more years – was the squire's son Adam. He was a strong, self-confident youth who would follow in his father's footsteps and eventually own the Horrocks' farm, taking his place among the more prosperous farmers of Wollaston.

It seemed that young Adam had made up his mind for he had asked his father's permission to pay court to the fair Miss Pond. The squire and his wife were rather doubtful, especially Mrs Horrocks. The girl was undoubtedly pretty and had pleasing manners and a sensible head on her shoulders, but what a dismal prospect for their son, to marry the daughter of a poor parson and gain a mother-in-law like Mrs Pond. Besides, the boy was not yet twenty-one and had not seen much of the world beyond Wollaston. At the same time, the squire thought that it might be as well for Adam to stake his claim, as it were, before a more impatient suitor appeared and carried the girl off. Adam was therefore told that he should not marry for at least two years, but that he might become acquainted with Miss Pond, and see how he liked her.

Adam therefore arranged to be strolling outside the vicarage school when the object of his affections emerged at the end of classes. He raised his hat to her and began to engage her in polite conversation, in which he was not very fluent.

'I trust that your parents are well, Miss Pond?'

'Yes, thank you for your kind enquiry, Mr Horrocks, they are both well,' she answered with a shy smile. 'And the squire, is he well? And Mrs Horrocks and your sisters and brother – are they not also in good health?'

His reply was unexpected. 'By heaven, Miss Pond, you are the handsomest girl I ever did yet behold! And the sweetest. May I be allowed to call you Elizabeth?'

She looked up into his flushed, eager face and blushed crimson.

'I beg your pardon, Mr Horrocks, I'm obliged to you, but . . . you may call me by my Christian name if you wish, but now I must be getting home. Good day to you, Mr Horrocks.'

She walked away so smartly that he knew it would be unwise to follow her; he had so clearly been dismissed, though she had not been entirely unkind. At least she had given him leave to call her Elizabeth.

Elizabeth's thoughts were in a whirl when she reached home. She was flustered and disturbed by the encounter, but not displeased – how could she be by such a flattering address? On reflection she decided that Adam Horrocks had meant well, but she knew that she had no wish to leave her father's house yet. Her dear papa would miss her and there would be nobody to ease the burden of Mrs Pond's scathing tongue. And besides, her young heart was not yet awakened.

When the mourners had left Sally's graveside, refreshed by the tea, lemonade and yarrow beer served by the Miss Buxtons, Herbert Pond did not go home straightaway. Instead he went and sat in the empty church. It was his habit to take refuge here and let the silence of the centuries flow into his troubled mind.

St Bede's was a fine example of a medieval church with a square tower and intricate stone carving, such as the fearsome-looking gargoyle waterspouts projecting from the roof gutters. A fourteenth-century wall painting showed a haloed shepherd holding a sheep, with three other strangely human-faced sheep looking on, probably inspired by the days when Wollaston had been an important stopping place on the wool trade route. Herbert Pond felt honoured by God for the privilege of serving the parish from such a splendid building. He constantly prayed for wisdom to carry out his duties to his flock and in particular he prayed for more patience at home. In recent years he had found it harder to continue to love his wife, the servant girl he had selfishly taken in a moment of blind passion all those years ago, and whom he had then married for the sake of her virtue and his vocation as a preacher. It had been a false step, yes, but what happiness had come to him as a result of it. He never failed to thank God for his darling, the apple of his eye, his lovely Lizzie. How great was the love of God, who, while taking away with one hand, had so freely given with the other!

Pond was also grateful to the Miss Buxtons who had proved a blessing to the parish in general and to his daughter in particular. In addition to about a dozen village girls with an age range from six to twelve, the ladies also offered weekly board and lodging to three older girls, daughters of clergy in other parishes who could not walk to Wollaston and back each day. Of the village girls, half were farmers' daughters and the rest came from respectable tradesmen's homes. Mr Pond could not have wished for more pleasant employment for his daughter; even Mrs Pond had to admit that Lizzie had done well for herself.

'Lizzie dear, I want you to come with me on a visit this afternoon. It's all right, I've spoken to the Miss Buxtons – and there's no need to bother your mother.'

'Why, Papa, what's the matter?' cried Elizabeth, alarmed by the gravity of his tone.

''Tis poor Mrs Venn who's taken to her bed. She must have good reason for doing so. Young Joshua told Squire Horrocks that Zack has sent for Meg to come home from Flaxford and I fear things are going badly with them. There's this bad feeling between Zack and the de Bovilles over the enclosure of common land.

'Oh, Papa, I must see Meg!' exclaimed Elizabeth with self-reproach. 'I haven't been near their cottage this great while, ever since she went into service at Flaxford, but I should have called on Mrs Venn. The trouble is, he's so bad-tempered.'

'Yes, my dear,' said Pond with a sigh. 'I've been turned away from the door on more than one occasion. Zack Venn can be obstinate, but I hope your presence might gain me entrance.'

They set out for Cove Common, Pond in his threadbare black coat and gaiters, crowned with a shovel hat, Elizabeth in her brown cloak and hood, for it was a blustery day. She had taken three eggs from the china crock in the pantry as an offering to the Venns, for Zack no longer kept chickens. Mrs Pond had counted the remaining jars of blackberry and apple jelly on the pantry shelf and had probably counted the eggs too, but Elizabeth was resigned to facing an angry accusation on her return; eggs would be welcome in a house where there was sickness. She carefully wrapped them in a soft cloth and placed them in her leather bag.

It was a twenty-minute walk, going at a good pace, and Pond braced himself for a hostile reception at the ill-fitting door that hung by one rusty hinge. To his relief it was opened by Meg, who stared for a moment at the parson, and then exclaimed at the sight of her childhood friend.

'Lizzie! Oh, I'm that glad to see ye – an' Mr Pond. It's good that ye've called for I been thinkin' o' sendin' for ye.' She lowered her voice. 'Was it Joshua told ye that Ma's ailin'? She be worn to a shadow an' can't get 'erself up off the bed hardly!'

She suddenly realized that they were still standing at the open door. 'Oh, come in, come in – Pa's out at the back seein' to the poor ol' pig, so ye can see Ma before 'e comes in.'

They followed her through a cluttered, stale-smelling living room where wet clothing hung from a length of rope, through to a dim inner room containing a low wooden bed and two straw mattresses covered with blankets. On the bed lay Mary Venn and Elizabeth had to stifle a gasp at the sight of her thin deathly-pale face. She stared blankly at her visitors without recognition and turned her hollow eyes on Meg.

''Tis the good parson come to see ye, Ma,' said Meg quietly. 'Him an' Lizzie both.'

'Ah!' the woman made a wordless sound in her throat and tried to sit up. A faint smile lit her wasted features and she held out a skinny arm to Pond. 'Ye've come,' she whispered hoarsely. 'Ye must've heard me.'

Pond leaned over her and took hold of her hand. 'Don't bestir yourself, Mary – don't try to speak. I have come to see how you do. You've been very ill, I hear, and—'

'Yer a man o' God, Herbert Pond,' she interrupted. 'I been prayin' for the sight o' ye. Give me a blessin', that's what I'm wantin'. F–forgive me my sins . . .' Her voice trailed away and she closed her eyes, wearied by the effort.

Falling on his knees beside her, Pond's eyes filled with

tears, but a smile of understanding lit his face as he assured her, 'Your sins be forgiven, Mary, in the name of the Father, the Son and the Holy Ghost. Christ our Saviour welcomes you and blesses you, my dear sister. May He grant you His peace.'

Mary Venn did not open her eyes again, but her calm expression showed Meg and Elizabeth that the parson's prayers had not gone unheard. They joined with him in saying the Lord's Prayer and then he rose from his knees and leaned over to kiss Mary's forehead. He could see that the end was near, but he had done his duty now. Meg Venn stifled a sob and whispered that they had better go before her Pa returned.

It was too late. Zack was already in the outer room, raising his voice in an angry bellow.

'Who've yer let in, Meg? Who's come sniffin' round 'ere like one o' them 'ounds o' the Deboffles?' He meant the de Bovilles. 'Oh, ah, I might've known,' he growled when Meg led the parson and his daughter out of the room where Mary lay. 'Who sent *you*, yer cantin' fool, to come 'ere mouthin' over my wife? Nobody asked yer to come now!'

Parson Pond looked the man straight in the eye. 'The Lord ordered me to come here this afternoon, Isaac, and I've seen Mrs Venn and given her what the Lord sent me to give to her.'

'Well, now yer can get out an' leave us to starve, same as all the rest,' said Venn in a surly but quieter tone, for the parson's mild face had a certain calm authority.

'We'd best be going, Papa,' murmured his daughter. Elizabeth drew a little cloth bundle from her bag. 'Here are three eggs, Meg – maybe your mother—'

'To hell wi' yer damned eggs, yer dolled-up miss!' snarled Venn, though Meg picked up the eggs with alacrity. 'Ye're very fine these days, trippin' about the village, hobnobbin' wi' them two ol' maids! Not once have yer shown yer face up 'ere, not since Meg went to Flaxford to wait on the so-called gentry for a few miserable pence. Hang 'em all, I say!'

'You've turned me away from your door with harsh words, Isaac,' said Pond gently. 'I could hardly send my daughter to be turned away in the same manner knowing that Meg wasn't here.'

'Huh! Her's been willin' enough to simper at the Horrocks's son, I hear! Ye'll make a fine match there, Lizzie Pond, an' go bowin' an' scrapin' to them – them cursed Deboffles. Them 'as stolen our grazin' land an' brought us so low that even the pig be starvin'.'

Pond's face had coloured indignantly at this slight on his daughter, but Elizabeth laid a hand on his arm and whispered, 'Hush, Papa.'

Meanwhile Venn stormed on. 'D'yer think I'm proud that my Joshua labours his guts out for that damned squire? My Sam ain't goin' to bow 'is back for 'em, no fear o' that. He's gone off to Colchester to sign on as a soldier.'

'May he prosper in that, Isaac, and come safely home to you,' said Pond, though the rebellion of the American colonies was something little understood in remote rural places like Wollaston.

'Home? Call this hovel home? Them bloody Deboffles've taken away me only means o' livin'!' shouted Venn, bringing his fist down on the rickety table. 'Do they care for the peasant farmers what've grown their veg'ables an' grazed their live-stock on their rightful strips o' common land fur 'undreds o' years, now left to starve or take to the road an' beg? My wife be wearied to death, poor wretch. She's struggled on beside me 'til she couldn't go on no longer, so she's turned 'er face to the wall. I ain't been a drinker or a waster, parson, so don't come round 'ere tellin' me that God's punishin' me – or that God's good. Not to *me* He ain't! Go on, get out – out wi' yer both!'

Meg spoke up at last, ashamed of her father's treatment of their visitors. 'Oh, Pa, don't forget Josh brings in a few pence, an' the squire often sends him home wi'n half a loaf or a bit o' bacon – an' Sir John once offered yer work on the estate.'

'Shut yer mouth, girl!' roared her father, enraged beyond control. To the horror of the Ponds he tried to strike Meg across the mouth but she ducked away from him. 'Don't ye dare mention that devil's name, don't *say* it, not if yer wants to stay under this roof, such as it is! I'd cut me throat 'fore I showed me face on that cursed estate, to take orders from that bastard, that scourge o' the poor an' 'is damned puppy of a son. Gallopin' everywhere on 'is bloody 'orse—'

'Hush, Isaac, you'll disturb your poor wife. We'll leave now. Good day to you, Miss Venn – come, Lizzie.' Pond spoke firmly.

He would have opened the door himself, but Meg stepped forward and pulled it open. She drew back in surprise at seeing the blacksmith's apprentice standing outside; the broad-shouldered young man was holding a wooden pail. He had clearly been waiting until the shouting died down before presenting himself, but at the sight of Meg and the Ponds he set down the pail. There was deep concern in his wide grey eyes.

'G–good good day, M–m–miss V–V–' He pointed to the pail. 'F–f–for th–the p–p–' He could manage no more words, but Meg was deeply touched.

'Oh, bless ye, Billy, ye're a true friend, ye've remembered our poor ol' pig!' He handed her the pail and she looked down at the scraps he'd foraged from the hedgerows. 'It's good o' ye, Billy!'

'G–got s–some s–s–sn–' He pointed to the pail.

'Aye, ye got some snails too! Ye must've picked 'em off the wall be'ind the ivy, for there ain't many of 'em about yet.' She turned to her father and pointed at the pig's dinner.

Zack stared at the young man and swallowed, as if stifling his anger. 'Aye. Ye're better'n a hundred damned Deboffles, Billy, poor simpleton though yer may be.'

'Shame on you, Isaac Venn,' cut in the parson sharply. 'William Siggery's the best of Wollaston's young people – and he can read and write, which is more than your Joshua or Samuel can. I know, I taught him myself, the only boy to pay any attention to the lessons.'

Zack turned surprised eyes on Pond, the humble parson who had listened in silence to insults directed at himself and his daughter without protest, yet who now rebuked him on account of Billy Siggery, the blacksmith's stammering assistant. He gave a dismissive shrug.

'Oh, aye, 'tis good o' the lad, and . . . er . . .'

'And we thank ye, Billy. Ye're very kind,' added Meg warmly.

'And now we really must be on our way, Lizzie,' said Pond. 'Maybe young Mr Siggery will walk with us as far as our paths run together. Good day to you, Isaac – and Meg. May the peace of God rest upon Mary and this house.'

Privately he felt certain that he had made a last farewell to Mary Venn, but he said nothing of this as the three of them set off down the long slope of the Common, Billy swinging the pail, for Meg had emptied it into the pig's pen.

'How's your mother keeping, Billy?' asked the parson conversationally. Young Siggery pointed to his left hip.

'Sh–she h–has p–pain an' ne–needs a–a s–st–stick t–to w–walk.'

'I'm sorry to hear that, Billy. Poor Widow Siggery, she's had a hard time of it over the years.'

As soon as the words were out of his mouth Pond regretted them for it sounded as if Billy himself were a hardship to the poor widow. His daughter noticed his mistake and tried to make amends.

'May I say, Mr Siggery, that your speech is much better now that you're older! I can understand you very well. Your mother must be very pleased with you.' And as soon as she had spoken, Elizabeth felt that her words had been patronizing, emphasizing his imperfect speech. She glanced at her father who gave a slight cough and spoke again.

'Tell your mother that I'd like to visit her one day when she's at home,' he said, and his daughter added her goodwill with a smile. Billy Siggery, whose mother had always understood him perfectly, was so overcome by shyness that he could not utter another word for the rest of their walk, not even a stammered 'goodbye' when they parted company. Pond shook his hand warmly and the thought crossed the parson's mind that if such an open, honest face and strong frame belonged to any other young man, he would be pursued by all the young women in Wollaston.

Mary Venn lay back on her hard bed consoled by the divine blessing and receiving forgiveness for her sins. Peace filled her heart and mind, and all pain and discomfort fled, so she did not hear Zack's angry outburst on the other side of the door. When Meg went to see her after the Ponds had left, she saw her mother sleeping, her face calm and untroubled. During the night her breathing became shallower and shortly before dawn Zack was suddenly awakened, not by a sound but by a silence. He leaned across to touch his wife, to put his calloused hand upon her forehead and whisper her name. But it was all over. Mary Venn had finished her life of poverty and suffering, and her husband was left to ponder silently on his regrets. Not until first light did he wake Meg, who slept on a straw mattress beside her parents' bed, and

Joshua who was bedded down on blankets in the only other room.

'Meg, ye must go fur ol' Granny Mason to lay 'er out. Ye can go to work as usual, Joshua,' he said gruffly, his eyes hard and tearless. 'There's nothin' yer can do 'ere an' we need every penny ye can bring in. Stop off at the parson's an' tell 'im there'll be another funeral for 'im. Life's got to go on, whether she be 'ere or no.'

Joshua was almost relieved at being thus dismissed, for his father's mood was strange, and he seemed to be wrapped up in his own grim thoughts. In fact Isaac Venn had made up his mind to leave Wollaston. He had lived here all his life, but in latter years he had known only grinding poverty, hunger and despair. He had seen his wife die from it and now he wanted to get out of the place and never set eyes on it again.

Joshua went first to his place of work, not wanting to rouse the parson's household at such an early hour and call down the wrath of Mrs Pond upon his head. As he approached the farmhouse, he saw Adam Horrocks breakfasting alone through the window and they waved to each other. The two young men were not exactly friends but they worked well together and shared a ribald joke or two. Today their greeting was sombre, and Adam, once he heard the sad news, was surprised that Joshua had come to work though he realized that it was probably the best course. He at once took upon himself the duty of messenger and said that he would call upon Parson Pond. He put on his three-cornered hat and buttoned his long jacket, hoping he would see the fair Elizabeth.

Herbert Pond woke early and lay in his narrow bed to say his morning prayers, rather than getting out and kneeling beside it. He feared wakening Mrs Pond in her room at the back of the house, for she would fill the air with her strident tones, rousing Elizabeth and Jenny the little maid-of-all-work who slaved for them in return for her keep.

Poor woman! he thought for the thousandth time of his wife. He had wronged her and felt he had failed her as a husband. He would always be a poor parson, unable to keep proper servants or a carriage, not even a two-wheeled gig. Even the Miss Buxtons sported a pony trap, but Mrs Pond had to walk wherever she wanted to go. As she so often pointed out to him, she was expected to keep up an appearance of gentility, a style of living that was beyond their means.

As he forced himself to concentrate on the psalm he was reading, trying to apply its precepts to his life in Wollaston, his ears caught the sound of footsteps in the lane. Then he heard the front gate being opened and closed and the footsteps approaching the front door.

In a flash Pond knew what the news would be: that Mary Venn had gone. It must be Joshua coming to tell him. He got out of bed and called softly out of the window.

'Don't knock, my boy, don't knock! I'll come down to see you.'

The early caller looked up and Pond saw that he was not Joshua but Adam Horrocks. The parson's heart gave a dolorous thud, for he understood at once that young Horrocks had taken this opportunity to be the bringer of news in place of Joshua, not out of sympathy but to see Elizabeth, to gain admittance to her home and cultivate his acquaintance with her.

Adam waited for the parson to go down and let him in. Pond took down from its hook on the door an old woollen wrap that he used when it was necessary to see visitors who had got him out of bed before he'd had time to dress. Pulling the wrap tightly around his nightshirt, he silently descended the uncarpeted stairs in his bare feet and unbolted the door. Adam stood on the doorstep looking suitably grave.

'Good morning, sir.' In other circumstances he would have said 'Good morning, parson', but he was addressing the man who he hoped would be his father-in-law. 'I am the bearer of sad news.'

'Yes, yes, Adam, I shall not be surprised to hear that poor Mrs Venn has gone to her rest.'

'But how did you—?'

'I saw her yesterday afternoon,' replied Pond, wondering if good manners required him to ask the messenger to step inside. 'As you can see, I'm not yet dressed, Adam, and my household is not yet risen. I will visit the cottage – the house of sorrow – as soon as I can this morning.'

Would the boy take the hint and have the sense to retreat after leaving his message? Pond wondered. Apparently not, for he continued to stand on the doorstep looking expectantly at Pond, who felt obliged to be hospitable. He reproached himself for his discourtesy when he should be turning his thoughts towards the bereaved family.

'You'd better come into the study, Adam, and wait while I . . . er . . . I can offer you only a glass of yarrow beer – unless you will take Mrs Pond's dandelion wine?'

'Please don't trouble yourself, sir,' said Adam, following the parson to the study, wondering how long he could prolong his visit in the hope of setting his eyes on the girl of his dreams. 'I have already breakfasted. Please don't let me put you to any inconvenience.'

As if this isn't inconvenient enough, thought Pond to himself, closing the study door behind him as he made for the stairs. And there, coming down in her house-gown, was Elizabeth.

'What's happened, Papa? I heard the front door. Has somebody called at this hour? Oh, is it about Mrs Venn?'

'Yes, my dear, the poor woman is at rest. I shall have to go there again this morning.'

'Let me come too, Papa, and see Meg!'

'The Miss Buxtons will be expecting you, Lizzie. There will be time to see your friend soon enough, for the funeral will not be long delayed. Go back to your room, Lizzie,' he ordered, anxious to get rid of Adam as soon as he could.

'But there is something else troubling you, Papa. Was it Joshua who brought the news?'

He hurried up past her on the stairs. 'I said go back to your room, Lizzie.'

'Papa, it is very plain to me that something else is the matter,' she said, raising her voice. To Pond's utter dismay their voices were heard and Mrs Pond appeared on the landing.

'What's goin' on here? Can't a body awake and rise in peace? Sounds as if the 'ouse is full o' gabblin' – good grief, aren't yer even dressed, Herbert? S'pose somebody was to come to the door and 'ear all this 'ullaballoo!'

Pond winced at her coarse accent, like a serving maid in a tavern, which became more pronounced when the lady was annoyed. 'My dear Mrs Pond, please go back to your room,' he begged.

'Don't you dare give *me* orders, Pond! You're hidin' somethin', you sly dog. Don't try to hoodwink me!'

There was a click as the study door opened and Adam Horrocks emerged. He had heard everything. Three pairs of eyes stared down at him from the stairs and landing. Then four pairs as little Jenny left her tiny room and joined them. Adam bowed. 'Forgive me, Mr Pond, Mrs Pond, Miss Elizabeth. I see that I have come at an inconvenient time. With your permission I will take my leave. I bid you good morning.'

Young Horrocks went out of the door, only just managing to keep a straight face, for he would have found the situation highly comical if it had not been for poor, pretty Elizabeth. It would be a kindness to rescue her from such a household!

The Miss Buxtons had willingly given Miss Pond the necessary time to attend the funeral and be with her distressed friend Miss Venn in that sorrowful hour. Meg wept bitterly as the coffin Billy Siggery had made without charge from cheap planks was lowered into the ground, while Joshua stood in sombre silence, wishing that Sam was beside him. Sam and Chopper had gone to enlist as soldiers, and there was no way of letting him know that his mother was dead. A few neighbours who had known Mary all her life had come to make their farewells, including the Widow Siggery, accompanied by her son who stood with bowed head, full of pity for the Venn family. Zack stood apart from the others, dour and as blank-faced as a statue.

Herbert Pond did not allow his own heavy heart to distract his attention from the prayer book, open at the Burial of the Dead, and the sorrowful faces around him. The Lord had called him into the Ministry and had upheld him throughout the trials and tribulations of an unhappy marriage. The parson had always resolved that he must put God first in his life, serving the folk he called his flock as well as he could, cheered and consoled by his beloved daughter, as loving in nature as she was lovely to look upon. The hateful morning scene two days ago had shaken this resolution. Mrs Pond had stormed and railed against him for frightening away 'the best chance Lizzie was likely to get'. Worse still, Lizzie herself had been rather cool towards him. Poor Herbert Pond took this to mean that she really liked young Horrocks and had been humiliated by both of her parents. He regretted with all his heart the way he had received Adam, and the farcical scene that had occurred.

The obsequies duly completed, the small gathering began to break up, and it was then that Pond saw two young men standing at the lychgate, just outside the churchyard. One was Adam Horrocks and the other was young Richard de Boville who attended St Bede's every Sunday with his parents, sisters and younger brother, taking position in the gated de Boville pew.

Herbert Pond experienced a pang. What was it? Anger? Fear? He was not sure what he felt. Adam Horrocks's admiration for Elizabeth had not been quenched as Pond had secretly hoped it would. Was the fellow never to leave them alone? He glanced at his daughter, but she was walking with an arm around Meg's shoulders, oblivious to all else.

Elizabeth was watched by the two young men with great interest.

'D'you see her there, Richard? The one attending to the Venn girl. Isn't she the handsomest creature you ever saw?'

'Mm–mm, yes, a sweet girl indeed,' replied his friend who at seventeen had not yet had any experience of women, though girls frequently turned their heads to admire his dark eyes and the hair that curled over his high forehead. 'And you say she loves you in return?'

'I have every reason to believe so.' Adam could not conceal his pride. 'Ah, look, they're breaking up and going their separate ways. She must come to this gate.'

No refreshments had been planned for such a poor funeral, but the parson had provided bread, cold mutton and yarrow beer to serve in the church porch. Pond knew that the poor were always hungry so a plain but substantial repast would be welcome. Sure enough, Joshua and his friends did justice to it, as did the Siggerys and their neighbours for whom this time of year meant empty larders and no fruit and fresh vegetables. Meg could eat nothing, and turned away from all offers of 'a bite and a sup' from the Miss Buxtons. Herbert Pond also declined to partake and took himself into the church to pray, while Zack Venn, stonefaced, strode away towards the lychgate. Meg saw him and called to Joshua.

'Come on, Josh, we'd best go with Pa! We can't let 'im go off on 'is own.' She and Elizabeth took a short cut across the churchyard, arriving at the gate just in front of Zack.

At this point Mr Horrocks made it obvious he was waiting to speak to Elizabeth. Meg, not wanting to join in any social exchange, disengaged her arm from her friend's and went to her father's side. Adam stepped forward and bowed.

'Miss Elizabeth, I beg your pardon for speaking to you on such an occasion as this, but I have to apologize for the inconvenience I caused to you and your parents on Wednesday morning. I was much at fault and am sorry, though it was not intentional. I would be grateful if you would convey my apologies to Mr and Mrs Pond.'

Elizabeth could only be gratified by such a courteous speech, especially as the Wednesday morning fiasco had definitely not been his fault.

'That's all right, Mr Horrocks,' she said hastily, with a little inclination of her head. 'Pray say no more about it.'

'Thank you, Miss Elizabeth. And may I present my companion, Mr Richard de Boville?'

Elizabeth looked up into a pair of dark eyes, twinkling with good-natured curiosity. She dropped a brief curtsey.

'Indeed, I see you every Sunday in church, sir,' she said.

Before Richard could answer, a furious Zack Venn strode forward and grabbed him by the lapels of his blue, brass-buttoned coat.

'Every bloody Sunday at church, eh? And every bloody day o' the week gallopin' yer 'orse over folks' property, yer useless young puppy!'

The bystanders gasped as Zack shook the boy like a rat, and deliberately blew into his face, sending a shower of spittle over him. 'I *spit* on yer, Deboffle spawn! I *spit* on yer 'ouse, yer father an' all o' yer!'

Heads were turning as Zack's curses echoed across the churchyard. Meg and her brother stood rooted to the spot while some of the bystanders muttered that Zack Venn had gone completely mad, and might attack them all.

It was a cool, clear female voice that broke in on Venn's stream of rage.

'Let him go at once, Isaac Venn. At once, do you hear me?' ordered the parson's daughter. 'Have you no shame in front of your son and daughter? Have you no respect for your wife, committed this hour to the earth? Stop it, I say! Let him go!'

Venn turned and looked at her, standing beside Meg. There

was a silence while the onlookers held their breath, and Richard de Boville felt hard fingers against his throat; his face started to turn blue.

Elizabeth stepped forward and laid her hand on Venn's arm. 'Stop this desecration of holy ground, Isaac. Stop this blasphemy *now*!' she ordered.

He tried to shake her off, but she kept her hand upon him. His bloodshot eyes met hers for a long moment, and then with a howl like a wounded animal he threw young de Boville against the ancient wood of the lychgate. Every hearer shivered at the yell of anguish. Zack bellowed something incoherent and fled, half-running, half-stumbling, towards Cove Common, his worn-out boots pounding the stony lane. The group at the lychgate stared after him until he disappeared from sight, an outcast among men.

Hearing the commotion and recognizing Elizabeth's voice, Pond emerged from the church to see young Horrocks helping de Boville to his feet. The boy was gasping for air, clutching at his throat, but he was able to turn and thank his fair rescuer.

'Miss Pond, my dear young lady,' he panted. 'How – how can I ever thank you?' He attempted to take her hand with the intention of kissing it, but she drew away.

'You can surely not be surprised at that poor wronged man, Mr de Boville. You had no right to come near his wife's funeral,' she rebuked him. 'Come, Meg, you shall rest and refresh yourself at my father's house, shall she not, Papa?'

Pond nodded, though he dreaded what Mrs Pond would say. He need not have worried, for Meg shook her head.

'No, Lizzie, I can't leave Pa. He's goin' off to London, now that poor Ma's in her grave. He says 'e'll find work at a coachin' inn, an' – an', Lizzie, I have to go with 'im. Josh is movin' into the stables at Horrocks's farm an' God only knows where Sam is.'

'But dear Meg, you have no money.'

'I know, Lizzie, we'll 'ave to beg our way to London, and 'eaven knows whether we'll get there or what fate awaits us.'

Herbert Pond stepped forward and laid his hands on her head. 'May God take care of you and your poor father, my dear child.'

'Oh, Papa, why don't you try to stop her facing such dangers?' cried Elizabeth.

He shook his head sadly. 'She will not forsake her father,

my dear, and she may be his only hope of salvation. Let her go, and we must go home too.' He took her arm and led her away, leaving the remaining bystanders discussing the eventful funeral.

One onlooker had stood apart from the rest in watching the whole drama. When Elizabeth Pond commanded Zack Venn to let de Boville go, the watcher had been prepared to step forward to defend her if he needed to, holding his breath until Venn released the boy. In his mind he saw that fighting, kicking, calico-clad girl; that had been seven years ago and then she had been defending him, Billy Siggery.

'She be not changed,' he told his mother that evening. 'She be not changed.'

He did not even notice that he had not stammered.

Two

A Summer Idyll

April–September, 1777

The blustery winds of March continued into April which
came in with lowering skies and heavy showers, bad news
for farmers who needed to sow their spring oats and barley.
The great shire horses plodded up and down the muddy fields;
on the de Boville estate they pulled a seed drill which let fall
a row of seeds at intervals, while the smaller farmers still kept
to the biblical way, sowers scattering seed in handfuls over
the ploughed earth, where all too often the birds of the air
swooped down and gobbled it up.

Elizabeth Pond continued to miss her friend Meg and to
worry about her. There had been no news of Zack Venn and
his daughter for a month and there was unlikely to be any.
Meg had never been to school so could hardly write her own
name. Elizabeth had no idea where to send a letter, and began
to face the fact that she might never see her childhood friend
again. After all, Zack had sworn he would never return to
Wollaston. It would be bearable, thought Elizabeth, if she could
only have news of the Venns. She would be happy if she knew
that Meg was not lying in some ditch somewhere but had found
employment, perhaps as a maidservant in some inn where
Zack was an ostler. Joshua knew no more than she did; he
was happily absorbed into his life as one of Squire Horrocks's
outdoor labourers. He was becoming a good all-rounder and
was likely to be promoted to groom or stockman in due
course.

One late afternoon in the watery April sunshine Elizabeth
went walking by herself on Cove Common. She had had a
melancholy impulse to see the Venns' humble cottage, so

recently vacated. To her astonishment it had completely gone; it had been pulled down and its bricks and beams carted away. Gone were the two rooms where a family had grown up, gone was the strip of land tended by Zack for so many years, and gone was the pig pen. Tears filled Elizabeth's eyes as she stared at the desolate land, where lately a home had stood, ready for the plough which would turn this piece of common into a field of corn.

Hugging her cloak around her, she made off in the direction of the scattered cottages that formed the tail end of the village. In one of these lived Widow Siggery, and Lizzie knocked on her door to ask if there had been any news of the father and daughter. Mrs Siggery bobbed a curtsey to the parson's daughter, for there were fine gradations of rank in the rural community, where the de Bovilles were above the Horrockses who would have been on a level with the rector, Dr Webb, if he had chosen to live in his parish. The Horrockses were above the poor parson and less prosperous farmers, along with the tradesmen. At the bottom of the pile came the peasant farmers, farm labourers and servants such as Widow Siggery, whose curtsey showed her deep respect for Elizabeth's father.

'Miss Pond, ye do us an honour! Wait while I call my good lad. He be seein' after the pig!'

This was news to Elizabeth, because the Siggerys hadn't owned a pig. When Billy hurried in from the yard he stopped short at the sight of her, his speech deserting him.

'I–I–I made a–a st–sty for th–the p–pig, Miss P–Pond. W–we sh–share 'im wi–with—' He broke off, wretchedly ashamed of his stuttering speech, and looked towards his mother who explained that it was the half-starved pig that had belonged to the Venns. Billy had tied a rope round his belly and neck and walked or dragged him across the Common to the Siggerys' dwelling, where he had made a sty for him.

'We has to share 'im with our neighbours an' we all feed 'im, Miss Pond,' she said. 'When 'e be killed 'e'll be shared out among the cottagers.'

Elizabeth nodded, glad that the pig had found a new home. 'Did you see Meg before she left, Billy?' she asked.

'Y–yes, m–miss, they s–said w–we could have th–the p–pig,'

he answered. 'An'–an' th–they went f–f–first thing n–next
mornin', c–carryin' b–bun-bundles.'

'They was carryin' everythin' they could heave on their backs,
Miss Pond, an' 'im as surly a man as ever lived.
Yet poor Miss Meg, she would go with 'im, though she could've
gone back to Flaxford. That was the last we saw of 'em. God
'elp that poor girl. I pray she may be kept out o' danger.'

Elizabeth declined a cup of tea, knowing how precious it
was; the cook and housekeeper at Oak Hall surreptitiously
gave the washerwoman little gifts of tea and sugar wrapped
in a twist of paper. She exchanged a few more words with
them and answered the widow's polite enquiries about her
father whose recent visit had given the poor woman much
satisfaction.

'Now, Billy, ye can see Miss Pond safely back to the village,
can't ye?' his mother ordered.

Though Elizabeth protested that it was not necessary, Billy
put on his broad-brimmed hat and set out beside her. Talk
between them was limited, though she was able to understand
or anticipate most of what he said. She told him how much
she missed Meg and he nodded with understanding. Dear
Billy! she thought; far from being embarrassed by him she
found his company both undemanding and restful.

So different from Adam Horrocks who took every opportunity to meet her and walk with her. His conversation was
somewhat limited to farm matters, the weather and the new
developments in agriculture. He had also remarked knowingly
that the war against the rebellious American colonies would
be over before the year was out. She knew nothing about the
conflict so was unable to contradict him. From time to time,
when there was nothing else to talk about, he would compliment her on her looks which he often declared far exceeded
those of all other young women in Wollaston. He had told
Elizabeth that his mother would be happy to receive her at
the farmhouse for tea one afternoon, but she steadfastly
declined this invitation. She felt it would commit her to
accepting him when his two years of waiting were over and
he was officially allowed to ask Parson Pond for her hand. It
was very trying! Her father disliked and discouraged these
meetings with Adam, while her mother encouraged them,
being all in favour of a match with the squire's family. Elizabeth

avoided speaking to either parent on the subject as she was far from knowing her own mind.

Halfway through April the skies cleared, the sun shone, and the earth awoke to new life. It was an annual miracle that both Elizabeth and her father enjoyed, when the drab greys and browns of winter gave way to all the hues of spring: the tender new leaf-buds, the drifting, delicate fruit-blossom, the dancing daffodils. Elizabeth's heart gave a leap at hearing the first unmistakable, audacious call of the annual visitor – 'Cuc-koo! Cuc-koo' – about to intrude on other birds' nests. She taught the girls at the vicarage school how to recognize the many different bird calls and songs, for she had always loved them.

One Sunday morning at the end of the service, when the congregation was streaming out of the dim interior of St Bede's into the warm sunshine, a voice spoke close to her ear.

'Miss Pond, I beg your pardon, Miss Pond, but may I present you to my mother?'

Elizabeth spun round to see not Adam Horrocks but young Richard de Boville holding out his hand to her. She hesitated, somewhat abashed by the trio of haughty-looking women just behind him, and taking her silence for consent he touched his mother's arm.

'This is Miss Pond, Mamma, the daughter of Parson Pond. She is the lady who saved me from being throttled! She ordered that fellow to let me go and he did so, but it was a close-run thing, for he would listen to nobody else! Miss Pond, this is my mother, Lady de Boville, and these are my sisters, Miss Frederica and Miss Georgina de Boville – and my young brother Edward, known as Teddy, the youngest of us!'

Elizabeth looked down on a bright-faced boy of about nine and curtseyed to the ladies, who looked somewhat bewildered. Sir John de Boville came up to the group, stared at Elizabeth, and then nodded his approval.

'Oh, so that's the girl! Do you remember, my love, that fellow who gave me so much trouble over that wretched dwelling, though I offered him work on the estate, much against my better judgement?'

The ladies inclined their heads slightly and allowed themselves to unbend a little.

Lady de Boville addressed Elizabeth. 'I am most grateful
to you, Miss Pond, for using your influence with that villain.
Richard is quite sure he would have been strangled if you had
not intervened.' Her expression was one of lofty distaste, but
Richard smiled and bowed again to his rescuer.

'You not only saved me, Miss Pond, but you rebuked me
for going near to the funeral of the man's wife, and of course
you were right,' he added unwisely.

His sisters were horrified. 'A girl of her station rebuking
our brother!' they murmured to each other, too quietly for
Elizabeth to hear. 'Whatever is the world coming to?'

'I believe that the man has completely lost his wits, and
should be locked up in a madhouse,' said Sir John. Turning
to the parson he shook his hand. 'I am obliged to you, Pond.
You have reared a girl of spirit – and so pretty!'

Lady de Boville and her daughters turned away, saying that
their carriage was waiting at the lychgate, but Richard was
delighted with his father's compliment.

'Is she not so, Father? And she has many talents, and also
teaches at the vicarage school!'

'Indeed,' replied Sir John casting an amused look at the
trio, for Mrs Pond had joined her husband and daughter.
'Come, Teddy, and you, Richard, we must be going.'

Shepherding his two sons away, Sir John walked down the
path, leaving Herbert Pond uncharitably annoyed at the condescension he'd shown towards his daughter rather than a proper
appreciation of her brave action. Mrs Pond on the other hand
was all smiles and gratification, having curtseyed three times
to the baronet's family.

'Really, Pond, you're the limit,' she scolded. 'You should've
showed a bit more respect, seein' as Lizzie'll be hobnobbin'
with them when she's married to a Horrocks! You ought to
be keepin' in with the gentry, 'stead o' wastin' your time on
the undeservin' poor o' the parish!'

Pond did not bother to reply. He had an unpleasant premo-
nition that his daughter would be further involved with the de
Bovilles in some way. He gave a grunt. Huh! At least there
would be no question of a 'match' from that quarter!

Elizabeth was silent on their short walk home. She had hardly
noticed the de Bovilles's disdainful attitude or her mother's
servility towards them. She had only seen the look in young

de Boville's dark eyes and the feel of his hand on hers. He had held it longer than was strictly necessary for a mere handshake. Everything about him betokened a gentleman – his looks, build, clothes, manner. In every way he was a far superior man to Adam Horrocks.

But he was a de Boville, she told herself. She should not indulge in silly dreams, though she privately decided that she did not want to marry the man whom everybody, including her dear papa, seemed to think was destined for her.

'Miss Pond's playing is much improved,' remarked Miss Buxton to Miss Letty Buxton. 'I think we should give her the opportunity to teach the older girls some songs. She has a pretty voice, and may be able to teach them to sing part-songs.'

Neither of the sisters were singers, and knew little about music other than hymns. Miss Pond was of course delighted to be asked to teach singing, and asked her father if she might borrow *Songs from Shakespeare* from his small library. He had willingly lent it to her, imagining the school girls singing such ditties as 'Hark, hark, the lark at Heaven's gate sings'.

In fact Miss Pond taught the three boarders a different kind of song; the music was written for two voices and she adapted it for four. They learned quickly, with many a smile and glance at each other as their teacher's hands danced on the keys with only an occasional wrong note.

> It was a lover and his lass,
> With a hey and a ho and a hey nonino,
> That o'er the green cornfield did pass,
> In the spring-time, the only pretty ring-time,
> When birds do sing, hey ding-a-ding-a-ding,
> Sweet lovers love the spring!

'Oh, please, Miss Pond, may we sing it again? *Please!*' begged the girls, and so when Miss Letty Buxton happened to pass by the open door, she heard a sprightly rendering of Shakespeare's tribute to the joys of spring. She waited until the end of the verse, and then entered the room.

'A moment, please, Miss Pond! You all sing very well and

your playing is much improved, but I wonder if that song is quite suitable for young ladies?'

Miss Pond looked up in surprise. 'My father lent me the song book, Miss Buxton, and the girls have learned it well, as you can hear.'

'Be that as it may, Miss Pond, but would Parson Pond agree with your choice of song? Hand it to me, please, and I will consult with my sister.'

The girls' faces fell, and Miss Pond had to fall back on *The Children's Song Book* until her father's book was returned the following day.

'We have looked through the songs, Miss Pond, and have found a number that would be suitable. Here is a list, and we look forward to hearing our older girls singing them.'

The girls were disappointed. 'Full fathom five thy father lies' seemed a mournful dirge and Miss Pond found the refrain of the banned song continuing to run through her head; and when she closed her eyes she saw the sweet lovers passing o'er the green cornfield, with a hey and a ho and a hey nonino! It so well expressed the way she felt about the glories of the season, the awakening earth that found an echo in her own heart where strange, unnamed stirrings seemed to respond to the natural beauty all around her. She could not remember having had these feelings during previous springs, this tremulous anticipation of she knew not what. Her father noticed her happy smiles, though her mother accused her of daydreaming. Mrs Pond also objected to her daughter taking long walks on Cove Common and in the lanes between the hedgerows where the May blossom was coming out.

'That girl's got somethin' on her mind, and I ain't so sure it's good for her,' muttered the parson's wife darkly. 'Always walkin' up on that common – an' talkin' with that blacksmith's lad, I shouldn't wonder. She'd better watch her step – no tellin' what 'e might try.'

Her husband sighed and made no reply, knowing that there was nothing to be feared from the gentle, thoughtful young man whom some people still called silly Billy Siggery. True, there might be dangers from other wanderers on the Common, but Pond was sure that Siggery would always treat his lovely Elizabeth with care and respect.

One fine afternoon towards the end of May, as soon as

Elizabeth left the school, she felt compelled to make her way straight up to the furze-covered common. There her destiny awaited her; she knew him as soon as he appeared, riding towards her on a chestnut mare. She knew that he was going to rein in beside her, yet her heart fluttered when he did so.

'Good day to you, Miss Pond! I observe that you are also enjoying this fine spring weather. Surely this must be the queen of seasons!'

'Mr de Boville,' she said, unable to think of anything else to say to Sir John's elder son. She blushed.

He dismounted, sliding expertly down the mare's gleaming flank, then holding the reins in his right hand as he addressed her.

'May I walk a little way with you, Miss Pond? Which direction are you taking?'

'I–I had no special direction in mind, sir,' she answered confusedly. 'I came up to the Common just for the air, the open heath. 'Tis all so – it is so different in springtime.'

What a silly thing to say, she chided herself. Why had she said 'different' when she could have said 'beautiful' or 'lovely' or even 'heavenly'. How stupid she must appear!

'Ah, it is exactly that, Miss Pond, an excellent choice of word,' he said, smiling as he strolled beside her, the mare ambling behind them. 'Different indeed from the bareness of winter – and the cold! Is there not a verse in a psalm that says, "Behold, I make all things new"?'

''Tis in the Book of Revelation, sir,' she told him, returning his smile and remembering too late that she had forgotten to curtsey. 'And 'tis just what I was thinking, for I love the springtime. Every year it's a surprise, as if we're seeing it for the very first time.'

He laughed delightedly. 'You make me think of a song,' he said. 'It's from a play called *As You Like It*, by the great Shakespeare. It goes rather like this, if I can remember it. "*It was a lover and his lass . . .*"' He took her right arm as he sang the familiar words that had been running through her head ever since the Miss Buxtons had banned it. He knew it well and sang with perfect pitch. She joined in, continuing the verse that he had begun, and their voices blended on the clear air.

When birds do sing, hey ding-a-ding-a-ding,
Sweet lovers love the spring!

Richard stopped, glancing at her upturned face and their eyes
met as their two voices sung together. They were in love from
that moment, at least they had already realized they had fallen
in love, but only now did they acknowledge it.

'I tried to forget about you, Elizabeth, but could not wait
to see you again.'

She looked up at him with a sweet smile that told him all
he wanted to know.

'Your eyes are two deep blue pools,' he told her wonder-
ingly. 'A man could drown in them.' He dropped the mare's
reins and put both his arms around Elizabeth's trembling body.
'You are so beautiful,' he whispered and kissed her forehead
with something like reverence.

She closed her eyes and felt that she would have fallen to
the ground if his arms had not been around her. Seeing her
eyes shut he ventured to touch her lips with his own. It was
her first experience of a kiss from a man – a lover's kiss.

Richard de Boville was younger than she, though he would
be eighteen at the end of the year, and he was far above her
in society. Nevertheless, he loved her and she returned his
love. They walked together, arms entwined, the patient mare
following them.

'How many other lovers have walked across the grass here,
dearest Elizabeth? There must be many in past ages, the shepherds and their pretty sweethearts!'

'Oh, yes,' she replied eagerly. 'The shepherds in their smocks
and straw hats.' She stopped, suddenly aware of his white shirt,
frilled at the neck and wrists, his buff breeches and stockings.
He wore the clothes of a gentleman, in contrast to her clothes:
a serviceable pale-grey cotton skirt that she had stitched herself
and a muslin kerchief around her shoulders and neck, covering
and yet revealing the swell of her small breasts. I am no more
like a nymph than he is like a shepherd, she thought to herself.
Richard asked her why she was smiling.

'I–I was just thinking,' she said a little hesitantly. 'I'm really
Miss Pond the good parson's daughter and an assistant teacher
at the school and—'

'Call me Richard, my Elizabeth.'

'Richard, I'm far below your station in life, though my father is as good as any man.'

'Of course he is. And you are a respectable young woman,' he said teasingly, tightening his arm around her waist. 'And young Adam Horrocks openly admires you and reckons to make you his wife in less than two years' time. But he cannot have you! Oh, my Elizabeth, do you think I care a fig for your station in life? Have you not read Spenser's advice to lovers?'

'My papa introduced me to the metaphysical poets – Spenser, Dryden and Donne. They are great favourites of his and I enjoy reading them too, though there is more than worship and praise in their verses, is there not?'

'They were men of faith, but also men who had great zest for life. I could talk to you all day and all night, because I see that we were meant to meet and know each other. We have so much to share!'

'But time waits for no man, Richard,' she said with a regretful smile. 'My father will be expecting me home.'

He sighed. 'Ah, yes! "*At my back I always hear Time's wingèd chariot hurrying near*". Poor Marvell, he was impatient with his coy mistress! Are you coy, my Elizabeth?'

'I–I have not acted coyly this afternoon, have I?' she replied with a shy smile, for she felt able to talk, discuss, argue or tease on any subject with this young man.

'I cannot imagine you being anything other than perfection, even in coyness,' he told her.

'But now I must take my leave of you, sir – Richard!' She held out her hand. How comely he was! His dark curls framed a bright, boyish face and his lively dark-brown eyes were fringed with lashes a girl might envy!

'I cannot wait to see you again, Elizabeth. When will it be? This evening? We could meet at the bottom of Mile Long Lane, and—'

'No, Richard, I have to stay at home.'

'Then make it tomorrow afternoon at three. I shall be at the bottom of the lane. Do, *do* say you can, and we can discuss poetry or sing songs, whatever you wish. Your wish is my command, my Lady Elizabeth!'

She dropped a low curtsey, and held out her hand. 'Goodbye until tomorrow, Richard.'

He took her hand but drew her to him in an embrace and kissed her. 'Until I see your lovely face again.'

There was now no turning back. They met whenever they could, snatching precious hours or half hours, long enough to exchange a line of poetry, a song or a story. They constantly surprised each other by their similar thoughts, the shared pleasures of the English language, from Chaucer to their contemporary Dr Samuel Johnson. They especially loved John Donne, who had also known the ecstasy of love for a woman. Parson Pond's little library of well-thumbed books came into its own, for Elizabeth could now relate the poets' imagery to Richard and herself. Sir John's large collection of classics had hitherto been seldom disturbed, but now yielded up the wisdom of the ages to this pair of lovers.

Parson Pond felt less apprehensive about his daughter's meetings with Adam Horrocks, for he and his wife assumed that was where she went on these expeditions. Mrs Pond raised no serious objections because she was entirely in favour of the match.

At Oak Hall Sir John de Boville thought his heir was out riding, idling with friends and perhaps sowing a few wild oats. Well, it was time for the boy to gain experience, there was plenty of time for him to make a suitable match.

Elizabeth and Richard often walked up the bracken-covered rise to Foxholes, a thick stretch of woodland where the tall oaks and elms formed a green cathedral roof, dim and cool, inhabited by all manner of wild creatures. Their scamperings and rustlings were scarcely noticed, for the lovers only had eyes and ears for each other.

They lay in each other's arms in the long grasses of the de Boville meadows on drowsy summer afternoons, and there came a time, as Elizabeth had dimly known that it would, when she gave way to the strange longings this spring and summer had aroused in her young body. Wordlessly she let herself be taken by this adoring boy, who having had no more previous experience than herself, and guided only by love, at length gained entrance to her secret woman's place. Richard's persistence at last brought her to a pitch of pleasure so exquisite that she cried out, and found that he too was groaning as he reached his climax. They clung together as the tempest passed over them; surely no other lovers had ever known such happiness!

Of course it could not last forever, and the lovers were to learn that time never stands still, nor does it go backwards, but forever marches forwards. Inevitably they were seen walking together, first by a gamekeeper on the de Boville estate who had come up with his gun to shoot rabbits, and then by a pair of ploughboys on the Common, sporting with their sweethearts, who were vastly amused to discover a de Boville with the same idea. There was another witness who saw them walking with their arms around each other, but the blacksmith's apprentice kept his pain to himself and told no one. He could never aspire to the sweet girl he had always worshipped from a distance, but it grieved him to see that she had given her heart to the heir of Oak Hall, a boy who could never make her his wife.

Eventually Adam Horrocks began to be suspicious, and one day he followed Elizabeth down to the bottom of Mile Long Lane, and then up the steep rise to Foxholes where he saw the lovers greet each other with tender embraces. He would have denounced them then and there if he had not been so bitterly humiliated by his intended wife and the companion he had considered his friend. He crept away without being seen, but from then on he ignored her when they met after church, and gave her no more compliments. While this was in one way a relief to Elizabeth, as she had never felt attracted to him, his studied avoidance now made her uneasy. If he had heard something about her or seen her with Richard de Boville, it would only be a matter of time before his father and mother started to question him about his change of mind. Then sooner or later he would tell them how she had betrayed him.

It happened just as she feared: suddenly the whole of Wollaston knew. It was at first whispered, then gossiped about over tea cups and in the Fox and Hounds over mugs of ale. There was every kind of reaction, from shocked surprise to ribald amusement. Young women secretly envied Elizabeth while young men envied Richard.

At Oak Hall Sir John did not take it too seriously, though

he reprimanded his son and called him a young fool to take up with poor Pond's daughter, adding that it wasn't fair on the girl because there could never be a future for such a clandestine affair. Lady de Boville was far more angry with her son, and insisted that he be sent away to stay with her elderly but stern mother at Diss, over the Norfolk border and only approachable by winding cross-country roads.

'And then he can go to Cambridge University at the start of Michaelmas term,' she declared.

Though Richard protested furiously, in the end he had to agree because of his youth and lack of means. He could not afford to elope with Elizabeth and had nowhere to take her. Nevertheless he swore to her that as soon as he attained his majority, he would return and marry her in the face of all opposition.

'Though by that time my father may well be persuaded that you are my only love and I will have no other, my Elizabeth.'

He wrote a letter to Parson Pond, expressing the same intention, and apologizing for his present situation.

I love her with my heart and soul, and will keep my promise, as God is my witness, he wrote. Herbert Pond gained some comfort from the words; the revelation of the secret meetings had been a great shock. Pond's first reaction had been rage against the de Boville boy, as he called Richard. As for Elizabeth, her tears earned her his instant forgiveness.

'Though you will have to face condemnation from your mother, my dear. She feels greatly shamed by what she sees as a scandal, and the way it will reflect on her. And my dear Lizzie, you will have to forget the de Boville boy, but I shall be very glad to have you here at home for a few more years. I never did like the idea of you marrying young Horrocks.'

'I'll never be able to hold up me head again in church, with that lot lookin' at us and talkin' behind their prayer books!' stormed Mrs Pond. 'I never knew a daughter o' mine could be so sly and shameless. A fine thing for the county to chew over, a squire's son jilted by a parson's daughter who then dallies with a son o' the gentry, one 'ardly out o' short breeches! We'll never be on civil terms with the de Bovilles or the Horrockses now, thanks to you, young madam!

Goodness only knows what the Miss Buxtons'll say, but one thing's certain, they won't want a hussy like *you* teachin' their girls!'

In fact the Buxton sisters were actually in a quandary as to whether they should quietly dismiss their young assistant or keep her on and wait for the storm to blow over. In the end her melancholy pallor and the shadows under her eyes which often filled with tears won the day. They agreed that the less said the better. They told their neighbours it was for the sake of the poor parson, but in fact they knew their school girls would be very upset if they lost Miss Pond, and they too would miss an excellent assistant.

Meanwhile time went on; the farmers talked of harvesting before the end of August, while the weather was still fine and dry. It was the busiest time of the year, and all hands were required in the fields, when the swoosh of the men's scythes cut the corn and the women gathered the sheaves into stooks, keeping a few themselves to winnow and grind into flour. At the end of the harvesting, Sir John de Boville invited the whole village to partake of supper in the courtyard of Oak Hall. A whole pig and a sheep would be roasted for them, with freshly baked bread and jugs of ale.

'*We* won't be able to show our faces there, not after all this trouble with Lizzie,' grumbled Mrs Pond.

'I shall be thankful to be spared from it,' answered her husband. 'The farmhands are inclined to get noisy and silly after quaffing all that ale.'

'Oh, well, you *would* say that,' she snapped, but it takes two to make a quarrel and her husband refused to give her the chance.

How was Elizabeth, whose letters from Richard de Boville, exiled in sleepy Diss with his grandmother, had to be sent via her father who opened them before sharing them with her? Similarly he read her own letters before posting them off, knowing that they would be perused by Richard's grandmother, Mrs Tarrant, so the young couple could make no secret plans.

Elizabeth was grateful for her father's sympathy, mostly shown in mute glances and quiet gestures like placing a hand on her shoulder, but she was of little use in the harvesting and felt that she might be going into a decline, as little Sally Partridge had done. Her monthly flow had not come on in July or August, and she felt nauseated and faint in the heat. If only there was a kindly older woman in whom she could confide! The Miss Buxtons were spinsters, and she did not know any of the tradesmen's wives well enough; her position as parson's daughter set her apart from other village women. She decided to call on Mr Palfrey the apothecary to see if he could make up a herbal remedy for her, but after questioning her gravely, he told her she had better go to Granny Mason, the old handywoman who attended births and deaths. She had laid out poor Mary Venn in her coffin, and her birthing skills were respected; she could usually tell whether a sick child was likely to succumb or recover.

The handywoman lived in an ancient cottage with a profusion of flowers in her garden – hollyhocks, rosemary and lavender – while her rustic porch was covered in honeysuckle. She looked surprised to see the parson's daughter on her step, but cordially invited her in and beckoned her to a chair.

'Take a cup o' peppermint tea, my dear, 'twill help to settle your stomach,' she said kindly.

Elizabeth felt a certain relief, and found that she could talk freely to this wise old woman whose questions were more searching than Mr Palfrey's enquiries. By the time she left she knew what she had to do straightaway. Within the hour she was sitting in her father's study.

'There is something I have to tell you, Papa.'

'My dear child, what is it? I know you are still grieving over young de Boville, but believe me, time will be the best healer.'

'No, it is not that, Papa, though God knows I think of him every day and hour,' she replied. 'I have not been feeling well lately, and without asking your permission I went to see Mr Palfrey for his advice. I hoped he could make up a remedy . . .'

She broke off as she saw her father's face go deathly white. He half-rose from his chair.

'No, my child, *no!*' he groaned, remembering little Sally Partridge. 'Don't tell me that you are ill – God couldn't be so cruel as to take you from me – oh, my child, I could not bear it. Say it is not consumption, for mercy's sake!'

'Hush, Papa,' she said, getting up from her chair and gently guiding him back to his seat. 'I have not got consumption, but oh, dearest papa, I am with child.'

Three

An Interrupted Journey

March–September, 1777

'C'mon, girl, we better get goin'.'
    Meg shivered involuntarily, but forced a smile. 'Aye, Pa, I be ready.'

Her last night in the only home she'd ever known had not been restful. Grief for her mother and fear of what might lay ahead had brought troublesome dreams, and she was almost relieved when she heard her father moving around before dawn.

'Shall I make tea, Pa?' she asked, gathering up the blankets under which they had slept.

'Gimme those, an' I'll tie 'em up in two bundles, one for each of us. No, water'll do for me, no time to get a fire goin'.'

Folded within the two rolled-up blankets he intended to carry on his back, Zack had packed a saucepan and two thick earthenware mugs, a second shirt and a pair of breeches as shabby as those he had put on; his knife he put in his pocket. In Meg's one blanket was rolled what clothes she possessed, her mother's shawl and a handful of rags to use when her monthly flow began. She also put in a half loaf of bread and a couple of slices of mutton, taken from the refreshments that the Miss Buxtons had served to the mourners at her mother's funeral the day before. She had also added a twist of tea leaves and another of sugar, given to her by neighbours in Wollaston. Her father carried a stone jar of yarrow beer, and she carried a bottle of water. He put the bundle on her back, securing it with a length of rope around her waist and shoulders, just as he had tied on his own larger burden.

'C'mon, Meg, the sun's up, time to set out. We got a long way ahead.'

'No, wait a minute, Pa, there be somebody at the door.'

'Who the devil's come to pester us at this hour?' growled Zack. 'If it's any nonsense wi' them Deboffles . . .'

'It must be Joshua come to bid us goodbye, Pa!'

But when Meg pulled back the rickety door, it was Billy Siggery who stood on the step. He too carried a bundle tied up in a huckaback towel.

'M–mother s–sent th–this,' he told her, holding out the bundle. 'F–f–for th–the p–pig.'

For a moment Meg was confused but then she realized that this offering was in payment for the pig, and took it from him. Opening the towel she found a loaf of barley bread, some oatcakes, about a pound of cheese, and, wrapped separately, a bar of hard yellow soap.

'Oh, Billy, that's so good o' yer ma!' Meg exclaimed, and even Zack's harsh features softened a little at the sight of these luxuries, precious to the penniless Venns. And there was more: Billy drew two guineas from his pocket and handed them over.

'F–for the p–pig,' he said with an attempt at a smile, though his grey eyes were full of concern. He handed Meg a sheet of paper.

We had a collection round the cottages and in the Village and Noah Reeve made it up to two Guineas and changed it for these to make it easy to carry.

Meg could have wept at such kindness from their old neighbours; and to think that as a child she had looked down on Billy Siggery as an idiot to be avoided for fear of some unnamed harm he might do!

The gifts were duly added to Meg's rolled-up blanket. Zack pocketed the money, transferring the two gold coins to a worn leather purse.

'Yer mother be a better woman than any other in Wollaston, Billy. Thank 'er for this, an' Noah.' He took Billy's hand and shook it. Meg did likewise. How many times, she wondered, had Billy turned up on their doorstep with scraps for their pig? And now he had brought food for them as a parting gift and money for their journey! On an impulse she raised her face and kissed his cheek, her eyes full of tears. Little did she know that Billy had contributed one guinea himself, his savings from working at the smithy for nearly three years. Noah Reeve, the blacksmith, had no regrets about taking him on for the lad had proved to have a natural way with horses. He had never ever been kicked as he hammered an iron horseshoe into an upturned hoof.

'Reckon the 'osses don't mind 'ow 'e speaks or 'ow 'e walks!' Noah had declared.

Billy watched as Zack refastened the bundle to Meg's back, threading the rope through the firmly rolled blanket.

'Come on, then, girl, don't delay any longer. Farewell to yer, Billy Siggery.'

'Goodbye, Billy, ye've been a true friend to us in our trouble,' she said. Billy stared at them both, unable to utter a word, though his pitying look spoke his thoughts to them as well as any words could have done.

And then they were away, father and daughter taking their first steps on what was to be a long and hazardous journey. It was the last week of March, and the morning air was chilly. The flat countryside stretched before them, dotted with isolated farm buildings; much of what had been common land was now enclosed and ready to grow wheat, barley, oats and rye. A few farm workers were already out in the fields with ploughs and horses, but apart from birdsong there was silence over the land.

Until suddenly a red and brown streak flashed across their path, heading for a clump of trees, and a pack of foxhounds came into view, barking excitedly as they pursued the scent of the fox over the fields, followed by half a dozen fine horses at full gallop, making the earth vibrate beneath them. Their riders wore the traditional red coats and hard black hats; they shouted to one another, and there was a long, wavering blast on a horn. The hunt was in full cry, galloping over grass and stone, skirting the edge of a newly ploughed field, and coming straight towards the rough track on which the two travellers walked.

'Look out!' Zack cried, grabbing her arm, and they both leapt out of the path of the approaching hunt into the surrounding heathland.

'They'd've trampled us underfoot an' not looked back, the bastards!' muttered Zack. 'Be yer all right, Meg? Bastards! I wish 'em all broken necks, the lot of 'em!'

'I–I'm all right, Pa, but see over there – that one jumpin'' over the ditch, see?'

'Bloody fool,' growled Venn, but following her horrified gaze, he saw that a horse had caught its foreleg in the ditch, lost its balance and rolled over on to its side. The rider had been flung several yards away and lay still. Most of the hunt moved forward in pursuit of their prey, but a couple of them reined in, dismounted and went to the fallen man.

'Oh, Pa, d'yer suppose 'e's dead?'

'Maybe 'e is, but they ain't all stopped, so 'e must be only a groom,' replied her father grimly. 'Come on, Meg, keep goin', leave 'em be. That sort wouldn't stop for us, not even if we was trampled on. We'd just be left to die.'

He strode on ahead and Meg hurried to catch him up, casting a few glances back; the fallen man had not got up, and the two attending on him were attempting to lift him.

'Don't mind 'em, Meg, just keep goin', like the ol' fox, wherever 'e is. I 'ope he gets away.'

'They'll be the Wollaston Hunt, Pa. Out early this mornin'.'

'Why the devil should we care, girl, 'tis them as made us beggars,' Venn replied in a surly manner.

He continued to stride along, spurred on by his anger and seemingly oblivious of the bundle on his back. Meg found hers increasingly heavy and irksome, though she hurried to keep pace with her father. They passed only a few people on the track: a couple of army officers on horseback, formidable in their red coats, and a burly farmer, leading a bull with a ring through its nose.

Meg ventured a timid greeting as they passed their fellow travellers, who smiled back at her but looked askance at Venn. They skirted the village of Bramfield, but Meg shrank away from begging yet as they carried enough food for two or even three days and could replenish their bottles from a stream.

At midday they sat down on the bank of a brook to refresh themselves with bread and cheese, after which they washed their hands and splashed their faces. Zack nodded towards a slight dip in the ground where wild blackberry bushes provided a screen.

'I'll go down there, Meg, and you can go behind them bushes yonder.'

Meg walked some distance to find a spot where she could not be seen, and warily squatted down to relieve herself. Then to her dismay she heard voices; two loud-voiced youths were approaching the bushes. When they were within earshot she realized that they were spying on her. What should she do, stand up or keep low, she thought panicking, horrified by what she heard them saying.

'D'yer see what I see, Ned? Ain't she the prettiest little thing, hidin' herself behind them thorns?'

'Watch out, she's 'avin' a piss,' warned the other.

'So we'll be polite an' wait till she's done, and then we'll 'ave some fine sport with 'er. Don't forget I saw 'er first! Stand back while I introduce meself!' said the first one in a gloating tone that made Meg's heart race with fear. She stood up and rearranged her gown and petticoat. Then a hand grabbed her arm, her cloak was pulled off, and her bundle rolled away. Another hand was thrust down inside her bodice.

'Come on, yer little beauty! Where've yer sprung from, sweetheart?' A mouth was pressed over her own, so firmly that she could not shout. She struggled violently, kicking out with her feet. *Where was Pa?* Had he left her to be forcibly taken and ravished by two men?

'Come over 'ere, Ned, and grab 'er legs – this is a four-'anded job to get 'er down!' shouted her assailant breathlessly. 'Damn these bloody thorns!'

There was a scuffle, and then suddenly both lads felt Zack's fists in their faces. So intent had they been on subduing Meg, they had not noticed the tall, black-browed man silently creeping up on the scene. Standing over them, flailing his powerful arms, he was a sight to strike fear into any opponent.

'Get orf, yer filthy beasts, take yer dirty 'ands orf 'er!' he bellowed. Grabbing the first one by the scruff of his neck, he heaved him headfirst into the blackberry bush. He turned to deal with the other one, but the fellow had taken to his heels.

Meg burst into tears of shock and trembled from head to foot.

'Why didn't yer call out to 'em, Pa, 'stead of comin' up on 'em while I was tryin' to fight 'em orf?' she reproached him bitterly. 'I thought I was goin' to be . . . to be . . .' She could not bring herself to utter the word, and Zack put an awkward arm around her.

'If I'd shouted, they'd've run orf 'fore I got me 'ands on 'em, girl. I wanted to give 'em summat to remember me by. Don't cry, Meg, yer put up a good fight, and they've gone now. Young scoundrels!'

He would have proceeded on his way, but Meg was in no state to continue their journey without having a rest to calm herself. Zack gave her a little yarrow beer to drink, and refilled the water bottle from the brook.

'Come on, girl, we got to move on,' he said after about fifteen minutes. 'We ought to get to Saxmundham 'fore the day's out.' He helped Meg to her feet, retying the bundle on to her back before they went on their way. Meg had been thoroughly unnerved by what had happened, and would not let her father out of her sight again.

Where would they spend the night, Meg wondered. How would they keep warm if they had to lie down in the open, even with three blankets to share between them? Her courage seemed to have deserted her after that horrible encounter, and she trudged after her father as they covered as many miles as they had in the morning. Toiling over a stretch of moorland in the late afternoon, she felt that she could hardly drag one aching leg after the other, and the bundle on her back was surely as heavy as the burden carried by the pilgrim in the amazing story that Lizzie Pond had told her, written by a man in prison a hundred years ago. I think I'd prefer to be in prison now, thought poor Meg, for I can go no further.

'Pa, I be that wearied, I can't go on,' she gasped. 'An' me head aches as bad as me feet.'

Zack slackened his pace slightly. 'Don't give up, girl. Once we get over Middleton Moor we'll be in sight o' Saxmundham. We done above a dozen miles today, an' we'll find somewhere there to stay the night.'

The thought of arriving in a town cheered Meg's spirits and gave new strength to her legs, but Venn's expectations of seeing Saxmundham were not fulfilled for another hour or more. At last, when Meg thought she would drop where she stood, the little market town, hardly more than a village, came into view, its ancient church spire pointing upwards to heaven. Meg gazed on it thankfully. She knew Parson Pond would have said that it was a sign of God's presence with them, a promise that they would reach the end of their journey in due time. Dear Lizzie, thought Meg, so clever at her reading and so devout in her faith! How kind she and her father had been on that last visit before Ma's death; would she ever see her friend again?

'Where'll we go, Pa? Can we stay at an inn? We got them two guineas, ain't we?'

'Aye, an' I'm keepin' 'em hidden 'til we need 'em in a sudden 'urry,' replied Zack firmly. 'I got a few pence in me pocket, an' we'll look for an alehouse to rest oursel's an' take a drink with our bread an' cheese – then tonight we'll look for cover at some farm. There'll be a cow byre or a haybarn where we can lay our heads if we wait 'til dark an' nobody's about.'

Meg's heart sank again. Even the straw mattress at their poor cottage had offered more comfort than a smelly byre with cows for company. And suppose there were barking dogs to warn of the approach of strangers? It was a constant complaint of Wollaston farmers that vagrants crept into barns and stables to sleep during the winter. We'll catch our death of cold on a chilly, showery March day like today, she thought, and tried to remind herself that it would soon be April, and that in any case beggars couldn't be choosers.

The alehouse they entered was fairly quiet, and the hostess's curiosity was aroused by the two strangers. Zack left Meg to do the talking – 'Don't tell 'er too much!' – while he sat in a dark corner drinking from a pint mug. The hostess questioned Meg closely, and quickly ascertained that they were a father and daughter from Wollaston, made homeless by the enclosure of common land, and that they were on their way to London in search of a new life.

'Yer poor little wench!' the woman said, shaking her head on which she wore a large mob-cap. 'I'll make up a bed for yer tonight with the maidservants if yer like.' She looked doubtfully at Zack. 'I won't want *that* one under me roof, but there's an outhouse at the back where we keep coal an' kindlin'. He can lay 'is head in there.'

Meg lowered her eyes in embarrassment, but was obliged to ask the all-important question.

'Are yer sayin' we can lodge without payin', mistress? I'd sleep in the outhouse along wi' Pa.'

'Bless yer, poor gal, yer can bed with the maids for nothin', an' yer pa'll keep dry wrapped in 'is blanket, but 'e can't come within doors. I won't turn a poor gal away to sleep on hard stone, for I know an honest woman when I see one!'

'Thank yer – oh, thank yer, mistress,' said Meg gratefully. The landlady was as good as her word. It was to set the pattern of the Venns' long journey: Zack would protect Meg from harm of all kinds, and she would gain them charity from strangers. Each of them needed the other, and though not as openly affectionate as the parson and his daughter, Zack and Meg were just as close in their way.

Meg found herself bedded down in a room with two young maidservants and an older one who eyed her suspiciously. She seemed to be in charge.

'Is 'e yer father, 'im outside in the yard?'

'Yes, er, Mrs . . . er . . . that he be,' answered Meg.

'Where're yer bound?'

'We're goin' to London,' said Meg cautiously.

'Yer ain't run away from 'ome, then?'

'No, Mrs . . . er . . .' Meg didn't like to ask the woman's name or her position at the alehouse.

'Yer ain't got a child in yer belly, then?'

'No, that I ain't!' replied Meg indignantly, and the others giggled. She closed her eyes, longing for sleep, but had to listen to the chatter of her companions, their frank comments on the travellers who had stopped at the alehouse that day. They were still talking when she fell into an exhausted sleep, and a deep sadness wrapped around her like a fog as she saw her mother's face in her dreams – so pale, so far away.

She was awakened the next morning by a clanging handbell wielded by the older woman whose name was Greta.

'Wake up, Doll! Get up, Poll! Time to shake yer feathers!'

The other two groaned, yawned and stretched. 'What about 'er? Don't she 'ave to get movin', same as us?'

Meg sat up quickly before she was told to do so. Grief for her mother still hung over her, and she ached all over. She sat on the chamber pot after the other three had used it, and was the last to splash her hands and face in a large basin of cold water fetched up by one of the two younger maidservants. She dressed quickly and followed them when they trooped downstairs and each one set about her daily duties, raking over the ashes in the grate and laying newspaper and kindling sticks to start a new fire. Curtains were drawn back and tables wiped;

one of them emptied chamber pots and washing bowls, and as soon as a fire was burning Greta set a pan of water on it to brew tea and then make porridge with coarse oats.

The hostess appeared and nodded to Meg, then went into a huddle with Greta. In the general bustle Meg slipped out into the yard to find her father rolling up his blankets and their contents. She hurried to his side.

'Oh, Pa, how are yer? Were yer cold in the night? They're gettin' breakfus' ready – ain't yer comin' in?'

'Is she givin' us a place at table, then?'

'She ain't said otherwise.'

'Yer better ask.'

The hostess told Meg she could breakfast with the maids, but would have to take her father a bowl of porridge to eat in the yard. 'He'd get no breakfus' at all, nor yet a night's lodgin' if 'tweren't for yeself,' she said. 'But if yer lookin' for work, I'll take yer on today if ye've a mind. Better for yer than takin' to the road again with that one.'

When Meg thanked her but said she had to stay with her father, it was made quite clear that they must be on their way as soon as breakfast was finished. They refilled their bottles with water, Zack tied Meg's bundle on to her back, and they left the house, Meg gratefully thanking the hostess for her generosity.

'That be some score o' miles from here to Ipswich,' said Zack. 'If we keep goin' at a steady pace we could make it by evenin'.'

Meg was determined that today she would keep up with her father. She smiled up at him and answered, 'Aye, Pa, best foot forrard!'

Their southward course brought them to the hamlet of Farnham and then to Wickham Market where they stopped to rest and eat the oatcakes with the remainder of the cheese, now somewhat past its best. The weather had brightened, and the sight of catkins, like curling silver caterpillars, nodding on the branches of willow trees before the new leaves had formed, were another reminder to Meg that spring was coming. Wild daffodils were lifting their golden heads, and in one cottage garden a tree was covered with early pink almond blossom, making Meg suddenly long for Wollaston. Those days were gone for ever with her childhood, she thought, and her mother was no longer there. Everything was changed, so she tried to set her thoughts towards London and whatever awaited her there.

Zack continued to stride on silently, and Meg did not speak her thoughts to him, fearing that she might shed tears that would distress them both. For all his dour expression and harsh words, Meg sensed that Zack Venn was sorrowing inwardly, and dared not allow himself to lose control of his reined-in emotions.

A knot of villagers had gathered in the little market square.

'There be folk enough round 'ere as could spare a coin or two, girl, if yer was to ask 'em,' Venn muttered, and Meg knew the shame he felt in asking her to beg, though by now she was ready. She thrust her shoulders back and raised her chin. Nearby to them stood a pleasant-faced young woman neatly dressed in a wool worsted gown with a white apron; she wore a becoming white cap edged with frills, and held the hand of a little girl of about three who wore a pretty smocked dress and a hooded red cloak.

'If yer please, lady,' Meg began, and stopped when the little girl looked up at her with wide, solemn eyes. 'If yer please to give a penny for bread to a hungry man turned orf his land . . .' She glanced at Zack who stood glowering at the little group. 'I be his daughter, mistress, and me poor mother dead this last week.'

She blushed with shame at the sound of her own whining words, the cringing tone she had heard from beggars at Wollaston; she had refused them, thinking how hard her parents worked in conditions of wretched poverty. Now she was no better than any of them. Her shoulders drooped and she lowered her head.

The young matron's face was sympathetic. 'You poor girl,' she said with a smile, and taking a drawstring purse from the basket she carried over one arm, she fished out two half pence and a farthing.

'Here, take these for yourself and your—' She glanced uneasily at Venn. 'For you and your father.'

'Thank yer kindly, mistress, that be good o' yer,' replied Meg, hardly able to raise her eyes. She held out her hand, but felt a sudden, stinging slap on it, making her draw back hastily.

'Shame on yer, Jane, throwin' away my son's hard-earned wages on a pair o' beggars!'

A large woman, wearing an enormous mob-cap tied with ribbons and lace, had seen the action of the younger one and rebuked her loudly and publicly.

'Ye're too soft, my girl, listenin' to every hard luck story you hear! That man looks a villain, and there's nothin' to stop him earnin' his own living – and a girl like her could find honest work anywhere if she bothered to look for it.'

The young woman coloured and turned away from Meg and her father, pulling the child after her.

'If I had *my* way, I'd have 'em whipped an' driven out o' the parish!' continued the lady whom Meg guessed was the mother-in-law of the young mother called Jane. 'Such sturdy beggars should be made to work for their bread!'

Heads were turning to look in their direction, Meg seized her father's arm.

'C'mon, Pa, let's get out o' this place. I couldn't bear to beg again, not here.'

'Old bitch!' muttered Zack. Meg saw that he too had been shaken by the scolding and was equally ready to wipe the dust of Wickham Market from under their feet.

And so they continued along the road, not saying much to each other; Meg was struggling against the despair that threatened to overwhelm her; her grief at the loss of her mother, the shame of having to beg, the uncertainty of the future and a secret fear that she would not have the strength to hold out until they reached Ipswich, let alone London. Venn was consumed with murderous anger against the de Boville family, and Sir John in particular, whose selfish action he felt had brought his own family to desperation. He noticed that Meg was in distress and holding her side as she walked. He slowed his steps to match hers.

'Not much longer to go now, girl. Here, gimme yer 'and.'

She looked up at him imploringly. 'Oh, Pa, I can't . . . I can't go on, not today. I have to rest.' She suddenly stumbled and would have fallen if he had not put out his arm to steady her. Her body sagged against his and he had to set her down on the damp grass at the side of the road.

'Let me take the bundle orf yer, I can carry both,' he said, though he was at a loss as to what they should do if she was really unable to walk further. They had no time to stop if they were to reach Ipswich by nightfall. His eyes roamed over the flat, empty landscape and spied a farmhouse and its adjacent barn away to their left. A deep, narrow lane branched off towards it, and he decided very reluctantly to throw himself on the mercy of whoever lived there and beg a night's lodging for Meg. He had the two guineas as yet unused.

'C'mon, girl, we'll try our luck with 'em. Can yer get up on yer feet again?'

He helped her to her feet and, transferring her bundle to his own back, he supported her on the half mile or so trek to the low-roofed whitewashed farmhouse. There was no sign of life except for a few cows grazing in a field to one side of the lane, and a couple of horses and a donkey in another. Zack looked at the barn, which was higher than the house, and wondered if they might creep stealthily into it to sleep overnight without being discovered. He directed Meg's steps towards it, pushed open a wide door and entered the large wooden structure with crossbeams supporting an upper storey which he rightly assumed to be a hayloft, at this time of year almost empty of hay. Spades, hoes and pitchforks were lined up against one wall and a large wooden feeding trough stood on the opposite side. Farm implements, wagon-wheels and part of an old ploughshare littered the space between, and the place was obviously used as both a cow byre and storage shed, for the stone floor was thickly covered with straw and cow dung. A thick rope hung down from the loft, but there was no sign of a ladder.

'Just lay yerself down here, girl,' he said, lowering her to the floor. 'I'll shin up to see what's above.'

Up the rope he went, hand over hand and gripping it between his knees – and there was the ladder, kept in the loft to prevent easy access. Venn put it in position, climbed down and within five minutes he had managed to help Meg up to the loft, supporting her from behind on the precarious rungs. He then pulled it up.

'They'll likely bring the cows in 'ere for the night, but if we don't make a sound they won't know we're up 'ere,' he whispered to her and he opened his bundle to get out one of the bottles of water. Meg sighed and closed her eyes, thankful just to be lying down under cover on a reasonably comfortable bed of hay. She was getting ominous cramps in her belly which warned that her monthly flow was due soon.

Meg turned over and fell asleep almost at once, while Zack sat up listening for any sound of activity – and sure enough, as the spring dusk settled over the quiet countryside he heard the lowing of cattle being brought into the barn by two men. He sat with bated breath, thinking that if they came up to the loft, he and his daughter would be lost . . .

They were not discovered; two women joined the men, accompanied by a clanking of pails and some good-humoured banter soon followed by the hiss as streams of milk were drawn from udders.

'Ol' Daisy ain't givin' as much as she used, is she?' said a female voice. 'An' Sally's in calf, so that's only Snow an' Speedwell to do after this.' There followed more clattering and some laughter, and at last the evening milking was done.

'Dan'll go an' put the 'orses in the stable and we'll go an' get our supper,' said the older of the two men. Then the four left the barn, closing the wide wooden door behind them.

That's us shut in for tonight, thought Venn, longing for some of the fresh warm milk for Meg and himself. Still he thanked Parson Pond's God for the hiding place and, rolling himself in his blanket, he too slept through the hours of the night in the hay.

When he awoke it was still pitch dark and, apart from occasional grunts from the animals below them, all was silent. Now would be a good time to leave their hiding place, Zack thought, before the household began to stir, farmers being traditionally early risers.

He sat up, staring blindly into unrelieved blackness. He put out a hand and touched the ladder where it lay; to lower it to the floor below would be hazardous in the dark, and to attempt to get Meg down it too dangerous to contemplate. Besides, it would disturb the cows who would start mooing and alert the farmer. No! Better to wait until morning, when the barn would be opened and the cows let out. The morning milking would be around six o'clock, twelve hours after the last one. He heard Meg sighing in her sleep, and in the next moment she awoke with a cry.

'Ma! Oh, help me, Ma!'

'Hush, girl, we'll 'ave to wait 'til the cows are out o' here,' he said. 'Then we can go down the ladder and be off.'

Meg answered hoarsely, 'Ay, Pa.' They lay awake in their

unfamiliar surroundings as the sky brightened; they had to relieve themselves in a corner of the loft, and to Meg's dismay she found her undergarments were soaked with blood.

As Venn had anticipated, the barn was opened for the morning milking, and one by one the cows walked out and back to the field. Venn retied the bundle to Meg's back and picked up his own, and two minutes later he had put the ladder in place. He went down a few steps, then told to Meg to follow.

'I'm right underneath yer, girl, so yer won't fall,' he told her, though he gasped and clung to the ladder when she missed a rung and almost fell on top of him. With a thudding heart she reached the bottom, and Zack gave her a grim smile. 'We done it, girl! Now heads down and—'

'Ho there! Who are yer and what be yer doin' in my barn?' called a loud male voice as they ran towards the lane. 'Dan, d'yer see them two as just crawled out o' the barn? Must've been there all night. Ho, there! Stop!'

'Damn it, they seen us,' muttered Zack. 'This where yer say yer piece, Meg girl, plead for mercy on us both. Go on, don't be afraid.'

Meg's head ached, her empty belly rumbled and her throat felt sore. A ruddy-faced man was running after them, and a younger one followed, wielding a pitchfork. Hearing the noise, a stout woman appeared at the kitchen door.

'Stop, yer dirty beggars! What've yer stolen?' roared the farmer. Meg was too weak to run, and her father could not leave her, so he stood his ground.

'We ain't stole nothin',' he said, facing the two men squarely. 'We just needed a place to lay our 'eads, that's all.' He looked at Meg, and she made an effort to speak.

'Me father's tellin' the truth – we ain't thieves or gipsies, we been turned orf the land an' lost our 'ome, an' . . . an' we got no food left!' she groaned, bursting into tears. The two men looked at each other awkwardly.

'Best just to let 'em go, Father,' said the younger man, but at that moment the farmer's wife, who had been watching this exchange, came towards them.

'No need to be hard on the girl, Enoch,' she said, and ignoring Venn, spoke kindly to Meg.

'What be the trouble, miss? Who be this man? Is he makin'

yer go with him?' Her question could have had two mean-
ings: either that Meg was having to travel with Venn against
her will or that he was forcing her to lie with him unlawfully.
Or it could have meant both.

'No, no, mistress, let it never be said!' said Meg sobbing.
''E's me father, an' a good one. We been turned orf our bit
o' land, an' . . . an' . . .' She could say no more.

'Well, now, that's hard on yer,' said the woman, indicating
to her husband that she would deal with Meg. 'Where's yer
bound, sweetheart?'

Meg was about to say London, but changed her mind and
replied, 'Our next stop's Ipswich, mistress.'

'Then ye'll come an' take a bite o' bread afore ye go.' She
put her arm around Meg's shoulders and led her to the kitchen
door, leaving Venn to explain himself to the men. Shabbily
dressed, smelling of unwashed flesh and cow dung, and with
a week's growth of black beard, he scowled at the father and
son.

'I'll wait down the lane while she's bein' seen to,' he told
them, at which they looked at each other, shrugged their shoulders and said he could stay for breakfast, but he would have
to eat out in the yard. Hunger won over pride and Zack tore
at the warm crust of bread and drank greedily the milk he
was given.

The farmer's wife meanwhile had noticed that Meg's skirt
was stained with blood.

'Here's some fresh bandagin' for yer, miss, an' yer can have
this old petticoat,' she said. 'An' yer won't have to walk to
Ipswich, 'cause Dan can take yer in the farm cart. I got some
cheese an' preserves to sell at an inn there.'

She went to the door to call for her son. 'Dan! Where are
yer, Dan? I got some stuff to take to the Sun Inn an' yer
father's got some kindlin' sticks. Make sure yer get a fair
price, an' take this young woman with yer. Maybe Mrs
Bourne'll give her some more vittles.'

'Ay, Mother, I'll hitch Brownie to the cart an' bring it round,'
replied Dan, delighted at the prospect of a drive to Ipswich
and back. 'Er – what about '*im*?' He indicated to Venn who
stood at the top of the lane leading to the main Ipswich road.

''E ain't ridin' in my cart,' said Enoch sharply. 'If 'e wants
to go, 'e can walk alongside it.'

And so the journey to Ipswich was accomplished, Meg sharing the farm cart with several large cloth-wrapped cheeses, a wooden box full of jars of home-made blackberry jelly and pickled onions, and a pile of kindling wood. As soon as they were out of the lane and back on the Ipswich road, Dan nodded to Zack who was walking beside the horse-drawn cart.

'Yer might as well get up along o' her,' he said, but Zack shook his head.

'I'd as soon walk,' he said dourly, hoisting the bundle on his back. Having been told that he had to walk, he was not in a mood to accept any more favours.

They arrived in Ipswich at midday. It was a bustling town where everybody seemed to be going about their business, either on foot or in carriages, gigs or pony traps. They drew up outside the imposing Sun Inn, and Dan got down to speak to the landlady, Mrs Bourne.

'Reckon we'll lodge overnight 'ere, girl,' said Zack, thinking of the two guineas secreted in his inner pocket. 'Then yer can 'ave a proper night's sleep. Go in an' order a room for yerself, then we'll 'ave some dinner.'

Feeling faint and light-headed, Meg climbed down from the cart. 'I'll ask for two rooms next to each other, shall I, Pa?'

'Nah! I don't need no bed. I'll go round to the stables an' see if they'll let me sleep along wi' the 'orses.'

He was in luck. The Sun had recently lost two horses to thieves who had broken into the stables at night, so a night watcher was needed in return for a cold supper every evening and breakfast in the morning.

Mrs Bourne took one look at Meg, and shook her head doubtfully; she did not want any sickness in the Sun Inn. However, when she saw the golden guinea available to pay for Meg's lodging, she took it and put the girl straight to bed. Meg's head was throbbing, and she fell into a fever, alternately shivering and sweating. Her thoughts wandered down strange pathways in which she saw her mother slicing a loaf in their old home, and then the faces of Lizzie Pond and Billy Siggery; they were saying something to her and laughing . . .

She was only dimly aware of Mrs Bourne standing at her side, and a grey-haired gentleman all in black who shook his head and said something about inflammation of the lungs.

Days and nights blended into each other as Meg muttered incoherently, and for two weeks Zack Venn waited for news as he guarded the stables through the long watches of the night, wondering with each new dawn whether Meg still lived or had gone to join her mother. If so, Zack knew that he would soon follow them, for his life would become scarcely worth living with them gone.

Then, on a bright, sunny morning, when the two guineas had been almost used up in payment for Meg's care and the physician's visits, Mrs Bourne came down to the stableyard and told him the crisis was over. Meg was once again in her right mind and was asking for her father.

'Ye might as well come up with me to see her,' said the landlady, who had grown fond of her charge, and when she saw the lean, unkempt man kneeling down beside his daughter's bed and taking her hand, she turned away from their reunion to hide her misty eyes.

By the beginning of May, Meg was not yet fit enough to continue their journey on foot, but felt able to work as a maid-servant, waiting on travellers who stayed at the Sun Inn.

Venn had proved himself to be a fierce guard of the horses and was taken on as an ostler. It was not London, but Ipswich, and here the father and daughter stayed throughout the summer months, working for a very low wage in addition to their bed and board. Meg gradually recovered strength, and began to take an interest in the bustling town, a flourishing centre for the trade and export of various goods being shipped to London. She and her father occasionally snatched a half hour to take a Sunday afternoon walk down to the docks where great seagoing merchant vessels came to unload their cargoes and take more on board.

It was a tolerable life, and Meg's memories of Wollaston gradually faded into the background, though she could never forget her friend Lizzie, and wondered if they would ever meet again.

Four

Two Angry Wives

September, 1777

Herbert Pond folded his daughter close in his arms, his heart full of thankfulness that he was not about to lose his treasure, but at the same time aching with love and pity for her.

'You poor child,' he whispered. 'My poor, dear child.'

For a time he held her close while thoughts whirled through his head, adjusting to this totally unexpected turn of events. He had received a shock, it was true, but he was not dismayed by it, not as he would have been if his beloved daughter had been in a decline.

'Is it young Richard de Boville?' he asked quietly.

'Yes, of course, Papa, who else would it be? And do not blame him any more than me, for I am older than he and shouldn't have allowed it to happen. I can see that now, Papa, but, oh . . . it seemed so right and natural, for I love him with all my heart.'

'And does he know that you are with child?'

'No, Papa, for I only knew it myself for certain today, after visiting Granny Mason.'

'Then I shall write to him at Diss to inform him of it. I'll write this very day,' said the parson emphatically, his mouth set in a straight line.

'Please don't put all the blame on him, Papa,' she begged again. 'I know that he'll have to be told and face Sir John's displeasure – and Lady de Boville's – but I know he won't forsake me.'

'My child, he is but a boy and may not marry without his father's consent,' said the parson, unable to envisage such consent being given. 'We shall have to wait and see what the de Bovilles decide, and I shall demand that they face their responsibility for their son's misdoing.'

'Oh, Papa, if Richard be not allowed to marry, let me go to the House of Industry and work there until the child be born,' said Elizabeth who was just beginning to realize what the effect on her parents would be if Richard was not permitted to marry her. 'Granny Mason thinks that three months have already passed and says there will be another six – so 'twill be born next March and all the parish will see my – my . . .' She stopped speaking, remembering the appearance of village women when they were great with child.

'*No,*' said her father decidedly. 'Never will any relative of mine seek refuge in the workhouse, Lizzie. You will remain at home, and the parish may say what it pleases, for I take no notice of gossips and shall rebuke them openly. I shall protect you and . . . and the child, of course.'

'But my mother will have a great deal to say, Papa, won't she?' Elizabeth's voice faltered a little as she contemplated her mother's reaction. She thought she would rather face village gossip than such a confrontation.

'Your mother may say what she likes, my dear, I am well used to her ill-humour. If the de Bovilles do not act justly, you will remain here with us in this house, and Granny Mason will come here to attend the birth, as she did at yours. Let a few days pass before I tell your mother of this, and meanwhile I shall write to Richard and walk up to Oak Hall this afternoon to tell Sir John. When the family understands the situation and have talked it over with the boy – with young Richard – then I shall tell Mrs Pond.'

Elizabeth watched as he took down his black shovel-hat from its hook, and buttoned up his coat. 'You sit here in my study, Lizzie, until I return. Your mother is busy preserving fruit in the kitchen and Jenny's with her. If she comes looking for you, give her what help she wants and say as little as you can. If she asks about me, tell her I'm visiting in the parish.'

Elizabeth sat looking out of the window at her father's retreating back in the mellow warmth of the September afternoon. The sun still shone with golden light over stubbled fields and the darker, dustier green of the trees and hedgerows. A few of the leaves were just beginning to turn, and the days were drawing in. Summer was over and with it the happiness she had known with Richard seemed banished from sight, and yet she felt curiously detached from her situation, the respectable daughter of a clergyman, assistant teacher at the vicarage school, with child by the heir to a baronetcy, a young man not yet eighteen. Her thoughts turned to the new life growing within her, Richard's child, her father's grandchild. Dear, kind Papa! His relief at knowing she was not consumptive had not closed his eyes to the nature of her predicament, but he had assured her of his firm intention to stand by her. She sat back in the chair and drifted into a dream of her lover: when he received her papa's letter, she knew that he would return to her and tell his parents that he loved her and would have no other.

He loves me, she thought, a soft, sweet smile upon her lips.

'Pond? D'ye mean the poor parson? What in God's name brings him to Oak Hall at this time of day? I've only just got back from a day with the hounds and must take my boots off. Tell him to wait in the drawing room, Hetty, and I'll be with him in about ten minutes.'

As the maidservant was showing Mr Pond into the drawing room, Lady de Boville appeared at the foot of the stairs and frowned at the sight of the black-clad figure.

'Not the drawing room, Hetty,' she said sharply. 'Show him into the small parlour.'

'Yes, ma'am.' Pond was redirected into a much smaller room, furnished with hard, cane-bottomed chairs and a plain square table with an inkstand that evidently did duty as a writing desk.

'If ye'd wait 'ere for Sir John, Mr Pond, 'e'll be with ye in a few minutes. 'E knows ye're 'ere.'

'Thank you, Miss Hetty,' he replied courteously, though he did not sit down but waited, hat in hand. Twenty minutes later Sir John breezed in, ruddy from a day spent in the open air.

'Good day to you, Pond! I hope it's not bad news that brings you here. Sit down, sit down!'

He sat himself on one of the chairs and gestured to the parson to take another, but Pond remained standing.

'Good afternoon, Sir John. I have unwelcome news for you, I fear, and the sooner you know of it, the better, which is why I've come straight here.'

'Good heavens! What am I about to learn?' asked the baronet, a flicker of apprehension on his face.

'It concerns your son Richard, at present residing with his grandmother at Diss.'

'Yes, yes, what about him? We both know the reason why he was sent away from Wollaston,' answered de Boville, frowning. 'Have you heard ill news of him? What can you know of my son that I do not? Speak, man, speak!'

'My daughter Elizabeth is with child by him, sir,' answered Pond steadily, looking down at the seated Sir John. 'It is regretful, but—' He broke off as Sir John leapt to his feet in great perturbation.

'What? *What* did you say, Pond? Good God! How do you know this?'

'From my daughter. She has seen the midwife who says that the child will be born some time in March, sir.'

'Indeed! And how do you know it is Richard's child? I knew there was some tomfoolery going on between him and your girl, but I believed that both of them had enough sense and self-control to avoid this . . . er . . . mischief. My son is not yet eighteen, and has had no experience of women – and I've always regarded your daughter as a modest, devout sort of creature, for all her good looks, though she did manage to get that villain – what's his name? – to let go of Richard's throat at the church gate. But I ask you again, Pond, how can you be sure that this is Richard's child and not young Horrocks's or some other fellow? Devil take it, what am I to say to Charlotte – to Lady de Boville?'

'My daughter has been with no other man but your son, Sir John,' replied the parson levelly, looking the baronet straight in the eyes. 'It is to be regretted, but it has happened, and you must send for your son and question him.'

'What? You're rather free with your orders, Pond! I shall certainly have the girl here for questioning by Lady de Boville, but until that has been done Richard will stay where he is.'

'Very well, in that case I shall write to him myself by tomorrow's post, Sir John,' said Pond, showing neither fear nor servility. 'And not until he has been questioned by you will I allow my daughter to be questioned by your wife. I bid you good day, sir.'

The baronet was left standing open-mouthed with astonishment at this unexpected defiance from the poor, henpecked
parson.

Sir John de Boville did not look forward to telling his wife,
but it had to be done. She would be furious if she learned the
news from anybody else and in another month or two it would
be all over Wollaston.

'Damn the man! Damn him and that wretched girl for
getting herself in cub like any cunning vixen,' muttered Sir
John. 'God knows how I shall break this to Charlotte – she'll
hardly be able to keep her hands from boxing the girl's ears.'

He strode up and down the library of Oak Hall, where his
wife and daughters would soon appear. He couldn't tell her
in front of the girls, so thought it had better be left until after
supper, when he could ask her to step into his study for a few
minutes. The baronet's heart sank at the prospect of her furious
reaction and he felt that he simply could not face her wrath
tonight. He decided he would leave it until tomorrow, perhaps
wait a day or two, until Richard had received Pond's letter.
The boy would then either defend himself against a false accusation or he would cut loose from Diss and return to Wollaston
and talk a lot of nonsense about marrying the girl. Sir John
sighed heavily. Why the devil couldn't Richard have practised
the art of love on some willing maidservant or milkmaid as
he himself had done in his youth? But as Pond rightly said,
this had happened, the mischief had been done and could not
be undone. Damn and blast it to hell! He would definitely
postpone the moment of revelation to his wife. Next week
would be early enough, there was no need to meet trouble
halfway.

Unfortunately Lady de Boville had seen the black figure
of the parson being shown into the small parlour, where Sir
John had joined him and closed the door. Before her husband
left the library, she bore down on him like a bird of prey.

'What did that canting fool want with you, John?' she
demanded. 'Why did he come here at such an inconvenient
time? What's going on?'

Sir John had no alternative but to break the news then and
there. 'If you will just step into the study, my love, I will tell
you what his message was.'

Standing facing her, he told her briefly that the parson's daughter was three months gone with child, and that she had named their son Richard as the father.

'*What*? God help us all! *What* an insult – trying to involve our son in her misconduct! Why did you not order him straight out of the house? Oh, my God! All the time you two men were talking in that room with the door shut I guessed it must be something serious, some injury to our son at Diss, some complaint about debts he might have run up – but *this*! Just let me get my hands on that lying hussy, I'll soon get the truth out of her! Oh, John, why can't you exercise your authority over these people? It's as if you enjoy lying down and letting them trample all over you! Oh, John, John!' Her voice rose to a shrill, angry shout.

'Hush, Charlotte, your voice will carry. Pray let us say no more of this tonight. We shall draw up a plan for tomorrow. Until we know the truth we must not condemn the girl.'

'Not condemn her? I wish I could have her put in the old village stocks and pelted with rotten fruit and eggs! She'd better not show her shameless face anywhere near Oak Hall!'

'But, my love, she says she has been with none but Richard and she has always been a truthful, modest girl—'

'Pshaw! Modesty, I'm sure! If you believe that, you'll believe anything. The scheming wretch has got her sights on becoming Lady de Boville one day. Oh, my *God*, what effrontery! We must see that not a word of this reaches Richard.'

'But my love, Parson Pond is going to send him a letter by tomorrow's post, telling him that the girl is with child,' Sir John said helplessly. 'That will give him an opportunity to deny what she says if it is false. If it is true, then I know my son and he will come back to Wollaston. Nothing will keep him away.'

'Do you mean to tell me that this miserable parson is sending our son a letter? I'll tell you what, John, I will see that Richard never receives it, not if I have to stop the post-chaise myself. It's a winding, cross-country way 'twixt here and Diss, and—'

She suddenly stopped, her eyes glinting with a sudden idea. 'Leave it to me, John, I shall see that our son never receives that or any other letter.'

'My love, I don't think we should—' began Sir John, feeling that Pond and his daughter should at least be given a fair hearing, and that his son should be questioned and given a chance to admit or deny his culpability in this matter.

Lady de Boville had already left the room; he could hear her rapid footsteps descending the stairs. He shrugged. When Charlotte had the bit between her teeth there was no stopping her. Yet sooner or later Richard would have to accept his responsibility for the child if it was indeed his – and Sir John was now inclined to believe that the girl was speaking the truth – whatever Charlotte said or did.

Lady de Boville went out through the kitchen door and swept towards the stables, a part of Oak Hall that she seldom frequented.

'Ho, there!' she called with a clap of her hands. 'I need a horseman to deliver a letter for me tonight! Where are you all?'

Two stable boys who were idly talking hastily stood to attention, touching their forelocks.

'Yes, ma'am,' said one. They had never been addressed directly by the mistress of the house before. The only time they saw her was when she stepped into or out of the family carriage.

'Where is the groom – what's his name – Brad something?'

'Brandon be down at the Fox an' 'Ounds, ma'am.'

'Well, go and fetch him here at once. He's no business to leave you boys to laze and loaf about. Get him here,' she snapped. 'I have a letter to write, and by the time I've written and sealed it he must be here with a swift horse saddled and ready to go. Do you hear?'

Lady de Boville returned to the house and went into the small parlour where her husband had interviewed the parson. She wanted to avoid the comments of her daughters as she took paper from a drawer, lifted a quill out of the ink pot and began to write rapidly.

> *My compliments to you, dearest Mamma,*
>   *Tomorrow a letter will arrive from the parson of St Bede's addressed to Richard. Please prevent him from seeing it at all costs, for it is full of false allegations. I beg you say nothing to my son, but—*

She hesitated a moment, then crossed out the word but, and continued.

> *...for the time being Sir John and I are arranging*
> *for him to travel to London and stay with my cousin*
> *Lennox in Bedford Row.*

Again she paused and frowned, wondering how best to persuade her mother that it was necessary to despatch Richard to his prestigious relations. The old lady could be stubborn in a disagreement, and Charlotte de Boville needed her entire support in the matter.

> *As you are already aware, dear Mamma, Sir John and*
> *I have hopes of an engagement between Frederica and*
> *young Charles Lennox. It would be as well for Richard*
> *to meet his cousin and share the company of Charles's*
> *friends. The boy sees little of the world in Wollaston,*
> *which is partly the cause of this unfortunate attachment.*
> *I am sending this in haste, dear Mamma, by a horseman,*
> *and beg that you will let the man rest overnight at Diss*
> *and send him back in the morning.*
> *I am, dear Mother, your loving and obedient daughter,*
> *Charlotte de Boville*

She sealed the letter in an envelope with the de Boville crest stamped on it. Hurrying down to the stables she found the groom Brandon ready to set off on his cross-country errand.

'Mind that you give this letter to no hands other than Mrs Tarrant, my mother,' she warned. 'If you see Mr Richard, say nothing about it. Tell him . . . er, tell him that I have asked her advice on . . . on trouble with servants. And when you return there will be a good reward for you.'

'Very well, Lady de Boville,' replied Brandon, touching his cap with his left hand, because his right shoulder was still stiff after the accident back in March when his horse had tripped in a ditch whilst out hunting with Sir John's pack. It had dislocated his shoulder, and although Mr Palfrey had with difficulty replaced the bone in its socket and bandaged it tightly in position, he still suffered weakness and pain in that shoulder.

As he rode off, Lady de Boville walked rather slowly back to the house, deep in thought. She now had to tell her husband her plan for Richard to spend the winter in London with distant cousins; her best ploy would be to remind him of her hopes for a match between Frederica and young Charles. She would have to use all her powers of persuasion, but she felt reasonably confident: Charlotte de Boville usually got her own way.

No sooner had Herbert Pond re-entered the cottage and hung his hat up on its usual hook, than Mrs Pond was demanding to know where he had been.

'It's about time yer showed yer face, Herbert! A fine thing, you an' Lizzie sittin' talkin' in the study 'alf the afternoon, an' then you go out an' she falls asleep in a chair while I work me fingers to the bone!'

'Where's Lizzie now?' he asked sharply.

'Doin' a bit o' work for once, washin' pots an' jars in the kitchen. Look 'ere, 'Erbert, I want to know what you an' that girl've been plottin' for hours on end!'

'I have something to tell you, Connie, so I must ask for your full attention,' he said gravely.

She stared at him. 'What's this, then? What's given yer this Sunday face? Out with it!'

'Come and sit down in the study, and close the door,' he said in the same serious tone.

'Don't order me about, 'Erbert Pond! Yer can tell me standin' up as well as sittin' down.'

'No, Connie, we need privacy for this. And you must be brave, for 'twill be a shock to you.'

Now alerted to hear bad news, Mrs Pond flounced into the study and banged the door shut. They stood facing each other.

'Let's hear it, then,' she said.

'It concerns our daughter Elizabeth,' he said quietly.

'Lizzie? Oh, well, in that case I can guess – them de Bovilles've found out she's been writin' letters to that useless son o' theirs and 'e's been writin' back to 'er. I warned yer not to let 'em, but would yer listen to me? No! There's no talkin' sense to yer, ye're so soft with that girl . . .'

'Connie, just stop talking, sit down and listen to me.' He broke in with a sternness she had never before heard in all their years of marriage. Her jaw dropped in astonishment, and she sat down heavily.

'Go on, then. Say what yer got to say.'

'Elizabeth is with child, and three months have already

passed. I am going to write to young Richard de Boville. He has to be told of it.'

For once Mrs Pond was lost for words. The colour drained from her face, and she gave an involuntary groan. 'Oh my God,' she whispered. 'I never thought – I wouldn't've known.'

He laid a hand on her shoulder. 'All right, Connie, don't distress yourself, it's not the end of the world, it's happened before. We'll take care of her and protect her.'

Just for a few hopeful moments Herbert Pond thought that their daughter's predicament might have the effect of drawing them together in adversity and bringing a new meaning to their marriage. This hope was soon dashed; Mrs Pond rose trembling from the chair and looked at her husband in utter dismay.

'So what're we goin' to *do*?' she asked wildly. 'Three months gone already, yer said? Where can we send 'er afore she starts to show? There's my sister Taylor over at Beccles, we've lost touch but yer could write an' say we've got . . . we've got . . . oh my God, the shame of it!' The thought of confessing their plight to a distant sister was too much for Mrs Pond. She looked almost pleadingly at her husband.

'Have *you* got any ideas, Herbert? She'll 'ave to go *somewhere*. Oh, I never would've thought it of 'er, never!'

There was silence in the study for a full minute while Mrs Pond sighed and wiped her eyes. Then Herbert Pond spoke quietly and clearly.

'Elizabeth is not going anywhere, Connie. She is staying here with us, her father and mother. I've been to see Sir John de Boville who was naturally shocked and said some unkind things in the heat of the moment, although I believe he will be fair-minded when he has thought it over. And I shall take care to inform young Richard.'

'But she *can't* stay 'ere, the whole o' Wollaston'll see 'er an' know our disgrace!' she wailed. 'How am I to face all them busybodies? I can't an' I *won't*!'

'If you can't and won't face the village, Connie, then it is *you* who will have to go and stay with Mrs Taylor or whoever will take you in. Elizabeth stays here.'

There was a finality in his tone that convinced Mrs Pond that he meant what he said, but she was not yet ready to yield up the sovereignty of years.

'Oh, go on, then, Pond, make us the talk o' Wollaston an' bring shame an' dishonour on a parson's family, us who's s'posed to set an example to the parish,' she said bitterly. 'But let me tell yer, Pond, I won't pretend to be pleased about it, I shan't walk down the street with 'er, the brazen *slut* – an' I'll tell 'er so to 'er face! She's no daughter o' mine!'

Her words hung in the air between them, followed by an almost palpable silence. She was about to leave the room when he reached out and took hold of her arm, gripping it like a vice.

'Stay and hear this, then, Connie Pond. If I ever hear you calling my daughter such a name, or if I overhear you referring to her in such a way, I promise you I shall announce to the parish from the pulpit that *you* were in the same way eighteen years ago. They shall all hear of it, the Miss Buxtons, the Horrockses and every family in Wollaston, how in a moment of madness I got *you* with child and had to marry you and endure a loveless marriage for the rest of my life.'

She flinched from his words as if they were stones being thrown at her and stared at her husband in utter disbelief.

'Yer couldn't do that, Pond. Yer wouldn't tell 'em . . . that.'

'Oh, yes, I would, and I will. I don't mind who hears it, I'm used to being a figure of fun. But my consolation in life – my *only* consolation – has been that same child conceived out of wedlock – my beautiful Elizabeth.'

His voice shook on the last few words, but Connie Pond knew that he spoke the truth. He would do exactly as he said. She turned away from his wrath and silently left the room.

Viscount Lennox was thankful for a quiet evening with no other company than his wife. After a good dinner he had loosened his waistcoat, discarded his wig and stretched out his legs in front of the leather-backed chair he preferred to the lightweight, elegant chairs that Lady Lennox favoured. A glass of claret stood on the small circular table at his elbow.

'Read it through again, Bess, and tell me what you think she truly means,' he said with an amused expression.

Lady Lennox picked up her eyeglass and studied the letter she had received from her Suffolk relative.

'She is simply asking us a favour, James. She wants us to

receive their son Richard and daughter Frederica for the winter season.'

'Hah! And does Sir John agree to this?'

'It is to be presumed that he does. She has written on behalf of them both.'

'Hmm. When did we last see the de Bovilles, Bess? It must be ten years since we stayed a night with them on our way to King's Lynn.'

'Less than that, James. Frederica was fourteen, and now she's . . .' She looked down at the letter. 'And now she's twenty-two.'

'Ah, yes, a pretty little thing who knew her manners. And has she no suitors?'

'Apparently not. They are buried out there in the country though, the only family of any consequence in – let me see – Wollaston. They are of an ancient line and date back to the Norman conquest.'

'Indeed! And yet young Richard has got himself into some scrape, she says?'

'Yes, it seems so – an unfortunate liaison with some girl in the village.'

Lord Lennox chuckled. 'Hah! I wonder how far it has gone. What age is this young Lothario?'

'He will be eighteen at the year's end.'

'Upon my word, he's starting early. I could wish that Charlie was in the same sort of scrape! Twenty-three and not a girl in sight. I'm not even sure that he's ever—'

'Fie, James, don't talk so – and don't call him Charlie now that he's a grown man. He will find the right girl in due time,' replied his wife with a slight frown. 'If all the young blades about town were as scrupulous as he, there would be a welcome drop in the number of bastards born to foolish girls.' She looked thoughtful. 'I wonder if Richard has actually got this village wench with child? Charlotte does not say so. But look, James, this could be an opportunity for Charles to learn how to conduct himself with a young lady. He could do worse than form an alliance with the de Bovilles.'

'Hah! I dare say that is what Charlotte has in mind,' said Henry, taking a drink from his glass. 'So, are we going to agree to this visit, my love?'

'Yes, James, I shall write back to Charlotte to tell her we

shall be delighted to receive Richard and Frederica here for
the season. Charles can take them to see the Tower of London
and Vauxhall Gardens . . .'

'And the coffee shops and taverns, no doubt,' added her
husband. 'And Frederica can exercise her country charms on
Charles. How could we refuse our relations?'

His mission accomplished, Brandon rode back across the flat
autumnal countryside, having slept in an attic room of Mrs
Tarrant's house, and had his breakfast brought to him there,
to prevent him being seen by Mr Richard. He had received a
half-guinea from the old lady who had given him a letter to
take back to her daughter who had given him a whole guinea
for his silence. To be a courier of secret messages was clearly
a lucrative occupation and he looked forward to more errands
of this sort.

Within two days of receiving a letter from London, Lady
de Boville had packed a large travelling trunk with both Mr
Richard's and Miss Frederica's winter clothes. Early on a
chilly, misty morning Sir John and his daughter left Oak Hall
in the family carriage and travelled first to Diss where Mr
Richard, looking unhappy and bewildered, took leave of his
grandmother and joined his father and sister on the long
journey to London.

Frederica could not hide her excitement at the prospect of
spending the winter in fashionable London. When her brother
questioned her about Miss Pond, she told him, as she had
been instructed by her mother, that the parson's daughter
had been seen in the company of Adam Horrocks and they
had resumed their courtship.

Richard received this information in stunned silence, then
turned to stare unseeingly out of the carriage window to hide
his unshed tears. How *could* Elizabeth prefer the company of
Adam who had always bored her with his limited conversation and total ignorance of any poetic sensibility? And they
had made love so passionately! Was it possible that such a
lovely woman could be so fickle?

Frederica saw the effect of her words and tried to persuade
him to be philosophical.

'Perhaps she simply tired of an absent lover, and Horrocks
saw his opportunity again, Richard,' she said. 'And she must

have known, just as her father would know, that any idea of marriage between her and a de Boville is entirely out of the question. That's the reason why Mamma and Papa decided to take you straight to London from Diss, to save you the embarrassment of going back to Wollaston.'

Sir John de Boville overheard this exchange; Frederica had not been told of the Pond girl's condition, but the baronet's conscience smote him when he thought of what Parson Pond must think of the de Bovilles. How could he face the man again in St Bede's on Sundays?

Having had no reply to his letter, Herbert Pond wrote again to Richard de Boville at Diss, and again received no reply. He had no choice but to tell Elizabeth, who wept silently, unable to believe that Richard had ceased to love her. A grey cloud seemed to descend over the parson's house; Herbert's heart ached for his daughter in her sorrow and disappointment over a false love and Mrs Pond was grimly silent. The Miss Buxtons remarked on their assistant's melancholy looks and reminisced to each other on the pangs of unrequited love.

One afternoon, near the end of September, Elizabeth went straight from the vicarage school to Cove Common where she and Richard had walked and talked and sang together in the happy summer days. She headed for Mrs Siggery's cottage, hoping that as the widow worked at Oak Hall she might have some news of Richard.

'Oh, Miss Pond, what a surprise! Come in, come in,' said the washerwoman cordially. 'Will ye take a cup o' tea? I was just goin' to brew a pot.'

Elizabeth entered the neat, clean little room with the widow's treasures on display – the carved wooden animal figures that Billy had made.

'Sit yeself down, Miss Pond. Billy's down at the smithy. Noah's made him a big boot to fit over his left foot, an' he's walkin' better for it,' said Mrs Siggery in her friendly manner. Then she caught sight of her guest's pale face and the strain in her blue eyes.

'Is there somethin' I can do for ye, Miss Pond?' she asked, remembering the recent gossip in the village when Master Richard had been sent away to his grandmother's. The girl must still be grieving over the loss of her sweetheart, she thought, and of course she realized the de Bovilles would never have allowed such an alliance.

Elizabeth looked up into the woman's face. 'Thank you, Mrs Siggery. You've been at Oak Hall today, and . . . and I only want to know if there is any news of . . . of Mr Richard de Boville.'

Bless the poor girl, she doesn't know, thought the widow.

'Haven't ye heard that Mr Richard and Miss Frederica have gone off to London with their father, Miss Pond?' she asked gently.

'No. W–when did they go?' asked Elizabeth hoarsely.

''Twas early yesterday mornin', Miss Pond. It all happened very quick.'

'Do you know how long – how long they'll be away, Mrs Siggery?'

'I don't know for sure, me dear, but I heard it was for the whole o' the winter, but I don't know for sure,' said the widow, alarmed at the look of anguish on the girl's face. 'An' I'm that sorry to be the one to tell ye, truly I am. Now, let me make ye a cup o' tea or would ye prefer a glass o' parsnip wine?'

'Thank you, Mrs Siggery, I'm obliged to you, but I'd better go now,' whispered Elizabeth, heaving herself up from the chair. At that same moment Mrs Siggery suddenly understood everything: this girl was in the worst kind of trouble.

'I'm that sorry to tell ye, sweetheart,' she said helplessly, opening the door for Elizabeth who walked away as slowly and dejectedly as an old woman.

'The poor girl,' she murmured to herself. 'And the poor parson. Whatever will they do?'

When Billy got back from the forge that evening, he immediately sensed his mother's uneasy state of mind. She told him about Elizabeth's visit and he asked eagerly how she had seemed.

'She wasn't well, Billy, not well at all. An' she got it out o' me that Mr Richard and Miss Frederica de Boville both be gone to spend the winter in London.'

'Oh, M–Mother, is that t–true?'

'It is, Billy, an' I told 'er . . . she made me tell 'er. And looked as if I'd cut her to the heart.'

'It m–may be all for the – all for the b–best, Mother. Sh–she will get over the sh–shock in time,' stammered Billy, feeling a kind of relief, almost a guilty thankfulness in his heart.

'No, son, yer don't understand,' replied his mother in some embarrassment, not wanting to go into details of what she called 'women's talk' to her son. 'I reckon the poor girl to be in the same way as that young maid the Horrockses had, the one they had to send to the workhouse.' She shook her head sadly. 'And her a parson's daughter – poor Mr Pond!'

Billy stared at his mother, remembering how the maidservant of whom she spoke had been sent to the House of Industry when it became apparent that she was with child. He also remembered the scandal that had raged, prompting young Adam Horrocks to stand up in church and publicly state that he was not responsible.

Speech completely deserted Billy. He turned on his heel and left the cottage as dusk was falling and limped to the Common where little Lizzie Pond had defended him all those years ago. What could he do for her now? Nothing. Oh, poor, sweet, beautiful Elizabeth, that such a calamity should happen to her of all people! By what his mother had said it seemed young de Boville had deserted her. Billy could have wept in both pity and anger.

Young Billy Siggery had learned hard lessons in his twenty years of life. Undervalued from birth because of his deformed foot and imperfect speech, he had been the butt of the dull and ignorant, regularly tormented by louts and unthinking children who saw only his outward appearance and not the perceptive honest man within. Disillusioned with people, he had turned naturally towards the world of animals and birds, with whom he had developed a special bond. Creatures did not fear him as they had learned to fear most men, for he felt their sufferings as keenly as his own and they seemed to know they could trust him. At the forge Noah often remarked on how gently Billy dealt with nervous carriage horses and the patient, lumbering shires. His heart went out to overworked, ill-treated donkeys who also had to be shod, closing his ears to the taunts of passers-by who shouted, 'Hee-haw! Hee-haw! Can't tell which one's the jackass!' He would pat the patient beast and whisper, 'There y'are, ol' fellow, ye–ye'll go miles with–without stoppin' with them sh–shoes on yer feet!'

He would pet the pariah dogs that nobody owned, beaten

for stealing scraps to fill their hungry bellies. He felt sadness for the birds whose nests had been plundered by thoughtless young egg collectors. And perhaps his pity was most stirred by the shouting of men and baying of hounds chasing a fox to a hideous death at the end of a good day's hunting by Sir John de Boville and his red-coated friends. For there was nothing Billy could do to save the exhausted animal.

Just as he was unable now to help Elizabeth Pond in her distress – and her disgrace – when the village gossips saw how matters stood. O cruel world! Billy Siggery would have given anything to comfort her, but what could he, the limping, stammering village fool, do? Nothing!

Five

Ipswich Encounter

September, 1777

Frederica's excitement was becoming somewhat blunted by the lack of enthusiasm in her two fellow travellers. As the hours went by and the carriage rolled along for mile after mile between flat, stubbled fields ready for the plough and thick hedgerows laden with berries, she found the journey tedious with nothing more to look at than an occasional church spire pointing up from a little village or a windmill with slowly turning sails in the still air. It was an uneventful countryside, touched by the autumnal colours of leaves soon to fall.

Frederica tried to concentrate her mind on the delights of the winter season in London: the balls, the fashions, the young gentlemen wanting to dance with her. She especially thought of Charles Lennox, son and heir of a viscount. Her younger sister Georgina had been satisfyingly envious of Frederica's good luck, but now Frederica could almost have wished that Georgina had come with her. They'd have spent the journey speculating about London life and the social round that awaited them in Bedford Row . . . but then she thought that perhaps Georgina might have caught the eye of young Charles Lennox and been preferred above herself. What a disaster *that* would have been!

Her attention was suddenly caught by a couple of puppies, playing and rolling over each other on a bank beside a stream. Then she noticed they had red coats and pointed faces – and magnificent fluffy tails – and realized they were not dogs.

'Look, Richard, is not that a fox – two foxes – over there, see?'

'What? Yes, Freddie, I see them,' her brother replied wearily.

She turned to her father sitting in the opposite corner. 'D' you see the little foxes, Papa? Don't they make you wish you were out with the Wollaston Hunt?'

Her father nodded. 'Good sport for the local pack. Where are we now? Such a dashed dull road, this. We must be near Wickham Green, so this land will be old Thoroughgood's, if he's still up to hunting.' He sighed heavily. Frederica was right, for he heartily wished himself out in the fields with the hounds on an autumn day like this, instead of going on what he saw as a most embarrassing errand.

Then the carriage rolled on, both father and son were preoccupied with the same disquieting thought: the parson's daughter. But whereas Richard was sad and disillusioned by the girl he had loved so passionately, Sir John was struggling with his conscience. He felt guilty about the deception being played on Richard, though Charlotte had insisted that they were doing their duty in protecting their son's future. 'After all, John, he is but a boy,' she had said. Yet he had fathered a child on a girl, and the baronet was troubled by her present plight. In the eyes of Wollaston she would be 'ruined', and the shame of it would fall on Pond, poor devil, as if he had not got trouble enough already with that wife of his.

And what of the child? It would be his own first grandchild. Was he to disown it? Richard had been told that the girl was keeping company again with young Horrocks, the squire's son, who was likely to be squire and a prosperous farmer in due time. If indeed the young man could be persuaded to take her on as his wife and call the child his own, the Pond girl would not do too badly. In fact both of them could do a good deal worse, reasoned the baronet, and privately decided to seek out young Horrocks for a quiet word; money would change hands if the young fellow agreed to save the girl's name and marry her. Sir John felt a little more hopeful, and he was prepared to be very generous in the matter.

By early afternoon they were all thoroughly uncomfortable, having been jolted up and down and from side to side for hours on hard leather seats; dozing was impossible, and when they arrived at Ipswich Sir John said they had travelled far enough for one day and would stay overnight at a coaching inn situated in St Stephen's Lane.

'It was recommended to me by Dr Webb – you know, he holds the living of St Bede's, though he lives in Ipswich. He said it was rather old-fashioned but known for its home comforts and food cooked by the landlady herself, a Mrs Bourne. And it will be good to stretch our legs!'

Frederica's spirits rose as Brandon guided the two horses into the inn yard, and she stepped down from the carriage into the bustle of a hostelry where Sir John gave instructions for the horses to be fed and stabled. He stood in the yard speaking with Brandon while Frederica and her brother entered the inn to order dinner. The landlady curtseyed and showed them into a pleasant small parlour where glasses of ale were brought to them by a maidservant with dark, curly hair. She told them that dinner would be ready in ten minutes. Frederica replied that they would wait for Sir John de Boville to join them.

The girl stared at them for a moment, then nodded and left the room.

'I don't think much of that girl's manners. Did you see the way she gaped at us?' said Frederica with a frown.

'Freddie! She is from Wollaston, I declare!' answered her brother with sudden eagerness. 'Her face is familiar. Don't you recognize her?'

Frederica shook her head. 'No, why should I? She probably reminds you of some serving wench you've seen at home.'

'I shall mark her when she returns,' replied Richard, quite roused from his lethargy. When the girl reappeared with a water jug, he frankly stared at her, and she returned his look with what Miss de Boville thought was undue boldness.

'Are you an Ipswich girl by birth?' he asked her. 'I seem to remember your face from somewhere else.'

'I be down from Wollaston, sir, these six months past,' she replied.

'I knew it! What is your name? No, wait, I remember now – you are called Meg. You are a friend of . . .' He hesitated, not willing to say the name of the girl he had lost to another.

'Aye, sir, I'm Meg Venn, and I was friends with Lizzie Pond,' she answered, her eyes lighting up with interest.

'Oh, Meg, do you remember me? I'm Richard de Boville and I saw you with Miss Pond at a funeral. That was when – oh, my God, I–I . . .' He faltered, remembering what had happened on that day.

Meg's face coloured as she turned accusing eyes on him. 'That were my poor mother's funeral, an' 'twas the de Bovilles who turned us from our poor cottage on Cove Common.'

'Yes, Meg, I do remember,' he said soberly. 'And you and your father left soon after. Elizabeth – Miss Pond – told me that you'd gone to London.'

'Aye, we was goin' to London, but I took very sick with lung fever, so we've stayed 'ere all summer, workin' for Mrs Bourne. But have yer news of Lizzie, sir? How does she do?'

'Good heavens, Richard, she's the daughter of that madman who tried to kill you!' cried Frederica in horrified realization.

Meg Venn turned to her indignantly. 'Me father be no madman! I don't know who *you* are, ma'am, but we was turned off our land an' made beggars by—'

'Let us not talk of that now!' Richard almost pleaded. 'Have *you* any news at all of . . . of Elizabeth Pond?'

'How could I? It was March when I was last in Wollaston, sir, an' she was courtin' with young Mr Horrocks then, the squire's son. She may be married to 'im by now for all I know. I only wish I knew.'

Frederica could contain her indignation no longer. This serving girl had no sense of her place, and she was furious that Richard was talking to her like an equal.

'You are forgetting yourself, Richard,' she said coldly and ordered the girl back to the kitchen. Richard was about to protest when they were interrupted by a great shouting and scuffling in the inn yard. Men's voices were raised to bawl orders which were clearly not being obeyed, for the disturbance grew louder, and a cry of ''E's killin' 'im! 'E's killin' 'im! Get 'im orf, pull 'im orf!' brought the landlady to the scene. They heard her shrieks, and Richard rose from the table to go and see what was happening, as did Meg. When they reached the inn yard they found themselves in the middle of a brawl. On the ground lay Sir John, blue in the face and fighting for his life, and on top of him knelt Zack Venn, his hands on the baronet's throat, squeezing the breath from his windpipe.

'In God's name, can nobody call him off?' cried the distracted

Mrs Bourne, though two men were already on their knees, tugging at Venn's shoulders and arms with shouts of 'Let 'im go, let 'im *go*, yer madman!'

If Venn heard or felt them he took no more heed than he would of a fly. He growled deep in his throat as he felt Sir John's body go limp beneath him.

'I'll do for yer, ye cursed Deboffle, I'll do for yer,' he panted. 'Ye'll rue the day yer follered me, yer scoundrel, yer robber, yer scourge o' the poor!'

A sharp blow on the back of his head with a horseshoe wielded by an ostler put an end to his vengeance. He fell forward and his hands lost their iron grip. Sir John struggled to breathe in air; his throat was bruised, he was unable to speak and his swollen features put some of the spectators in mind of the hangman's noose, but gradually he began to revive. Venn had been knocked unconscious by the blow and was dragged to a corner of the yard, where Meg wept over him and chafed his hands, begging him not to die.

'Wake up, Pa, wake up, *please*, Pa. Ye're all I got in the world.'

Nobody took any notice of her as they attended Sir John who was soon sufficiently recovered to stand up and be helped indoors. The landlady tearfully apologized for the attack made upon her distinguished guest and the bystanders were up in arms.

Having assured himself that his father had survived the attack and was being cared for, Richard heard the piteous pleas of Meg Venn. He thought quickly, counted the money he had in his purse, and went over to where Venn was beginning to regain consciousness. Meg gave a sigh of relief, then realized with alarm that Richard de Boville was at her side. He hastened to reassure her.

'They've sent a pot boy to fetch a constable to take him to the town gaol, Meg. I'll try to persuade the man to take him to the docks instead, and put him on a cargo vessel bound for London,' he told her in a low, rapid tone.

'But he can't go without me, he's me father and I ain't leavin' him,' she answered with a sob.

'I know, I know, Meg. He was ill served by my family, and you've had to share his fate. Go and pack your belongings as quickly as you can and come back here – and hurry!'

With a despairing look at her father, Meg did as she was told. After hastily throwing her clothes into a bag she dashed down the stairs – and ran straight into Mrs Bourne.

'Meg, my girl, there's no need for *you* to leave us,' said the red-faced landlady, her cap askew and her hair escaping from its pins. 'Yer don't have to go 'cause o' yer father. They'll cart him off to gaol or—'

'I'm obliged to yer, ma'am, for all ye've done for us,' said Meg breathlessly. 'But I got to go with Pa.'

Without waiting she ran down to the inn yard where Richard was talking earnestly with a self-important bailiff who had been called to take charge of the troublemaker. A high-sided cart stood at the entrance to the inn and a rough-looking driver with a red scarf round his head was perched up behind the one horse. Zack Venn was slumped in the cart, his face cut and bruised, his eyes half-closed. Richard was talking to the bailiff.

'Can't you see the wisdom of it, officer?' Richard said. 'To throw this stranger into the town gaol would make him a charge on the law-abiding citizens, whereas by despatching him off to London you'd be rid of him. D'you want the likes of him living on funds meant for the sick and needy of Ipswich? Put him on a cargo ship for London and let him take his daughter with him!'

The bailiff scratched his stubbly chin and looked thoughtful. This well-turned-out young gentleman obviously had some self-interest in the case, he reasoned, probably linked to the distraught girl who had just come into the yard. He gave Richard a sly sideways look.

'And who's goin' to pay for the ruffian's transport by sea?' he inquired with his head on one side.

'I shall pay whatever is necessary,' replied Richard, and holding out his hand he produced two guinea coins which the man grabbed and pocketed. It was sufficient to change his mind.

'Come on, girl, get up along o' yer father,' he said to Meg, taking his own place behind the driver. As Richard helped Meg up into the cart, he slid his third and last golden guinea into her hand. She turned to him with a look of astonishment, but he frowned and put a finger to his lips.

'Make haste, man, an' get to the docks,' barked the bailiff

to the driver. 'We don't want felons livin' on the toil of honest men! Don't yer worry, sir, we'll be watchin' 'em close as cats watchin' mice 'til they're stowed away on board for London – they won't give yer no more trouble!'

As the cart trundled off, Richard de Boville watched it go with some misgiving. He had not a penny left in his pocket and could not explain to his father how quickly he had parted with three guineas.

Miss de Boville and Mrs Bourne begged Sir John to stay a second night at the Sun Inn to rest and recover from his almost fatal encounter with the mad stableman, and he allowed himself to be persuaded. Mrs Bourne put him in the best room she had, and mixed him egg and milk noggs with brandy, to slip easily down his still swollen throat. Frederica fussed over him and when he felt able to get up, took him out for gentle exercise in the September sunshine. The baronet had been more shaken by the attack than he admitted.

'Has the man been taken to the town gaol?' he inquired of the landlady who assured him that he had. Frederica noticed that the impertinent maidservant had also disappeared; when she asked her brother if the girl had gone to gaol with her father, Richard could only say that Meg had not wished to stay at the inn after the incident.

After two nights at the inn, the de Boville carriage took to the road again with its three passengers and their driver. Frederica found her companions more taciturn than ever, each with his own reflections on the unfortunate coincidence that had led them to Isaac Venn and his implacable hatred. It troubled Sir John, and not just because of the grievous physical injury inflicted on him; he had always looked upon himself as a beneficent landowner and a fair Justice of the Peace. Now he had to face the fact that he had made a bitter enemy of the cottager Venn, who vehemently wished him dead. It was a sobering thought.

Richard silently asked himself why he had intervened on behalf of his father's enemy, saving him from being thrown into gaol. He concluded that it had been for the sake of Meg Venn, simply because she had been a close friend of Elizabeth Pond. It was something he knew neither his father nor sister would understand; in fact he scarcely understood it himself.

Much as they desired to reach London and Bedford Row,

Richard persuaded his father to break their journey at Chelmsford for a night, more or less halfway along the seventy miles still to be covered. When they set out the following day on the remainder of their journey their spirits began to rise in anticipation. Frederica found that her brother was as interested as herself in the changing landscape they passed through: the cattle markets, the smell of brewing beer, the corn mills powered by water rather than by wind. There was much more traffic on the road, stage coaches and post-chaises vying for space with farm carts and wagons as they passed through Brentwood and Romford where house building was taking place. They emerged at last on the outskirts to the east of London, and then travelled closer to the centre where there were many grand, newly built houses in wide streets and open, tree-lined squares. There was an air of affluence about the area. When at last the carriage drew into Bedford Row, Frederica could hardly believe her eyes.

'Oh, look at those houses, Papa! They must all belong to persons of distinction!' she cried, gazing up at the elaborately stuccoed façades, the carving over the doors, the wrought-iron balconies to the first-floor windows. 'I wonder which one is . . . oh, Papa!'

Words failed her as Brandon reigned in the horses outside a four-storeyed house in a row of similarly handsome dwellings. He climbed down to open the carriage door and let Sir John descend to the pavement. She suddenly felt apprehensive; both son and daughter hung back while Brandon raised the brass door knocker to announce their arrival. The door was immediately opened by a liveried footman who held wide the door and bowed to Sir John.

'I will inform his Lordship and her Ladyship,' he began.

At that moment a very grand lady appeared and he stood aside while she greeted her guests.

'Dear Sir John! We have been somewhat concerned because we expected you earlier than this. Has there been a delay on the road? Oh, there is Miss de Boville and Richard . . . come here and show yourselves. My word, how well you have grown! It must be the country air of Suffolk – do you not think so, James?'

Lord Lennox appeared beside his wife and agreed wholeheartedly with her. Lady Lennox led them upstairs into a large, airy room where a tall young man and a pretty girl of about sixteen stood ready to shake hands with their visitors. Frederica curtseyed low in the manner she had been shown by her mother – she had been practising for days – and noted from the corner of her eye that Charles Lennox had a somewhat prominent nose and a high forehead crowned with fine, light-brown hair. The Honourable Miss Julia Lennox held out her hand to Richard with a winsome smile, and he hardly knew how to respond; he took her proffered hand and held it briefly to his lips.

'I thank you, Miss Lennox.' His gallant gesture seemed to be well received and they exchanged a smile. He then turned to the son of the house, shook hands and, with a little bow, said, 'I'm happy to make your acquaintance, sir.'

'Pray call me Charles, and . . . er . . . oh, yes, we're all glad to meet our . . . er . . . cousins from Suffolk – from the country,' replied the Honourable Charles Lennox rather awkwardly.

Richard could not help noticing that his palms were moist and his pale-blue eyes had a worried look.

'It must be very pleasant to live in a lovely county like S–Suffolk,' Charles continued nervously. 'Perhaps one day I shall be able to . . .' he said, rubbing his hands together.

Richard surmised that he was feeling shy at meeting Frederica, especially if his parents had dropped a hint about future matrimonial prospects.

Lady Lennox was smiling benignly on them all, but on Frederica in particular, enquiring about Lady de Boville's health and expressing regret that she had not been able to accompany them to Bedford Row. Frederica explained that her mother had taken the opportunity to visit her widowed mother at Diss in Norfolk, adding that the old lady was not in the best of health. Lady Lennox sympathized and expressed the hope that Mrs Tarrant's health would be improved by her daughter's visit.

'And meanwhile, my dear Frederica, you will be my special charge throughout the winter season,' she continued. 'It will be my pleasure to chaperone you to social assemblies of all kinds – the galleries, the theatre and concerts. To introduce you to the best of London's society. You shall have my own maid to dress you and –' she glanced down at Frederica's gown – 'we must make a few trips to Layton and Shear's.'

'It's most kind of you, Lady Lennox,' faltered Frederica, blushing. 'I'm most obliged to you, most obliged.'

Lady Lennox smiled and gave the girl a strangely knowing look. 'And it may be, my dear Frederica, that you will do *me* a kindness by allowing Charles to escort you wherever you wish – whether to church on Sundays or to the Duchess of Devonshire's delightful balls.'

Frederica lowered her eyes modestly, but her heart leapt at the prospect. There was no doubt at all of Lady Lennox's approval and actual cooperation in making an advantageous match for her son. She looked across the room and saw Charles and Richard talking amicably together in a corner, and her eyes brightened: Charles was heir to a viscountcy. She was ready and willing to fall in love at exactly the right time.

'Ho, Watkin! Got a pretty pair o' passengers for yer!' Meg heard the bailiff shout. 'What time d'yer sail?'

'On the night tide – an' I ain't got no room for fellers on the run,' came the reply.

'What're yer carryin'?'

'Grain, twenty sacks o' best local grown wheat for Queenhithe. We're already overloaded.'

The bailiff got down from the cart, and exchanged some talk in a low tone with the owner of a moored vessel with one tall mast. Meg could only make out a word here and there. 'A troublemaker', 'Not a bad lookin' girl', ''Ow much've they paid yer?', 'Well, if they keep quiet'. Then she heard the sound of coins clinking. The bailiff returned to the cart, having parted with two silver crowns.

'Right, out yer get, and on to that rig – quick! He says it's grain in them sacks. Ye'll have to bed down among 'em an' keep yer mouths shut. Come on, feller, get a move on!' he shouted to Venn, and as soon as the pair were off the cart he led them down a short flight of steep wooden steps where they were helped, none too gently, into a vessel that rocked alarmingly as they set foot in it.

'Ye'll 'ave to get below along o' them sacks when we cast orf, an' be'ave yersel's, or ye'll be thrown over the side – won't they?' the trader said to another man who appeared to be all the crew he had. Both men gave a loud guffaw which somehow took the threat from the words, and Meg began to hope that they really were going to London, their original destination, thanks to the intervention of one of the 'Deboffles' so ferociously hated by her father.

Until they set sail, which Meg gathered would be around midnight, she and her father were allowed to sit on a hard wooden seat in the stern of a ship called *Northern Queen*. They watched as a triangular sail was rigged up, along with a larger mainsail. The hours went slowly by, and Meg felt stiff all over; she could hardly keep her eyes open, and her head drooped.

'Lay yer 'ead on me shoulder, girl, an' see if yer can doze orf,' said Zack, and put his arm around her. She was at once fast asleep, only to be woken by a shout from Watkin. They were on their way and the Venns had to descend into the hold, pitch dark and crammed with its cargo of grain. They both coughed in the dust-laden air, and later Meg was emboldened to go aloft and ask for some water. Around them the sea was calm, and stars twinkled above, obscured at intervals by high, scudding clouds. Out at sea all was dark, but a few lights glimmered on the shore.

'Eh? What yer want?' Watkin said, glaring. 'Keep yer voice down, we don't want no trouble.'

Meg moistened her dry lips. 'Pa an' me's that thirsty, can yer spare us a drop o' water?' she pleaded.

Watkin heard her and moved to fill a mug from a small cask.

'Only a drop, mind,' he said, filling a tin mug. 'Reckon that'll do for the two o' yer.'

Meg croaked her thanks and took the mug down to her father who gulped half of it and handed it back to her.

''Ave some yersel', Meg. Thanks. Ye're a good girl,' he said with more emotion than she had ever known from him. Having shared the water, they settled themselves on or between the sacks, and drifted into a fitful sleep, lulled by the regular rocking of the ship.

At first light they awoke with dry throats and Meg again ascended the steps. The two traders were shortening sail and expertly tying ropes together. Meg saw that they were now sailing on a vast stretch of water, but the shore could just be seen on either side. Vessels were passing them in both directions: a great ocean-going clipper, several long barges and little coasters seemed to be multiplying as they proceeded up river.

'Where is this?' Meg asked Watkin.

'Mouth o' the Thames, where did yer think it was?'

'Really? Does this mean we're nearly there?'

'Nah, we got a fair way to go yet. D'yer want some more water? There, that's the last of it.'

She returned to her father with the mug, and found him stretching and rubbing his sore head.

'We're at the mouth o' the Thames river, Pa, an' we're goin' to pass under two bridges,' she said eagerly. 'I've never seen anythin' like it. Come up an' see!'

As the sun rose and the sky brightened the river narrowed and the traffic on it became so thick that the water seemed completely covered with masts. Meg could see flat green land on either side and dwellings began to appear; further up still there were great wharves on either side. The larger vessels were drawing in to a number of quays, each of them dealing with different commodities. She could smell spices and coffee mingling with the salty, fishy tang of a busy river port. She and her father stood looking in wonder at the busy and varied scenes they passed until they saw what looked like a great, grey, forbidding castle on the right of a huge bridge across the water.

'That's the Tower an' Tower Bridge,' Watkin told them, quite pleased to share his knowledge with his astonished passengers. 'An' we got London Bridge to go under 'fore we're there.'

Under the second bridge they went. The autumn sun lit upon the water as the *Northern Queen* turned into an ancient quay on her starboard side and was moored beside a jetty. Men on the shore were preparing to unload her cargo and carry it to one of many warehouses along the waterfront. They had arrived at Queenhithe.

'Yer get orf 'ere,' said Watkin. Looking at Zack, he added, 'Yer could get taken on as a stevedore – all yer need's a strong arm an' stay at a job 'til it's done. No questions asked.'

Father and daughter looked at each other, and she fingered the guinea coin under her bodice.

'Thank yer, Mr Watkin, but first we'll find a place where we can get breakfast. Come on, Pa.'

'So we got 'ere in the end, eh, Meg?' Venn's harsh features softened as he spoke.

She nodded and her courage began to rise despite the ordeal they had come through and whatever fortunes or misfortunes might lie ahead.

'Aye, Pa, let's see if we can find another inn like the Sun.'

Six

Home and Away

1777

S ir John de Boville stayed in London for six days, and then returned to Wollaston. His spirits rose considerably at the sight of the familiar Suffolk countryside in autumn, serenely flat beneath the vault of the wide ever-changing sky. In London there was no time to note the sky or the season, for the days seemed all taken up with social arrangements, visits and calls, introductions and invitations. Frederica had been thrilled by the life of the *bon ton*, but her father preferred taking a glass of best Madeira with Lord Lennox and talking about the progress of the war against the rebellious American colonies. It seemed that all was not going as well as the newspapers reported, and the highly respected Earl of Chatham had stood up in the House of Lords and made an impassioned speech against the war – calling for British troops to be withdrawn.

This was of little interest to Lady de Boville, and in response to her eager questions Sir John reported that the Honourable Charles Lennox was a likeable young man, though with no claim to dashing looks or ease of manners in company. Privately Sir John thought him awkward and gangling, and although he had appeared anxious to please Frederica and escort her to social gatherings, his conversation was limited.

'He is said to resemble a Lennox ancestor whose portrait is on the drawing-room wall,' Sir John told her. 'I could certainly see a resemblance to the nose, which is rather prominent, but the portrait shows a commanding air of authority.'

'Has Charles not the same commanding air?' asked Lady de Boville.

Her husband had to reply that he had not. In fact he considered young Charles anything but commanding. However, as he was heir to a viscountcy and all the wealth and prestige that Lord Lennox would bequeath to him, Charlotte de Boville saw more than sufficient compensation in that.

'And how are things in Wollaston, Charlotte? How are the Horrockses – and Parson Pond?'

Her Ladyship's brow darkened. 'I am almost inclined to attend St Werburgh's on the other side of Cove Common, rather than sit beneath the pulpit at St Bede's and be preached at by Pond,' she replied. 'Thank heaven we have sent Richard out of harm's way to London! And do you know, when I sent for that Pond girl to attend me, her father had the impertinence to scribble a note to say that he would not allow her to be questioned!'

Sir John cleared his throat. 'I have had a thought, my love, that young Adam Horrocks might yet be willing to marry her. I shall have a quiet word with him about the . . . er . . . possibility.'

'What? Why on earth should a decent young man like Adam, who will be squire in the course of time, why should he marry a worthless creature who is carrying another man's child?'

'Because that child is my grandson, Charlotte,' he replied promptly. 'And I would like to see it properly provided for.'

'You amaze me, John. I do not believe that the child is Richard's. Let us at least wait until it is born – I cannot imagine that Squire Horrocks would approve of such a plan. He was in no hurry for his son to marry that girl earlier in the year, if you remember.'

Sir John sighed. 'I shall have a word with Adam, nevertheless. He will not find me ungenerous.'

Lady de Boville sniffed. There was an awkward silence between them. To fill it and change the subject, Sir John began to speak again.

'Oh, by the way, we had a rare adventure on arrival at Ipswich! You remember that cottager, name of Venn, who disappeared with . . .'

He stopped, aware that she was not listening. When Sir John hesitated, she looked up at him blankly.

'I beg your pardon, John, my mind was elsewhere. What did you say?'

'Oh, nothing – nothing of importance,' he said, suddenly deciding that the less said about Venn the better.

At the parson's house the chill October wind and rain reflected the atmosphere within. Herbert Pond struggled with his feelings of pity for his daughter and his contempt for the man who had betrayed her love. The news that Richard de Boville had gone to London on a long visit seemed to confirm that he no longer loved Elizabeth, though the parson was certain that he had been sent away by his parents to ensure that all contact with Elizabeth should be stopped. The boy was barely eighteen, and still subject to his parents, though Pond despised him for not standing up to them. The parson had resolved to look after his daughter in the face of all the scandal and speculation that would ensue once her condition became known. But after the baby was born – what then? Would his grandchild grow up under his roof? What alternative was there? Who would want to marry a woman with a bastard child? She would be unable to support herself so Pond's meagre stipend from Dr Webb would have to feed another mouth.

Elizabeth saw the anxiety in her father's eyes, and it hurt her far more than her mother's silent anger. Mrs Pond barely spoke to her and household messages tended to be passed though Jenny, the maid-of-all-work who toiled from morning till night for very little more than her board and lodging.

Returning from the school one gusty afternoon, Elizabeth let herself in at the back door, hoping that her mother would not be in the kitchen. Jenny was there, washing pots at the stone sink, and Elizabeth smiled at her as she passed through into the narrow hallway, took off her hooded cape and sat down heavily in her father's study. She let her head fall forward and rest between her hands.

'O Lord, help me,' she whispered, using the diction of the psalmist. 'Only Thou canst help me in my sore distress.'

'Is that you, Herbert?' she heard her mother call from the top of the stairs.

Elizabeth raised her head. 'No, Mother, it's me,' she answered wearily.

Mrs Pond's footsteps clattered down the stairs and approached the study door, where she regarded Elizabeth with a frown.

'Ye might as well sit in the parlour, seein' there's a fire in there,' she said. 'Gets on my nerves the way yer coop yerself up in this study, as if there wasn't another room in the house.'

'Yes, Mother.' Elizabeth got up and took her cape to hang in the narrow hallway before going into the parlour. Her mother followed her.

'An' if I'm allowed to say so, ye'd better tell the Miss Buxtons afore they can see for 'emselves,' she continued. 'An' that won't be long.'

'Yes, Mother.'

Mrs Pond shook her head, slammed the door, and went back upstairs, leaving Elizabeth alone with her thoughts. She had in fact told the Miss Buxtons of her situation that day, after declining her father's offer to do so. The three of them had just finished their light midday repast and, as they were about to rise from the table, Elizabeth politely asked if they would wait a minute as she had something to tell them. The sisters stared at her in astonishment.

'Why, what is the matter, Miss Pond?' asked Miss Letty. 'We had noticed that you have not been in your usual good spirits lately, although we knew you had . . . well . . . a disappointment, but . . . er . . .' She looked helplessly at her sister who finished the sentence for her.

'We hoped that you were getting over your disappointment, Miss Pond. Are you not well?'

Miss Pond averted her eyes. 'N–no, I'm not ill, Miss Buxton, but I am with child – and there is no question of marriage.'

For a few moments there was an incredulous silence, then Miss Letty exclaimed, 'Oh, poor Mr Pond!'

'Poor Mr Pond indeed!' repeated her sister. 'The shame of it – the disgrace!'

They did not seem to know what else to say. As respectable spinsters they felt they could not possibly ask about the father of the child.

'Are you *sure*, Miss Pond?'

'Yes, Miss Buxton, I am,' she answered quietly. 'I am very sorry. The child is due to be born some time in March, so I can no longer stay on at the school. I'm so very sorry.'

'We would never have known . . . I mean we would never have believed it, Miss Pond,' said Miss Letty in confusion.

Both sisters shook their heads. It was one more reminder to Elizabeth of the harm she was doing to her father's ministry. Nothing else hurt her so much as that knowledge.

'What does your father say, Miss Pond?' asked the elder sister.

It occurred to Elizabeth that no mention had been made of her mother – the shame that would be brought upon *her* in this crisis. Both Miss Buxtons' concern was for Parson Pond. The two sisters often deputised for Mrs Pond at weddings, funerals and any special event connected with St Bede's. Mr Pond's gratitude was their sufficient reward.

'My father has shown me nothing but kindness.' Elizabeth's voice was hardly more than a whisper. The sisters nodded at each other, trying to imagine the reaction of Mrs Pond. 'Pray give me leave to go home now that I have told you.' She rose from her chair. 'Good day to you both, and thank—'

'No, wait a minute, Miss Pond,' said the elder Miss Buxton, who was recovering from the initial shock of the news. 'We must make some sort of arrangement for you to be replaced.'

'We shan't be able to find anyone as half as good,' broke in Miss Letty sadly.

'How long could you stay at the school before . . .?' Miss Buxton could think of no delicate way of referring to the change in size of a woman carrying a child. 'Could you stay until the end of this month . . . er . . . the end of October?'

'If you really wish me to, I could,' said Elizabeth in a flat, weary tone. 'If it would not offend the parents of the pupils.'

'As a matter of fact, Miss Pond, one of our pupils is the natural daughter of—'

'Hush, Letty, it is our duty to keep such matters secret,' said Miss Buxton with a frown. 'Then let us say the matter is settled, Miss Pond. You will stay with us until the end of the month or possibly a little longer if you are not . . . er . . . and, of course, the pupils must not be told.'

Elizabeth could only thank them humbly, guessing correctly that it was their devotion to her father that had influenced them. Now sitting mournfully in the parlour at home, she heard a timid knock at the door. She raised her head. 'Yes?'

Jenny the maidservant entered with a little tray on which a tin tea pot had been placed, together with a cup and saucer and a small jug of milk.

'Oh, Jenny, that's just what I need!' cried Elizabeth. 'But didn't you ask my mother first?'

'No, miss, she's abed an' wouldn't've let me, so I done it meself. Shall I pour it, miss?'

'That's very kind of you, Jenny. Thank you.' Elizabeth's eyes filled with tears, and she reproached herself for not hitherto taking much notice of the girl Mrs Pond had got from an orphanage at fifteen, to take the place of an older girl who had given notice because of the long hours and Mrs Pond's ill temper.

'My mother will scold you for making tea without asking first,' Elizabeth went on, taking the reviving cup from Jenny's hand. 'You must tell her that I asked you to brew it.'

'Bless yer, miss, it all goes in one ear an' out the other,' said Jenny. 'I jus' wanted to do summat for yer, miss, 'cause yer look so poorly sad.'

Elizabeth was deeply touched. For the second time that day she had been shown unexpected kindness, and she felt warmed by it. She stared at the girl, as if seeing her for the first time.

'Are you happy here, Jenny?' she asked, sipping the tea.

'Aye, miss, I am that! Parson Pond's as good a master as ever was. I get good food an' a bed o' me own to sleep in. It's a sight better'n the other place I was in.'

'Where were you born, Jenny?'

'In the work'ouse, miss, the 'Ouse o' Industry as they call it, but there wasn't nobody to take me 'ome with 'em, so I got sent to that place at Flaxford. There was a lot o' other children there, an' I nearly died o' the white throat when it broke out. Lot o' children was taken away in coffins, but I got over it. One day Mrs Pond came an' 'ad a look at us bigger gals, an' she took me. This is a fine place I be at, miss, an' Parson Pond's a good 'un. *An'* I like goin' to church Sundays!'

'Oh, Jenny, what a sad life you've had!' exclaimed Elizabeth, regretting her former indifference to the maidservant. 'Have you any relations?'

'Nary a one, miss, but I got Parson Pond an' you, miss, an' nobody was ever as kind to me as you two been. An' I seen yer was sad, miss, an' sometimes cryin', an' it makes me sad, too.' The broad smile that accompanied these words could hardly be called sad, but Elizabeth judged that it was gratitude for the attention being shown to her.

'So you like going to church, then, Jenny? I've heard you singing the hymns and saying the prayers. Who taught you to read?'

'Bless yer, miss, nobody never learned me 'ow to read! I got 'em orf by 'eart, an' I can say 'em or sing 'em 'cause I got 'em all in me 'ead! But I can't read nothin'!'

An idea came to Elizabeth. 'Would you like to learn to read, Jenny? Soon I shall have to finish teaching girls at the vicarage school so I'll have time on my hands. I'd like to teach you.'

Jenny looked doubtful. 'The missus keeps me at it all day, miss, an' if she saw me sittin' down to read, she'd give me more work to do.'

'Then I'll help you with your work, Jenny, and when we've finished, we'll sit down together and I'll teach you. What do you say to that?'

'That'ud be right good o' yer, miss, an' I'll do me best,' said Jenny gratefully. 'Thank yer, miss!'

'Please call me Elizabeth, Jenny, and let us be friends,' said the parson's daughter to the girl who had lived under the same roof for nearly a year neither noticed nor appreciated.

As the year declined into winter, Elizabeth's shame was no longer a whispered secret but revealed to all. To Mrs Pond the disgrace was every bit as humiliating as she had expected, and her eyes were bleak as she considered the tittle-tattle. The Reverend Herbert Pond, on the other hand, went about his duties in exactly the same way; whereas his wife averted her face and Elizabeth walked with head downcast, he looked his parishioners straight in the eyes. He discovered that he was loved and respected by his flock more than he had realized. Even the men who had laughed at the threadbare, henpecked parson with his good intentions, now shared their jokes with him in a good-humoured way.

Elizabeth saw this and was comforted. Her father had always been able to bring out the best in people, just as her mother brought out the worst. There were a few women who muttered and pointed when she walked out in a high-waisted, loose-fitting gown with a cape drawn over it, but for her father's sake they mostly remained silent. The Miss Buxtons' discreet reticence on the subject of their former assistant also had an effect, for the parish looked up to the worthy sisters and followed their lead. As Mrs Pond had feared, some mocking remarks were made and unpleasant epithets were uttered, but this mostly happened behind closed doors.

One person certainly benefited from the Ponds' misfortune, and that was little Jenny Tasker. When Elizabeth left the vicarage school she kept her promise to help Jenny with her work, which was mostly sweeping, dusting, scrubbing and polishing, and in the afternoons the two girls sat down together in the parlour to pore over a reading primer. Jenny wrote her first letters of the alphabet on a slate supplied by the parson. She was fairly quick at learning from Elizabeth, her patient teacher, though Mrs Pond was disgusted by the sounds of shared laughter that sometimes pealed from the parlour in the afternoons. Herbert Pond's heart rose at the sound and he thanked God that his daughter and maidservant had now become teacher and pupil, to the advantage of both. The old saying was true, he thought, that it was an ill wind that blew nobody any good!

Winter brought with it the traditional pleasures of the hunt. Sir John happily led his hounds out on frosty mornings with a dozen or so other riders in their scarlet jackets and hard black hats. He was glad to get away from his wife's constant reference to the Pond girl.

On one particular day near the end of November, when the Wollaston Hunt had thundered over field and farmland all day in pursuit of three foxes, one of whom had got away, Sir John deliberately arranged to ride beside young Adam Horrocks on the weary homeward trot. He began to talk about local news and farming matters, which rather bewildered the young man; never before had he been singled out by Sir John. Parson Pond's name was mentioned, and his popularity in the parish, during their conversation.

'Although heaven knows Pond has his cross to bear,' said the baronet. 'That wife of his is such a shrew, and with this latest misfortune in that household –' he gave Adam a quick sidelong glance as he spoke – 'this . . . er . . . mischance must make his burden even heavier. He dotes on that daughter of his – she is indeed a beautiful creature.'

Adam felt distinctly embarrassed by this turn in Sir John's

conversation. 'She has turned out to be a great disappointment to her father, sir,' he said. 'Beautiful she may be, but her conduct tells a different story.'

'I think we should not be too hard on her, Adam, for equal blame rests on whoever . . .' Sir John stopped short of mentioning his son's name, for that would be an acknowledgement of Richard's guilt. Adam thought he saw the direction in which the baronet was heading.

'If that is meant as a caution to *me*, sir, you are entirely wrong! I have already had to protest my innocence in the matter of a maidservant – and if *that* is what rumour is saying of me now, I shall stand up in church again and deny it on oath!'

'My dear boy, you misunderstand me completely,' blustered Sir John. 'As it happens, I believe Elizabeth Pond to be a sweet girl with a loving nature, perhaps too loving, who is having to pay dearly for her mistake. I would like nothing more than to see her decently married and accepted in the parish.'

Adam was even more astonished. 'But the man responsible is no longer here to marry her, is he?' Like Sir John, he hesitated to name the false lover, though they both knew that Richard's name was on the tongue of every gossip in the parish.

'Ah, it's not for us to judge, Adam,' the baronet said seriously. 'Elizabeth has much to commend her, and any young fellow looking for . . . a . . . helpmeet who will be obedient and loving . . .'

Adam's expression showed that realization was dawning in that young man's eyes. He hurried on to his main point.

'I can tell you, Adam, nay, I can *assure* you that such a man's reward would not only be an amiable wife. There would be security, a suitable house and secure tenancy, to live in with her and . . . er . . . any children she might bear you.'

Too late he realized that he had said the word *you*. He stopped speaking and wiped his brow with a large handkerchief. Adam's face was flushed, and his expression showed his fury.

'You undervalue me, sir. I am not so bereft of self-respect that I'd stoop to marry a woman carrying the fruit of another man's sowing! Especially when that other man has publicly deserted her. I thank you, Sir John, but I'm not tempted by Richard de Boville's leavings!'

Adam galloped off in the direction of his father's farm, rather than return with the rest of the hunt to Oak Hall for claret and rich fruit cake.

Sir John cursed silently to himself. He had been made to feel foolish and feared that the story would be passed around the village – another juicy titbit for the women to gossip over. He could hardly ask young Horrocks not to repeat what had been said and ground his teeth at the thought that the boy would probably tell his parents.

Judging from the odd look he got from Squire Horrocks in church the following Sunday, and the half-amused, half-defiant look that Mrs Horrocks gave Lady de Boville, it seemed his fears were not unfounded. And to add to his chagrin, word had also got around about the eventful meeting with Venn at Ipswich – how Sir John had nearly been throttled, but for the timely intervention of his son, now openly referred to as the father of Lizzie Pond's child.

'Damn the man, I told Brandon to keep quiet about that,' raged Sir John, but his caution had come too late, for the groom had told his tale as soon as the carriage had reached Oak Hall. The gossip had reached Joshua Venn at Horrocks's farm and in no time at all it was all over the village, along with news that Sir John had offered young Horrocks a handsome reward for marrying the parson's erring daughter.

When the story reached the forge the blacksmith passed it on with a grin to his apprentice.

''E'll be askin' *you* next, Billy!' he teased. 'Would yer give 'im the same answer?'

Billy Siggery blushed to the roots of his hair. This amused Noah, who did not realize that the flush was as much due to anger as embarrassment.

If only such an event were possible! If only he, Billy Siggery, had been given the chance of marrying the girl he adored. How he would guard and cherish her, how he would protect her with his love and shield her from such vulgar talk. How gladly would he accept the other man's child as his own. But he was only Silly Billy, who could not walk or talk like other men.

One part of the story of the de Boville's journey to London

caught Billy's interest: Sir John had been attacked by Zack Venn at an Ipswich inn where his daughter worked and it was said that Venn had been taken off to the town gaol, and the Venn girl had also disappeared. Billy knew Miss Pond would want to hear this news, and when he saw her passing the forge, he looked up from the horse's hoof he was shoeing.

'G–good morning, M–Miss Pond.'

She turned to him with the kind of smile she gave Jenny and those for whom she felt no fear or distrust. 'Good morning, Billy.'

He was about to ask if she knew that her friend Meg had been working at an Ipswich inn, but checked himself. She would ask how he knew, and then he'd have to tell her Brandon's story of the attack on de Boville by Zack Venn. There was too much bad news to add to the good, so he just smiled again and resumed his work on the horseshoe.

Elizabeth walked on, a little puzzled by Billy's manner; it was as if he had had something on his mind that he could not tell her. *Dear Billy!* she thought. If only there were more of his kind in the world . . .

Frederica de Boville's anticipations of life in fashionable London were more than fulfilled. Every day brought new delights and Lady Lennox's generosity was overwhelming. Miss de Boville was often taken to stroll in the pleasure gardens at Ranelagh in Chelsea, said to be less raucous than the similar park at Vauxhall. Arm in arm with the Honourable Charles Lennox she wandered among its grottoes and groves by day, and listened to orchestral performances in the dark evenings, followed by supper under the great dome of the Rotunda, one of many places where the *bon ton* met to rub shoulders with the best of London's society.

One evening she was taken by the Lennox family to the Theatre Royal at Covent Garden where the viscount had a box. The play was *The Winter's Tale*, and it was the very same performance that the King and Queen had chosen to attend. The royal box was next to the proscenium, and as the royal couple came in sight of the audience, everyone stood up and applauded. Carriages and phaetons were waiting outside the theatre when the performance ended, but Lady Lennox insisted that Frederica and Charles should be carried home in a sedan chair. She hoped that the close intimacy of its interior would stir Charles into a little flirtation with his pretty country cousin, but apart from taking her hand in his own, he simply asked her if she had enjoyed the play.

'Oh, yes, indeed, Charles, I most certainly did!' she enthused, taking his cold, bony hand in both of hers. 'It was wonderful, was it not?'

'Er . . . yes, very well done, but I . . . er . . . there were so many characters and changes of scene, that I rather lost the plot,' he admitted. 'But it was happiness to sit beside you,' he added as his mother had rehearsed him. Frederica had to be content with that.

Richard de Boville escorted the Honourable Miss Julia Lennox on walks in St James's Park and to afternoon tea at the homes of her mother's friends. It was at one of these that he fell into conversation with a young army officer, the nephew of their hostess. He looked very fine in his red jacket, having removed his high peaked cap in deference to the ladies.

'Yes, I'm finishing soon at the Royal Military Academy at Woolwich,' he told Richard, 'and any day now I'm expecting to be called to serve with the Sixth Royal Artillery Regiment in Delaware under Sir William Howe.'

Richard could only stare in admiration. 'How are things going over there?' he asked, trying to sound as if he had followed the course of the war from its beginning two years ago.

'We're getting there,' said the young officer confidently. 'We have borne with those damned insurgents for long enough, and that fellow Washington needs to be taught a lesson! He may have scored a victory in Princeton, but he got a good drubbing in September at Brandywine Creek!'

'I heard that the war was expected to be over by Christmas,' ventured Richard. 'D'you think we're nearly there?'

The officer shook his head. 'No, they've put up a fair resistance, give them their due. It's more likely to be some time in the spring.' He laughed. 'As long as it's not all over by the time I reach the other side of the Atlantic! Excuse me, will you, there's a girl over there I want to catch before my aunt does!'

At the beginning of December the Lennoxes were invited

to a masked ball at Devonshire House, the magnificent town residence of the Duke and beautiful Duchess of Devonshire. Lady Lennox helped Frederica to choose an evening gown in the very latest fashion. The pale mauve silk clung to her youthful body, and the low-cut neckline showed off her shoulders to perfection.

'Does my dress suit me, Richard?' she asked, turning round in front of her brother, and gracefully gesturing with her painted fan.

'It's more like an *un*dress,' he replied moodily. He longed for the Suffolk countryside, and could not forget Elizabeth Pond, though she had played him false. His thoughts returned to the young army officer who was soon to travel a great distance for a noble cause.

Frederica was quite dazzled by the glittering ball, and curtseyed low when introduced to the Duke and Duchess. And she could not help noticing the admiring glances turned in her direction by the young men, many of whom were uniformed officers. One of them boldly came over to request a dance with her, and she hoped that Charles would notice. Her young admirer whirled her round and round until the brilliant chandeliers seemed to be whirling also.

'Charles, aren't you going to ask me to dance?' she asked, arriving back at his side, flushed and breathless.

'I–I'm not very nimble on my feet, I'm afraid,' he apologized, but a stern glance from his mother made him take Frederica's hand and lead her into the dance. His self-deprecation proved to be all too true, and in spite of his efforts to keep time to the music, and Frederica's valiant attempts to steer him round the room, he managed to trip over his own feet and tread on hers.

'Oh, I say, I'm sorry! Are you all right?' he asked, and as she smiled and assured him that she was, they almost collided with another couple.

'She's very good with him, James, and he'll get the idea in time,' muttered Lady Lennox behind her fan.

Her husband gave a non-committal grunt. Privately he was of the opinion that what Charles needed was instruction in the art of love by an experienced older woman. If he could be initiated into manhood, such social graces as dancing and flirting would follow with the increased confidence that the experience would give him. Little Frederica did her best, of course, but the viscount was becoming rather worried about Charles's awkward lack of response to the smiling eyes of young ladies out to catch a wealthy heir.

'C'mon, yer pair o' peaches, jump to it! There's another big'un just unloaded, an' the Jack Tars' throats'll be middlin' dry!' called the landlord.

'All right, Mr McSweeney!' chorused the maidservants, smoothing their aprons over their low-cut gowns.

Betty signalled Meg to go into the stone-flagged front parlour which had room enough for a score of sailors from the brigs and barges that docked at Queenhithe. Sailors congregated there at all hours, demanding good English ale poured by a pretty serving wench into their pewter mugs. The Drummer Boy inn was well known, situated as it was between a labyrinth of passageways and alleys off Thames Street and the waterfront.

Nervous and wary at first, Meg Venn had settled quite well into the day-to-day life of the Drummer Boy, for Mr McSweeney treated his servants fairly, though he had strict rules that had to be followed. He prided himself on the respectability of his house from which the bells of St James's Garlickhythe could be clearly heard. It was not a coaching inn, so had no horses to be stabled, and the pretty, smiling maids knew exactly how far their customers could go. Warm hands might stroke their shoulders and maybe pull at the kerchiefs that covered their bosoms; but if any hands tried to lift their skirts and feel for what lay beneath, that was the moment to withdraw.

'If one o' the fellers with a bellyful of ale comes on too strong, yer can come to me an' I'll send Tom to deal with 'im,' McSweeney had told Meg when he took her on. 'But I don't like a lot o' complainin', it's bad for business, an' a smart gal knows how to look arter herself. If ye're daft enough to meet any one of 'em outside the 'ouse arter hours, don't come to me if yer end up wiv summat yer 'adn't bargained for – understand?'

The other maidservant, Betty, taught Meg how to lean forward when pouring ale, to show just enough of the cleft between her young breasts and no more.

'Roll yer sleeves up above yer elbows,' advised Betty. 'They likes pinchin' a pretty arm, an' it's better'n pinchin yer arse.' She laughed. 'An' take it from me, Meg, them in the back parlour's just as bad as them in the front, though they ain't as honest. They'll try to get yer to meet 'em after hours – the dirty devils – an' even if them looks like gen'lemen, the answer's always *no*. Only remember to keep that smile on yer face! We want to keep 'em comin' in 'ere, but we ain't whores.'

Meg was getting more accomplished at such coquetry. The inn was not as clean or as homely as the Sun Inn at Ipswich, and there was no kind Mrs Bourne to care for her maidservants. Mrs McSweeney was nearly due to deliver her sixth or seventh child, Meg was not sure which and did not care to ask the good lady who sweated out of sight in the kitchen. Betty was friendly and Tom, the dour-faced aproned manservant, never tried to take advantage of the girls. Life could be a good deal worse, but Meg found herself longing for Suffolk, the wide sky above Cove Common, the freshness of the air, the peace of the countryside in winter. But her mother was dead and her home was gone, and she had lost contact with both of her brothers. The only soul in Wollaston who would be truly glad to see her was Lizzie Pond. How she would love to meet again with her childhood friend! Was Lizzie still being courted by Adam Horrocks who was waiting two years for her? How long ago it seemed! And what would Lizzie, the parson's daughter, think if she could see Meg now – a serving wench fending off advances in a London inn?

So why didn't Meg beg or work her way back to Suffolk? Because of her father. She had thrown in her lot with him, and had never been tempted to desert him. She knew that he now needed her as much as ever. She worried about him more with every passing week. He had found work as a stevedore, loading and unloading cargoes, and discovered that Watkin worked a profitable sideline in smuggled French brandy; but although Venn was strong and never left a job until it was finished, he had been involved in a couple of fights with other men who had teased him about his speech and his savage mutterings about 'them damned Deboffles'.

'Papa, you must forget about the de Bovilles now,' pleaded Meg. 'We've left them behind – there's no sense in dwelling on the past.'

'That Deboffle came after me to Ipswich, didn't 'e? I know 'is sort better'n you do, Meg, an' 'e'll be after me again, an' this time I'll throttle the life out of 'im, the villain! Just wait 'til I get me 'ands on 'is throat again!'

'Papa, ye've *got* to put the past be'ind yer, for 'twill do yer no good to keep dwellin' on it!' she begged, but to no avail. His mind was not to be diverted from his hatred and Meg began to fear for his reason. And that was not all. At first McSweeney had allowed Venn to sleep in the coal house, but as the man had no opportunity to wash in clean water he had begun to smell. He had grown a black beard which made him look more unkempt than ever and when Mrs McSweeney caught sight of him through the kitchen window, she was frightened about the effect he might have on her unborn child.

''Twill be born wiv the mark o' the devil,' she complained to her husband.

So Venn had been banished. Having lost his work through his quarrelsome nature, he had taken to scavenging the muddy banks of the Thames when the tide was out, picking up the odd coin or objects lost from the mass of ships that crowded the river. Meg was horrified, but could do nothing to help him.

'Don't fret yer 'ead over me, girl, I'm better on my own,' he told her. 'Yer got a good place at the tavern, an' I got somewhere to sleep down there by the water. One o' them sheds where they keep grain an' stuff. No good tryin' to beg, so I don't say nothin' to nobody – except for Watkin, who ain't a bad bloke. 'E gives me a tot o' brandy some nights to keep out the cold.'

Meg sighed; she passed him the odd penny or two from her meagre wages each week. The weather had turned very cold, with frosty nights, and as Christmas approached, Venn's prospects appeared bleak.

Parson Pond was pleased to see that every seat in St Bede's was occupied at Morning Prayer on Christmas Day. He knew every face that rose to sing the opening hymn, and noted that the strong male voice rising above the rest belonged to Billy Siggery, standing beside his mother. Like many other stammerers, Billy was not troubled by his defective speech when singing, and had perfect pitch. Below the pulpit Pond saw his daughter in the usual front pew, between her mother and little Jenny. Elizabeth's eyes were downcast, and her mother's face was averted during the Gospel reading of the day which referred to the Virgin Mary as being 'great with child' as she accompanied her husband to Bethlehem for the census. Now close to seven months into her time, Elizabeth felt that all eyes were upon her and she must look shamefully big to the congregation, and tears brimmed in her eyes. Jenny shot her a quick glance, while her mother sat as immobile as a statue.

I mustn't weep, for Papa's sake, she told herself silently. *I must think of his love as being like the Lord's love for me, and be thankful.*

And then the strangest feeling stole over her. Her sorrow over Richard and her shame suddenly lifted from her like vapour in sunshine; she felt as if borne up on angel's wings and, for a few blessed moments, a kind of happiness filled her heart.

This must be in answer to Papa's prayers for me, she thought, looking at her father in gratitude; but he was not looking at her. He was looking across the congregation to where Widow Siggery sat with her afflicted son.

If ever Herbert Pond saw steadfast love transform a human face, he saw it then, directed towards his daughter from the boy. He wondered why he had never realized it before.

My poor child, he thought sadly. If only the de Boville boy had loved her half as much . . .

Seven
Midwinter

1777–1778

A thick mist hung over the river as the low December sun rose on the masts of small craft crowding between the banks of the upper pool above London Bridge. Further down, below Tower Bridge, ocean-going merchant ships lay at anchor, waiting to discharge their cargoes on to lighters, small flat-bottomed barges that could dock at the many quays along both sides of the Thames. Visibility was very low, which suited Watkin on this particular venture. The sails of the *Northern Queen* were folded away, for she was propelled by two oarsmen who could row silently into the deserted quay. Her present cargo was not grain or cheese, but sugar and rum from a moored merchant ship whose crew had gone ashore, leaving only a few watchers who could be bribed by the night plunderers, of whom there were many.

The oars splashed softly, and they were drawn in; the mooring rope was unwound and thrown ashore by one of the rowers. The other was a burly lad who had never been heard to speak.

'Good lads. Quiet now an' quick,' whispered Watkin. 'Take 'em up to the shed. Mind 'ow yer carry the skins – we don't want none of 'em burstin'!'

Each of the three men carried a sack filled with a hundred pounds of dark muscovado sugar; the rum had been tapped from casks into wine-skins which could be carried without noise until transferred to glass bottles by the innkeepers who paid Watkin well for it.

Nobody who mattered heard the arrival of the *Northern Queen*, but Zack Venn's ears pricked up. He had been unable

to sleep in his damp, draughty shed. He stretched and eased
himself upright, opened the door and raised his hand. Watkin
gave him an answering wave, and the three men entered the
shed and put down their burdens. The wine-skins full of rum
would be taken away on a cart hired for the purpose.

'Ho, there, Zack. How're yer doin'? By God, it's raw this
mornin',' muttered Watkin, somewhat taken aback by Venn's
skinny frame and red-rimmed eyes. 'That black beard o' yourn
frightens me more'n any pirate!'

When the three sacks were stowed in a corner of the shed,
Watkin again looked hard at Venn, and saw that he was
trembling.

'Yer can't stay 'ere, mate, it'll kill yer,' Watkin said bluntly.
'Yer need to be tucked up warm an' dry. What about that girl
o' yours? She still at the Drummer Boy? Can't she get yer in
there for the winter? Ye'll be a goner else.'

'Ooh-ah,' replied Venn, scratching his head, around which
he had tied a grubby scarf.

'Look 'ere, I'll get rid o' these skins an' then come back
an' take yer up to McSweeney's.'

'Nah! Not *there*,' growled Venn. 'Meg's got 'erself bed an'
board an' I ain't goin' to mess it up for 'er.'

Watkin did not bother to argue, but paid off his rowers and
made for the Drummer Boy, to make an agreement with
McSweeney over the price of two quarts of best Jamaica rum.
He caught sight of Meg while he was there and beckoned to
her for a quiet word.

'Yer pa'll be goin' out on the ebb tide, nothin' so sure, if
'e stays down there in winter, miss. Yer better see McSweeney –
ask if he can't stick 'im in the coal 'ouse again, eh?'

Meg's eyes filled with dismay; McSweeney was not given
to acts of charity. She and Betty had been busier than ever
since Mrs McSweeney had been delivered of a son, and the
landlord was having to manage with a hired cook who lacked
his wife's skill with mutton chops. It was not a good time to
beg for favours.

Sure enough, he frowned and stuck out his lower lip when
she approached him, but he knew Meg to be a hard worker
and a girl who had just the right attitude to amorous advances:
she knew how to smile as she gave a firm refusal.

'All right, then, just for a couple o' days – only 'e's to stay in the coal 'ouse an' yer can take 'im any leftovers when the dogs've finished their dinner. But I don't want to see 'im, understand?'

Meg was tearful in her gratitude; as soon as the midday rush had been dealt with, she put on her cape and ran down to the quayside. Venn was dozing in the shed with his head on a sack of sugar, a good deal harder than grain. Horrified at his condition, Meg would not stop to argue with him. 'Ye're comin' with me *at once*, Pa, no shilly-shallyin' – I'm goin' to look after yer. McSweeney says ye can sleep in the coal house, an' I'll be able to bring ye somethin' to eat. Come on, get up, Pa – *now*!'

Shivering and muttering under his breath, Venn let her take his hand and lead him through a narrow, winding alleyway and up a short flight of steps to the inn.

''Ere yer be, Pa, the coal 'ouse ain't cold, 'cause it's next to the kitchen. I'll bring a blanket from off my bed. Come on, lay yeself down, an' I'll see what I can find for yer to drink. Only ye must stay in 'ere – don't show yeself in the yard.'

Poor Meg. No sooner had she settled her father in a corner of the coal house than Tom the manservant came out with the coal scuttle from the back parlour.

'What's goin' on 'ere? Who the hell are *you*, yer stinkin' ol' villain? Be orf with—'

Meg opened her mouth to say that her father had been given permission by the landlord, but Venn suddenly sprang up to defend himself. He looked hard at the manservant who drew back slightly from the glittering, red-rimmed eyes.

Meg hastened to explain. 'He's me father, Tom, and Mr McSweeney says—'

'So yer come after me again, yer cursed Deboffle!' roared Venn. 'I knew yer would – an' this time I'll throttle yer!'

Meg shrieked, and threw herself between the two men, catching a sharp blow from Venn to the side of her head.

'Stop, Pa, *stop!* He ain't no de Boville! Run away, Tom, run away 'fore he goes for yer throat!'

But Tom was not one to run away from intruders. Instead he shouted to Meg to get out of the way. She had a sickening sensation of déjà vu as Venn lurched at him roaring, 'Damned Deboffle!'

Mrs McSweeney, feeding her baby upstairs, heard the shouts and looked out of the window. She began to scream at the top of her voice.

'Help, help! Murder! For God's sake, help, help!'

McSweeney came running out, followed by a couple of sailors from the front parlour. It took all four men to restrain Venn who continued to shout and hit out with his fists.

'Damned Deboffle, I'll kill yer!'

'Look out, 'e's gone berserk!' gasped one of the sailors, fending off blows. ''E's a mad dog! Fetch a rope to tie 'im up!'

The noise of the scuffle began to alert the locals – the idle and the curious came running to the scene, drawn by the sport of a brawl. Venn was overpowered and his hands tied behind his back with a rope.

'Fetch ol' Tollett's dung cart an' take 'im orf to clink!' shouted McSweeney, while Meg reeled against the wall, her head spinning from the blow.

'The Fleet! Take 'im to the Fleet!'

'No, Newgate's the place for 'im! They'll string him up!'

Venn was dragged out of the inn yard, and bundled on to a ramshackle cart. It had no need of a horse, being pushed along by the swelling crowd. This was a London mob in full cry, howling and picking up more followers as they proceeded up from Thames Street like a pack of hounds following their quarry, to skirt St Paul's Cathedral and surge towards Newgate prison. Venn was then thrown inside and locked in a cell to await trial. Meg was ignored, left to wail and wring her hands; there was nowhere for her to go, except back to the Drummer Boy, where she faced the wrath of McSweeney.

'A fine carry-on, bringin' a ravin' lunatic into a respectable 'ostelry!' he began. The rush of patrons back from the hue-and-cry interrupted him and he ordered her back to work.

'But don't yer dare bring that madman round 'ere again, or ye'll be out on yer arse! Bloody lunatic!'

Meg needed all her self-control not to break down and weep while serving ale, some with a tot of best Jamaica rum. As she hurried between the kitchen and parlours, refilling her jug, a lady came forward and gently drew her aside. She wore a black velvet cape, edged with fur, and her broad-brimmed hat was trimmed with three ostrich feathers. She was an unlikely patron of the Drummer Boy, and Meg, in spite of her anxiety for her father, felt quite overawed.

'Forgive me, my dear, for introducing myself at such a sad time,' said the lady. 'My name is Duvall, Mrs Duvall, and I believe that your poor father has been taken to Newgate prison.' She laid her gloved hand on Meg's shoulder for a moment. 'Try not to worry too much, my dear. I will find out the sentence of the court and let you know of it.'

She pressed a half-guinea into Meg's hand, smiled and went on her way with a gentleman. Astonished and bewildered, Meg was comforted to know that there were still some kind people in the world – even in lawless London.

Christmas in Bedford Row brought more social activities. Frederica de Boville continued to enjoy her life as prospective daughter-in-law to the Lennoxes; but her brother Richard found no pleasure in the endless round of parties. He felt that he was wasting his time, though there was nothing to entice him back to Wollaston where Elizabeth Pond may already have married Adam Horrocks. A daring idea was forming in Richard's mind – but he had nobody to ask about the information he needed. Then one afternoon at the very end of the year, he was asked to accompany Julia to the home of an aunt of hers, a Mrs Seward, who had married Lady Lennox's half-brother. She was now widowed and lived alone in Clerkenwell.

'I simply cannot put her off any longer, Frederica,' Lady Lennox said, half-apologetically. 'Mrs Seward is a good sort of woman in her way, but lacks that degree of refinement one could wish to see in one's family. I have another engagement that afternoon, but I know I can rely on you to chaperone Julia, and Charles and your brother will also be there.'

On entering the drawing room of Mrs Sophia Seward's house in John Street, Richard at once saw two red-coated officers, one of whom was introduced to him as Captain Oliver Seward, son of their hostess. Mrs Seward was a friendly, neatly dressed woman in her forties with no social pretensions and she was genuinely delighted to meet the de Bovilles. Having been introduced, Frederica did not spend much time in conversation with her, but Richard noticed that Charles seemed much more at ease in her presence and addressed her as Aunt Sophie. She called to Oliver and his brother officer, known as Toby,

to meet young Mr de Boville, and after exchanging pleas-
antries the three young men settled in a window seat. The two
officers could talk of nothing else but their inclusion in a plan
to sail for America and fight under the British flag.

'Of course my mother is utterly opposed to my going,'
Oliver confided. 'She doesn't mind me being in the Guards
here at home, though we seem to spend half our time pursuing
ruffians and breaking up brawls – that isn't what I joined the
army for.'

His friend laughed in agreement, leading my Richard to
tentatively ask about the army as a career.

'Get yourself down to Woolwich, young man, and enrol at
the Military Academy,' Toby said grinning. 'If you survive a
couple of months' training, and putting down the odd riot or
two, apply for active service. We're short of decent officers
to take charge of the riff-raff who've taken the King's shilling!
I take it you're old enough to enrol without your father's
permission? Eighteen? Oh, that's all right.'

'But what will my uncle Lennox say?' asked Oliver.

Richard shook his head. 'He won't be able to stop me.'

'Maybe, but you'd better tell the old fellow of your plans,
and at least let your parents know,' Oliver cautioned.

'Certainly I will,' replied Richard. But not until I've been
accepted for service abroad, he thought to himself.

Meanwhile Charles Lennox was talking with his aunt.

'I envy Richard living in Suffolk,' he was telling her. 'And
I think I was intended to be a farmer.'

Sophia Seward laughed aloud, looking on him fondly and
then across the room at Frederica. A pretty girl with a charming
manner, she thought, and obviously favoured by the Lennoxes
as a wife for Charles, but would they make each other happy?
She couldn't picture Frederica as a farmer's wife nor Charles
as a dashing young husband in London's brilliant but shallow
society.

Similar thoughts had been going through Lord Lennox's head.
Here they were, nearly into a new year, and no official
announcement had been made. Was the boy normal? Lennox
shuddered his disgust at the very thought. No! I shall have to
take matters into my own hands, he decided. If he hasn't
declared himself to the girl by the end of January, I shall carry

out a little plan of my own. Only I'll have to find a worldly-wise woman. And it was something he could not possibly discuss with his wife.

Three days had elapsed since Zack Venn had so unceremoni-ously been carted away to Newgate. Meg's pale cheeks and hollow eyes betrayed her sleeplessness and constant anxiety. Betty was curious to see the prison and offered to accompany Meg on a visit to her father, but McSweeney kept both girls working from morning till night and had forbidden Meg to leave the inn.

On the third day after the brawl, Mrs Duvall paid another visit to the Drummer Boy, this time alone. She spoke to McSweeney and a coin was placed lightly in his palm; he transferred it at once to his pocket.

'Meg's a good girl, an' I wouldn't like to see 'er come to no 'arm,' he said dubiously. 'An' I s'pose yer know that 'er father's a stark, starin' lunatic?'

'Indeed I do, Mr McSweeney,' she replied. 'And I have news for Meg on that matter. So may I claim her for an hour?'

McSweeney shrugged, thinking of the half-guinea in his pocket.

'All right, then, take 'er and bring 'er back within the hour,' he replied with a show of concern for Meg. 'This is 'er only home, yer know, an' I has to keep an eye on 'er.'

'Very commendable of you, Mr McSweeney. I do under-stand that you are her guardian now. Thank you, then, I'll take her and bring her back to you safe and sound.'

She swept away to find Meg, leaving the innkeeper looking distrustfully at her retreating figure.

'Ah, there you are, little Meg. I've come to give you news of your father.'

'Oh, how is he, Mrs Duvall? Have yer seen him?'

'Listen, dear, McSweeney has given me leave to take you out for an hour or two. My carriage is waiting in Thames Street, so take off your apron and put on your cloak.'

Meg's heart leapt, but she suppressed her questions until they were seated in the carriage; she heard Mrs Duvall tell the coachman to drive them to Bethlehem Royal Hospital.

'Hospital, Mrs Duvall? D'ye mean Pa's in a place like St Thomas's or St Bartholomew's?'

'Yes, in a way, my dear. Your father's case came up before the judge yesterday, with a handful of other . . . with a dozen or so felons. One of them was sentenced to be hanged, the rest to be returned to Newgate – except for your father. He was sent to Bethlehem Royal Hospital in Moorfields. It is a very beautiful building, designed a hundred years ago for the accommodation of persons troubled in their minds.'

'Oh, Mrs Duvall, is that where we're goin'? To see Pa in this hospital?'

'Yes, my poor girl,' answered her companion softly, putting an arm around Meg's shoulders and drawing her close so that she was enveloped in the lady's expensive perfume. 'And I have to tell you, dear, that Bethlehem Royal is a madhouse.'

'Oh, no, not a madhouse, Mrs Duvall!! Say it's not true!' implored Meg.

'Ssh–ssh, my love, at least he will be kept safe there,' the lady said calmly. She went on to explain that the original hospital had been founded by a monastic order in medieval times, and called St Mary of Bethlehem. After the dissolution of the monasteries, it had been moved to this new building in Moorfields.

When they arrived at the imposing entrance, which had two life-size statues on either side, Meg's spirits rose, for this was not at all like Newgate. She followed Mrs Duvall into a high-ceilinged hall where the lady bought two tickets from a man at a desk. He directed them down a long corridor which met with another at a T-junction. Meg could hear strange voices. It was not a pleasant sound; a mixture of shouting, howling, weeping and hysterical laughter. The noise grew louder as they left the corridor to enter a ward. Here a sight met Meg's eyes which she was never to forget.

The inmates were kept separate from the visitors by an iron railing which reached up to the ceiling. Behind this barrier men and women sat or walked or gambolled like wild animals. They sang and shouted, waving to the visitors, and Meg and Mrs Duvall averted their eyes from a woman who was stark naked, sticking out her tongue and muttering obscenities. Further along an elderly man grinned and exposed his genitals, for which he got a whack across the shoulders with a whip held by one of the warders in charge of this band of lost souls. The smell was sickening, and some visitors held handkerchiefs over their noses; they were pointing at the antics of the inmates, exchanging comments and exclaiming. One man sat with a sketch book on his lap, drawing pictures of the dreadful spectacle.

'They come here to look at the lunatics, Meg,' explained Mrs Duvall in a low tone. 'Not so many as in the past, because entrance is now by ticket only. The money goes to help run the place and they're not supposed to use whips any more, only when necessary.'

They continued to walk along beside the barrier, Mrs Duvall's arm around Meg's shoulders. The girl was speechless, dreading what she might see next, until they came to Zack. He was chained by his right leg to an upright iron post and his arms were pinioned close to his sides by an iron ring locked around his body. His beard had been shaved off and he had obviously been washed but he was being tormented by a circle of grinning inmates who stood around him, just out of reach of his one free limb, his left leg, with which he kicked out at them.

'Deboffle! Damn' Deboffle!' they shouted, and Venn howled like an animal, clenching his fists uselessly at his sides.

'I say, look at this fellow,' said a visitor, a young man who had come for the entertainment. 'They told us about him, didn't they? You've only to shout "Deboffle!" at him, and he roars the place down.'

He turned towards Venn, putting his face up close to the bars. 'Watch this . . . Deboffle, Deboffle, come and get me!'

And sure enough, the wretched man grimaced and ground his teeth in frustration.

'Wonder what it means?' laughed the group, and walked on, leaving Meg too shocked and horrified even to weep. Her father's eyes were wild, with no sign of recognition, and she could not say a word to him. Instead she clung to Mrs Duvall, hiding her face in the lady's cloak.

'All right, my dear, you have seen enough. Let me take you out of here.' Supporting Meg with her arm, she led her out of the place they called Bedlam.

Once they were in the carriage, Mrs Duvall spoke softly and kindly. 'I'm very sorry I took you there, you poor, dear girl, but I felt that you needed to see the condition of your poor father. Now, listen to me. I will have him removed from

Bethl'em, and placed in a private asylum where he won't be gawped at like an animal in a zoo. I know of a quiet little place for distracted persons which will be much better for him. Oh, Meg, dear, don't cry, I'll get him out of there tomorrow, I promise.'

Meg had laid her head on Mrs Duvall's shoulder, but she now looked up into her face and asked the obvious question.

'Oh, Mrs Duvall, what a friend you've been to me, but why? *Why* are yer showin' such charity to me and me poor father?'

Mrs Duvall smiled and placed a lavender-scented glove on Meg's arm. 'Because I am drawn to you, dear little Meg. You are a sweet country girl – so young and innocent. It quite breaks my heart to see you slaving away at that low tavern, being pawed by the lecherous ruffians and smugglers that trade with that man McSweeney. You are worthy of a much better life than he can offer, and I have a proposal to make. I have a charming, spacious house, overlooking the park in Marylebone, and it so happens that I am in need of a young woman to serve as a maid to some of my many visitors – I might add that New Road is quite an exclusive address – and I can gladly offer you this advancement. No, no, please, little Meg, don't cry. I don't need an answer now, but I beg you to consider it. And meanwhile I shall arrange for your poor father to be transferred from that place to a private asylum where you may visit him without such distress.'

What could Meg say? She was overwhelmed by such generosity and nearly agreed to Mrs Duvall's offer immediately. There was just one question she needed to ask.

'So what exactly would yer want o' me, Mrs Duvall? Will I still be a servin' maid?'

The lady gave a little silvery laugh. 'If you care to look upon your work as being that of a maidservant, Meg, I suppose you would be, but to a much more select clientele than at the Drummer Boy! My establishment is known by gentlemen of the highest repute: city bankers, lawyers, a few Members of Parliament and sometimes by special arrangement, members of the aristocracy. Oh, yes, Meg, my pretty, fresh, rosy-cheeked country girl, you will be much admired and respectfully addressed, I can assure you!'

'W–what shall I say to Mr McSweeney?' asked Meg. 'He's

been good to me in 'is way, an' I don't want to leave 'im in the lurch.'

'La! McSweeney can pick up a working girl anywhere, and pay her low wages to work all hours – don't worry about *him*!' Mrs Duvall looked thoughtful for a moment. 'Though perhaps your best plan would be simply to walk quietly out of the Drummer Boy without telling anybody where you are going. My carriage will call for you at an arranged time. You won't need to look back, sweet Meg, only forward, to a new life!'

The letter that arrived at the end of January from Lord Lennox had a devastating effect on the de Bovilles – and set the servants whispering behind closed doors. Charlotte de Boville was almost hysterical.

'Gone to *enlist*? Gone to train to be an officer in the British Army?' she gasped, her eyes wide. 'How could the Lennoxes have allowed him?'

'They didn't have much choice in the matter, my love,' replied her husband. 'He's eighteen and may do as he pleases. James is full of regrets and apologies, but we can't really lay the blame at their door. Look here, Bess has added a few words of her own, addressed to you.'

Charlotte snatched the small sheet of paper from his hand, and read aloud.

> I blame myself, Charlotte, to some degree, though I never intended it to happen. I allowed your son to accompany Julia to an afternoon tea party at the home of a distant relative by marriage. Frederica and Charles were also there, but I was not; it was this woman's son and a brother officer who persuaded Richard to take this course. I shall never acknowledge her again, but I humbly beg your forgiveness for something that has shocked me as much as it has shocked his lordship.

'There you are, John! He was lured away, pressed into it, while away from home. Oh, my poor, foolhardy son! I suppose he was seized by a taste for adventure.'

'Calm yourself, my dear,' soothed Sir John. 'I am inclined to think that he was more influenced by the ending of the affair with the Pond girl. I believe the boy to have been more deeply affected than was realized, and if he had known the truth, that she was with child, I am sure that he would have come back to Wollaston.'

'What nonsense, of *course* we did right in not telling him!' Lady de Boville snapped. 'Did you expect him to come back and *marry* the girl, a mere parson's daughter, and he the heir to a baronetcy and all the responsibilities it carries?'

'Maybe not, but he could have given her some support,' said the baronet quietly. 'I would gladly have helped him with money, for the child is of my own blood. And he could have acknowledged his part in the matter.'

'Oh, John de Boville, I despair of you sometimes!' she cried, almost beside herself. 'I cannot understand why that silly fool of a parson and his shrew of a wife have not sent the wretched girl away. Parading her condition in the village and in church every Sunday when she's not fit to be seen!'

'Richard's responsibility for her condition is also public knowledge, and he is not commended for it,' Sir John replied. 'Perhaps it is as well that he will be away for a year or two.'

'A year or two? What do you mean? Oh my God, if my boy is sent across the Atlantic ocean to America to do battle with those damned rebels – if he should be . . . oh my God.'

She burst into tears. Sir John had to comfort her as well as he could, though his thoughts were as heavy as hers.

Ill news travels fast, and loses nothing in the telling. From the servants' hall to every farmhouse kitchen, and from gossiping housewives to the gatherings at the Fox and Hounds, it became known that young Richard de Boville had chosen to join the army and fight in America rather than face the accusations of Wollaston. Widow Siggery heard the news and sadly passed it on to her son, although Billy had already heard it from Noah Reeve who had been at Oak Hall to re-shoe one of Sir John's best hunters.

'I–I think I–I'll go f–for a walk on – on the Common, M–Mother.'

'What, at this time, Billy? It's black as pitch out there, an' bitter cold.'

'Th–there's a half-m–moon. I–I'll be all right.'

Mrs Siggery's heart ached for her son. She had endured the pain of his birth, and seen how the midwife's face had fallen at the sight of his grotesque club foot. In every other way her baby had seemed healthy and contented, though he had been slow to learn to talk. The doctor had looked into his mouth and found no 'tongue tie' to cut; Billy could shout and sing like any other young child, but when he tried to make simple sounds like 'ma-ma', 'da-da' and 'ba-ba', the impediment was revealed. Billy's father succumbed to smallpox before he reached thirty, leaving his wife to struggle on alone, working to support herself and her son. No man was interested in a widow with an idiot son – for so Billy was thought to be, a limping, stuttering child, a butt for the cruelty of other children. And yet as time went by, she had begun to realize that there was a quick brain and a loving spirit concealed beneath his imperfections. Parson Pond had agreed with her, and had offered to teach Billy to read and write, and he had proved to be the brightest and most thoughtful of all Pond's pupils. By the time Billy was apprenticed at sixteen to Noah Reeve, he had become a familiar character in the parish community, tolerated by most, patronized by a few and accepted by all. He did not expect to marry, or be loved by any woman other than his mother, but this did not mean that he was unable to give love. Widow Siggery, like Parson Pond, knew that Billy's heart had long been given to a girl who in turn had given hers to another, with tragic consequences.

January passed in ice and snow; February came in with a thaw and the days began to lengthen. The first snowdrops appeared; the Miss Buxtons picked them from their garden to offer to their former assistant teacher when they saw her in church. They seemed to show their continued concern for her, and frankly it puzzled Mrs Pond, who had been expecting to be cold-shouldered. Not everybody was as kind, however.

'The parson's girl be a fine size now, i'n't she? Can't be long now 'fore she's brought to bed,' observed the cook at the school.

Neither Miss Buxton made a reply. They only shared their thoughts with each other, and agreed that few confinements in Wollaston had been awaited with more curiosity.

* * *

It was just as Mrs Duvall had said: 43 New Road was a fine house, one of a line of elegant new houses built only a year or two previously. There was a carved stone arch over the front door, leading to a hallway decorated tastefully in dove-grey and duck-egg blue, a theme echoed in the well-appointed drawing room where Mrs Duvall sat each morning to deal with her correspondence and accounts.

'You will be my own personal maid until you get settled in,' Mrs Duvall informed Meg. 'You will bring trays of coffee or hot chocolate to serve to my morning guests. My young ladies have a habit of lying in bed, and joining us at midday in the dining room. In the evening there is a cold supper set out on a table for guests to refresh themselves if they so wish, and . . . oh, but you will be wanting to see your poor father, won't you, little Meg? I have ordered the carriage for this afternoon. I will come with you on this first visit; after that you may visit as often as you wish. Please don't thank me, Meg, for I can see a splendid future ahead for you!'

Myrtle House was situated in a quiet spot, half-hidden by trees on the lower western slope of Primrose Hill. The propri-etress received them, and escorted them upstairs to a clean, plainly-furnished room where Zack Venn sat staring out of the window. He was alone.

Meg went at once to his side and knelt down. 'Hallo, Pa, d'ye know me?'

She took hold of his hand and he stared at her for a long while before croaking, 'Meg.'

'Yes, Pa, it's me, Meg, an' I've come to see yer.' Her voice shook and her eyes brimmed.

He nodded slowly. 'You an' me've come a long way to get 'ere, girl, but we got 'ere in the end. Ye're a good girl, Meg, like yer mother.'

Mrs Duvall tactfully left them alone together. Not much more was said between the father and daughter, though Meg told him she had a good place to work in now, and that Mrs Duvall was very kind. She kissed him and promised to come again soon. Mrs Duvall smiled and shook her head when Meg thanked her.

'I've told you before, little Meg, I am drawn to your sweet nature, and happy to do you a favour, bless you!' The lady put an arm around Meg and kissed her.

The first month with Mrs Duvall was very easy for Meg after the hectic atmosphere of the Drummer Boy. She rose at seven each morning, and breakfasted with Mrs Duvall in a small room overlooking the garden at the back of the house. At nine the lady took herself off to the drawing room where she did her paperwork and interviewed gentlemen, some quite elderly and distinguished, who were then offered coffee or hot chocolate brought in by Meg on a silver tray. Sometimes Mrs Duvall nodded to Meg as a signal for her to leave the room and wait until summoned back in; and if a gentleman eyed Meg admiringly and tried to talk with her, the same rule applied: Meg was dismissed until recalled.

There were five other ladies living in the house; one of them, Mrs Vinery, was in her forties, the rest were quite young and pretty though Meg did not get much chance to talk with them. They offered her sugared almonds and preserved plums, treating her rather like a child. Often her remarks made them giggle and glance knowingly at each other. In the evenings they dressed in gowns of silk and velvet, and curled each other's hair. The supper table was laid, and more bottles of wine produced, but Mrs Duvall sent Meg to the small back room to take her supper and practise embroidery.

The front door bell began to ring as guests arrived, and men's voices could be heard mingling with the ladies at the lavish supper table. Footsteps went up and down the stairs, and Meg wondered idly why she was not called upon to serve them at the table; but her thoughts always returned to her father, whom she visited every afternoon. He seemed to be calmer in his mind, and had put on a little weight.

Then came the moment when, late one February afternoon, Meg went into the kitchen and overheard the two stout kitchen maids talking, their mob-caps wobbling as they stood at the sink with their backs to her.

'Shockin', innit, a pretty little thing like 'er, brought to a place like this, an' no idea what madame's up to. Downright wicked, I calls it!'

'Well, she'll 'ave to know some time, won't she? A tasty little morsel like 'er can name 'er own price!'

'Nah, it's madame what rakes in the silver, an' I'll wager she's savin' up little Meg as a virgin, fresh from the corn-fields for some ol' lecher!'

All at once Meg stood still, as if turned to stone. A terrible realization dawned on her, like the scattered wooden pieces of a puzzle coming together and making a picture: an unbelievably horrible picture. She heard, she saw, she understood – her unasked questions were suddenly answered. She had only one idea in her head – to escape. She went straight to the drawing room where Mrs Duvall sat drinking tea by the fire. She looked up, saw Meg's horrified face and smiled, for she had anticipated this sooner or later. Little Meg had been surprisingly slow.

'Mrs Duvall, I know why the ladies sleep 'alf the mornin', an' dress 'emselves up at night when the gentlemen start comin' in!' cried the girl, white with shock.

'Now, now, my dear, don't jump to conclusions,' the lady replied calmly. 'My establishment is absolutely exclusive. Nobody is admitted without a prior appointment. This is not one of those disreputable places down on the south bank. You have seen how well I look after my ladies, and I can tell you that more than half of them go on to make good marriages. And you've seen the kind of gentlemen who come to avail themselves of my services for themselves or their sons, and all with the means to pay me very well.' She smiled, looking Meg up and down. 'And you, my dear, are very special, the kind of girl that some discerning gentlemen prize above all others.'

'What, *me*?' cried Meg. 'Oh, I must leave this place at once!'

'And where will you go, may I ask? And what about your father? You don't think I'd go on paying the fees for Myrtle House if you left, do you?'

Meg stared. Her kind Mrs Duvall had turned into Madame Duvall, hard and businesslike.

'And now it's time you started working for your keep, Meg, and your father's. I have a cabinet minister coming here tonight, and *you* are going to make yourself agreeable to him.'

Meg saw that she had fallen into a trap. If her father was not to be turned out of Myrtle House, she would have to become one of Madame Duvall's 'ladies' – offered as a sweet, innocent, fresh-faced virgin to satisfy some middle-aged parliamentarian.

'Come, take some wine to steady your nerves, Meg,' said Madame Duvall, pouring out a glass of best claret. 'And don't try any tricks like running away. By working here you will be doing a public service to the nation, and with much benefit to yourself. Go on, drink!'

And in desperation Meg accordingly drank all that was offered her, and the next few hours passed in a haze of wine. Her senses were reeling when she was suddenly handed into the care of Mrs Vinery.

'You'll have to take charge this evening, Vinery, for I have received an urgent summons, which is a damned nuisance,' Mrs Duvall said, frowning. 'Remember *this* one's booked for Sir Gideon Draynes, and there are three young blades coming, all paid for – one o' them is yours by his father's special request, the others can have Belle and Susie.'

'Very well, madam,' Meg heard Mrs Vinery reply. Other female voices came and went, now close to Meg's ear, now far away.

'Help me to undress her, Belle – we must put a white gown on her. Hand me that brush and comb, Susie, and be quick – the sooner she's in the bed, the better.'

'She'll be wasted on Sir Gideon in this state,' remarked Belle.

'I don't suppose he'll mind, he might have had a fight on his hands if she was sober – and he'll've downed a few glasses himself, I dare say!'

'What a pretty creature she is! D'ye think he might want to take her away with him?'

'And how would he explain her to his lady wife? This way suits him better.'

Meg felt too giddy and bewildered to ask questions, and swayed against Mrs Vinery.

'Can she walk?' asked Susie.

'No, we'd better carry her – we don't want her falling down and hurting herself on her first go!'

'Is she to go in the Silver Room?'

'No, the Gold. Nothin' but the best for Sir Gideon,' replied Mrs Vinery with weary cynicism. 'I've got a young puppy to instruct in the art of love, I'll take him to the Silver Room. You and Susie can take yours to the Red and the Blue. They've all been paid for, so no awkward mention of money. I'll take the old man upstairs when I take mine up. Come on, the supper table awaits, and there's the first one at the door!'

Meg woke in the Gold Room with its richly draped curtains and hangings. She was wearing nothing but a simple white gown, signifying her virginity, and her dark hair had been combed through and spread over the pillow. There was a scent of rose water and lavender, and she felt slightly sick. She sighed and turned over, promptly falling asleep again.

At the supper table it was the rule for the gentlemen to help themselves to refreshments in the company of the ladies assigned to them. When they had eaten and taken wine, they were led by the lady to one of the five rooms above. The Right Honourable Sir Gideon Draynes had agreed with Madame Duvall to be called plain Mr G, and there were three younger gentlemen, Mr X, Mr Y and Mr Z. The first two were in high spirits and laughed a great deal, teasing Mr Z who looked most uncomfortable in such an establishment, in spite of the wine he had taken. Gideon Draynes was unexpectedly interested in Mrs Vinery, and asked if she had been an actress at the Theatre Royal. He complimented her on her looks, and she smiled; and as he continued to talk with her, she saw her opportunity. Married he might be, but she stood a fair chance of becoming his next kept mistress if she pleased him well enough. She was tired of being at the beck and call of Madame Duvall, and having to take charge at short notice without any extra payment. To hell with the awkward, tongue-tied Mr Z!

'I'm taking Mr G to the Silver Room now, and you will oblige me by taking Mr Z to the Gold,' she whispered to Belle, who was sitting on the knee of Mr X. The four young people had taken supper, and were more than ready to ascend the staircase for the main business of the evening.

Belle went up with Mr Y holding her right arm and she beckoned to Mr Z to take her left.

'Excuse me for a moment,' she said to Mr Y. 'I have to deliver your friend to the sweetest, prettiest girl of us all!'

Having shown Mr Z into the Gold Room, she rejoined Mr Y in happy anticipation.

Meg was suddenly reawakened by the sound of men's ribald laughter; there were footsteps on the stairs. The effect of the wine was wearing off, and she remembered her discovery earlier that day – she was now one of Madame Duvall's 'ladies'.

Something had been said about a cabinet minister, and some-body was at the door!

'Oh, Lizzie Pond, if yer could see me now!' she groaned. ''Tis the lowest I ever been.'

The door opened and the Honourable Charles Lennox was pushed into the room, flushed and extremely apprehensive at the prospect of being instructed by Mrs Vinery.

'Enjoy yerself, Mr Z!' said Belle gaily, shutting the door behind her.

Eight

A Rescue and a New Arrival

1778

E lizabeth Pond had felt out of sorts all day, after a night disturbed by a dull, dragging ache in her back which persisted. A few days ago she had thought that the labour pains were beginning, and asked that Granny Mason be sent for. Her father had rushed to the handywoman's cottage, and the midwife had come out at once, only to inform Elizabeth that these were merely 'false pains' and would occur again – much more strongly – when the time was right. Mrs Pond had complained loudly about the waste of everybody's time, and Elizabeth was determined not to say anything again until she was really sure. She was finding Jenny Tasker's lessons in the afternoon rather tiring.

'Your reading is much better, Jenny, and now I would like you to try writing.'

'Oh, can I write a story, Miss Liz'beth?' asked Jenny eagerly. 'A story about a pretty girl from an orphanage, who falls in love with a handsome m—'

'No, Jenny, we will copy out a story about a little prickly hedgehog who has slept all through the winter, and wakes up feeling hungry – and goes outside to see all the fields and woods waking up to the spring . . .'

Jenny's face fell. 'That sounds like summat for children, Miss Liz'beth.'

'Children's stories are a very good way of learning to read and write, Jenny, because they're simple and easy. And it's time for me to talk a little bit about basic grammar.'

'What's that, Miss Liz'beth?'

'It's about the correct way of using words, Jenny, and not

easy to explain.' Elizabeth gave a gasp at a sharp stab of back-ache. 'We're going to study grammar by writing out this story about the hedgehog, and talking about the way it's been written. First of all—'

'How much longer is that girl goin' to sit on her backside?' called an impatient voice from the kitchen. '*Very* sorry to interrupt, I'm sure, but *I'm* left with all the housework to do!'

Jenny rolled her eyes, but Elizabeth closed her book and folded away the paper she had been using. 'You'd better go, Jenny. We've had quite a long time today.'

Jenny reluctantly rose. 'We'll 'ave another lesson tomorrow, won't we, Miss Liz'beth?'

'No, Jenny, tomorrow's Sunday – and the first day of March,' said Elizabeth smiling, thinking to herself it was the month her baby would be born.

'Are you comin' to 'elp me or not?' roared Mrs Pond from the kitchen. Jenny hurried off, to Elizabeth's secret relief.

She rose awkwardly, clutching the side of her father's desk, and went into the hall passage, taking down her hooded cloak from its hook. Should she tell her mother that she was going for a walk? No, she decided, for there would only be a sarcastic retort and a warning not to go up on Cove Common.

She made her way straight to the Common. Here she could walk freely and take deep breaths of fresh, cool air, away from Wollaston folk who stared at her and asked when the baby was due.

Her spirits lifted a little as she gazed all around at the awakening earth. Already the gorse was showing the first early yellow blooms that she and Meg had called 'butterflies' when they had played on the heath as children. It was a sign of the golden glory to come later.

Meg Venn! Where was she now? And what would she think of Lizzie Pond, heavy with a bastard child? Surely Meg would be sorry that her friend's first love had ended in such a way. And where was Richard de Boville? On his way to America, maybe already there? Did he ever give a thought to the girl who had walked on the heath with him, sharing poetry and murmuring words of love? Tears filled her eyes.

These reflections were cut short by a sudden sharp pain in her belly. She gasped and put her hands over it: the muscles had

tightened to a board-like hardness, which gradually softened as
the pain eased off. She had better retrace her steps and go home,
she thought, for this was no false alarm: she knew she would
soon need Granny Mason.

She had not taken many steps before the pain seized her
again, and she doubled up, groaning loudly. Again she clutched
at her hardened belly, and when the pain had ebbed away, the
continuous backache remained, making it difficult for her to
walk. When another pain began, she cried out aloud, afraid
that she might not get home in time. She gritted her teeth and
forced herself along, but just as the next pain began she felt
a sensation of something happening down between her legs,
followed by a gush of warm fluid, soaking her underwear and
dripping over her shoes. In her fear she cried out, 'Oh, Lord
have mercy on me, forgive me my sins and save me – *help*
me, Lord!'

Straightaway she felt a strong arm around her swollen body
and a voice spoke in her ear.

'Lean on m–me, Miss P–Pond, I–I got hold o' ye, d–don't
worry.'

'*Billy!*' she groaned, leaning against him. 'Oh, Billy, I can't
walk any further.'

When he withdrew his arm she cried out in fear. 'Please
don't leave me!'

'Never, I'll n–never leave ye, Elizabeth my love. I–I'm
going to c–carry ye now, we're not far off m–my mother's
home.'

The word *love* was out of his mouth before he realized it,
and whether she had heard or not, he did not know. He swept
her up in his arms, and despite his limping foot, he moved
rapidly towards home. His work at the smithy had strength-
ened his whole body, and his shoulders were broad. She put
her arms around them, and even when she cried out with pain,
he kept going until he came within sight of the Siggerys'
cottage.

'Nearly there, M–Miss Pond – ye'll be safe s–soon, with
my m–mother to look after ye.'

And then they were on the doorstep, and Billy knocked
instead of walking straight in as was his usual habit. His
mother came hurrying to answer, and as soon as she saw the
parson's daughter in his arms, she understood the situation.

First she helped Elizabeth to lower her legs to the floor as Billy's arms relinquished her, and after removing the girl's cloak, she led her through to a bed.

'Lie down there, me dear, an' let me lift yer petticoats – oh, ye're all wet, so yer waters've broke. Hush! Just let me see,' she said gently but firmly.

'I–I'm getting another pain, Mrs Siggery, help me, oh, help me!'

'I'm here, sweetheart,' said the widow soothingly. 'Ye're safe here, ye're all right.' Turning away briefly from the girl, she called to her son who was pacing up and down in his agitation.

'What can I do–do, Mother? Sh–shall I fetch the p–parson?'

'No! Go an' fetch Granny Mason – tell 'er to come at once, Billy, d'ye hear? Fetch 'er as quick as ye can, my son!'

Meg sat up in the luxurious feather bed, clutching her hands tightly round her knees. Her head still whirled, but she was able to focus her eyes on the anxious-looking young man who stood irresolutely at the foot of the bed. They stared at each other, neither knowing what to say; then Meg felt an ominous churning of her stomach.

'I'm goin' to be sick!' she mumbled, putting a hand over her mouth. The man glanced wildly round the room, and saw a marble-topped washstand in a corner; on top of it was a large decorated basin and pitcher, and beneath it a chamber pot. He grabbed the latter, and rushed to the side of the bed, holding it out just in time to catch the stream of sour-smelling vomit. Meg gasped and groaned, then gave another convulsive retch and spewed forth the rest of her stomach contents.

'Ugh,' she whispered, letting her head fall back upon the pillows. 'Ugh, I'm sorry. Too much to drink.'

'Er – yes, I understand, Mrs . . . er . . . I've drunk too much, too,' he replied, for he had also come near to throwing up his supper. 'Are you feeling better now, Mrs . . . er . . .?'

Meg nodded, for the emptying of her stomach had given her relief. Her head was clearing – but how shameful!

He put the pot down on the floor in case it should be needed again and looked at the girl lying against the pillows. Her eyes were closed, her face was pale and glistening with drops of perspiration; clumps of her dark hair clung to her forehead and cheeks. She hardly seemed like the experienced older woman he had been led to expect, a skilled courtesan who would rouse his passion. This girl was young; she did not give an impression of being well versed in the art of making love. Should he speak to her or quietly leave the room to allow her to sleep? He could wait downstairs for his two companions. A more practical idea came to mind: to wash her face and hands after the bout of vomiting.

He went to the washstand and poured some water into the basin. There were two huckaback towels hanging on a wooden rod at the side of the stand; picking up one of them he carried the basin to a small table by the bedside. He dipped a corner of the towel in the water.

Meg kept her eyes closed to avoid seeing the man who must be the cabinet minister Madame Duvall had mentioned. Perhaps after this humiliating scene he would be so disgusted that he would go away and let her sleep.

Then she felt a cool, tentative touch on her forehead and around her nose and mouth as her face was gently wiped with a damp towel. It felt refreshing, and she opened her eyes.

'That's better,' she whispered.

'Give me your hands and –' he lifted the basin and steadied it on the bed – 'dip them in the water.' He waited while she dabbled her hands, then wiped them on the dry end of the towel he held out for her.

'Thank yer, sir.' She looked straight at him. 'Are yer Sir Gideon Draynes?'

'What? Certainly not, he's a fearful old rake. My name's Lennox, and I was expecting . . . er . . .' He stopped speaking while he recalled what he had seen at supper.

'Draynes was at table this evening, talking to one of the . . . er . . . ladies, a little older than the rest, in fact I thought that she would be coming to join me. Tell me, were you truly expecting that horrid old man to come to you?'

'Yes, I s'pose so,' she answered. 'Mrs Duvall said I'd be 'aving a cabinet minister. It's my very first time, yer see.'

'Oh, my dear girl, thank heaven for the mix-up! I just shudder to think of that old lecher . . . he must have chosen the other lady instead – and you got me! Don't worry, I won't harm you.'

He smiled down at her, thinking how sweet she seemed. 'May I ask your name, then, Miss . . . er . . .?'

'Me name's Venn, sir. Meg Venn. Me an' me father came down to London after 'e was turned orf his bit o' land, 'cause o' the enclosures. Me poor mother died, and Pa's lost his mind over it, an' was put in Bethl'em, a horrible place like a zoo where people come to watch the sufferin' of others. Mrs Duvall 'ad 'im taken out o' there an' put in a private asylum, and I can visit 'im there. She's been very good to me, sir.'

'And in return she procured you for Draynes. Oh, Meg, you've escaped such a fate! Tell me, where do you come from, you and your father?'

'From Wollaston, sir, a little place in Suffolk.'

'Good heavens! Of all the amazing things! Did you say Wollaston? I know a girl from there, a sort of cousin by marriage – and I'm supposed to marry her, but I'm full of doubts. She likes the town life, the parties and social events. I'm useless at that sort of thing, like a bull in a china shop – or so I've been told.' He smiled ruefully. 'I think I was meant to be a countryman.'

It was Meg's turn to be curious. 'What's she called, sir, this girl from Wollaston?'

'Frederica. She's a pretty, well-mannered girl, and comes of an old family, the de Bovilles.'

'*De Boville?* Oh, I can't believe it!' exclaimed Meg, her eyes wide. ''Tis the very name – the very same as turned us orf our bit o' land. The ones as killed me mother an' drove me father crazy. Oh, sir, don't go marryin' a de Boville!'

He stared at her. 'No, Meg, I'm not going to. But what am I doing? I should be getting you out of this ill-famed place. Are your clothes here somewhere?'

'No, they're in my room, sir, on the other side o' the 'ouse.'

'Can you creep downstairs and fetch them? I'll come with you in case there's anybody on the prowl who'd try to stop you. And then we'll get out and find a sedan chair to take us.'

'Take us where, sir? To where yer live?'

'No, Meg, not there. I think I know of somewhere you'll be safe. Come on, let's find your room and get you dressed.'

She pattered down the stairs barefooted, and he followed her. They hurried along a ground floor corridor towards the kitchen and entrance hall, then up another flight of stairs to her room next to Madame Duvall's.

'I'll wait outside the door for you, Meg,' he whispered. 'Dress as quickly as you can . . . put on a coat or something, it's a cold night.

As if in a dream, Meg tore off the white gown, and put on a petticoat and thick stockings. She pulled a woollen gown over her head and drew a shawl around her shoulders. Over this went her cape and hood. As soon as she came out of the room he hurried her down the stairs to the front entrance. But before they could open it, footsteps approached from the outside.

'Somebody's coming in!' he hissed.

'Quick, let's get under the stairs,' said Meg, leading him to a small, cramped space half full of boots, brushes and brooms. 'Sssh! It must be Madame Duvall comin' home.'

She was right. The lady's key scraped in the lock; then she entered the house, turned round and closed the door, drawing two bolts across. Off came her cape, hood and gloves which she threw down on the low, padded ottoman in the hall. She then disappeared down the passage leading to the kitchen.

'Now, Meg, let's go out before she comes back in!'

Out they came and made for the door. It unlocked with a click, and Charles bent down to draw back the bottom bolt while Meg drew back the top one. It was an unmistakeable sound, and they heard Madame Duvall's voice crying out, 'Who's there?' Her footsteps came running towards them.

'Quick, Meg, quick!' But the lady had rushed into the hall.

'What the devil—?' she began. 'Meg Venn! Where d'you think you're going?'

Meg shrank back from her fury, but Charles Lennox spoke up clearly.

'I'm taking this innocent girl away from this house and the likes of Gideon Draynes.'

'Oh, are you indeed? And who might you be?'

'Call me Mr Z. I'm taking her to where you can do her no harm.' He hurried Meg out of the front door. 'Goodnight, Mrs Duvall.'

'Your father will be back in Bethl'em tomorrow morning, Meg!' she shouted.

'No, he won't. I shall take it upon myself to pay for his care,' Charles answered. 'Now, come along, Meg, we must get away from—'

Madame Duvall cast aside her dignity, yelling after him like a fishwife. 'You've got a brass neck, young Lennox, coming here to lose your precious male virginity and running off with a silly girl I've been grooming for better things! Ha! I doubt if Lord Lennox will give her bed and board!'

The heated exchange had brought others to the scene, for it was scarcely nine o'clock, and a brawl outside Madame Duvall's establishment was an unusual attraction. Charles saw a two-wheeled trap drawing up, and taking Meg firmly by the hand, he hailed the driver. 'Have you room for two?'

'Two, sir? Get up, the pair o' yer. Where d'ye want to go, apart from away from here?'

'John Street in Clerkenwell,' replied Charles.

'That'll be a fair way, sir. Both o' yer?'

'Yes, you'll be paid for two – now let's get moving.'

While Meg wondered where they were going, Charles summoned up his courage to throw himself on his aunt Seward's good will. He hoped that her preference for him would make her amenable to taking in a penniless girl for the night and possibly longer. He would have to say that he had found Meg wandering homeless in the streets – and insist that she was not a prostitute – and that her father had lost his mind due to hardship. It was a sad enough story, and he felt confident of his aunt's kind heart.

He turned to Meg as they bowled through the dark streets, and put his arm around her for extra warmth. She nestled against him trustingly, and he smiled to himself. His visit to Madame Duvall's establishment had not been a complete failure after all; on the contrary, it was turning out to be quite an adventure. All the more satisfying to know that he had saved a girl's innocence from being despoiled.

The Lennoxes were completely baffled. And angry.

'I simply cannot understand him!' exclaimed her ladyship. 'All these months he has escorted her everywhere – and been seen by everybody. He has given her every hope of a proposal before the end of the winter season, and now says he does not want to marry her! Think how the poor girl's reputation will suffer when there is no announcement. How I am to tell her parents . . . I do not know!'

'We must put it around that the decision was made by them both,' said Lord Lennox. 'By mutual agreement – that will at least save her pride.'

'But what will Sir John and Lady de Boville say to that?' asked his wife. 'They have already lost their son to the army. No, James, we shall have to tell her parents why she is returning to Wollaston broken-hearted and humiliated. Oh, how *could* he? Why has he changed his mind? Why, why, why?'

The viscount shrugged and did not answer. There were certain facts that Bess did not know. He had gone to considerable subterfuge and no small expense to arrange Charles's visit to Madame Duvall's establishment – and Madame herself had promised to introduce him to a woman of the right age and experience to turn him from a boy into a man. Yet it was immediately after this night out on the town, from which Charles had returned home before midnight, that he had sprung this change of heart upon them.

'I shall have to break it to poor Frederica as gently as I can,' said Lady Lennox, shaking her head, 'and as soon as possible.'

And *I* shall have something to say to Charles in private, thought the viscount.

A maidservant was sent to request Frederica's attendance in her ladyship's bedchamber, and tea and fruit cake was ordered to be brought to them. When Frederica arrived, rather breathless and with shining eyes, Lady Lennox braced herself for her task.

'My dear Frederica, I have come to regard you as a . . . a close relative, a dear niece, which makes it all the more difficult to give you news which I know will distress you,' she said with due seriousness.

The girl's eyes flickered in sudden alarm. 'Is it news from Wollaston, Aunt Bess? Have you had word from my parents?'

'Oh, no, my dear, nothing of that kind,' replied Lady Lennox, thankful to have no family calamity to report. 'It is simply that Charles, our son Charles, has informed us that—'

Lady Lennox saw the girl's countenance brighten momentarily, then resume an expression as grave as her own.

'He has informed us, my dear, that he has no plans for marriage as yet. I might add that his father and I are deeply disappointed in him, particularly in the circumstances – the singular attention that he has paid to you over the past months – and we—'

She stopped speaking, watching Frederica's reaction, fully prepared to take the girl in her arms if there were tears. Apart from turning a little pale and clasping her hands tightly together, the girl kept her self-control.

'Of course you will want to return to your parents, my dear, and they will no doubt feel the same indignation as we feel at Charles's behaviour. I suggest that we let it be known that this is a decision made by both of you – mutual agreement. I dare not imagine what Sir John and Lady de Boville will think of us, first Richard joining the army and now this – this extraordinary attitude of Charles.' There was silence for a moment or two, and her ladyship began again. 'Would you like me to write to your parents, my dear? To prepare them? I shall be willing to do whatever you wish. You have only to mention it . . .'

Her words tailed off, knowing how she would feel in Frederica's position; but the young girl was quickly adjusting to this new situation.

'If you would not mind, Aunt Bess – I mean Your Ladyship – I would prefer to stay here at Bedford Row for a few weeks longer.'

'Certainly, if that is what you wish, my dear,' replied Lady Lennox, assuming that Frederica must feel embarrassed about returning to Wollaston and her parents' sympathy. 'Of course I would love to have you here for as long as it pleases you, but remember that you will no longer have Charles to escort you.'

Frederica inclined her head in a little bow. 'Of course, Your Ladyship.'

Unable to think of anything further to say, her ladyship poured out tea and handed Frederica a slice of cake.

Viscount Lennox had summoned Charles to walk with him that morning in Lincoln's Inn Fields, so they would be out of earshot of anybody at home. For a while they strode in silence, then Lord Lennox began abruptly with a straight question.

'What happened at Madame Duvall's last night?'

'Er . . . nothing that would be of interest to you, sir,' faltered Charles.

'Don't be impertinent. I sent you there in order to educate you in the ways of men and women. Did you or did you not take a woman to bed and perform a man's natural duty?'

'No, sir, I did not.'

'Then what in God's name *did* you do there? Madame Duvall assured me that she would introduce you to a woman of the right age and experience who would instruct you. Did you meet such a woman?'

'I believe there was some kind of misunderstanding, sir,' said Charles, feeling extremely awkward, but not wanting to lie to his father. 'Madame Duvall was called away on urgent business, and I have reason to believe that the woman intended for me went with Sir Gideon Draynes.'

'*Draynes?* That old lecher? What was *he* doing there?'

'He was on the same errand as the other men who visit such houses, sir.'

'Don't try jesting with me, Charles. So what happened to you?'

'I was shown into a room where I found a girl who should never have been there. An honest, innocent country girl who had been tricked by Madame Duvall into that life. I did not touch her.'

'What in hell was Duvall thinking of, to allow such a fiasco?' said his lordship, fuming. 'I wish to God I had never sent you there!'

They walked on for a while in silence, and then Charles ventured to speak. 'Perhaps some good has come out of it, Father.'

'What? How on earth do you mean, Charles? What possible good might come out of such a farce? It's like one of those indecent plays by that fellow – what was his name? – Congreve or Wycherly or somesuch. Well, go on – what *good* are you thinking of?'

Charles drew a deep breath, and chose his words carefully. 'Well, perhaps the experience brought me to a realization of myself, Father – to make me consider what I truly want in life. And it is not a town life such as Frederica enjoys. She is a pretty and accomplished girl . . . she will make some man an ideal wife. But I suspect she would not give me a glance if I were not who I am, your son and heir. Surely you must have seen that for yourself, Father?'

Lord Lennox made a vague non-committal gesture with his hands, for he could not truthfully disagree with this appraisal of the de Boville girl.

'So what sort of a girl *would* make you an ideal wife, then?' he asked irritably. Charles made no answer. 'I suppose you mean this honest, innocent country girl who was palmed off on you at Madame Duvall's, the one you say you did not touch?'

'That's true, sir, I did not, though we talked for quite a long time. She and her father came down to London from Wollaston, of all places, after being turned off their piece of land by . . . who do you think? The de Bovilles!'

'Good God, is that a fact? Are you sure?'

'She was sure enough of it, Father, and mentioned the name without any prompting from me. Her father's mind has cracked under the strain. He was in the Bethl'em hospital until Madame Duvall had him placed in a private asylum – and then used that to threaten the girl, to stop her from absconding. I took the liberty of saying that I would pay the fees for the asylum.'

'The devil you did, Charles! Well, if that's the way you want to squander your money . . .'

'Surely better that losing it at cards, Father. And I did not leave the girl there. I took her to a house where I know she will be safe.'

'I simply do not believe what I'm hearing, Charles. *What* safe house? Tell me!'

'I took her to my aunt Seward's house in Clerkenwell, Father, and begged her to look after the girl until a suitable place can be found for her as a maidservant.'

Lord Lennox was dumbfounded. 'Mrs Seward, your mother's cousin by marriage? They're not even on speaking terms, not since young de Boville ran away to join the army.'

'All the more reason why my mother need not know, Father.' Charles gave a rueful little smile. 'The only lie I told was to my good aunt. I said I'd found the girl homeless and wandering after her father had been thrown into Bedlam.'

'She'll find out the truth some day, nothing so sure!' declared his lordship.

'She probably will, Father, some day. But I could hardly tell her I'd taken the girl from a brothel I'd visited, could I? And that you had arranged it and paid for it!'

Lord Lennox stood and gaped at his son – and then saw that Charles was smiling.

'You young dog!' Lord Lennox clapped his son on the back, and they both laughed aloud.

'Not a word of this to your mother!'

'Not a word, Father.'

If Billy Siggery had made good speed carrying Elizabeth in his arms, he covered the ground twice as fast on his descent from Cove Common. He half-ran, half-walked, stumbling at intervals but never falling, even when he slid on the dismembered body of a hare. The Wollaston Hunt had thundered across the Common that morning in loud pursuit of a fox, and the unfortunate hare had diverted some of the baying hounds from their quarry.

Granny Mason's cottage was one of several dwellings on the eastern edge of Wollaston, on a bend of the lane that went off to the little hamlet of Cove.

Billy knocked at the door, which was opened at once. Now in her sixties, Granny Mason lived alone with her two cats and was a figure of some authority in Wollaston. She had taught herself the rudiments of reading and writing, sufficient for keeping an ill-spelt record of births and deaths. She had no close friends, but knew everybody and was used to being obeyed.

When she saw Billy, her features softened. 'Who sent ye to me, Billy? Take a good, deep breath and say one word at a time.'

'M–my mother wants yer to c–come to M–Miss Pond at our h–home.'

'Pond? Ye mean the parson's girl? She at yer mother's?'

Billy nodded. 'P–please come now.' His eyes pleaded with her.

'Right. I'll fetch me cloak an' bag, while ye go over to Tom Saunders an' ask to borrow his donkey cart.'

Billy nodded again, and promptly crossed the triangle of open ground to a cottage opposite Granny Mason's – only to be met with the news that Tom's donkey had reached the end of his hard-working life, and lay dying in the shed that served as a stable.

'Can't lend ol' Bob out any more,' Tom told Billy mournfully. 'Ain't Noah Reeve got a hoss or a pony as can pull the cart?'

It was now getting dark, and the smithy was locked until Monday. Billy drew another breath.

'Can yer l–let me b–orrow the c–cart?'

'Who for?'

'Granny M–Mason. She's got to g–go up the C–Common.'

'Course she can. It be round the back, an' I'll fetch it. Poor old Bob won't draw it no more.'

Out came the donkey cart, and to Tom's astonishment Billy placed himself between the shafts, holding one on each side with his powerful arms.

'Gawd 'elp us, Billy, you ain't goin' to pull that cart up the Common?'

But the man-drawn cart had already set off, to Granny Mason's admiration when she saw it. She climbed up with alacrity, and threw her bag into the cart, taking her driver's seat behind Billy.

'Gee-up, Billy, ye're a good'un!' she joked. 'All I need now's a whip!'

It was hard work ascending the grassy slope to Widow Siggery's cottage. A candle was burning in an uncurtained window, and the door was opened by Billy's mother, long before they reached it.

'Thank God for the sight o' ye, Granny! The pains be hard upon her, an' I can't do more'n hold 'er and tell 'er ye're comin'!'

Granny Mason practically jumped down from the cart and hurried indoors. Billy was sweating and his breathing was rapid from the exertion of doing a donkey's work. His mother brought him a mug of water, which he drank gratefully. 'W–what next, M–Mother?'

'Can ye go to the Ponds an' tell 'em, Billy?' she asked apologetically. 'Poor Parson Pond'll be beside himself with worry.'

Billy smiled and nodded, then squared his shoulders and set off again, this time without the cart.

He found the parson's home in chaos. Pond had just returned from another fruitless search for his daughter, Jenny was crying, and Mrs Pond greeted Billy angrily.

'What d'*you* want? We got trouble enough 'ere already!'

Billy began to reply, but his arm was seized by the parson, his eyes full of terror.

'Have you news of Elizabeth, Billy? Tell me, is she alive or dead?'

'Y–yer daughter's s–safe with my mother,' replied Billy. Herbert Pond wept with relief.

'Thanks be to God! Oh, thank God! How is she?'

'M–Mother has sent for G–Granny Mason, and she—'

'I must go to her!' The parson grabbed his coat and hat, which he had thrown over a chair. 'Are you coming, Connie?'

'No, I'll stay 'ere and wait,' she replied in an aggrieved tone. In truth she was secretly thankful that the birth was not taking place at home – she had no wish to be ordered about by Granny Mason or be under obligation to Silly Billy Siggery's mother.

Herbert Pond did not linger further, but strode out of the house towards the Common. Billy joined him and took his arm to steady him over the rough terrain in the dark. Within twenty minutes they reached the cottage, and were let in by a neighbour who had come to help. From an inner room they could hear Elizabeth's agonized groans and the voices of the two women in charge of her.

'There y'are, Mr Pond, a cup o' tea for ye,' said the neighbour, and poured out a small beer for Billy, because the tea was scarce and expensive. 'Her's doin' well, an' won't be long.'

The next five hours passed slowly for Herbert Pond and Billy. Nine o'clock came, then ten, then eleven . . . the parson sat with his head between his hands, praying, and Billy, also suffering at the sound of those intermittent groans of pain, kept his hand on Pond's shoulder.

Soon after eleven they heard purposeful talk between the two women.

'It's time to push down *hard*, Lizzie Pond,' said Granny Mason. 'Take a big breath in and hold it – no, don't scream, *hold* yer breath an' *push!*'

'Have a sip o' water, my love,' said Mrs Siggery.

'Another pain – come on, push down hard! Look, Mrs Siggery, there's the top o' the head.'

By midnight there was further progress. 'Get 'er on to 'er

side, towards you, and take hold of 'er right leg – hold it up – come on, Lizzie Pond, we're nearly there. Another push!'

'I can't, I *can't*, Granny, my body's splitting in half. Oh, help me, help me, show me mercy!'

Parson Pond groaned and sank to his knees in prayer.

They heard another drawn-out cry like that of a wounded animal. Billy knelt beside Pond and put his arms around him.

'There's the head – keep hold o' that leg, Mary Siggery,' Granny Mason said, 'an' now the body – oh, there we are, a boy! Lizzie Pond, ye're the mother of a son.' And then there was another sound, the 'Lah! Lah! Lah! Lah!' of the newborn.

'A *son*? Did she say a son, Billy?' whispered Pond. 'Then 'tis my grandson, thank the Lord.'

Elizabeth said weakly, 'A boy? Can I see him? Hold him?'

'In a minute, sweet, when I've cut the cord. Have ye got a name for 'im?'

'I'll call him Andrew, after the disciple,' said the new mother.

'Andrew, did ye hear that, boy?' said Granny Mason to the baby. 'Andrew Pond ye may be, but ye're a de Boville, an' no mistake. See that nose an' the shape of 'is head?'

'Let me hold him – oh, let me see,' begged Elizabeth, holding out her arms.

Mary Siggery came out of the bedroom twenty minutes later and smiled at the two men.

'Mr Pond, ye can go in an' see yer daughter an' grandson. 'Twas yer prayers that helped her through.'

Pond needed no second bidding, and went to kiss his daughter and bless his new grandson. He thanked Granny Mason and Mrs Siggery from his heart, and agreed that Elizabeth should stay at the cottage for a few days. He said he would send Jenny up to help.

Meanwhile Mary Siggery spoke tenderly to her son.

'Ye can't go in there, Billy, but she's told me how ye carried her all that way when she was in travail, an' you with yer poor foot an' everythin'. I'm that proud o' ye, Billy.'

'Thank ye, Mother. I–I'm just grateful that I was at–at hand when she needed me.'

He rose and went outside to offer up his thanks under the night sky in the first hour of that Sunday morning.

Elizabeth, holding her newborn baby and smiling down at

his little face, remembered something Billy Siggery had said as he carried her.

Elizabeth my love. Or had she just imagined that she'd heard it?

Nine

Forbidden Love and Love Revealed

1781

Constance Pond looked out of the kitchen window, her face set in the aggrieved expression that had become habitual with her. Her husband was in the garden, sowing and planting another season's crop of vegetables. She watched him straighten his back and fold his hands over the handle of his rake. His eyes were alight and his features softened into an indulgent smile as the little boy came running up to him.

'Gaffer! Gaffer! I digged wif my spade!' cried Andrew excitedly, brandishing the child-sized wooden spade that Billy Siggery had made for him. 'I been *busy*, Gaffer!'

Constance saw her husband drop the rake and hold out his arms to pick up his grandson.

'Have you, my busy little boy? Take care with that spade – you mustn't hit Gaffer over the head with it! My word, you're getting heavy – such a big boy!'

'I'm a big boy 'cause I'm free! Where's Mama? Put me down to fetch Mama!'

'No, no, Mama's busy at the piano – can't you hear it playing? Listen, Mama's teaching another big girl how to play her scales: doh, re, me, fa, so, la, te, doh!' sang Pond.

Andrew tried to do the same. 'Doo, ray, doo, me . . .'

'You're not ready for the church choir yet!' his grandfather said laughing. 'Your mama will teach you your scales when you're bigger. Down you go, now, I must get on with planting my runner bean seedlings. They look small now, but they'll grow up and up and up, and be taller than me!'

The little boy stared at the row of seedlings planted in a

well-manured shallow trench. 'As big as a beanstalk?'
Pond laughed again.

God knows Lizzie's had it easier than I have, thought
Mrs Pond bitterly. At least I was married to Pond when she
was born, though I've paid a price for it ever since. *She*
flaunts her child all over Wollaston, just as if he'd been
born in respectable wedlock. Herbert dotes on him, and that
Siggery woman's always coming here with titbits for him,
talking just as if *she* were his grandmother. Everybody smiles
on Herbert and Lizzie and the boy, but what about *me*, his
true grandmother? I've borne with the shame and disgrace
without complaining – why aren't *I* appreciated for all I've
endured?

No answer was forthcoming. Herbert Pond and his grandson
continued to talk in the April sunshine, and Elizabeth had
another hour of teaching piano to the village girls. She also
took a class of younger girls to teach them basic reading,
writing and enough simple arithmetic to deal with money
thriftily. These lessons and her father's classes for boys helped
to bring a little extra income into the house, but it was *she*,
thought Constance Pond, *she* who had to make it stretch to
keep them all fed and clothed.

'Haven't you brought in that washin' yet, Jenny?' she called.
'Should've been brought in an hour ago – it'll be too dry to
iron prop'ly!'

Andrew suddenly caught sight of a familiar figure at the
back gate, and ran towards him.

'Look, Gaffer, look, there's Billy! How d'you *do*, Billy?'
he said in the polite way he had been taught to greet visitors.
'Pleased to meet you, Billy! Where's Ladyfox?'

'Hello, Andrew, p–pleased to meet you, t–too, and Mr
P–Pond. I'm on m–my way home, and G–Granny Siggery's
got L–Ladyfox,' said Billy shyly.

'Take me up to see her!'

'N–next time you c–come up with your m–mama,' answered
Billy, lifting up the child and making a seat with his hands
for Andrew to sit on, his back to Billy's strong chest.

'How's life with you, Billy?' asked the parson pleasantly.

'Another s–six weeks to J–June, an' I'll be d–done,' replied
Billy with satisfaction.

'Ah, yes, your seven long years of apprenticeship will be

finished,' said Pond. 'What will you do then? Set yourself up in a smithy of your own somewhere else?'

'N–no, N–Noah wants me to s–stay an' help him to make a b–bigger smithy, and t–take charge when he g–goes to Oak Hall, seein' to the h–hunters.'

'That's very good news, Billy. We've been wondering how Noah would manage without you.'

'I–I don't want t–to leave W–Wollaston, Mr Pond.'

'And 'tis certain Wollaston doesn't want to lose you,' the parson said, though he knew Billy's real reason for staying in Wollaston.

'Can I come up an' see Ladyfox tomorrow, Billy?' Andrew asked.

'Y–yes, if your mama an' gaffer d–don't mind you comin' up to G–Granny Siggery's.'

Suddenly their attention was diverted by another visitor. Mrs Pond craned her neck to see Sir John de Boville standing at the back gate and beaming down on the little assembly. Mrs Pond wondered why on earth he had gone to the back gate like any travelling pedlar, instead of coming to the front door where she would have greeted him with suitable words and a curtsey.

'Good afternoon, Pond. I've brought over those documents you were asking me about,' said the baronet in a casually friendly way, as befitted a senior churchwarden. 'I wrote to Dr Webb about the choir stalls, and he sent me the details of when they were carved, and how much was paid for them.'

Sir John was addressing the parson, but his eyes were fixed on the parson's grandson, held aloft by that strange blacksmith fellow who was so good with the thoroughbred hunters.

Andrew's bright, intelligent eyes brought Richard's face so vividly to mind that Sir John's heart lurched. The boy had inherited his mother's golden hair and blue eyes, but his features were his father's. He's a handsome child in every way, thought Sir John with a pang. There had been no news of Richard for over two years. They had received one letter to say that he was serving under General Cornwallis, but news of the war was confused and contradictory – a growing faction in the House of Commons thought it should be brought to an end. General Clinton had eventually taken Charleston after a long siege the previous year, but with heavy casualties among the British. Sir John knew Richard could be dead or wounded, and he looked longingly at this small boy, possibly his son's only memorial.

'Thank you, Sir John, that's good of you,' replied the parson civilly but without subservience. He knew why Sir John had offered his services as churchwarden, which occasioned frequent consultations with himself. The baronet had also offered a regular allowance towards Andrew's upkeep, but Pond had so far declined it, not wanting to be under any obligation to the de Bovilles. Pond believed that the boy would be much happier with his mother, at least while he was young; circumstances might alter later when the question of his education arose. Relations between the two grandfathers were cordial, though their wives refused to acknowledge each other's existence.

Sir John now held out his arms to the boy. 'Come to me, young man, I'm your grandsire!' he called jovially, but Andrew clung to his seat in Billy's arms until relinquished and gently pushed in the direction of the baronet.

'How d' you *do*, gran'son?' he asked politely. 'Pleased to meet you, gran'son.'

Which made them all laugh, except for Constance Pond, who stood well back from the kitchen window so as not to be seen.

'You are forever going to visit that wretched parson, Sir John,' remarked Lady de Boville with a frown. Her inward grief over the uncertainty of Richard's fate had hardened her features and sharpened her tongue, whereas Sir John had shown his sadness by ageing ten years in the space of three; his movements had slowed, and his hair was thinning and turning grey.

'As a churchwarden I have regular business with him – and of course I see the boy,' he confessed.

'And his mother. And that obnoxious Mrs Pond.'

'No, I did not see either woman. His mother was teaching piano and Mrs Pond was indoors, I believe, keeping out of the way.' He paused. 'Young Siggery was there.'

'What? That stammering fellow with a deformed foot? What was *he* doing there?'

'He and Pond have always been close – Pond taught him

to read, y'know. And he's a splendid smith, so good with my hunters.'

She did not reply, and he deliberately changed the subject.

'Has there been a letter from Frederica? It must be a month since we last heard from her.'

'We must remember that she leads a very busy life,' the lady replied, 'giving dinners and supporting Theodore in his business matters – all those meetings he has to attend with the governor general and the other commissioners. It's a very large and important company, is it not? Theodore serves it well.'

And rakes in an enormous revenue for the East India Company, with no small gain to himself, thought Sir John. Aloud he said, 'Yes, our daughter has done well for herself after that unfortunate business with Lennox's son. She made a good choice in Theodore Carr, and titles are not everything. And you never know, he could be in line for a knighthood for his exertions to the company.' He saw his wife's face brighten at the thought. 'Georgina seems to be yielding to young Wilborough's entreaties,' he continued.

Lady de Boville made a very slight grimace with her mouth. 'I could have wished better for her than an attorney's clerk, though at least Beccles is not so far away as—'

She left the sentence unfinished, but Sir John knew what she meant: not as far away as America or London or Cambridge where their younger son was at school.

'I like Wilborough well enough,' he said. 'Comes of good yeoman stock, and he'll be an attorney-at-law himself one day, with his own firm.' He smiled as he spoke, though his wife was silent, and he went over to her and put a comforting hand on her shoulder.

'Charlotte, my love, we still have Teddy. Perhaps we should start calling him Edward, now that he's nearly thirteen, and maybe—'

'You mean he may sire the heir to the baronetcy, seeing that Richard's son is a bastard with no rights at all.'

Sir John winced. 'I will say one thing, Charlotte. If God is merciful and returns our son to us again, he will see that he has a son, and know that he was deceived by us. I hope that he may forgive us, and I would have no objection whatever if he then chose to marry Elizabeth Pond.'

Charlotte de Boville shrugged, but her answer was sincere. 'He could marry whomsoever he pleased, if we could only set eyes on him again.'

For Mrs Frederica Carr life was undoubtedly eventful, but today she was feeling out of sorts. Her husband was kind and indulgent, it was true, and the house in Southampton Row was all that she could wish for in luxury and elegance but it was not enough. Her magnificent wedding at St Margaret's Westminster had been a triumph, coming so soon after her crushing humiliation at the hands of that pitiful fool Lennox, the whole winter season during which she had willingly endured his awkwardness, his clumsy efforts to dance, his inability to flirt in spite of all her encouragement – and then to think that he had dismissed her! How *dared* he? Would she ever forget Lady Lennox apologizing for his behaviour, assuming that she would return to Wollaston and face the disappointment that her parents would feel?

Frederica had gritted her teeth and refrained from showing how deeply her pride had been hurt. Lady Lennox had been surprised when she had asked to stay, not knowing that the girl had noticed the attentions of Theodore Carr, a self-made merchant who had become very rich as a commissioner for the East India Company. Once freed from her supposed engagement to Charles, Frederica set about responding to Mr Carr's advances and securing his affections; a proposal was made and accepted, and a mere two months after Lennox's rejection of her, she became a radiant bride.

Viscount Lennox and Lady Lennox had been invited to the wedding together with the Honourable Charles and Julia, and her parents had come from Wollaston to see her married. She remembered with cold satisfaction the moment when she had driven past the Lennoxes' house in Bedford Row, seated beside Mr Carr in his open-topped landau, and had waved a condescending hand to Charles, standing on the front doorstep looking vague and uncertain as usual. If, as was predicted in some circles, Carr's exertions on behalf of the East India Company earned him a recommendation for a knighthood, Frederica's happiness would be crowned.

Since her marriage, however, there had been disappointments: she had conceived twice, but both times had ended in miscarriage. And now, after two years of wifehood as an acknowledged beauty and charming hostess, her husband seemed less confident about the future. He had spoken of the need for economies, of difficult times for the East India Company, and false accusations made against its commissioners. He had become absent-minded and frowned when she bought new clothes and planned dazzling dinner parties for his associates. Somehow the life of the *bon ton* had lost its lustre, along with her husband's early adoration of her, and for a woman like Frederica, it was inevitable that she would find other admiring eyes. She found herself light-heartedly competing for the attentions of a man of wealth and power, experiencing again the delights of flirtation, of inviting with her eyes but refusing to yield with her lips. What would the next step be?

Seated in front of her mirror, Frederica smiled at her pretty reflection as her maid adjusted the high-piled, powdered wig. Yes! If Theodore had become so obsessed with the East India Company that he started to neglect his lovely wife, he must not be surprised to find that other men, and one in particular, was more appreciative of her charms.

Rumours that all was not well with the Carr marriage had begun to circulate, and reached the ears of Mrs Seward through one of her former maidservants, now married. The good-natured lady had been pleased when Frederica found a rich and devoted husband, and Charles told his aunt that he too was happy that his cousin had found a more suitable husband. But now it seemed that she had become bored – and was playing with fire . . .

Charles had drawn closer to his aunt after her son Oliver had joined the army and disappeared from the London scene to fight in America. Mrs Seward confided her fears about the war to her nephew, who visited her regularly. And there were other subjects of conversation.

'Thanks to you, Charles, I've befriended that poor girl you brought here,' she told him. 'She's a willing worker, and has told me the most interesting tales of her country life at Wollaston, and how her father lost his mind after being driven off his piece of land by the de Boville family. Aren't you glad you did not marry their daughter, Charles?'

Charles coloured and looked distinctly embarrassed by her teasing tone.

'Yes, you may well blush, nephew, for I've discovered that *you* have been paying the fees of a private asylum for her poor father. I have gone with Meg to visit him. Sadly his body is wasting and weakening with his mind, and I fear he will not live much longer – but meanwhile *I* shall take over the fees for Myrtle House. I commend your charity, Charles.'

Her prediction proved true, for Zack Venn did not survive the winter but died in his sleep on a raw February day. Mrs Seward accompanied Meg to the funeral and paid for the coffin and a headstone; she touched by the girl's grief.

'Me mother's gone, an' now me pa, an' I don't know where Sam is, an' Josh don't keep in touch,' she sobbed. 'It's 'ard when yer can't read or write.'

'You're a good, cheerful worker, Meg, but I agree that much of the world is closed to one who cannot read,' said Mrs Seward sympathetically. 'How would you like me to teach you?'

The offer was gratefully accepted, and in the course of the lessons Meg's grammar improved, and her speech became softer, though she did not lose her lilting Suffolk accent. This was not lost on Mrs Seward's only manservant, Peter Coleman, who began to take notice of the pretty girl up from the country. He started to engage her in conversation, and told her of his wish to move out of London and take up employment as a butler in one of the great country houses.

'They often take on a married couple as butler and 'ouse-keeper,' he told her. 'Makes for better discipline among the other servants. D'yer think ye'd like that sort o' life, Meg?'

Meg listened and followed the drift of where he was leading. Peter Coleman was a steady, honest sort of man, and the possibility of such a partnership was quite appealing; but for the present she was content with her life at John Street and Mrs Seward's kindness.

In the summer of 1779 a scandal had rocked London, the kind of salacious story that the general public loves to read or talk about, shaking their heads over the goings-on of people who should know better. It seemed that a certain young nobleman had been robbed of a considerable sum of money whilst visiting the establishment of a Madame Duvall in Marylebone. His purse and pockets had been emptied by the woman with whom he had spent several hours, after which he found that over fifty pounds in bank notes was missing. Duvall had vigorously denied the charge when he first complained, but had been summoned to meet him at his lawyer's office. She had refused to make any payment, and told him that if he persisted with his accusation she would name him to the *Morning Post*, and disclose that he had visited her establishment.

Madame Duvall was to learn that it is a mistake to make threats in the presence of a lawyer. The next week the *Morning Post* carried a scandalous exposé of Madame Duvall, named as 'a notorious brothel keeper', and described in lip-smacking detail how she lured young girls from the country and taught them how to satisfy the carnal appetites of lecherous old men. The scandal raged for days, and the many revelations lost nothing in the telling.

At John Street the morning paper was read aloud by Peter Coleman to the cook and the two maidservants, Biddy and Meg.

'Cor! I bet there's a lordship or two shiverin' in 'is shoes in case 'is name comes out,' Peter said grinning. 'Serve 'em right – show 'em all up!'

He stopped chuckling when Meg turned very pale – she looked as if she might faint.

'Quick, get 'er a drink o' water!' ordered the cook. 'Ought to be ashamed o' yerself, Coleman, readin' out that sort o' stuff in front of a girl like 'er. Biddy, go for the missus!'

Mrs Seward took Meg to a small sitting room where the girl could lie on a couch while her mistress questioned her, kindly but persistently. Was she not feeling well, was her monthly flow due, did she have any other symptoms? Meg could not lie to her, and the truth came out – that Meg had been employed in Madame Duvall's establishment when Mr Charles Lennox had found her there and rescued her. He had then brought her straight to his aunt Seward to stay until she could find work as a maidservant.

'And here I've stayed, Mrs Seward, an' you've been that good to me, and I'm grateful, but . . . but now this awful story's come out in the paper.' She burst into tears.

Mrs Seward was indeed shocked, and sent Meg to her bed, saying that she would need to think the matter over. Then she despatched Coleman to Bedford Row with a brief note requesting Charles Lennox attend her immediately. This request annoyed Lady Lennox, but he presented himself within the half hour.

'Sit down, Charles,' ordered his aunt, and for once her friendly smile was absent. 'I want to talk to you about this scandal over a brothel keeper in Marylebone. Meg Venn almost fainted when my manservant read about it in the *Morning Post*, and she now tells me a very strange story of your first meeting with her. I have often wondered about your account of how you found her wandering homeless and penniless in the street, but I saw no real reason to question either of you about it. Besides, I have always known you to be truthful, Charles. I will now give you another opportunity to tell me again about the circumstances of your meeting with the girl.'

In great confusion, and blushing to the roots of his hair, Charles told his aunt the true story of how he had met Meg and rescued her; it corroborated exactly with Meg's account.

'I apologize, Aunt Sophie, for not telling you the truth that night, but I feared that you would not accept her if you knew,' he said humbly. 'But I gather that she has been a satisfactory maidservant, and that you are teaching her to read – and you know her to be innocent.'

'I have indeed come to realize that Meg is a good girl – I can see that she was trapped by an artful woman into a life of vice, from which you rescued her,' replied Mrs Seward. 'My only question now is to ask what you were doing, Charles, visiting a brothel. Will you tell me that?'

Now this question was a trap into which Charles might or might not fall; Mrs Seward had heard the whole story from Meg, of how Charles had been sent to Madame Duvall's at the insistence of Lord Lennox who wanted his son to have experience with an older woman.

'Well, Charles, are you going to tell me?' demanded his aunt sternly.

'I–I felt that I needed some experience of – of what happens between a man and a – a woman,' faltered Charles, lowering his head and avoiding her eyes. 'I realize now that it was a wrong thing to do, Aunt Sophie, and I'm very sorry.'

'Well, as long as you are truly sorry, Charles, and Meg has every reason to be thankful that you were there at that particular time,' said Mrs Seward in a softer tone, while inwardly she commended her nephew further for not betraying his father. 'As I have said, Meg has proved her worth as a servant, and I am happy to keep her here. But nobody – absolutely *nobody* – must ever know where you met her. I shall never disclose it.'

'Thank you, dear Aunt, and I am forever in your debt,' replied Charles with emotion. 'And before I go, may I speak with . . . with the girl – with Meg Venn?'

'Is that necessary, Charles? Both of you have separately told me the real truth, so surely there is nothing left to be said.'

'If you please, Aunt Sophie, I wish only to see her – to ask how she does and offer my services in any way useful,' said Charles awkwardly.

'You have done her the greatest service already, Charles, and it would be best to let the matter end there,' his aunt said seriously.

'Yes indeed, Aunt, you are right, I know, but if I might see her and offer her my good wishes, I would be most obliged to you,' pleaded Charles.

Mrs Seward agreed to send for Meg and allow Charles a brief interview in her presence.

While Biddy went to fetch Meg from her room, Mrs Seward waved aside her nephew's thanks. 'Let me remind you, Charles, that although you met this girl in strange and highly improper circumstances, you are still an heir to a viscountcy and she is but a poor, uneducated servant girl. It would be most unfair to give her any ideas about . . . well, any kind of friendship between you.'

'I had no such idea, Aunt,' he protested.

'I'm glad to hear it. Perhaps I should tell you, Charles, that Meg has been noticed by my manservant Coleman, and I suspect that they will be married in the course of time. He wants to leave London for a place in the country, and so I shall lose two honest, reliable servants – but it may well be the best future for Meg.'

'Oh, indeed, Aunt, yes, I suppose it may well be,' answered Charles unhappily.

There was a soft knock at the door. Mrs Seward called, 'Come in!'

Meg entered, looking nervous, and her eyes opened wide

at the sight of Charles Lennox, though she quickly lowered her head and curtseyed.

'Yes, come in, Meg, and you may be seated. Are you feeling better now?' her mistress enquired.

'Yes, thank you, ma'am.' Meg sat down, keeping her eyes lowered.

'Mr Lennox has confirmed your account of what happened at that woman's house.'

'Yes, ma'am,' answered Meg in a whisper.

'As far as I am concerned, that's an end to the matter, and I wish you to remain here as my personal maid. However, my nephew wishes to see you, and I've agreed to a short interview.'

Mrs Seward nodded to Charles, and remained firmly seated, for she had no intention of leaving them alone.

Charles rose and held out his hand to Meg. She took it and they shook hands.

'I hope I find you in good health, Miss . . . er . . . Venn?'

'An' I hope ye're the same, sir.'

'It is good to know that . . . to see you here with my aunt, Meg, and I'm glad too. I would like to give you my best wishes for the future.'

'Thank ye, sir, an' I give ye mine.' As their eyes met Mrs Seward noticed the look that passed between them.

'If – if I could be of any service to you, Miss Venn, I mean – I remember you said you had two brothers, and . . . and is there any message I could take to them?'

An eager look came into Meg's eyes.

'Why, yes, sir, there's my older brother Joshua who works for Squire Horrocks in Wollaston, and there's my younger brother who went off to join the army. Sam may be in America by now, an' I don't s'pose ye could track 'im down, but if ye could tell Joshua that I got a good place here an' tell him that Pa died. Oh, yes, an' the parson at Wollaston, good Parson Pond. If ye could ask him to tell his daughter Lizzie—'

'I think that's enough, Meg,' Mrs Seward broke in, glancing at Charles, whom she knew would have no pleasure in visiting Wollaston with its associations of Frederica. 'It would probably be best, Charles, if you wrote to this Squire Horrocks and told him to pass on the messages to Meg's brother and the parson – that would be quite sufficient.'

'Very well, Aunt Sophie. I will see that your messages are delivered, Meg – I mean Miss Venn.'

'Thank ye, sir – an' ma'am.'

'You may go, Meg,' ordered Mrs Seward.

'Yes, ma'am. Good day t'ye, sir.'

'Good day, Meg.' Charles took the hand she held out to him, and raised it, pressing it to his lips. Mrs Seward stared in astonishment, but nothing more was said for there was no need: their eyes said it all.

Elizabeth's last pupil had left, and the house was silent; she had heard the voices in the garden earlier – her father, her son, Billy and Sir John. Parson Pond had come indoors, washed his hands and replaced his boots with slippers, and she guessed that he would be in his study now. She wondered if she should brew a pot of tea, expensive though it was. She tapped lightly on the study door.

'Sssh!' hissed her father, opening the door and pointing at Andrew who lay curled up fast asleep in the window seat, his grandfather's garden jacket tucked around him. His eyelashes brushed his soft cheek, his rosy mouth half-open as he slept, and Elizabeth marvelled for the hundredth time at her beautiful child.

'He's had two visitors this afternoon,' whispered her father.

'Yes, I heard them, Papa. What did Billy and Sir John want with you?'

'They didn't want anything with *me*, my dear. They came to see *him*, and he wants to see Ladyfox. I said you'd most likely take him up to Siggery's tomorrow afternoon.'

'Ah.' Elizabeth looked thoughtful, but did not answer.

'That pretty little vixen is as cunning as any monkey,' the parson continued. 'She follows Billy wherever he goes, and the cottagers give her titbits and treat her just like a puppy – and she knows it! She's much changed since Billy found her, a helpless little orphan cub after the Wollaston Hunt got her mother and the rest of the litter.'

Elizabeth said, 'Andrew would like her to come and live with us.'

'No, 'twould be too much of a sideshow, the village lining up to see a domesticated fox! And besides, your mother . . .' He shrugged.

'D'you think Ladyfox will ever go back to the wild, Papa?'

'Wouldn't be surprised, when it comes to mating time – there is the danger of the Wollaston Hunt though. They'd get her as they got her mother, nothing so sure.'

Elizabeth frowned, began to speak and then changed her mind; she feared how her words might be received. Her father noticed.

'Come, Lizzie, what do you want to say?'

'I – oh, it's not easy to put into words, Papa, but sometimes I wish that things could always stay as they are now. Andrew is such a dear little boy, and . . . and Billy calling here to see him practically every day. I wish Meg could see him.'

'Yes, it was good to have news of her when that shy young gentleman came to Wollaston, stammering nearly as badly as Billy!' laughed the parson. 'At least you know that she's alive and well, and poor Zack has gone to his rest.'

'I wonder what Meg thought when he went back to London and told her that I have a child out of wedlock,' mused Elizabeth, again hesitating, then turned to her father and spoke plainly.

'Papa, I don't think I should take Andrew to see Ladyfox tomorrow – or any other day.'

'Really, Lizzie? Now why should you think that?'

'Well, because . . . oh, Papa, this sounds so presumptuous, I know, but—'

'Go on, Lizzie. You can tell me,' he prompted gently.

'Just lately I've thought that Billy Siggery has grown too fond of Andrew,' she said, avoiding her father's eyes. 'I mean, Papa, that they are like father and son.'

'Is that such a bad thing? And is it only Andrew you think brings Billy here?'

'Oh, Papa, I can't hide anything from you, can I? Yes, I fear that Billy may be growing too fond of . . . of *me!*'

'My dear girl, I've known that for years,' her father said with a smile. 'He has loved you from childhood, and I've seen it deepen since you have both grown up.'

'Papa!' She turned and faced him. 'Why have you not said this before?'

'It would have been unfair to give his secret away. I was waiting until you saw for yourself, my dear.'

'But poor Billy! He knows full well that we can never be . . . oh, Papa!' She clasped her hands together in her agitation, glancing at Andrew who remained fast asleep. Pond laid a hand on her shoulder.

'Why not, Lizzie dear? He loves you and Andrew, his apprenticeship is finished, and a good smith need never go short of work. And consider further – you are the daughter of an impoverished parson and a mother with little sympathy or understanding of you, and you have a bastard child. By contrast *he* is the most faithful, wise and devoted man you will ever meet. Think about that, my girl.'

Elizabeth drew in a sharp breath and put a hand to her heart. It was as if she had been blind for a long time, but now her father's words had opened her eyes so that she could see clearly. Not only Billy's love for her, but the love that had lain deep and hidden in her own heart.

'Tell me, Papa, what should I *do*?' she asked in a low voice.

'Be happy, my daughter,' Pond replied, his voice shaking slightly, and his eyes misty. 'Be happy with him.'

Ten

A Scandal and a Midsummer Celebration

1781

Elizabeth scarcely slept that night; she heard the bell of St Bede's mark each and every hour, and dawn found her still in a whirl of confused emotions. There was sheer amazement and self-accusation for her own blindness; there was uncertainty about the future – and something else that she could hardly name, so incredible and unlikely did it appear – something like happiness.

She had a class of four girls attending the lesson that morning, so had to give all her attention to them. Jenny Tasker, now a smiling eighteen-year-old, took over the care of Andrew at class times, and delighted in showing the pupils how well *she* had learned to read and write. On the whole the girls' parents were pleased with the progress they made, and there might have been twice as many pupils if the parson's daughter had not been 'ruined' and borne a bastard child, though such condemnation was rarely heard now; it had been replaced by a general admiration of the little fair-haired boy – so bright and friendly.

The class finished at midday, and the Ponds sat down to a repast of bread and cheese with the last of Mrs Pond's pickled onions, washed down with a mug of beer.

'Andrew wants to go up and see Ladyfox this afternoon, Lizzie,' said her father, wiping his mouth and setting down his mug. 'I must make a few visits to the cottages up there, so we'll take him together.'

'Very well, Papa.'

'Billy will be at the smithy, but Granny Siggery will be at home,' he added in a casual tone.

'I notice she's *Granny* Siggery these days instead o' Widow,' remarked Mrs Pond acidly. 'She's nobody's granny as far as I know.'

'She helped Granny Mason to bring Andrew into the world, and cared for him in his earliest days, so I think she has a right to the title, Connie,' her husband reminded her mildly. 'We all know that you and Lady de Boville share the privilege of being his true grandmothers.'

'*That* woman!' muttered Mrs Pond under her breath, but she said no more. Over the past few years she had learned the wisdom of guarding her tongue.

'Right, well, Lizzie, we'll be on our way, shall we?' said Pond, getting up. Together the father and daughter set out for Cove Common, with Andrew holding a hand of each. It was a fresh April afternoon, the time of year when the earth is young again in leaf and flower. The wide arch of the sky was pale blue, with high, feathery clouds which the parson called 'angels' wings' and pointed out to his grandson. He and Elizabeth scarcely exchanged a word, but Andrew was full of questions and wanted them to swing him backwards and forwards, lifting him off his feet while he yelled with glee.

Mrs Siggery was out of doors when they arrived, feeding scraps to the two pigs. Herbert Pond was astonished yet again to see Ladyfox running around as tame as any dog or cat that knows it can trust its owners. The pretty little creature had been reared from helpless infancy to a healthy, half-grown vixen with a soft reddish-brown coat and fine, bushy tail. At first she had been named Fred Fox, but after a certain discovery Mrs Siggery had changed her name to Flora. Andrew, however, chose to call her Ladyfox, and the name had remained.

Andrew let go of their hands and ran towards Mrs Siggery. 'Gammer!' he cried. 'How d' you do, Gammer? I come to see you and Ladyfox!'

Mrs Siggery and the parson exchanged a smile. Andrew was now able to pronounce the words 'Gran'farver' and 'Gran'muvver', but his first efforts had been adopted by them and they sometimes jokingly addressed each other as Gammer and Gaffer.

Elizabeth hung back a little, feeling self-conscious. When

her father and Granny Siggery had disappeared into the cottage, she was content to stay outside with Andrew and Ladyfox. She knew, without a word being uttered, that her father wished to speak with Mrs Siggery alone.

Inside the little living room the kettle simmered on the hob over a small fire. Mrs Siggery took two tea cups and saucers down from the sideboard. Herbert Pond inwardly prayed for the right words to be given him in an unusual and possibly painful talk with her.

'Andrew's a fine lad, and he loves your Billy as a son loves a father,' he began.

She gave him a surprised look, and occupied herself with brewing tea.

'That be true right enough, Parson Pond, an' likewise Billy loves him like a son.' There was a hint of regret in her voice, a sadness that did not escape Pond.

'And is there anything wrong with that, Mrs Siggery, that they should be so attached to each other?'

There was a pause, and then she spoke more forcibly. 'Well, yes, seein' as Billy must part with 'im in time. People in Wollaston are sayin' the de Bovilles'll take 'im when 'e's bigger an' send 'im away to school, an' we'll all lose 'im.'

'Really? Is that what they're saying?' asked Pond with an amused smile which did not please Billy's mother.

'Aye, an' the day'll come when the boy won't even remember poor Billy at all. It's a great pity, Parson, that my son must walk through this cruel world without ever havin' the blessin's that other men have, not half as deservin' as he! He must always give up to others, give up love, give up havin' a wife an' children of 'is own – it's not right, Parson Pond, it's not fair!'

She was weeping openly, wiping her eyes on the corner of her apron. Herbert Pond rose from his chair, and took her hand in his.

'Hush, Mary Siggery, and be comforted. I know that your son is as good as, or better than, any man in Wollaston, but those who know him best are not blind to his worth.' He spoke seriously, watching her face as he went on. 'My daughter Elizabeth is older and wiser than when she yielded to young de Boville, but she can now see where true goodness lies.'

She raised her head and looked at him sharply, a question in her eyes.

'Ah, Parson Pond, if only that girl knew how much she's loved, and for so long! My boy could get work in any place in Suffolk or beyond, but 'e won't leave Wollaston, just 'cause o' her!'

'I know, I know, Mary, in fact I've known for years,' he answered softly. 'But it's taken Lizzie time to see what we can see and know. And I've had to wait until she did so, just as we wait for a flower to bloom and unfold its petals – we can't pull them open or we'll damage it.'

'So – what are ye sayin', Parson?' she asked him directly.

'I'm saying, Mary Siggery, that the time has come. Your Billy may claim her whenever he pleases – this very day, if he cares to.'

'Oh, no, that can't be true!' she cried in disbelief.

'Hush, woman, I'm telling you it *is* true. Your son loves my daughter, and his love is returned by her. Let him ask her – let him be bold and come to her, this evening if he likes, for she is ready to accept him. *Tell* him, Mary, for heaven's sake, and let them wait no longer!'

Having stated his case, there was nothing more to be said, and the parson replaced his hat and bade her farewell. Outside of the cottage he called to his daughter.

'Come on, Lizzie! And you, my little man! We must be going, so say goodbye to Ladyfox.'

'Haven't you any more visits to make, Papa?' Elizabeth asked, a little surprised that Granny Siggery only waved to them from her cottage door instead of coming out to kiss Andrew and exchange a few words with herself.

'No, my dear, I think we should be getting back now.'

'Is Granny Siggery not well?'

'She is perfectly well, and we have had a very profitable discussion,' he answered with a smile and an air of finality, so that she asked no more questions. Andrew, as always, claimed all their attention.

The dim spring dusk was falling when the knock came at the door. Mrs Pond rose to answer it, but her husband said he would go. They heard the door open, and a hesitant voice spoke.

'Lizzie!' called her father. 'Come to the door.'

She obeyed, her heart fluttering, for she knew that this was to be a confrontation of some kind. And there on the doorstep stood Billy Siggery in his best Sunday clothes.

'William Siggery has come to speak with you, Lizzie,' said her father calmly. 'Fetch your cloak and bonnet, for there is no privacy to be had in this house.' He gave her a reassuring, knowing smile. 'Go walking with him, dear, and remember what we said yesterday. Good evening to you, William.' He closed the door, leaving the young couple to speak for themselves.

She looked at Billy, who gave her his arm to link with hers, and they walked along the lane beside the row of terraced cottages of which the parson's was the end one; then by unspoken consent they turned their footsteps towards the Common.

'It's a lovely evening, Billy,' she said, looking up at his face.

'A l–lovely evening to b–be with you, E–Elizab–beth,' he answered, and pressed her hand.

They continued to walk up the incline of the Common towards Foxholes, on the very same ground where Elizabeth had walked with Richard de Boville four years ago. She had been a young girl swept up in her first love, and he had courted her in the words of Shakespeare and the metaphysical poets. Looking back now with the wisdom of hindsight, she realized that since Andrew's birth her grief over Richard's desertion – and his possible death – had gradually faded into memory, while at the same time her love for the man now beside her had grown slowly and imperceptibly, recollected now in many little instances of his kindness, their shared smiles and observations, a rapt look on his face which she had sometimes suddenly surprised. He had become part of the fabric of her daily life, a constant presence, steady and reliable – and adored by Andrew.

Walking beside him now with arms linked, she felt enveloped in his love without words. And even if Billy Siggery had been able to speak fluently and clearly, he could not have expressed the tremulous adoration he felt, the overwhelming wonder of knowing his love to be returned.

At just the right moment they stopped walking and he drew her towards him.

'Kiss me, William.'

'I love you,' was all he said. Their first kiss needed no further words.

Mrs Pond was unbelieving at first, and honestly thought that she had not heard correctly when her husband told her that Lizzie had gone out walking in the twilight with a young admirer.

'Gone out walking with *who*, after dark? Has the de Boville's son turned up again? Or has Adam Horrocks changed his mind? Or has a stranger—?'

'No stranger, Connie. Young William Siggery.'

'William *who*? You mean some relative of Widow Siggery?'

'Yes, her only son, William. People call him Billy, but I shall call him William from now on.'

'Not Silly Billy Siggery?' Mrs Pond almost shrieked. 'Not the village fool?'

'Don't ever let me hear you calling him that again, Connie. I shall be proud to call him my son-in-law, and Lizzie could not have found a better man to be her husband. Many may agree with you, I dare say, for there are plenty of real fools around.' He gave a little smile. 'Heaven only knows what the de Bovilles will think of it – hah! They'll double their efforts to take Andrew away from us, but they shan't have him. Well, Connie, I'll wait up until they return, but there's no need for you to – not unless you're prepared to greet him with courtesy.'

Poor Mrs Pond could not trust herself to greet Billy Siggery as her future son-in-law, so without further comment she took up her husband's suggestion and went to bed.

As expected, Wollaston was stunned by the news that a June wedding was planned – the reactions were many and varied. The parents of Elizabeth's pupils hoped that she would be happy with her strange choice of husband, and also that she would continue to give lessons, for the girls came from the poorer cottagers' families rather than the tradesmen who could afford to send their daughters to the vicarage school. The Miss Buxtons wished her well: they represented a body of opinion who presumed that Miss Pond was marrying for security, seeing that a young woman with a bastard child was not able to pick and choose and was therefore thankful for the

young blacksmith's offer. One thing they were agreed upon
was that she was not marrying for money, and neither was
he, for Parson Pond would not be able to bestow much by
way of a dowry.

It was given out that the ceremony would take place quietly
at St Bede's, conducted by the parson, and that there would
be no wedding breakfast to follow. The Miss Buxtons assured
Mr Pond that they would serve light refreshments afterwards
in the church porch, as they did after poor funerals, but this
would be at their own expense as a gift, as much to him as
to the young couple.

At the Horrocks's farmhouse a debate took place as to
whether the squire and his family should attend, and it was
decided that they would all go, largely because the parson
was so well liked. A handsome present was sent to his house,
a strong oak chest filled with good quality linen and wool
blankets. When the news of this generous gift got around
Wollaston, there were a few spiteful tongues who said it must
be a thanks-offering for Adam's escape from marriage to the
parson's daughter who had borne a child to his one-time friend.

Lady de Boville was as incredulous as Mrs Pond.

'To think of our grandson living under the same roof with
that unfortunate fellow, Sir John – for I suppose they will
move into the washerwoman's cottage. Such a small and
cramped place for a boy to grow up in – and I've heard it
said in the stables that Siggery actually keeps a fox – a *fox*,
mark you – as if it were a cat or a dog. Just think of it, Sir
John!'

And indeed this item of news horrified the baronet.

'D'you mean to say that Siggery keeps such a creature in
the *house*, as a *pet*, Charlotte?' he gasped in disbelief. 'It can't
be true – nobody would be so foolish. Why, a bite from that
thing could give a person the dreaded dog's disease, and send
him to his death having fits and foaming at the mouth. I shall
speak to Pond about it.'

'For heaven's sake, John, you're a Justice of the Peace, and
you must *order* them to get rid of it. We can't allow the boy
to be subjected to such danger!'

Sir John sighed wearily. He did not remind his wife that
she had long refused to acknowledge Andrew as Richard's
son, and had dismissed him as a bastard with no legal rights.

That had continued to be her stance until the child had proved such a bright, healthy little boy, the very image of Richard. Now that Richard had been lost to them, and could be lying dead or fatally wounded on some remote foreign shore, she had completely changed her attitude and had begged Sir John to adopt the boy, though their younger son Edward would be next in line to inherit the baronetcy before Richard's bastard son. However, Sir John's lawyer had pointed out to him that just as Andrew Pond had no claim to the de Boville name or property, by the same token the de Bovilles had no claim upon the child – where he lived or with whom. In strictly legal terms a bastard child has no relatives except for his mother – and no rights.

It was a difficult time for Charlotte de Boville. Not only was she mourning the loss of her elder son, but she worried she would have to watch her grandson growing up in a hovel with a stammering cripple as a stepfather. And that was not all, for there was worrying news from London.

Since Frederica's two miscarriages there had been no news of any further hopes of a child. In fact they only received infrequent one-page notes from her, telling them about her busy social life: the latest ball she had attended, and how she had met and talked to the Marquis of Rockingham at a dinner at the Mansion House. She had also been introduced to Mr Charles James Fox at Devonshire House, where she had been a guest of the beautiful duchess. Sir John was a little surprised that his son-in-law moved in such exalted circles, and could have wished for more information, but his wife pointed out that Frederica's new life in London society was bound to be very different from that of the country. But then they received a disturbing letter from Lady Lennox.

'*Perhaps I should have let you know earlier,*' her lady-ship had written, '*but I think you should be aware that while Mr Carr has been away on business for the East India Company, your daughter has been seen in public attended by a cabinet minister of dubious reputation. They drive around town openly in his carriage, and he has escorted her to dinners and receptions at the Mansion House and Devonshire House. I do not wish to alarm you, but people are beginning to talk, and perhaps you should come on a visit to her and settle the matter, as there is very little that*

I can do. Believe me, dear Charlotte, I only wish for her
happiness and yours, but if she were my daughter . . .' The
letter continued in the same vein, and Lady de Boville's first
reaction was indignation.

'She's simply vexed that Frederica has made a much better
match than that booby Charles Lennox,' she told her husband.
'And she cannot bear the fact that any woman should outshine
the Honourable Miss Julia Lennox who can't even find herself
a younger son!'

Nevertheless she wrote a longer than usual letter to young
Mrs Carr, suggesting that she and Georgina might make a
visit to London to see Frederica, and allow Georgina a taste
of the *bon ton* by which her sister was so clearly captivated.

Frederica's reply was a long time coming, and lacked enthusiasm for the visit. She was very busy with social engage-
ments, she wrote, and the heat of summer in London was
oppressive and would weary her mother. There was not a
single mention of her affection for her mother and sister, or
the pleasure she would gain from seeing them. Regarding the
news of the parson's daughter, Frederica said it was a good
thing for the girl to marry Billy Siggery and go and live with
his mother up on the Common, taking her bastard son with
her.

While the de Bovilles tried to decide what should be done,
if anything, preparations for the June wedding went ahead,
and Noah Reeve came to a decision that filled young William,
as people were learning to call him, with great delight.

'I been thinkin' about givin' up work, an' now me rheumatics
is gettin' worse, I reckon Billy can take over the smithy, an'
I'll keep to servin' Oak Hall an' the Horrockses an' wherever
they got 'unters and carriage 'orses,' he announced. 'Billy be
as good a man with 'orses as ever I met, aside from meself.
So good luck to 'im an' Lizzie!'

It was good news for William in every way, for he had long
felt misgivings about attending the finely bred hunters that
were used to carry their owners to hunt foxes, deer and hares.
Siggery had always been sickened by the violent, painful deaths
suffered by the hunted animals after an exhausting chase, and
the matter had been troubling his conscience. Now he would
only have to attend the lumbering shire horses that worked the
land and the privately owned ponies and donkeys. His increased

income would enable him to buy a little cottage for Elizabeth, Andrew and himself; meanwhile they would share the available space in his mother's modest dwelling. Mrs Siggery said she would go to stay with her sister-in-law at Flaxford for the week following her son's wedding, so as to give the newly-wedded pair some time on their own at the start of their married life.

Then William received a note from Sir John de Boville, asking him to attend the baronet in his study. William had a shrewd idea of what Sir John would say, and sure enough, he was greeted cordially and told that he and Elizabeth could have a well-built, reasonably spacious cottage on the edge of the Oak Hall estate; there was, however, a certain condition to be agreed upon.

'No, Sir J–John,' replied William Siggery, politely but emphatically. 'I've promised to b–bring up Andrew as my–my own son.' And as there was nothing else to be said, the interview was brief and ended abruptly, without even mention of the pet fox. Sir John was disappointed but not really surprised. He did not care to stir up unpopularity against himself by pursuing an issue on which he had neither legal nor moral grounds.

No sooner had he imparted this news to his wife than another blow fell on the de Bovilles. Lady Lennox sent them a copy of London's *Morning Herald*, a newspaper known for its artful reportage of society gossip, and this particular issue carried a shocking story. Sir John and his wife spread the page out on his study desk and read together in mounting dismay.

> For some time now there has been speculation in some circles about a certain lady whose beauty and charm has evoked admiration in many quarters. We can now disclose on irrefutable authority that this brilliant jewel in the crown of London's society has taken the step of leaving her matrimonial home and taking up residence at an address in Great Smith Street, conveniently near to the Houses of Parliament where her patron and protector has important duties concerned with our country's good. The *Morning Herald* of course can only report what we know of the facts in this case, and must leave it to our readers

to surmise what must be the turmoil in the hearts of Mr C*rr and Sir G*d**n Dr*yn*s, also the feelings of a certain Mrs V*n*ry who has apparently vacated the position that Mrs C*rr now occupies. We hope to be able to keep our readers informed of any consequences or developments in this intriguing case.

Charlotte de Boville burst into tears. 'It was a mistake to send our daughter to London, Sir John,' she said, sobbing. 'And Richard, too. Bess Lennox is responsible for allowing him to enlist without consulting us, and be sent abroad to his death – and then marrying off Frederica to this Theodore Carr who cares for nothing but the East India Company! Oh my God, I wish we had never sent either of them away!'

Sir John put his arm around her, but could offer no words of comfort, for his shock was as great as hers, and was also mixed with remorse. 'We sent Richard to London to separate him from the parson's daughter,' he said heavily. 'We also told him that she no longer cared for him and never told him that she was with child.'

'But Frederica – there was every reason to hope that a good match might be made with Charles Lennox!' cried his wife with a fresh burst of tears. 'Oh, what a bitter blow, Sir John!'

Her husband did not reply, but kept his arms around her. To him this latest calamity seemed uncomfortably close to divine retribution.

Standing at his study window Herbert Pond thanked his Maker for the beauty of a fine May evening – not the least being the loving couple walking away up the lane with arms entwined. They would probably go up to Foxholes, he guessed, and his Lizzie would traverse the same gorse-covered Common she had walked with young de Boville four years earlier. Did she ever think of him now, her father wondered, the man who had seduced and betrayed her? He reflected that forgiving Richard would be easier now that Elizabeth was marrying a far better man; and Richard might be dead. He had after all been only seventeen when he'd drawn her innocence into deception and secrecy. William's love was open and honest, and an older Elizabeth, matured by experience and motherhood, joyfully responded with both heart and mind.

Even Pond could not guess the intensity of William's devotion, his yearning for that day in June when he would lawfully take the woman he had so long worshipped, to be his wife. As the May days lengthened, the natural world around him had never seemed so beautiful and new. After a day's work at the smithy, he would shed his leather apron, wash his face and arms in well water, and put on a clean shirt and waistcoat to make his eager way to the Ponds' cottage where *she* waited for him, her classes over and Andrew put to bed. They would exchange a chaste kiss, and she would put on her shawl and the straw hat that tied under her chin with a ribbon. The evenings were light and mild, with golden skies as the sun sank low over the horizon; in Foxholes they would stand still to listen to the nightingale's song, a waterfall of liquid notes to thrill the hearts of lovers. Then William would put his arm around Elizabeth's waist and lead her home, to part with her on the doorstep. He did not enter the house because of Mrs Pond's awkward silence, but exchanged a warm handshake with Herbert Pond, a man he already regarded as his father.

In the end Sir John de Boville decided to go to London alone, staying at a coaching inn rather than asking hospitality of Viscount Lennox. Standing at a second-floor window of the house in Great Smith Street, he wondered what his attitude should be towards his daughter. Should he be stern or should he obey his natural inclination and open his arms to her? He looked around the room into which he had been shown by a pert maid; there were floral prints upon the walls and an embroidered screen hid the fireplace. On the mantelpiece stood a small gilt clock and a pair of china dogs. Charlotte would think it pretty but too small for a drawing room. He clasped his hands behind his back and tried not to feel resentful at being kept waiting.

The door opened and Frederica entered. She was dressed in a pale green high-waisted gown with a sprigged muslin overskirt; a gauze scarf covered her shoulders, and a similar one was twisted around her head as was the fashion, allowing tendrils of hair to escape at the front and at the nape of her neck. She had clearly taken trouble but Sir John noticed only the changes that the past few years had made. Gone were her youthful features and there was tension in the set of her mouth; her eyes were wary.

'Frederica,' he said smiling, and held out both hands. 'Frederica, my daughter.'

She moved towards him and awkwardly took hold of his hands. 'Good day, Papa. Thank you for coming to see me. I trust that you and Mamma are well? And Georgina and Teddy?'

The formality of her words had clearly been rehearsed, and she sounded quite composed.

'We are all well, my dear,' replied her father. 'And you? Are you in good health?'

'Certainly, Papa, I thank you.' She let go of his hands. 'Pray be seated. Shall I ring for some refreshment? Tea or lemonade, perhaps?'

'Tea will be refreshing, thank you.' He sat down on a cane-bottomed chair, and she pulled on a bell-rope to summon the maid. While they waited for her to return, Sir John confined himself to small talk; they discussed the merits of coaching inns, the warm weather and his journey. The maid entered with a tray of tea and almond biscuits which she set down on a small table.

'Thank you, Susan. You may leave us. I am not at home if any other visitors call.'

'Very good, ma'am. Except for Sir Gideon, I s'pose?' the girl asked boldly.

'Sir Gideon is not expected. You may go,' said Frederica in a firm tone. The girl bobbed a curtsey, looked curiously at Sir John, and left the room. Frederica poured out two cups and passed one to him.

'Thank you, my dear. Now, then, I have not come all this way to talk of the weather. As your father I need to know your situation, and what you intend . . . er, how you intend to live in the future. Is this your address for the time being?'

'Yes, Papa. This is my home now, permanently.'

'And who is the owner?'

'Sir Gideon Draynes is in the process of purchasing it, Papa.'

'And you are . . . under his protection, then?'

'I am, Papa. I have left Mr Carr,' she replied with what he thought was an effort to be calm.

'But Mr Carr is still your husband?'

'I suppose so, Papa.' She shrugged.

'You *know* so, Frederica. You have chosen to put yourself outside the acceptable bounds of propriety. Society will close its doors to you.'

'I cannot agree, Papa. Sir Gideon escorts me to social events, more than I ever attended with Carr.'

'But not where members of the nobility are present.'

She did not answer, but busied herself with the teapot, and Sir John continued speaking.

'You have no legal standing if this man should withdraw his protection at any time. He has a wife, and I understand that you are not his first mistress. Lady Draynes is the only woman who has any legal claim upon him.'

Frederica's hands shook slightly as she took his cup to refill it. 'I am assured by his own promise, Papa, that he will continue to support me – whatever legality may dictate.' She raised her eyes to his. 'I have chosen my path, Papa, and shall not be dissuaded from it.'

'I am sorry to hear it, Frederica, and your mother will be sorry also.' He found that he could not keep his emotions under control, and spoke earnestly to her. 'Oh, my daughter, I beg you to reconsider. If Theodore Carr would take you back, or . . . or if you would return to Wollaston, I would find a house for you to live in – in seclusion – away from wagging tongues, because –' he paused, his voice shaking – 'your mother and I could not receive you at Oak Hall. You do realize that, Frederica? Only if you come to us as a lawfully married woman, not as another man's kept mistress. My dear girl, reconsider before your life is irretrievably ruined. I will speak with Carr, I will plead with him on your behalf to forgive—'

She interrupted him. 'Mr Carr is nothing to me, Papa, and I would not go back to him, not even if he would have me. I shall stay here under the protection of Sir Gideon. There is nothing more to be said!'

She was flushed but dry-eyed. It was Sir John's tears that could not be held in check. He put out his arms to embrace her, but she stiffened and drew away. He had no choice but to leave the house and the life his elder daughter had chosen. He knew that Charlotte would say that he had not made suffi-cient effort to save their daughter. She might even travel up to London herself. If so, he knew that she would have no better success. Frederica was lost to them.

The midsummer wedding at nine o'clock in the morning had been envisaged as a quiet occasion, attended only by the parents and a few close friends of the couple to be married. A limping, slow-tongued bridegroom taking to wife a woman with a child born out of wedlock was hardly an event to be advertised, and no bells were to be rung nor any music played.

The day arrived. Parson Pond in his white surplice made his way to St Bede's through the back gate he always used, accompanied by his daughter, who wore a simple dove-grey gown and the straw hat that tied with a ribbon. She carried her own black prayer book and no flowers, though her father eyed her fondly and thought how sweet she looked. As they reached the churchyard they were surprised to see a line of parishioners entering at the lychgate.

'I think there may be a few more there than we expected,' the parson told her gently, but when they entered at the west door they stared in astonishment at the backs of the packed congregation. A whisper ran round the assembly: 'She's here!' Two shepherds began to play music; one with his fiddle, the other with his flute, filling the church with an old Suffolk melody.

Taking his daughter's arm, Herbert Pond led her up the stone-paved aisle towards the man who waited for her. William wore a white shirt, brown waistcoat and breeches, and had eyes only for the girl advancing towards him. There were ripples of admiration around the church, and the ladies noted Mrs Pond and Mrs Siggery in a front pew with Andrew between them.

The parson took his place in front of the altar, his prayer book open at the Solemnization of Matrimony. He nodded to young Siggery to come forward and stand beside Elizabeth, and uttered the familiar opening words.

'Dearly beloved brethren, we are gathered here in the sight of God, and in the face of this congregation, to join together this man and this woman in holy matrimony . . .'

When it came to the point in the service when the clergyman asks 'Who giveth this woman to be married to this man?', Herbert Pond changed the words to 'I give this woman to be married to this man', quietly but audibly, and the service proceeded with the exchange of vows and the placing of the ring on Elizabeth's wedding finger. William repeated his words carefully and with only an occasional stammer; Elizabeth's responses were quiet and clear. Finally Parson Pond joined their right hands and made the solemn declaration, 'Those whom God hath joined together, let no man put asunder.'

They were married, and having put their signatures in the parish register, they turned to face the congregation and proceed slowly down the aisle between the rows of pews. At this point a joyous peal of bells rang out, bringing delighted smiles to all faces; more than half of Wollaston had turned out, including Sir John de Boville, who sat alone, his eyes lingering on the grandson he shared with Pond. His heart was heavy, comparing Elizabeth's radiance with the very different situation of his daughter Frederica.

The Miss Buxtons were wondering how they could possibly provide refreshments for such a large congregation, but they need not have worried; once outside the church there were baskets of home-baked bread, freshly churned butter and plates of cold mutton and Suffolk cheeses donated by the parishioners; yarrow beer was poured from earthenware jugs, and Sir John de Boville had anonymously donated a barrel of best ale. He shook hands with the new Mr and Mrs Siggery and bestowed a kiss on Andrew; then he untied the horse he had tethered outside the lychgate, and rode slowly back to the dark cloud that hung over Oak Hall.

Elizabeth greeted her friends with shining eyes. Many remarked on the pride in her husband's countenance as he gazed upon her.

'This is the h–happiest day of m–my life, dear wife,' he murmured close to her ear.

'And mine too, dearest husband,' she whispered back with an expression on her face that caused many a man to envy Siggery.

Joshua Venn, talking with Adam and the girl he was to marry later in the year, suddenly caught sight of a pair of ragged men hungrily tucking into the food. The taller one had lost a leg below the knee and walked with a makeshift crutch. They were stick-thin with straggly beards and grimy, leathery skin. Others had seen them, and drew away from their unwashed bodies and travel-stained clothes.

'What are those two vagabonds up to?' demanded Adam loudly. 'The brass neck o' them, helping themselves to food at a wedding party! Let me deal with them, Father – show them the way out of Wollaston. Come on, Josh!'

'But Adam, they may be soldiers returned from the war,' protested Joshua.

'Army deserters, more likely – scum!' At a nod from the squire, Adam strode off angrily towards the men. Parson Pond, always alert to trouble, put down his plate and went to see what was afoot.

But Joshua Venn reached them first, and the onlookers heard the urgency in his words.

'Leave 'em, Adam – *wait*! Let me see 'em . . . I think one of 'em might be my brother Sam, him who ran off to be a soldier!' He approached the shorter man and spoke anxiously to him.

'Is it – is it Sam Venn? My brother Sam who went for a soldier these three years back?'

A defensive look passed over the man's gaunt features. 'Aye, Joshua, I be yer brother Sam,' he said hoarsely. 'Me an' Chopper, we 'listed together, an' that's 'ow we stayed. 'Tis all over with the British in America, so we left 'em to it an' stowed away 'ome. Nearly starved to death we did, down in the 'old.'

Joshua's voice shook as he took his brother's hand. 'It's good to see yer, Sam.'

'Aye, but where be the others, Josh? Ma an' Pa an' Meg?'

Joshua's eyes filled as he told his brother that they were orphans.

'Pa went up to London after Ma died, an' Meg went with 'im, but 'e died there an' she stayed.'

Sam shook his head in resignation, and the bystanders crowded round to peer at him and his companion, both younger than they had at first appeared. Memories of them were not of the kindest.

'Sam Venn an' Chopper! Who'd 'ave thought it?'

'Never expected to set eyes on them two again – pair o' troublemakers – an' now back to take our bread as if they 'ad a right to it!'

'Remember 'ow they used to torment poor Billy Siggery? Cruel pair o' rogues they was!'

'Ah, but 'e's got the laugh on' em now, ain't 'e? Come on, lads, let's haul 'em up in front of 'im.'

And in spite of remonstrances from Parson Pond – who perhaps did not try quite as hard as he might have done to prevent it – a grinning ring of ploughboys and stable lads surrounded the pair and hustled them across the churchyard to where the wedded couple stood at the porch.

'Oh, William, look, 'tis those devils who used to persecute you when we were children!' cried Elizabeth indignantly. 'What are *they* doing back here?'

'Gawd's teeth, Sam, d'yer see who she is? That wild cat of a parson's daughter!' muttered Chopper, and Sam looked up to behold the formidable frame of William Siggery, tall and broad-shouldered.

'It's 'im right enough,' groaned Sam. 'We're done for, Gawd 'elp us.'

'Told yer we shouldn't't've come back 'ere.'

'Go on, Billy, give 'em a taste o' their own medicine!' roared the assembled crowd. 'Let's shove 'em in the stocks an' throw rotten eggs at 'em!'

This was greeted with a cheer, and Elizabeth looked at her husband to see if he consented.

But William was not inclined to take revenge. He remembered the boys who had taunted him, but his clearest memory was of the kicking, clawing girl in calico who had come to his defence. He turned to whisper in his wife's ear, and then spoke slowly.

'This is the h–happiest day o' m–my life, so I d–don't feel anger against any m–man, an' yer must've suffered a lot. So let's sh–shake hands, an' you may bow to m–my wife – and then go an' eat yer fill, for yer l–look nigh famished.'

The incredulity on their faces was almost comical; they muttered their thanks, bowed to the bride and shuffled off.

The wedding celebrations continued on a happy note, with much commendation of William's Christian forgiveness of his former adversaries. Parson Pond made no comment; he perceived that William Siggery had taken a far more subtle and appropriate vengeance.

There were some who stayed at the improvised feast until past noon, but the newlyweds had other duties to be done before the day was over. Noah Reeve had lent his horse-drawn cart for young Mrs Siggery to remove her possessions from the parson's house to the Siggery cottage on the Common. She sat smiling beside her husband as he drove to her new home.

Mrs Pond had made it clear that it would be difficult for her as a busy parson's wife to look after Andrew for a week.

Jenny winked at Elizabeth and promised Mrs Pond that she would help with the boy.

'It'll be an 'oliday for 'im, Miss,' she had whispered to Elizabeth, ''an' there's always his gaffer to make a fuss o' him!'

At last the husband and wife were alone together at the close of their wedding day, and by mutual consent they went for their evening walk to Foxholes where they had often stood to hear the nightingale's song. There was a glorious sunset and when the owls began their haunting call, William put his arm around his wife's waist and led her home: not to her father's doorstep, but to the empty cottage waiting for him to enter with his bride.

When at last they lay in each other's arms, Elizabeth's only wish was to please her husband, and she delighted in his body, exclaiming aloud at his eager response, his tender worship of her own welcoming flesh. For William Siggery, all the sadness of his lonely years was swept away in this joyous celebration of hearts and minds, two bodies becoming one.

Eleven

A Well-Chaperoned Proposal

1781

Mrs Sophia Seward was trying her best to rejoice in the happy situation of two of her servants who were planning a September wedding. Peter Coleman had been patient and persistent in his courtship of Meg Venn, and at last he had been rewarded: she had smiled, placed her hand in his, and they were now betrothed. Mrs Seward immediately said that they must be married from her home in John Street, with a hired carriage and a wedding breakfast in the servants' hall. Coleman's parents and his brother and sister-in-law would be invited to attend, and Mrs Seward would stand as Meg's patroness. Everything must be done to make it a happy occasion, and Sophia would smile and conceal her personal sadness at losing a maidservant who had become a real friend, one who could understand and sympathize with her daily sorrow at Oliver Seward's prolonged absence and the lack of news from across the Atlantic. Hopes of his survival and that of his friend Toby were fading, neither was there any news of Richard de Boville, whose enlistment had cost Mrs Seward the condescension of her Lennox relatives. They blamed her for allowing Richard to be influenced into joining the war as an army officer, just as the de Bovilles blamed them, and seemed to overlook the fact that her own son was also missing, for the young men would not be dissuaded from their course.

And now she was to lose Meg and Coleman who had obtained a place as under-butler and assistant housekeeper in a grand country house in Northamptonshire. They would have separate quarters of their own, and had good prospects of becoming head butler and housekeeper in due course. Mrs Seward tried to put on a happy face, but her heart was heavy; she told herself not to indulge in self-pity, but to put the happiness of others before her own inclinations.

It was while she sat at her embroidery in the little sitting room she preferred to the larger drawing room that the doorbell rang. Looking out of the window she saw her nephew Charles Lennox being let in by Biddy. Thankful for a diversion she put aside her work and stood up to greet her visitor with a genuine cry of welcome.

'*Charles*! I had half given up hearing from you again. When did you get home? My dear boy, sit down and tell me all about your travels – oh, this is such a happy surprise!'

'Hello, Aunt Sophie.' He kissed her affectionately and let her fuss over him, summoning refreshments, plumping up the cushions on the two-seater couch, and exclaiming at his improved looks.

'You look older, Charles – and I mean that as a compliment. You've filled out a little, and you have a different air about you from—'

'From the awkward, clumsy youth you remember, Aunt Sophie, after that wretched business with Frederica!' He smiled. 'The best advice I ever received was that which you gave me – to get out of London and travel. To see other parts of the country, and broaden my mind! And that's exactly what I've done. It was so good to get right away from the parties and the dinners, the social visits – and visiting cards! – oh, it was all so superficial, so trivial, so far away from what I wanted.' He checked himself. 'Forgive me, Aunt Sophie, I haven't asked you how you do. I take it there hasn't been any news of—?'

'No, Charles, there is no news of Oliver or Toby. Oh, this wicked, foolish, wasteful war! However did our King and Parliament get involved in such folly? Why could they not see that the American colonies were going to break their ties with Britain sooner or later? It all seems so futile now!'

Charles kept hold of her hand and looked grave. 'Yes, I agree with every word you say, Aunt Sophie, and we are not the only ones. Opinions are changing, and men in high places are coming round to the same viewpoint now that the war's dragging on with no decisive victory for the British, quite the reverse in fact. George Washington is no longer considered an upstart, but a very determined and capable general who does not intend to be beaten, or to agree to an armistice. He wants victory, and one cannot help but respect him – and now that the Spanish and Dutch have joined France on the side of the colonies, it means that the British navy is outnumbered. We've lost our supremacy at sea.'

He checked himself when he saw her face, and tried to be more encouraging. 'But we must not give up hope, Aunt Sophie – when the hostilities have ended, one way or another, there'll be a return of the fighting men.'

'Those who have survived,' she said in a low voice. 'There has been no news of our dear young men who went out there with such hope, little knowing what a defeat awaited them. Oh, for just a word, to know whether my son is alive or dead!'

'*All* news from America takes six weeks or so to cross the Atlantic, Aunt. Think how long it took us to hear of the defeat at Saratoga.'

'But why can't our rulers admit defeat and bring our dear boys back home *now*?' she asked, but then reproached herself. 'Forgive me, Charles, I have not asked you anything about your travels. Has it all been worthwhile?'

'Oh, yes, Aunt Sophie. When I rode off northwards on a hired horse I had no idea how much it would change my outlook. As you know, I went first to Wollaston to look for . . . for Meg Venn's brother and her friend the parson's daughter.'

'Oh, yes, Charles, she was overjoyed when you wrote to me and said that you found her elder brother Joshua was working for the local squire.'

'Yes, the younger brother is still away with the army.'

'Did you see anything of the de Bovilles?'

'Oh, no, I kept well away from Oak Hall! I called on that parson, Mr Pond, a most upright and good-hearted man, and we had a most profitable talk in his study.'

'And the daughter is still living at home, you said? Not married to the squire's son? Meg told me that there was an understanding between them.'

Charles hesitated. 'No, Miss Pond remains at home, and I spoke only very briefly to her. She seems a sweet, sensible girl, and teaches reading and writing to cottagers' daughters – also the piano. But – there was something I didn't tell you, Aunt Sophie, in my letter, because it did not seem to be right to do so. Miss Pond is indeed a beautiful girl, just the sort of friend I would expect Meg Venn to have, but she has been ill-used. She has a child, a son, by some well-born man who then deserted her.'

'Oh, my goodness!' exclaimed Mrs Seward. 'A bastard child to a clergyman's daughter? And you say she still lives at home? She hasn't been sent away?'

'No, she is fortunate in her father. I have the greatest respect for him, Aunt Sophie, and his staunch support of her in her trouble. She is a good mother to the boy, a fine, healthy little fellow, and she spoke most affectionately of Meg.'

Mrs Seward shrugged. ''Tis a highly unusual situation, Charles, and one on which I do not care to comment. Come, tell me what happened after you left Wollaston and continued on your journey. Where did you go next?'

'I turned north-west to the midlands, and went through Birmingham, then northwards again to Manchester, and east to Leeds. I saw a great variety of countryside, and prosperous farms increasing in size—'

'Yes, by enclosing the common land and robbing Meg's family of their livelihood,' interrupted his aunt. 'I've learned a lot from that girl, and the greed and heartlessness of the de Bovilles.'

'Yes, I know there are different viewpoints, Aunt Sophie, but I saw great improvements on the farms, new methods of agriculture and breeding of livestock. And it's going to be needed, for the population in the north is increasing rapidly. I wonder just how much our rulers at Westminster know of the new industry – new machines that can spin yarn, wool or cotton, at ten times the rate of a spinning wheel – there was a machine that weaves the yarn up just as quickly. I spoke to the owner of one of these manufactories, as they're called, and he told me how they use the power of water to work the machines, but there is talk of using the power of steam soon – and that will need more coal and more coal mines! This man said to me, "Factories and finance – that's the future!"'

'Oh, how interesting, Charles – and do you think the new ideas will replace hand work?'

'My dear aunt, they're already doing so. I got the impression that great changes are on the way, whether for good or ill I cannot say, but I know this much – change is inevitable.

People in London and the southern counties have absolutely no idea of what is happening in the north.'

'So, dear nephew, you have entirely recovered from the unfortunate business with the de Boville girl?' She smiled knowingly. 'May I ask if there were any romantic encounters in the course of your travels? Or are you still heart-whole?'

He looked very thoughtful, and answered seriously. 'There were no encounters of that nature, Aunt Sophie, but I cannot call myself heart-whole. There was . . . *is* one face I could not forget, one which still remains with me.'

'Oh, don't say you fell in love with that parson's daughter, the one with the child!'

'No, Aunt, I don't mean her, though I admired her greatly. I hope that some man will be sensible enough to see her worth and marry her one day. But on the subject of marriage, I'm astonished by what I've heard about Frederica de Boville – I mean Mrs Carr. My mother refuses even to discuss it and my father says that I was right after all to reject her! Tell me, what exactly happened?'

'Oh, it's been the most fearful scandal, and yes, maybe Lord Lennox is right, though perhaps things would have turned out differently if you'd married her – but nobody can know that.'

'Tell me, Aunt Sophie, for we were practically betrothed. Was the marriage to Carr not happy?'

'She was not contented with the marriage, Charles, and two unfortunate . . . er . . . miscarriages must have had an effect on her attitude. Mr Carr, a commissioner with the East India Company, was probably too wrapped up in his work, though the company has been in trouble as we now know. I suppose he just did not have the time to spend with a young wife. He must be about fifteen years older. She began to be seen in public with other gentlemen, and of course there was talk and a daily newspaper hinted at a liaison. Then she left her husband's home to stay in Great Smith Street, under the protection of Sir Gideon Draynes, a cabinet minister—'

'*Draynes*! Oh, surely not!' cried Charles, remembering the night at Madame Duvall's.

'Yes, Charles, Draynes. He's even older than Mr Carr, and a known profligate. Frederica became the target of all kinds of gossip, and my cousin – your mother – said she could no longer meet with her.'

'Oh, Aunt Sophie!' Charles was genuinely shocked.

'I believe her father came down from Wollaston to remonstrate with her, but all to no avail. She found society's doors closed to her, and her name taken off all the visiting lists. For the first time Sir Gideon found himself cold-shouldered, not only in society but among his fellow Members of Parliament – some would not allow their wives to sit at the same dinner table.'

'And what about Carr?'

'Well, the East India Company became a subject of speculation, as it seemed there had been corruption on a large scale. The company was deposing local Indian rulers and nominating new ones who would do their bidding. Anyway, Mr Carr's position as a commissioner seemed uncertain, and he sold his house and moved in with his elderly mother. They're sometimes seen driving out together.'

'Good heavens, what a story,' murmured Charles. 'I suppose she is to be pitied now.'

'Yes, poor Frederica has learned a bitter lesson,' Mrs Seward said, shaking her head. 'And the story isn't over, Charles. It seems that there was a great scene of accusation and recrimination between Sir Gideon and Lady Draynes when he discovered he could not depend on the support of friends to keep him socially acceptable. He has forsaken his old ways and taken up a new life of virtue, going with his wife to church every Sunday and denouncing all forms of self-indulgence. Ugh, the horrid old man! I don't know which is worse, the way he was before his change of heart or after.'

'And Frederica?' prompted Charles. 'What can she do now?'

'Her only hope is to disappear from London and settle herself quietly in the country somewhere, perhaps with a lady companion. I can't see her parents taking her in again, like that parson you spoke of. Poor Frederica.'

'I hope that I have not contributed in any way to her misfortunes,' said Charles.

'No, she chose her way of life. She must now live with the consequences. But tell me – you mentioned a face you could not forget. Am I allowed to hear that lady's name?'

He looked slightly taken aback, but answered promptly. 'Ah, Aunt Sophie, after all we have said about poor Frederica's disgrace, how different is the girl whose face I have kept in

my heart all the time I've been away. I'm sure you know who
I'm speaking of – and I would like to see her now, if you will
permit me.'

Mrs Seward drew a deep breath as she understood his
meaning. 'Oh, Charles, if you are still thinking of Meg Venn,
I have to tell you that she is to be married in September.'

'What? Who in God's name has claimed her?'

'My manservant Coleman, an honest and reliable man who
will make her a good husband. It is better this way, Charles,
for you must not think of marrying a maidservant. She will be
happy with Coleman, though heaven knows I will miss her.'

'Nevertheless, Aunt Sophie, I wish you would call her now
and let me wish her well.'

'Oh, Charles, you are not wise – but I can see that you
won't be satisfied until you set eyes on her again: I will call
her but I must ask you not to upset her. As before, I shall stay
to see and hear everything that passes between you. I won't
have that girl unsettled.'

She rang the bell, and Biddy appeared. 'Will you send Meg
here to me, Biddy? At once, please.'

Meg Venn was sitting by the open kitchen door darning socks;
nearby Peter Coleman whistled cheerfully as he cleaned and
polished shoes. She had noted the arrival of the Honourable
Charles Lennox and had felt her heart flutter. Quarter of an
hour passed, then half an hour and finally an hour since he
had arrived to visit his aunt. She knew Mrs Seward's opinion
about Charles's unsuitable attachment to herself, and besides,
she was now promised to Peter, a good man who would look
after her and treat her with respect. So it was most unlikely,
she thought, *most* unlikely that she would be sent for.

She heard the bell ring, and Biddy got up to answer it, and
came back with a curious look.

'Missus says ye're to go straight away to her sittin' room,
Meg. She's got that nephew of hers there with her.'

Meg rose, put down her needle and thimble, smoothed her
hair and checked that her apron was clean. Peter Coleman
looked up.

'Wonder what she wants with yer, Meg? Don't have any
talk with the Honourable Lennox, he's nothin' to do wi' you.
If he speaks to yer, just don't answer.'

Meg left the kitchen without answering, for this was a promise she could not make.

As soon as she entered her aunt's sitting room, her eyes met Charles's. He looked older and more confident but he was still the earnest young man who had rescued her from the brothel.

She has changed, and yet she has not changed, Charles thought at once. Bright-eyed and rosy-cheeked, her slim figure emphasized by a dark gown, white apron and a white frilled cap on her dark curls, she was still the same country girl he had taken from Madame Duvall's establishment.

She glanced at Mrs Seward, and curtseyed low to them both. Charles eagerly kept to his feet and held out his hand to her.

'Miss Venn!' he said with a courteous smile. 'Miss Venn! How have you been keeping all these months? I trust that I find you well?'

'Very well, thank you, sir,' she replied, looking again at Mrs Seward who sat still and unsmiling. Charles looked surprised as he seemed to notice Meg's softened tone, her sweet, clear voice that retained its lilting Suffolk accent. 'Have you enjoyed your travels, sir?'

He realized that he was staring, unable to take his eyes off her. 'Er – yes, indeed, Miss Venn, I have seen much of life, both in town and country, and I hope I have learned from it. Though I was never so happy as I am now, to be back in the place where I . . . where I met you.'

There was an awkward pause before Mrs Seward announced firmly, 'Miss Venn is to be married to Mr Peter Coleman in September, is not that so, Meg?'

'Yes, ma'am.' She looked at Charles in confusion. 'I . . . we are going to work in a country house in Northamptonshire.'

Charles faced Meg squarely. 'And tell me, Meg, are you looking forward to this change in your circumstances?' he said grimly. 'Are you happy to become Mrs Coleman?'

She hesitated, blushing painfully. 'Why, yes, I . . . but I shall miss the kindness shown to me by Mrs Seward, sir. I–I have been happy here, ever since you brought me here with you.'

She clasped her hands to hide their shaking, but she could not hide the tremor in her voice. Charles Lennox clenched his fists and thrust them into his pockets trying to stop himself from going over to her and taking her in his arms.

The tension in the room seemed almost palpable. Sophie Seward could not fail to be aware of it. She made an attempt to ease the situation by smiling in a good-natured way and keeping the conversation matter-of-fact.

'And I shall miss you, Meg, for you have been a good maid-servant – in fact more than a maidservant to me. It will not be easy to replace you – or Peter. But you do realize, don't you, my dear, that it is all for the best.'

'May I ask *what* is all for the best, Aunt Sophie?' Charles broke in, hardly able to restrain himself. The sight of Meg's downcast eyes and the white knuckles of her tightly clasped hands was almost more than he could bear, he had no taste for empty politeness.

'Why, the excellent prospects now opening to Meg,' replied Mrs Seward smoothly. 'A suitable marriage, a good position in a beautiful house, and in the course of time—' She broke off and spread out her hands.

'Yes, Aunt? In the course of time, what then?' demanded Charles. 'Children? Coleman's children? How many d'you think he might give her?'

'Charles, you forget yourself!' his aunt reproved him and aimed a warning glance at Meg. 'Such talk is most improper!'

'No, Aunt Sophie, let us speak the truth, improper or other-wise,' replied Charles, now determined to be heard. 'Enough time and effort was expended on trying to get me to propose to Frederica de Boville, now proven to be an adulteress, disgraced and deserted, an object of pity. Yet to prepare me for marriage to her, my father sent me to a brothel—'

'Charles, be *quiet!*' cried his aunt.

'No, I must speak – I must know Meg's heart before I go away and leave her to this manservant, if he is the one she chooses. She took possession of *my* heart on the night I first saw her at Madame Duvall's – and I have thought of her day and night ever since. After seeing many different ways of living, the prosperity and the poverty, the real and the false, what do you think I care for titles and the empty trappings of society? This dear, sweet girl is worth a hundred so-called genteel young women with their arts and accomplishments.' His voice rose almost to a shout. 'I am telling you, Aunt

Sophie, I care for nothing more in life – *nothing*! – than to humbly offer Meg my heart and my name and to cherish her for the rest of my life!'

He paused at last for breath, and Mrs Seward was visibly moved by his outpouring; she spent a moment or two composing herself, and eventually replied quietly.

'My dear Charles, if you feel so strongly, surely it is not I you should be addressing. I suggest that you repeat what you have just declared, only this time address yourself to the woman you love. Give her an opportunity to reply to your proposal with a yes or a no.'

Charles turned to look at Meg who slowly raised her head and their eyes met. Hers were brimming with tears, but her lips curved in a happy smile.

'Yes, Charles – oh, yes, dear Charles, let us be together!'

Mrs Seward unobtrusively left the room as the lovers drew together. She wiped away a tear of her own, and went in search of Peter Coleman.

Life in the Siggery cottage that summer was filled with busy but very happy days. Andrew played out on the Common every day with Ladyfox, who was growing into a fine young vixen.

''Tis as well that none o' the cottagers around here keep chickens,' Mary Siggery remarked, looking fondly on the boy and his lively companion. 'I never did see a fox so tame an' close to a body as she is to that boy!'

One Sunday afternoon every month Andrew was fetched by Sir John to take tea at Oak Hall. Elizabeth was always unsettled by his absence, though William tried to reassure her that Sir John was a good man at heart and would not attempt to keep the boy against his will for longer than the time agreed upon. Andrew was always as pleased to see his mother on his return as she was to see him. He would prattle happily about the big house, and how Aunt Georgie and Uncle Teddy had taken him for a walk and showed him the sheep and the cows in their fields. On one occasion another gentleman came with them, Mr Felix Wilborough, who had walked and talked with Aunt Georgie and made her laugh a lot.

'Ah, that'll be the one what's courtin' her,' said Grandma Siggery with a knowing nod. 'He seems a decent sort o' man, and Oak Hall needs a bit o' cheerin' up.'

Mrs Pond was a disproving visitor to the cottage occasionally, sometimes accompanying the parson, who visited almost daily.

''Tis most unhealthy, Herbert, the four of 'em all squashed up in that miserable hovel meant for just one ol' woman,' she said. 'Him an' Lizzie sleep with Andrew in what used to be the ol' woman's room an' she has a bed in the livin' room. It's not right.'

'I agree that there's not much spare elbow-room, Connie,' her husband answered, 'but the boy's out of doors more often than he's in, and William's at the smithy all day, so Lizzie's got room to teach her pupils. And Mary Siggery goes up to the hall on washdays.'

'That's all very well in the summertime, when they can all get out o' the place an' get some fresh air,' grumbled his wife. 'What about when winter comes with freezing cold winds an' ice an' snow – pitch-dark mornin's and evenin's – heaven knows it's bad enough in our own house, never mind a draughty place like that! What'll happen to the boy *then*?'

'Let's not meet trouble before it reaches us, Connie,' replied the parson. 'Noah Reeve will leave William the smithy in due course. Then they'll be able to live in his cottage behind it. *That*'ll be warm enough, even in winter!'

'Aye, but how long's it goin' to be before Reeve goes, Herbert?'

'I was not speaking of death, Connie, but the possibility of Noah going to live with his niece at Laxfield,' he answered. 'Let us rejoice that our grandson has a loving home with good parents. I notice he's always glad to come home from Oak Hall despite all its rooms!'

In spite of his reassuring words Parson Pond privately agreed that the cottage was too small for a family of four: Mary Siggery had told him in confidence that she would be willing to live with her sister-in-law at Flaxford, but she would lose the money she earned as washerwoman at Oak Hall.

'There be only the House of Industry at Flaxford,' the widow said with a shudder. 'That an' a few small farms. There's only the ol' ladyship left at Flaxford Manor, so there's no work to be had there.' She sighed. 'My Billy won't let me go an' live in poverty, an' I won't let him keep me, not with a wife an' child to feed, so I has to work, y'see.'

Herbert Pond nodded. The cottage was her home anyway, and she should not have to leave it unless she could be sure of security. He could only hope and pray that the Lord would make some provision for his loved ones. In the meanwhile he enjoyed the carefree summer days; he had never seen his daughter looking more beautiful than now. William looked so happy; some days he hardly stammered at all.

And then September brought news of the death of the old dowager at Flaxford Manor. There was much speculation as to what would happen to the handsome seventeenth-century house, and it was rumoured that it would be sold to pay the debts incurred by the improvident son of the old lady, due to his persistent gambling. Then it was revealed that new owners were expected to move in to the manor – and that all kinds of indoor and outdoor staff would be needed.

It also meant that Mary Siggery could go to live with her sister-in-law as suitable work was available. The Siggery cottage would have sufficient space for the father, mother, child and whatever other children might be born to them in the future. To Herbert Pond this was an answer to his prayer, for which he gave grateful thanks, kneeling beside his bed.

Twelve
The Return

1781

A fter the harvest thanksgiving service at St Bede's on the second Sunday in September, a traditional harvest supper was held on the following Friday at Horrocks's farm. Half an ox had been roasted and the meat freshly carved to serve with potatoes roasted in the dripping pan. There was a general conviviality as the ale flowed freely. The climax of the feast was the entry of Adam Horrocks and his bride, riding aloft on a loaded haycart. Miss Lydia Buxton was a niece of the Miss Buxtons, and she and Adam had been married at her parish church of St Mary's at Bungay two days' previously; now it was time for Adam to present her to his neighbours. The couple were cheered and complimented as they climbed down; Adam was popular and it was taken for granted that in due time he would take over the farm and become the squire.

Even Mrs Pond remarked on the excellent fare, tucking into a thick slice of roast beef.

'There's the de Bovilles over there,' she said, nodding to where Sir John stood talking to the squire. 'Him an' the daughter an' that attorney from Beccles. It's them who should be giving the harvest supper, like they've done every other year.'

'They've had a lot of trouble to contend with, Connie,' said her husband, 'and I think the squire was only too pleased to take over the supper, especially with young Adam getting married and wanting to show off his bride. She looks an agreeable girl, doesn't she?'

'She'll have to be better 'n that elder daughter o' the de

Bovilles,' Mrs Pond observed with a certain relish, for Frederica's disgrace was no secret in Wollaston.

Herbert did not reply, but pulled his grandson up to sit on his knee.

'No more for you, young glutton, or you'll go *pop!*' he said, to Elizabeth's amusement. It was a warm, fine evening, and most people seemed to be enjoying themselves.

Sir John de Boville was apologizing for the absence of his wife who he said was indisposed.

'She sends her good wishes, but I've brought Miss Georgina and Mr Wilborough. I . . . er . . . hope to see them follow young Adam's example soon.'

Horrocks nodded, but noticed the baronet's melancholy air, and guessed that he must be thinking of his loss of both Richard and Frederica.

'How's young Sam Venn doing as a stable-hand?' asked Sir John.

'Sam works very well with his brother,' answered Horrocks. 'Chopper didn't last long, though – took himself off after a couple of days, saying he could do better begging in the streets of Ipswich as a wounded war hero.'

Both men grimaced. Horrocks hardly knew what to say to his friend. Nobody expected to see Richard again and there had been no news of Frederica since her father's visit to London. Lady Lennox had no knowledge of her whereabouts, only that she was no longer at Great Smith Street.

'Is there any further news of the purchase of Flaxford Manor?' asked Horrocks, to change the subject.

'Only that the new owner's from London, and aspires to be a gentleman farmer, so I've heard.'

'Is he a family man?'

'I believe he's recently married,' replied Sir John wearily. 'No doubt we shall discover all we need to know when our wives go to call on them. I could wish that Charlotte had something to take her mind off . . . for my part, I'm more than ready to get out hunting again. Thank heaven for the start of the new season.'

A housekeeper moved into Flaxford Manor with two menservants and a cook. It was understood that though the new owners would bring their personal servants with them, other female staff were being recruited from the nearby House of Industry to be trained as housemaids. Mary Siggery presented herself to serve as a general domestic servant, experienced in the care of household linen, its laundering, starching and ironing. She was immediately accepted.

News took at least a month to cross the Atlantic, especially in winter storms at sea, and when it reached London it still took time for regional newspapers to receive and publish it. Sometimes the effects of happenings abroad preceded the official announcement of them at home, and so it was with the events on the seventeenth of October. Lord Cornwallis, after a protracted siege during which his men were literally starving, was forced to surrender ignominiously to General Washington at Yorktown. The news reached London on Sunday the twenty-fifth of November, and it was generally agreed that the war was lost. By the time the details of this crushing defeat filtered through to the provinces, some of the surviving, exhausted troops who had sailed on the ship bringing the news had already found their way back to the homes from whence they had set out so enthusiastically. One of these, a gaunt, bearded man, staggered into Wollaston on the evening of the first Sunday in December.

The maidservant who answered the knock at the door of Oak Hall screamed at the sight of the stranger, and ran back down the passage to the office where Sir John conferred with his bailiff and male staff members. A manservant came hurrying to see what had frightened the girl, and was about to tell the vagabond to be on his way when something in the man's face silenced him, and he shrank back as if he saw a ghost.

'Good God, this is a fine welcome,' said the stranger, hobbling into the entrance hall. 'Are my father and mother at home? Can somebody fetch them to me?'

Sir John de Boville wept at the sight of his son, and Lady de Boville fainted. It was left to his sister Georgina, helped by two menservants, to carry Richard upstairs, undress and wash him. His body was filthy and verminous, and he had a half-healed gash on the side of his head and blisters on both feet; they cut his hair and beard and re-bandaged his raw flesh.

Then they put him to bed and he lay between clean sheets for the first time in years.

On the following morning Parson Pond was called to the bedside of a woman dying of a foul canker that had consumed her left breast. He gave her absolution and Holy Communion in the presence of her family. On his way out he met Mr Palfrey who was also visiting her to apply a witch-hazel dressing. The two men frequently met in the course of their duties. Palfrey asked Pond in a low tone if he had heard the news at Oak Hall.

'Young Richard de Boville is home from the war,' said the apothecary. 'I've just been up there to look at his wounds, and I never saw such a change in a man. He's but twenty-one years old and looks like one returned from the dead.'

Herbert Pond took the news with outward calm, but inwardly his thoughts whirled alarmingly. Should he call at the hall to see if there was any spiritual counsel he could give? Palfrey urged him to do so, adding that Lady de Boville was deeply disturbed and would not leave her son's bedside. Pond decided to go and offer his services; he was after all Christ's representative, whether they accepted him as such or not. He pressed his hat more firmly on his head, braced his shoulders and set off.

'Oh, my God, Pond, you find us both rejoicing and sorrowing!' cried Sir John with visible emotion on Pond's arrival. 'Our beloved son we thought we'd lost has come back to us, but more dead than alive. Palfrey has been here and ordered rest and silence and bread soaked in warm milk with sugar – and I'm just going to get him a small glass of Madeira. Oh, my God!'

'I rejoice with you, Sir John,' said Pond gravely, 'and your son will no doubt recover his health with careful nursing. How is Lady de Boville?'

'She's with him now, hardly leaves his side, talks to him all the time, though Palfrey has counselled silence. Oh, Pond, my old friend, come with me and give him a blessing!'

Herbert Pond was a good fifteen years younger than the baronet who had never before addressed him as friend, but he followed the distraught father up the staircase and along a corridor to a room where there was a bed with its curtains drawn back, a fire burning in the grate and a familiar sweetish smell in the air that Pond recognized as the odour of sickness. A wasted figure lay on the bed, awake and clutching at the sheet: his red-rimmed eyes stared straight at Pond, and he gave a low groan. Lady de Boville sat on the other side of the bed, her hand upon her son's shoulder.

'Parson . . . Parson Pond,' whispered Richard. 'Father to Elizabeth, she that I loved so dearly.'

'Be at peace, Richard,' said Pond, laying a hand on the one clutching the sheet. 'You're home again now with your loved ones.'

'I loved her, Parson, though she played me false and married another,' said Richard hoarsely.

'Hush, dearest Richard,' said his mother, bending over him to kiss his forehead. 'We shall not speak of such things just now.'

Herbert was silent. He hated to hear such a false accusation made against his daughter, but he saw that young de Boville was extremely ill, and rambling in his speech, so it was not a time for an argument that would bewilder the invalid and incur the anger of his parents. There would be time enough for that later, if Richard survived.

He stepped forward and laid a hand on Richard's forehead. 'In the name of the Father, and of the Son, and of the Holy Ghost, Amen. Be at peace, Richard.'

The invalid closed his sunken eyes, but his thin features softened at hearing the words.

'Heaven bless you, Pond, you are the first to cause him to smile!' cried Sir John, then immediately lowered his voice to a whisper and apologized.

'I will leave you now,' said the parson, replacing his hat.

'But call again, Pond, call at any time!' urged Sir John. 'You have given us new heart, new courage – come again if you please, you are most welcome.'

Her ladyship said nothing, but gave all her attention to the son back from the dead.

Until the de Bovilles broke the news – and with servants whispering behind doors, this could not long be delayed – Pond did not feel free to tell anybody of Richard's return, including Mrs Pond. He did not care to have such a secret from his daughter and son-in-law – and heaven only knew how he would tell them when it became necessary – so for the time being he busied himself with parish duties and did not call at the Siggery cottage. But of course the news got out. House servants and stable staff spread it to the Horrockses, and Mr Palfrey's daily visits to Oak Hall were noted. Pond called again on the Wednesday, and found the atmosphere calmer.

'He's better, Pond, he's better, thank God,' said Sir John. 'He's taking some food and talking sensibly. Come with me – let me take you to see him.'

It was true. Richard was sitting propped up on pillows. His face was still deathly pale, but his eyes met Pond's with pleased recognition.

'Dear Parson Pond, your blessing restored me to my right mind,' he said weakly, holding out his hand. 'How are you after all this time? And Mrs Pond?'

'We are well, Richard, I thank you.'

'And your daughter Elizabeth – is she well also?'

'Yes, Richard, she is.' Pond caught Sir John's anxious look as he answered.

'She married Adam Horrocks, didn't she? That was a bitter blow to me, for I loved her dearly, and still do, and always shall, but I wish her no ill because her love failed. Is it well with her?' he asked again. Lady de Boville, standing on the other side of the bed, gave Pond a significant signal, putting a forefinger over her lips and shaking her head. It was a clear order not to tell Richard how matters really stood.

'She is well, I thank you, Richard,' Pond replied quietly.

'You must know that I've been through much hardship, Mr Pond, and I've come through it by the grace of God – but not all of us did. Poor Oliver died of a fever and Toby of his wounds, but I have been spared, Mr Pond, and I see life differently now. I have spoken bitterly of Elizabeth, it is true, but I can forgive her now. I have been spared, and so I can forgive any man – or woman – who has injured me in the past. I want to do good with my life from now on.'

'That is very commendable of you, Richard, and I have

no doubt that the Lord will direct you in the way that you must go,' said Pond steadily. Privately he thought that Richard would first have to know the truth, for it could not be kept from him for much longer. He gave a blessing and moved away from the bed, beckoning Sir John to follow him out into the corridor.

'He will have to be told the truth, Sir John.'

'Oh, no – not yet, he is too ill!'

'He must be told,' repeated Herbert Pond sternly. 'Sooner or later he must know that my daughter never played him false. On the contrary, she was deserted by him.'

'No, Pond, you do not understand—' began the baronet, but Pond interrupted him.

'I think I understand very well, Sir John, better than I did before. Your son must be told that Elizabeth is married, but not to Horrocks – and he must be told that he has a son.'

'No, *no*, Pond, for God's sake, he must not know that. Can't you see how it would affect him? Andrew is Siggery's son to all intents and purposes – that is how it must remain. Our son shall *not* know, Lady de Boville and I are quite determined about that.'

Herbert Pond looked straight at the baronet with a certain contempt in his eyes. 'Do you think that you can keep from your son what all of Wollaston knows? *I* shall not tell him, for it is not my duty to do so, that must be *your* confession. My concern is for my daughter who was always true to him. Think of the shock that *she* will have when she hears that he has returned – and my son-in-law, as good a man as I have ever known. You and your wife had better prepare yourselves to face the truth and face your son – and face Wollaston. You have heard Richard say that he is willing to forgive any man for any injury done to him, so may he forgive *you*! I pray that God will help you to do your duty.'

Turning on his heel, he left Oak Hall without a backward glance. Sir John de Boville stood watching him go, and felt a chill of fear at his heart.

As soon as the parson crossed the threshold of his home, Mrs Pond called out to him in fury.

'So, Herbert Pond, don't tell me any more lies about where ye've been, 'cause I *know*, the same as half Wollaston knows.

Ye've been up at Oak Hall, cookin' up a story to tell young de Boville who's come back from the war. Don't think yer can pretend that Andrew's not his son, 'cause ev'rybody knows he is, and a nice scandal 'twill be, all over again! I knew it was a mistake to marry her off to Siggery, but did yer listen to me? No! Ye're always so damned sure that ye're always right!'

'Oh, be quiet, Connie – just close your mouth,' he said, sighing, taking off his hat and coat and hanging them on the hook. He felt unutterably crushed in spirit as he went into his study. Just as he was closing the door, young Jenny Tasker put her head around it.

'Don't mind 'er, Mr Pond, I'll bring yer a nice cup o'best tea,' she whispered.

'Thank you, Jenny, you're a comfort to me,' he replied, then closed the door and fell upon his knees beside his desk. 'O Lord, look down on me – on us – on *all* of us, O Lord, in thy great mercy, and direct my path. Show me what I have to do!'

'But that is wonderful news, Father!' exclaimed Adam. 'After all this time – to be home again! I must go and see him at once – and take Lydia to meet him. *Sunday*, you said? Why has it all been kept so quiet, as if 'twere some strange misfortune?'

'I can only say that Sir John has forbidden all visitors to Oak Hall,' his father replied. 'The young man is in a very low state, and not in . . . not in his right senses, I gather. Only the parson and the apothecary are allowed to see him, at least until we are told otherwise. Even I am excluded from the sick room.'

Adam looked alarmed. 'Why, d'you think he may be disfigured, Father, scarred in such a way as to make him appear—' He stopped mid-sentence, not wanting to say grotesque. 'That would be terrible. Well, I won't clamour to see him but wait upon events.'

'That is what we must all do,' said the squire, though Sir John had said nothing to him about any disfigurement, only that Richard was 'very ill and not himself', which presumably meant he was raving. Even so, Horrocks felt that there was some mystery attached to the return, for Sir John had appeared nervous and evasive, though by now the whole village had heard the news.

'How long is it since Richard left for London, Father? In '77, wasn't it?' And just after that Sir John offered me "a home and security", as he put it, in return for marrying Elizabeth Pond, then known to be with child. Richard was much condemned at the time for deserting her.'

'I remember only too well, Adam,' said the squire grimly. 'He was but seventeen then, under his parents' rule, and I've sometimes wondered if he ever knew – but we never saw him again. Still, he has been spared and for that we must all give thanks.'

Richard had got out of bed and stood holding on to the bed-post while his mother watched with some trepidation. A stick was produced, and Richard hobbled around the room with its aid. He then wanted to dress, helped by a manservant, and the housekeeper appeared with clean clothes.

'I shall want my blue buttoned jacket to go out,' he demanded, but Lady de Boville would not allow him to venture outdoors.

''Tis cold and windy weather, my son. Last night a ship was overturned off Felixstowe in a fearful storm. You must stay indoors for at least another week.'

'I should go to St Bede's, Mother, and give proper thanks for my deliverance when worthier men perished. And if I can't go this Sunday, I shall make sure to be in the de Boville pew on Christmas Day. Nothing will keep me away.'

Sir John and Lady de Boville were in a quandary. Happy as they were at his restored health of body and mind, they knew there would be complications as soon as he appeared in public.

Wet and windy December weather kept Elizabeth and Andrew at home in the cottage on the Common. William went down to the forge each day, and he heard about young de Boville's return on the Tuesday. Like the rest of Wollaston he could not but give thanks for the man's preservation, though they had never been acquainted. All he truly knew about Richard de Boville was that he had fathered Elizabeth's child, and had left Wollaston at the time when her condition was first known. He had pondered long and often about the extent of Richard's guilt, having talked with his mother whose knowledge of the de Bovilles was more intimate than most of the villagers. She had always found Richard a pleasant, rather dreamy boy, she'd said, thoughtful and always honest. By contrast Lady de Boville could be devious; she had influenced her husband on occasion to suppress inconvenient facts when she thought fit.

What difference did Richard's return make now to himself and Elizabeth, his loving and dutiful wife? He looked upon Andrew as his own beloved son: the past was surely passed.

But was it? If de Boville now reappeared in Elizabeth's life, if he wanted to claim his own son, what would happen to their family? He felt a shiver of fear when he thought of Elizabeth finding out, as she would inevitably do. How would she react when she saw her erstwhile lover again, the father of her child? William knew that he must tell her, but his heart sank at the thought of the pain and bewilderment he must cause her. Perhaps she would rejoice at the return of the man who had first claimed her love.

William's thoughts went round and round in his head, and he did not know what to do or where to turn for counsel. He went home to the cottage that night and said nothing, but the next day he knew what had to be done. After leaving the smithy at noon, he washed and changed his clothes and set out for St Bede's and the little end terrace house where Parson Pond had recently returned from Oak Hall to be greeted by Mrs Pond's diatribe and Jenny's cup of tea. As the parson knelt praying there was a knock at the door. He stood up as he heard Jenny go to the door, open it and give a cheerful greeting to the visitor. In the next moment she had ushered William Siggery into the study.

'William, my son.' The two men spontaneously embraced and, after a quick discussion, decided to go up to the cottage and tell Elizabeth together.

Richard de Boville sat pensively in the drawing room with his father. Lady de Boville had gone to her room to rest, worn out by the excitement and activity of the past three days.

'If you won't let me go out, Father, at least let me receive visitors!' Richard said crossly.

'But, my dear boy, you must allow yourself time to get truly well.'

'People will be wondering what sort of a state I'm in, cooped up in here out of sight! And the friend I would most like to see is the one who married the girl I loved, Adam Horrocks. I want to shake hands with him – and his wife if she will allow me – to show that I bear them no grudge and wish them well. Surely you can grant me that much, Father.'

These were the words Sir John had dreaded to hear. It was just as Parson Pond had warned him. The truth had to be faced – and confessed.

'Why, what ails you, Father? You look as if there was something wrong. Is it Adam? Oh, Father, tell me, what has happened?'

It could be no longer delayed. Sir John's hands were trembling as he sat beside his son.

'I have something to tell you, my boy,' he said, his voice strained.

'Then tell it, in God's name!'

'Your friend Adam is indeed married, but not to Elizabeth Pond. He married a Miss Lydia Buxton, a niece of the Miss Buxtons who run the vicarage school.'

'Oh. Oh, I see. But I was surely given to understand that she had returned to Adam who was courting her before I supplanted him. I think it was Frederica who told me – I'm not sure. But what happened to Elizabeth? Where is she? Her father said she was well.'

'Yes, Richard, she is well. She married the blacksmith, Siggery, and I believe they are very happy.'

'Siggery? Surely that was the name of a simpleton who lived in a cottage on the Common.'

'He is no simpleton, Richard, but a good man who had the ill-luck to be born with a club foot and a severe stammer. He and his father-in-law, the parson, are as father and son.'

'Oh, I see, so that's the way it is. I thought you were going to say that she is still unmarried, but I could not expect fortune to be that kind. When did she marry this blacksmith?'

It was the question that Sir John feared, but it had to be answered.

'It was this year,' he answered heavily. 'On Midsummer Day.'

'As lately as that? Oh, if she could have but waited a few months more! And do they live at the old Siggery cottage?'

'Yes. His mother has gone to live with her sister-in-law at Flaxford.'

'Aaah.' Richard gave a long sigh. 'So my lovely Elizabeth is married to another. I suppose I must wish them both well. They seem happy, you say?'

'Yes, indeed they are, Richard – but I have more to tell,' said his father wretchedly. 'She never played you false.'

'What d'you mean?' asked Richard sharply.

'Your letters to her and hers to you were intercepted, both here and at Diss. Your mother and I . . . oh, Richard, forgive us if you can. We thought it an unsuitable match, and . . . and so we sent you to your mother's relatives in London, to . . . to . . .'

'To get me out of the way, Father, that's what you mean, isn't it? You deliberately separated us, and sent me with Frederica to the Lennoxes. I left that poor, sweet girl thinking that I had jilted her, as I thought she had jilted me. May God forgive you, Father!'

Sir John wrung his hands. 'Richard, I have repented often. Your mother and I have been punished by your enlistment and . . . and as we thought, your death in the war. God knows I've paid for that deception day and night, ever since.'

Richard's voice was toneless as he answered. 'I may be able to bring myself to forgive you, Father, but first I must see Elizabeth Pond and tell her—'

'Elizabeth Siggery, Richard, is a married woman now. It's too late to speak to her, and besides, there is another matter—'

Neither of them had noticed Charlotte de Boville entering the room. She stood just inside the door trembling at what she heard.

'*What* other matter, Father? Surely there can be no more blows for me to bear?'

Sir John drew a deep, shuddering breath. 'Richard, I have to tell you that you have a son, born to Elizabeth on the first day of March in 1778.'

There was a stricken silence for a few moments, then

Richard gave a cry, like the howl of an animal in pain. His father and mother hurried to his side, but he thrust them away.

'Oh, my Elizabeth, what you must have thought, what you have suffered!' he shouted, as if she were in the room and able to hear him. 'Forgive me, forgive me, I knew nothing of it, nothing, as God is my witness!'

In his weakened state, he collapsed into agonizing sobs. Lady de Boville also wept and Sir John walked up and down the room, wringing his hands in anguish.

Richard eventually raised his head and addressed them in a cold, hard voice they had never heard before. 'I will never forgive you,' he told them. 'No, keep away from me. Didn't you hear what I said? I will never forgive you. Never!'

In the little living room at the Siggery cottage Elizabeth was trying to comfort her son who had been in a tearful, unhappy state since discovering that Ladyfox was not in the little outhouse where she usually slept; in spite of repeated calling, the fox had not reappeared.

'Andrew, dear, she might have gone to live with her relations in Foxholes or some other place where foxes live,' said Elizabeth gently, for she and William had half-expected this. 'You know that foxes don't usually live with people, because they are what we call wild animals who would rather live with each other. Ladyfox has grown up and got bigger, so she might have said to herself, "I can't stay here any longer, but must go to live with my own kind." So you mustn't be sad for her, Andrew, just be glad that you loved her and gave her a good home when she was a little baby fox.'

'But I want her to come home, Mama!' wept Andrew.

Elizabeth could only hope that he would get over the loss of his pet in time. And may she escape the hunters with their hounds, she prayed silently, for that was the real danger of returning to the wild.

'Come, Andrew, you must be brave, dear,' she said.

She was holding him on her lap when she heard the knock on the door and William's voice calling her name softly. Her father was with him and both men looked grave. Putting Andrew off her lap she stood up, looking alarmed at their unexpected appearance at this hour.

'William! Papa! What's happened? Is it my mother?' she asked, her hand on her throat in sudden panic.

'Don't worry, my dear, nobody has been hurt or harmed, not in the way that you think,' her father said soothingly.

'Then what is it, Papa? What brings you here? Tell me, do!' she cried, turning to William who put his arms around her and held her close.

'Listen, my dear daughter,' the parson said. 'Richard de Boville has come back from the war—'

'*Richard!* Richard. Oh, heavens above!' she gasped. 'After so long!'

'Yes, Elizabeth, he has returned from the war in America, and has suffered a great deal – but I have seen him and feel sure that he will recover.'

'But . . . does he know that I . . . that I am married to William and – Oh, Papa, does he know that I have a son?'

As if he knew that something momentous was being discussed and that it concerned him, Andrew clung to his mother's skirt.

'I don't know whether he has yet been told, Lizzie, but he will have to know. It is only right that he should.' The parson's voice was regretful but firm.

Elizabeth turned to William who still stood with his arms around her, and to her horror, his face was full of fear. She put her arms around his neck and kissed him tenderly, whispering her love for him, close to his ear. Then she turned back to her father.

'You are mistaken, Papa. Richard de Boville has *not* got a son, not any more. He left Wollaston long before Andrew was born, and now he's William's adopted son, and no child could have a more loving father. I'm happy for Richard and his parents that he has come back home, but nothing is changed here.' And she kissed her husband again.

'Thank heavens!' exclaimed the parson, and bent down to disengage Andrew from his mother's leg and hold him in his arms.

'So if young de Boville comes looking for you, Elizabeth—?' he began.

'I shall speak civilly to him, Papa, you may be sure – but he must find himself another woman to wed. I'm wedded already.'

'Thank you, d–dearest wife,' said William, speaking for the first time. 'F–forgive me for–for being afraid.'

The two men exchanged a look of relief.

'But Gaffer, when is Ladyfox coming home?' wailed Andrew. Then the rest of their talk was not of de Boville but of the boy's pet fox, loved but now lost.

Thirteen

A Renunciation and Two Reunions

1781–1782

'Brandon! What d'you mean by letting those two go out riding at such an hour? Master Richard is not fit to mount a horse and Master Edward needs a proper watch kept on him!'

'I couldn't very well stop 'em, Sir John, Master Richard were that set on it an' Master Teddy was all excited,' the groom apologized. 'I talked 'im into taking ol' Daffodil, she's sure footed an' knows 'er way – an' Master Teddy went on Cleo.'

'Confound it, Brandon, you should have come and told me! Which direction did they take?'

'They rode off northwards, sir, on the Bungay Road, but didn't say where they was bound for. I couldn't very well ask 'em. Very sharp in 'is manner, sir, be Master Richard these days.'

Sir John de Boville closed his eyes in wordless exasperation. He questioned the man about what time the pair had come to the stables, but knew that the groom was not to blame. Richard's behaviour had been both headstrong and erratic during the three weeks since his return. Sir John knew that his wife would be horrified when she heard that her sons had gone out early, riding heaven knew where; Richard seemed positively to enjoy causing them disquietude. The family feared to argue with him in case he simply got up and walked out of Oak Hall.

Who would blame him if he did? thought Sir John, feeling his own blame more keenly than ever. He could not discuss this with anybody, least of all his wife, who wept at the very mention of the subject and tended to blame Lady Lennox for everything. The baronet knew that this was neither fair nor reasonable, and he took some comfort from Georgina, whose happiness with Felix Wilborough was a ray of sunshine in an otherwise clouded sky.

Sir John sighed deeply and muttered to Brandon that they could only hope that his two sons would return without incident.

'By Jove, this is more like it, Ted! Let's turn their heads round and gallop over to the beck, for 'tis not a great jump – and then follow the track where the ground rises up to the ridge and down into Westhall. Come on, old girl, let's put you through your paces!'

Daffodil and Cleo responded eagerly to this unexpected treat. They had passed their useful years as hunters, except to train young horsemen in riding to hounds, but they were still young at heart, and cantered along in the crisp morning air, their manes flying in the wind as their hooves thudded over the uneven terrain. Richard's spirits rose at the view of open countryside, the trees grey and bare under an arching sky, yet momentarily bathed in a burst of winter sunshine.

Young Edward, his cheeks reddened by the wind, was delighted that Richard had asked him to ride with him at such an early hour. He banished from his mind the confrontation with his father which he knew would await them on their return.

'I shall go out with the next Wollaston hunt, Ted!' cried Richard. ''Twill be good sport and good company, out with Horrocks and the hounds!'

'Will Father let me come too?' shouted Edward, his voice half carried away by the wind. 'Will you ask him if I can join the hunt?'

'You'll have to ask him yourself, Ted. Tell him you want to and then keep reminding him about it until he gives in.' Richard had no intention of begging his father for anything, not even on behalf of his young brother.

They continued riding for some six or seven miles before Richard began to feel the effects of the exertion. The strength seemed to drain out of him; he developed a pain in his side which took away his breath. He did not want to ask Edward to slow down, but merely suggested that they should now head for home to be back in time for breakfast.

'We'll go up over Foxholes and then down to the bottom of Cove Common,' he said, knowing that this would mean passing quite close by the Siggery cottage. When they reached it, Richard drew in his reins in the hope that Elizabeth might appear with her son – *his* son! His heart beat faster at the thought, but on such a cold day the occupants were indoors and the windows closed. The pain in Richard's side was getting worse; he could scarcely draw his breath when they reached the main street of Wollaston, which curved between St Bede's and the Fox and Hounds. They passed the forge with its furnace and anvil on which the horseshoes were hammered, and Richard gasped when he caught sight of the blacksmith. What a great, strong fellow he was! He made Richard feel like a poor, bony wretch. He was sick and giddy and wanted only to get back to Oak Hall and rest.

Edward, unaware of the tension, called out gaily, 'Hello, William! We've been over to Westhall – the wind nearly blew us away!'

The blacksmith looked up and immediately saw Richard beside his young brother. Their eyes met. Richard tried to say, 'Morning!' but felt his senses deserting him as he slid down Daffodil's side in a faint.

Edward gave a shout of alarm and Siggery dropped his hammer to rush out of the forge as fast as his club foot would allow, calling on the apprentice to follow him. Richard lay ashen-faced on the cobbles, and William put a hand over his heart.

''Tis beating, and he's b–breathing,' he muttered. 'I'll fetch Noah's c–cart to take him home. Joe, go for a horse b–blanket, and Ed-Edward, hold the reins o' both h–horses and wait by him till I b–bring the cart.'

In what seemed a matter of seconds the cart was there with the horse in the shafts, and William and Joe lifted Richard on to the cart while Edward supported his head. Richard moaned as his senses returned, feeling hands touching him, carrying him, voices close to his ear, the sky straight up above him; there was a jogging and a jolting while Edward held his hand. Then more voices, shouts of alarm, and somebody – was it his father? – exclaiming, 'Thank God!' He was home . . . somebody was thanking the blacksmith. As he became aware of his surroundings, he began to suspect that he had made a great fool of himself.

'It's very cold today, Richard, and there has been a heavy frost,' said Lady de Boville, standing at the foot of her son's bed. 'Your father and I think it would be most unwise for you to leave the hall in your present condition.'

'No, Mother, I will not be prevented from attending church on Christmas Day,' he said, though he still felt a weakness in his limbs and a lassitude of mind that made him unwilling to take part in any kind of social activity. Even a game of chess with Felix Wilborough had tired him and he had lost to his future brother-in-law in spite of that gentleman's kind efforts to let him win.

But going to church – that was worth getting out of bed for. For today he would see Elizabeth sitting beside her mother and husband, and accompanied by her son – *his* too! There might be an opportunity to speak to her at the conclusion of the service, for it would be perfectly in order for him to thank Siggery for his quick actions to save him a week ago. Yet the incident had had its good side, in that it had curbed his ill-humour and put him back on speaking terms with his parents out of sheer necessity, for he had been forced to take to his bed and resume the routine of an invalid.

In the matter of attending church he was adamant, so the whole family set out together, Lady de Boville in the family carriage while Sir John walked with Mr Wilborough and Georgina, to join the faithful that filled the pews of the ancient church.

'Let us therefore come and adore Christ the Lord, born in a humble stable to bring salvation to mankind,' said the parson, closing his sermon. 'God today has raised up the poor and humble, and cast down the proud.'

Seated in the gated de Boville pew, Richard's view of the congregation was limited, but as soon as the service ended he got up and went to stand at the door in the north transept through which most of the parishioners passed. And there they were, the man and the woman with the child between them – and there too stood Richard's father exchanging Christmas greetings with the Siggerys so that he could bend down and speak in a grandfatherly way to a bright-eyed boy in whose happy little face Richard saw his own. This child was indeed his own! As he stood watching them he felt his whole body tremble.

Mrs Elizabeth Siggery turned to him and smiled politely. 'Good morning, sir!' she said, and somehow he managed to make some sort of a reply. And then they were gone, the husband, wife and child, leaving him standing alone like one left out of heaven. He was then approached by his sister Georgina, who laid a hand upon his arm.

'Come, Richard, the carriage awaits us. I am to join you and our mother in it, and Felix will walk home with father.' Linking her arm with his, she led him down the path to the lychgate where Lady de Boville sat waiting for them in the carriage.

It had been only for a moment, but he had seen her and she had acknowledged him. He knew that he now had to show courage of a different order from that demanded of him in his years of hardship in a wasteful, discreditable war. His Elizabeth was married to another, and her son belonged to her husband; somehow he, Richard de Boville, had to rise above himself and let them go.

For such hardy souls who were prepared to linger at the church door in the freezing air, there was a fine piece of news to be passed around and talked over. Flaxford Manor was now occupied by its new owners who had arrived only a few days ago. They were said to be a pleasant, agreeable couple, recently married and as yet childless. There was much curiosity and speculation about them.

Sir John wore a thoughtful frown when he told his wife what he had heard from Mr Palfrey after the service.

'He says their name is Lennox, my love. A Mr and Mrs Lennox.' She looked up sharply.

'Does he? Well, they may be an offshoot of the Lennoxes of Bedford Row, but I doubt it,' she said with a shrug. 'I cannot imagine them to be closely connected. And you say there is no title, they are known as simply Mr and Mrs Lennox?'

'At present they are, Charlotte, but Palfrey says he is an Honourable, and heir to a viscountcy. I think he is probably your cousin's son Charles.'

Charlotte's face hardened. 'Fortunately Flaxford is six miles off, and we are under no obligation to visit them. I refuse to receive them here at Oak Hall. I have no wish to meet the man, honourable or otherwise, who jilted our daughter and set her on the path to . . . to . . .' She burst into tears. 'Why, oh, *why* did he have to come to Suffolk, and so near to Wollaston?'

Sir John could provide no answer. It was as well that Georgina and Felix were seated round the hearth roasting chestnuts, sharing conundrums and playing a game that Felix had introduced, called Consequences. Their peals of laughter lightened the atmosphere, and Richard was eventually persuaded to join them.

The new year came in with gusty winds and sleet which turned to snow, and for a week Wollaston and most of the county lay under a silent white blanket that made even short distances difficult to traverse. Food was short for men and animals alike and young Mr Horrocks and his wife were seen out visiting poor cottagers with soup and bread from the farm-house kitchen. The de Bovilles sent staff to call on their tenants to ask if they were in need of food or extra clothing. Sir John would not allow his womenfolk to go visiting in such weather, and said that some of the men were rude and uncouth. He had never forgotten 'the villain Venn', as he remembered him, who had assaulted both Richard and himself. The baronet believed that the lower orders should be fairly treated but not allowed to get above their station in life.

The St Stephen's Day Hunt had been a case in point. Sir John had ridden to hounds with the squire, Adam and young Mrs Horrocks; Miss Georgina and Mr Wilborough had attended, but were told to keep well to the back of the pack, not being much experienced. The numbers were made up with Joe, the apprentice, Joshua Venn, and Brandon the groom to deal with any unforeseen mishaps. At the end of the day they had lost the scent of the fox they had picked up earlier and old Reynard had got clean away. The hounds had killed only a couple of rabbits, digging them out of their winter burrows and tearing them apart to eat noisily. Sir John blamed their failure on Adam and young Venn for behaving childishly during the day; it had irritated him, and he longed for Richard to be able to join the hunt again. The boy seemed to be gradually getting back to normal health and strength, though he was very quiet and evaded questions.

Elizabeth Siggery was thankful that the snow had put an end to hunting for a while. She could not forget Ladyfox and the fate which might overtake her away from the domesticity of her life with the Siggerys. Nevertheless it was irksome to be shut indoors day after day while William was at the forge. She took Andrew out for short walks in the snow, which fascinated him. He loved to look back on his tracks in the whiteness. There were no classes to take, as the cottagers' daughters could not be expected to trudge up to the cottage in snow which could be treacherous when it thawed and refroze.

She was engaged one January afternoon weaving a wool blanket. She had put Andrew to bed as he was tired after a walk. The noon chimes from St Bede's had just floated out on the still air when she heard the sound of a horse's hooves, slowing as it approached the cottage. There followed the sound of somebody dismounting, followed by a pause while it was tethered to an iron ring set into the wall outside.

Who on earth might this visitor be? Elizabeth's heart fluttered at the thought of facing Richard de Boville. How would she deal with him? She left the loom and looked out of the window. The unexpected caller was a lady, smartly dressed in a dark riding jacket and skirt, with a tricorne hat on her dark curly hair. Elizabeth opened the front door before the visitor knocked.

'Lizzie Pond!' cried the lady, her eyes bright with emotion. 'Oh, what happiness to see you again after all this time!'

Elizabeth took in the merry face, the smile, and the sweet voice with a local accent – not so strident as her mother's or as slipshod as the cottagers' girls.

'Lizzie Pond, can you not recognize an old friend?'

'*Meg!*' exclaimed Elizabeth. 'Meg Venn! I never thought to see you again. Oh, Meg, come in, come in! I'll boil the kettle and make up the fire. Where have you come from?'

'Just now, from your father's house, for I thought you still lived there. I've come over from Flaxford Manor, my husband Charles and I moved in just before Christmas. The weather's been so bad that he wouldn't let me out until now – except to call on a few poor cottagers.' Her dark eyes danced. 'D'you know, we went out on a sleigh – yes, a real sleigh that my pony could draw across the snow, with me and my cake and cheese and stuff for the poor souls. Oh, Lizzie, it brought the past all back to me, and what my poor mother went through.' Her smile faded.

'But Meg, I don't understand. Flaxford Manor, you said? But I've heard it has new owners.'

'Yes, Charles and me! Oh, I have such a wonderful husband, Lizzie! He wanted to live a country life, away from the London social round, and *I* wanted to return to Suffolk – and when we heard that Flaxford Manor was up for sale it was an answer to our prayers.'

'But who is Charles, Meg? Where did you meet him?'

'He's the Honourable Charles Lennox, son of Viscount Lennox. Londoner by birth and upbringing. One day I may tell you where he met me but not just yet. It was arranged for him to marry Frederica de Boville, but at the last minute he backed out because he'd met *me*! It was love at first sight. His aunt, who's very kind and wise, advised him to go on a long journey to see if he'd forget me. I was her maidservant while he was on his travels. She taught me to read and write and speak more like a lady, and I was practically promised to a manservant of hers. But then Charles came back. Oh, Lizzie, we were as much in love as ever! And so we were married last year, and came here. But what o' you, Lizzie? What's this your father's told me about you marrying Sil – er, the blacksmith? And you have a little boy?'

'My husband William Siggery is a wonderful, wise man, Meg,' said Elizabeth seriously, for she had heard Meg's near slip of the tongue. 'You will remember him as Noah Reeve's apprentice, a young man much afflicted by a club foot and a stammer. I suppose you were very surprised when Papa told you we were married.'

Meg sat down beside her friend and took hold of her hand. 'No, Meg, I wasn't surprised, for I remembered you always defended Billy when we were children. I shall never forget that day on the Common when you flew at my brother Sam and that oaf they called Chopper. And later I found out for myself what a good heart he had, so kind to my mother and all of us. Even my poor father praised him when he hadn't a

good word to say for anybody else – remember how he used
to go mad about "them cursed Deboffles"?'

Elizabeth kissed her friend for her understanding, but did
not want to pursue the subject of the de Bovilles.

'And you've got a little boy, Lizzie. Where is he? Can I
see him?'

Meg's lively chatter had woken Andrew who came into the
room and stared at the visitor.

'Andrew dear, this lady is an old friend of mine,' said his
mother proudly. 'Now, what do you say to her?'

'Good day to you,' Andrew said immediately. 'How do you
do?'

'Very well indeed, kind sir,' Meg said laughing. 'Oh, Lizzie,
what a darling! I can see he has your eyes, except that they're
dark and yours are blue – and he's got your father's forehead.'

Elizabeth smiled but made no reply. She had discovered
that people saw in babies' faces what they hoped or expected
to see.

'What a little charmer! How old is he?' asked Meg, chucking
Andrew under his chin.

'He'll be four on March the first.'

'Oh? You've been married for that long? That's strange,
because when Charles came to look for my brother Joshua
and yourself, that must have been – let me think – two years
ago, he called on your father and said you were still living at
home. He must have made a mistake.'

Elizabeth smiled and gave a little sigh. 'No, Meg, he made
no mistake, though he obviously never told you that I had a
son. Andrew was about eighteen months old when ... er ...
Mr Lennox came here, and dear William and I were married
last midsummer. He calls Andrew his son, and cares for him
as well as any father, but Andrew isn't his by birth.'

Meg's jaw dropped. 'Never! Oh, Lizzie, you of all people –
and the parson's daughter! What a dreadful time you must have
had.'

'My father is a true Christian, Meg, and he didn't send me
away as my mother would have done. He stood beside me in
my trouble, and it wasn't so dreadful after all because he is
so much loved and most people admired him for his kindness
to me.'

'Oh, my dear Lizzie, I never would have believed it,' said

Meg, genuinely surprised. 'And was it some Wollaston man –
ah, Adam Horrocks! I remember he was courting you when
I left. Did his parents—?'

'No, no, no, poor Adam has been blamed for every bastard
child born in Wollaston, but I don't think he has sired a single
one,' said Elizabeth emphatically. 'It was . . . somebody else.'

'Ah. You're not going to tell me. Well, whoever he was, I
hope he got a just punishment. Men get off so easily in these
matters, leaving the woman to suffer,' Meg said with a stern
frown.

'He was punished,' said Elizabeth quietly, not willing to
confide further in her friend at that moment. 'No doubt you
will hear the story sooner or later.'

Meg was mystified, but did not press her friend for more
details. 'Anyway, Andrew's the most delightful, handsome,
bright little boy, Lizzie, and you must be so proud of him.'

'I am, Meg. I've been blessed in both my son and my
husband.'

'Bless you, Lizzie, I'm so happy that we've met again and
we shan't ever part. You must come over to Flaxford and meet
Charles again. He'll be a viscount one day and I shall be Lady
Lennox – isn't that a joke?'

She kissed her friend with a loving look, though Elizabeth
was amazed. 'Lady Lennox? Oh, Meg, if only your poor father
was alive to see how things have turned out. You'll have the
last laugh on the "Deboffles".'

Meg looked a little dubious. 'To be honest with you, Lizzie,
I don't think I shall have much to do with them. You remember
I told you that Charles was more or less betrothed to Frederica
de Boville – there was an agreement between the two families. Anyway, when Charles decided that he didn't want to
marry the de Boville girl, she rushed off to marry somebody
else, an older man with lots of money. But she didn't stay
with him, in fact she left his house after less than two years,
to become the mistress of a fearful old rake, even older than
her husband . . . ugh!' Meg shuddered at the very thought of
Sir Gideon Draynes and what might have happened at Madame
Duvall's. 'But he deserted her, as he'd deserted others, and
now . . .'

'Go on, Meg, what happened to Frederica?' asked Elizabeth
curiously.

'Well, it seems that she made friends with another woman who had been this old man's mistress, and they now live together in a house on the Marylebone Road and run it as a place of ill-repute.'

'What sort of ill-repute, Meg?'

'Oh, dearest Lizzie, I can see that you're still the same sweet, innocent country girl you always were! Let's just say we hope Sir John and Lady de Boville never find out what their poor daughter has come to. And now I'm going to play with this young man and ask him to show me what he can make with these bricks!'

'Do you know that your brother Sam is back from the war and working for Squire Horrocks?'

'*Sam?* Oh, my little brother Sam, I thought he must be gone for ever. Lizzie, what news you've given me on this day, I do declare! I must see him and speak to him!'

'I'm happy to give you good news, Meg. We've had our troubles, both of us, and I've missed you so much – but God has been good and now it seems we've come to safe harbour.'

As the light began to fade, Meg said she would have to be going or her husband would be upset at her for riding in the dark.

'We'll meet again, Lizzie. You and William must come to Flaxford Manor. Charles has asked his aunt to come on a long visit when the weather warms up. She's a widow, and broken-hearted at the loss of her son. I'm hoping that she'll come to look on Charles as a sort of son. The truth is, Lizzie, his own parents are not so happy about our marriage or the way he's left London to settle in the country. I can't imagine that *they* will want to come and stay with us!'

When William Siggery lifted the latch that evening and stepped into the welcoming warmth of home, he found his wife all smiles and excitement.

'Will! You'll never guess who's been here this afternoon to see me and Andrew. Someone we've always known since we were children!'

To her dismay he went pale, and clutched at her, holding her close in his arms. 'N–no, Elizabeth, not him! Not de Boville!'

'Why, Will dear, of course not! 'Twas a dear friend from

the past, my *best* friend that I lost – Meg Venn – you know, Joshua's sister.'

'Ah, Meg, yes.' He gave a long sigh of relief.

'Only she's not Venn any more but Lennox. She and her husband are the new owners of Flax— Will, how strange of you to think I'd receive de Boville here in our home.'

'Forgive me, d–dearest wife, but he's not just any m–man, he's the father of Andrew. I've often thought he might c–come lookin' to see the boy – and you. He's a gentleman full o' book learnin', and he . . . he was deceived by his parents about you. I've half-expected him t–to . . .'

'Hush, Will, how could you doubt me?' she asked almost accusingly. 'Richard de Boville belongs in the past, and . . . well, I know from my father that he has no designs on Andrew. He knows I'm happy with *you* and that Andrew considers you his father. Can't you believe that? Can't you understand?'

She drew herself back so she could look straight into his face. 'I care nothing for his book learning, Will. Your wisdom is greater than all his words. I love you, Will.'

'Ah, my love, f–forgive me.' He drew her close against him again. 'I–I couldn't bear to lose you, Eliz–Elizabeth, my dearest t–treasure.'

'Dear Will! You needn't worry, I'll never look at *any* other man as long as I have you.'

They kissed and clung together but it was as if a shadow had passed over their home, a wintery whisper of the frailty of human life and love.

'Mama! There's somebody at the door!' cried Andrew.

His parents opened their eyes and yawned, for it was not yet dawn.

'No, dear, there's nobody about at this hour,' said Elizabeth. 'Go back to sleep again.'

'But Mama, I *heard* – listen, somebody wants to come in, and I can't reach the latch. Come and open it, Mama.'

William Siggery heaved himself out of the feather bed in which he had made a warm nest against his wife's back. 'Now, Andrew, this is naughty. There's nobody there and it's not time to get up yet.'

'Please, Papa, open the door!' begged the boy. With a resigned sigh William drew back the bolt and lifted the latch.

The door opened inwards and in walked Ladyfox. 'As large as life and twice as natural,' Elizabeth later told Meg Lennox. Andrew gave a shout and his parents could no longer stay in bed, they were all so relieved that Ladyfox had not been taken by the Wollaston Hunt. Andrew was simply overjoyed at the return of his playmate.

Fourteen

Once Upon a Day in Springtime

1782

"'T is g–good to see the s–sun rising earlier!' said William
Siggery, standing at the cottage door in his nightshirt,
looking up at the sky. 'The old p–people used to say
Feb–February is the great l–light-giver, between its
b–beginning and its end!'

Ladyfox bounded forward, sniffing the air appreciatively.

'Ye–ye're a fine lady, a'n't ye?' he said admiringly, for she
had grown into a splendid animal with her reddish-gold coat,
graceful limbs and beautiful bushy tail; she seemed to have
gained an extra sheen since her return from the wild.

'Take care you don't get cold, standing out there!' called
young Mrs Siggery, drawing a woollen shawl over her plain
white nightgown and coming to watch the animal's antics.
'She's flirting with you, Will!'

'Sh–she's been f–flirting somewhere else, I think,' he said,
bending down to stroke the short, soft fur of the belly. 'Put
your h–hand here and touch her. C–can you feel any–anything?'

'Ah, yes, of course – she's in cub!' exclaimed Elizabeth.
'So that's what she was getting up to in the wild! Why,
Ladyfox, you cunning little vixen!'

'Not so l–little now!' chuckled William. 'Th–thank heaven
she'll be s–safe from the h–hunt. They don't kill vixens in
c–cub.'

'No, they've got their eye on the cubs for next winter,' said
his wife with a grimace.

William gently palpated the animal's abdomen. 'I c–can
feel three c–cubs, perhaps f–four. Yes, dear Eliz–Elizabeth,

our L–Ladyfox has come home t–to give birth b–because she
knows it's s–safe here.'

'When will she have them?' asked Elizabeth, thinking how
excited Andrew would be.

'When w–was she away? D–December – so some time in
Ap–April, I reckon.'

Andrew woke up and at once came out to join them, rubbing
the sleep from his eyes.

'You're getting *fat!*' he told the fox, and his parents
exchanged an amused glance. It was surely too early to explain
the mysteries of how new life was made and they nodded in
tacit agreement. Andrew looked up at them, his dark eyes
wide.

'Did you say she had four cubs inside her, Papa? How will
they get out?'

It was through the Wollaston Hunt that the de Bovilles had
to meet the Lennoxes, for Charles wanted to join the traditional country pursuit and his wife insisted on accompanying
him. Women, especially the younger ones, were gradually
becoming a familiar sight on the field. They quickly made
friends with the young Horrockses and word got around that
Mrs Lennox was sister to the two Venn brothers who worked
for the squire. It seemed to add insult to the injury the de
Bovilles had already suffered at the hands of the Lennoxes,
for there was no doubt that Charles was indeed the 'booby'
who had jilted Miss de Boville with such disastrous results.
Sir John felt fairly sure that Charles must know something
about the present whereabouts of Frederica, but it was far
beneath his dignity to enquire – and he feared what the answer
might be. A blanket of silence had descended between them
and their elder daughter; she had cut herself off from her
family.

For Lady de Boville the situation was intolerable. That Mrs
Lennox should be none other than the daughter of that
dangerous madman Venn was a bitter pill to swallow. To think
that such a common creature had been preferred above her
own daughter made it worse; her ladyship adamantly refused
to open the doors of Oak Hall to the couple.

'My God, what times we live in nowadays, John!' she would

say bitterly. 'What in God's name has the world come to? Our country no longer has any pride; our armies are routed by upstart American colonists, our noble families are degraded by inferior blood, there is no respect shown to gentry or the church.' On and on she would rail and lament, and her husband had no choice but to listen, keeping to himself his own sadness that Frederica was disgraced and Richard much changed by the hardships he had endured in America and the loss of the woman he loved.

'At least Richard was saved from marriage to Pond's daughter!' Charlotte would exclaim, not appreciating her husband's strong attachment to his bastard grandson and his lasting remorse at having conspired to deceive Richard.

Meanwhile the world went on turning and winter gave way to spring; once more the earth awoke to new life. Andrew's fourth birthday was a fine, blowy day. His mother took him for a walk up to Foxholes to find the first daffodils and purple violets half-hidden in the grass between tree roots. In the field and meadow they saw a few early lambs frisking on their spindly legs beside their mothers, which made Elizabeth think of Ladyfox and the growing cubs within her. The great shire horses dragged ploughs across the brown fields in preparation for another season of wheat, oats and barley; William was kept busy at the forge, hammering new iron horseshoes on to their powerful hooves, mending cartwheels and harrows.

'March comes in like a lion, and goes out like a lamb!' quoted Elizabeth gaily. 'And it certainly came in with new life four years ago, Will!'

He looked grave. ''Tis a night I sh–shall never forget, dear wife, for I was there with y–your father, here in this v–very place. I tried to c–comfort him when he heard your c–cries of pain and sank down on his knees. Oh, yes, my love, I was there when our ch–child was born.'

The implication of his words was not lost on Elizabeth, for he meant that he had been there in place of the blood father of Andrew who had been an ocean away. Elizabeth smiled and softly kissed his cheek.

'But that's all past, Will, and now it's March again, and into another spring, more beautiful than ever,' she said. 'Don't you notice how every new spring is like the first one, different from any other? The whole of nature seems to be rejoicing!'

He understood her for he had been close to the natural world all his life; wild creatures came to him as Ladyfox had come, trusting and without fear. They had always been his consolation, and now that he had been granted the incredible blessing of a loving wife and child, his cup of happiness brimmed over.

To Sir John de Boville and the Wollaston Hunt the spring meant the end of the season. Out in the hunting field he and Richard had regained something of their former comradeship, and unlike his wife he harboured no ill-will against the young Lennoxes. Mrs Meg Lennox was not after all responsible for her father's behaviour and Sir John was coming to realize that Venn had had a just grievance for the way he and his family had been treated. Meg was a pleasant enough girl, liked by Georgina who had introduced another young huntress to the circle, a Miss Diana Mulholland whose father ran a small private school for boys halfway between Wollaston and Bungay. Miss Mulholland seemed a jolly girl and was quite pretty. Sir John dreamed that one day – dare he even think of it? – she might make an acceptable wife for Richard.

A final meet for the Wollaston Hunt was arranged for the third Wednesday in March. Sir John anticipated a good turnout and the day would end with game pie, cake and wine at Oak Hall. The day dawned bright and clear, and the dew was still on the ground when the meet assembled in the stableyard. Sir John was not disappointed in the company, for there were a dozen mounts and fifteen dogs, barking excitedly and wagging their tails in anticipation. The boys had been out early to block up the known earths with stones and all the signs pointed to a good day. Old Major Forsyth had ridden over from Cove at the crack of dawn with his nephew, as had the Reverend Mr Thorne who was determined to catch an old dog fox which had so far evaded the hunt.

'The old devil got into my poultry shed last week. You never saw such carnage, Sir John. If we don't catch the old scoundrel today, I–I won't go home until I do, drat him!'

There was general laughter at this. Mr and Mrs Lennox had arrived early from Flaxford and were soon chatting happily with young Mr and Mrs Horrocks, Georgina who was with

Mr Wilborough, and Georgina's friend Miss Mulholland. Joshua Venn was mounted on one of Horrocks's best hunters. As if he were gentry, thought Sir John; but the baronet reasoned that Mrs Lennox's fortunate marriage was bound to pull her family up by its bootstrings. He just hoped that the young fellow would behave himself.

A manservant came round to each member serving a stirrup-cup of warmed mulled wine, then as the pack moved off, the hounds sniffing for a scent, Sir John's eyes rested on Richard. If the boy could distinguish himself in some way today, it would surely draw him closer to his father. At present he was riding with Miss Mulholland, near to the back of the pack.

Within half an hour the hounds picked up a scent, and went racing off northwards. The horses followed, with Adam and Joshua in the lead.

'A view! Halloo, a view!' cried Joshua as a reddish-brown streak was seen ahead, keeping close to a hawthorn hedge.

''Tis that old villain, for sure!' roared Mr Thorne, and urged his horse on, galloping just behind the two young men.

The old dog fox – if indeed it was he – raced ahead, cutting across towards Westhill Heights and down to a stream that meandered through meadows, gradually widening until it emptied into the Waveney.

'Cunning old villain, he's aiming to cross the water and throw 'em off the scent!'

'Go on after him! We don't need scent if we've got a sight – and the dogs'll soon pick it up on the other bank!'

Mr Thorne, the squire and the two young men were now in the lead, followed by Sir John, the major and his nephew. Richard was with Georgina, Wilborough and Miss Mulholland, while the Lennoxes brought up the rear. One by one they crossed the stream with much splashing, shouting and muddying of the ladies' skirts; and then the cry went up that there was a second fox, possibly a third. Sir John blew a long blast on the hunting horn and the air was filled with thundering hooves and barking as the hounds raced ahead at top speed.

Richard felt his heart beating faster and his spirits rose as his mount galloped alongside the hunter on which Diana Mulholland sat. Her own eyes were bright with the excitement of the chase, and she called out to him, 'This is fine sport, Mr de Boville!'

Fine sport indeed. Richard was at one with the English countryside that he had so sorely missed during his sojourn on the eastern seaboard of America. The sight and the sound of the Wollaston Hunt in full pursuit of its quarry was truly intoxicating, an exhilarating exercise for body and mind. Miss Mulholland also seemed at home in the hunting field, fearless and completely in control of her steed. He wondered whether he should make a good second choice, based on social equality and a mutual enjoyment of country pursuits. He threw a glance in her direction, and it seemed that he saw his own thoughts reflected in the brightness of her eyes, her English rose complexion flushed with both the exertion and the pleasure of the chase. Surely it would be right and sensible to look ahead rather than back. Richard did not want to become embittered like his mother.

'I'll have to l–leave ye for a bit, Joe,' said William with a frown at his own forgetfulness. 'This farmer wants his harrow m–mended today, and it needs a couple o' bigger l–links to go each end, them oval ones, an I left 'em up at the c–cottage. Sorry.'

''S'alright, Billy, don't 'urry,' replied Joe, who liked being left in charge. 'Will yer walk up?'

'B–better borrow Tom Saunders' donkey if she be there. Be b–back soon, Joe.'

The donkey being available, Tom saddled her and William patted her neck as he guided her gently with the reins. She trotted down the High Street, turned the corner at St Bede's and headed up to the Common. William could already see that his wife and Andrew were out of doors and smiled to himself at the very sight of his loved ones. He also saw Ladyfox loping up towards Foxholes, so he knew that the Wollaston Hunt was not in the vicinity.

But he did not see Ladyfox suddenly prick up her ears at a distant sound, a menacing vibration through the ground and on the air; and what William did not know was that while the main body of the hunt was pursuing two foxes six or seven miles away, there were three dogs at the back of the pack that had picked up a new scent and swerved away southwards to go after it. Mr and Mrs Lennox found that their horses seemed intent on following the dogs on this new trail, and not being well experienced in horsemanship they loosened the reins and gave their steeds their heads, galloping towards the ridge of the Common. Miss Mulholland, seeing them turn away from the pack, decided to follow them, and with sudden nameless apprehension Richard too changed course, leaving the others to go after the two foxes they could see streaking ahead. Richard charged after the three breakaway riders who were following the three dogs; they circled round the edge of Foxholes Wood, and then Richard's heart gave a leap, for there, straight ahead of them was a large fox, with a small child nearby. *His son.*

It all happened in a few moments, printed for ever on de Boville's memory. William Siggery, approaching the cottage, saw Ladyfox veer round in a semicircle, heading towards the safety of her earth – which for her was the little wooden shelter attached to the cottage wall.

Both William and Andrew could now hear the approaching dogs and horses getting nearer with every second. Three dogs appeared, followed by three mounted horses, and a fourth rider was yelling at them to stop. Andrew ran towards Ladyfox, shouting her name, and William dropped himself off the donkey and he too shouted at the top of his voice.

'Andrew! Andrew, go *back*! GO BACK! GO TO MAMA, RUN TO MAMA, ANDREW!'

Elizabeth ran from the cottage door, frantically calling her child's name. Andrew turned, bewildered at hearing his papa shout so loudly and without stammering. Seeing his mother, he ran towards her. The horses and dogs were now on the trail of Ladyfox, cutting her off from her refuge. William stumbled after his son to protect him with his own body, but his club foot tripped over a tussock of grass, and he fell headlong.

'Rein in! Rein in, for God's sake!' he heard a man's voice yelling. 'Stop, *stop!*'

The ground trembled beneath him, and he cried out one word, 'Elizabeth!'

The dogs came first, barking in pursuit of the fox. Then came the horses, galloping and trampling. Charles Lennox's steed reared, missed the child by a few feet, but a huge hoof came straight down on William's head as he lay on the ground, crushing his skull. A woman shrieked, but William Siggery did not hear. All was finished for him.

The Lennoxes at last managed to rein in. They dismounted, trembling with fear. Miss Mulholland pointed to the body and screamed again, turning to Richard de Boville, who had also dismounted. He brushed her aside and strode towards the still figure and knelt down beside it. The face was unrecognizable and the grass was rapidly staining with the dead man's blood.

Richard straightened himself up. He saw Elizabeth standing near the cottage door, holding her sobbing child. He gave a low groan, for he dared not go near her, but ordered Mrs Lennox to go and take her friend indoors. He gestured to a white-faced Charles Lennox to take Miss Mulholland away, and then remounted his horse to go down to Wollaston and order a cart to be sent to remove the body. Then he braced himself to face Parson Pond and send him to do what he could for his daughter.

It was some time before anybody noticed the work of the three hounds. They had gone ahead and caught up with their prey, slowed as she was by the burden within her. Desperate to save her cubs as much as to save herself, she fought valiantly, but was overcome by dogs who knew no better, having been trained to catch and kill. And there were not four cubs but five ripped from her belly and scattered over the grass, hairless, sightless, helpless, soon to be set upon and eaten by the dogs. Ladyfox lay like her master, torn and bleeding, her beautiful bushy tail wet with blood and her upper lip drawn back to expose her teeth in a snarl that she had never once shown in life.

To Elizabeth Siggery it seemed as if time had stopped, and only because of the weeping child in her arms who needed her protection – more than ever now – she clasped him to her breast but uttered not a word. There were no words to express the darkness that had fallen on the day, the complete emptiness in her heart. Meg Lennox led her indoors and spoke what words came into her head, though fear clutched at her own heart when she thought on what had happened and who was to blame for Siggery's death. She attempted to divert Andrew, but he clung to his mother, who remained silent and seemed not to see or hear anything other than her child. Only when her father came to her some twenty minutes later and held her in his arms did she begin to give vent to her loss.

Herbert Pond knew that with some kinds of grieving there was nothing that could to be done to comfort those who weep, except by weeping with them.

Fifteen

Afterwards: Another Summer

1782

A gentlemen's meeting was called in the library at Oak Hall on the day following the tragedy. Sir John had requested the attendance of all the men who had taken part in the last meet of the season. Mrs Lennox had begged to be allowed to speak on her husband's behalf, but Sir John had decreed that only male members of the Wollaston Hunt were to be present.

'Gentlemen, we are here on melancholy business,' he began. 'Yesterday a man was killed and we must discuss how it happened and decide on compensation for the man's widow and –' he hesitated momentarily – 'child. It was a tragedy which we all wish had never happened, but 'tis the way of the world that what's done cannot be undone.'

There was a subdued murmur of agreement.

'It appears that while the main body of the hunt was pursuing two foxes in the area of Westhill Heights, three dogs at the rear of the pack caught another strong scent and suddenly broke off from the rest. Four riders at the back of the pack turned their horses to follow the dogs – Mr and Mrs Lennox, Miss Mulholland and my son Mr Richard – isn't that so, Mr Lennox?' he said, turning sternly towards Charles Lennox, whose white face and horror-stricken eyes bore witness to his sleepless misery ever since that terrible moment when Siggery had fallen in front of him.

'I couldn't rein him in, he was going at such a speed, I was almost thrown, Sir John,' he said tremulously. 'Mr Richard was calling to us to rein in but I couldn't. I was clinging on as well as I could, but it was impossible. I could hear my wife and Miss Mulholland screaming, and I . . .' He covered his face with his hands.

'Let us be thankful that you managed to stay in the saddle, Mr Lennox,' said Sir John grimly. 'And Mrs Lennox, how did her mount behave? She was on the chestnut mare, wasn't she? Did that also rear?'

Richard had been the only other male witness.

'Mrs Lennox kept her seat, and the mare *may* have trampled on the – on Siggery's body, sir,' Richard replied. 'I cannot be sure. But in any case Siggery died instantly at the moment of impact.' Richard's expression was sombre, trying to control the turmoil in his mind.

'Why exactly did the three riders break away? To follow the dogs?' asked Adam.

'Mr and Mrs Lennox's horses took it into their heads to go after the three breakaway dogs who were on to the scent of the tame fox that the Siggerys kept as a pet,' said Richard wretchedly, because his evidence implied criticism of friends. 'Er – neither Mr or Mrs Lennox are long experienced in horsemanship or fully aware of the dangers. Miss Mulholland followed them to give support, and I–I felt that I should also follow and try to draw them off that area of the Common. I saw the boy and shouted to them to rein in, to stop – but Mr Lennox's horse reared, as he has said, and Siggery, trying to protect the child, fell headlong, and that was how he—' Richard's voice shook, and he drew a deep breath to contain his emotions. 'The horse missed the boy by inches, thank God, but Siggery died in saving Andrew.' He covered his eyes with his right hand for a moment, and then looked sympathetically towards Lennox. 'It was an accident, Sir John, an accident brought about by three dogs going off on another scent.'

'And that in turn led to the death of a vixen in cub,' said Sir John soberly. 'Abominable hunting practise and to be avoided at all costs. Beside the death of Siggery, of course, 'twas only a fox and a few cubs – was it four or five, Adam?'

'About that number, sir – the dogs had feasted on them by the time I got to see them.' Adam cast a somewhat contemptuous glance at Lennox. 'It was unfortunate in the extreme, and . . .'

'Let us not attach blame to any one individual,' the baronet cut in gravely. 'It could have been any one of us in the heat of the moment and we must be thankful that Mr Lennox was spared. It could be said that Siggery gave his life to save the . . . the child. He must be given due honour at his funeral.'

He glanced round at their solemn faces. 'Parson Pond informs me that the burial service is to be held tomorrow, Friday, there being no reason to delay it. It is indeed a sorry ending to the season, gentlemen, and perhaps it is just as well that the Wollaston Hunt will not be meeting again until the autumn.'

'I shall never hunt again, Father,' said Richard quietly but with emphasis.

'Neither will I,' came the muffled voice of Charles Lennox, his head still buried in his hands. 'What would have happened if my horse had trampled on the child? Oh, my God – my God!'

'Yes, be thankful that 'twas not Andrew,' said Richard grimly. 'But I shall never hunt again.'

At this point Charles Lennox excused himself and left the room to ride back to Flaxford Manor and the comfort of Meg's warmth and understanding.

Making no effort to detain him, Sir John had one last proposal to make.

'Regarding compensation to the widow, I propose that we each make a donation to provide her with an income over the first six months,' he suggested, at which they all nodded in agreement. 'I will visit Parson Pond to discuss the matter with him.' He did not say anything about his own intention to pay for Andrew's upkeep and education permanently. From now on he would treat his grandson as being on an equal footing with his sons.

'Well, gentlemen, I thank you all for coming, and bid you good morning.'

The meeting broke up, and as they rode back to Cove Common, Major Forsyth remarked to the Reverend Mr Thorne that it had been 'damned generous of de Boville' to compensate the blacksmith's widow.

'Ah, but he was a good one and won't be easy to replace,' replied the fox-hunting cleric.

*　　*　　*

Just as most of Wollaston had come to St Bede's to see Billy Siggery married to the girl he had always loved, so now, scarcely nine months later, did they quietly assemble for his burial. They came to honour him and pay their respects to his widow and mother – and his child, for so Andrew had come to be regarded.

In his funeral eulogy, Herbert Pond had spoken nothing but the truth, though there were some who found it uncomfortable.

'William Siggery left his mark on our village and parish. In boyhood and early manhood he was often mocked as the village fool, as halting in speech as in movement,' he said. 'But for the last seven of the twenty-four years he lived on earth, he came to be recognized as a man of deep wisdom and for the loving kindness he showed to all life – human and animal. As a blacksmith and craftsman he was painstaking and thorough; as a neighbour he was always ready to lend a helping hand – and he freely forgave those who'd mocked him in earlier years.'

Sam Venn hung his head at hearing the stern words, but knew that it was true.

Mr Pond then had to read the words of the Burial Service. The two Siggery widows stood silently side by side at the grave of William's father, now reopened to receive the coffin of the son. Mrs Pond had stood alone until Mrs Lennox had gone over to her and invited her to stand with herself and her husband Charles. The Horrockses stood a little apart from the bereaved family, and Sir John de Boville and Richard, following at the back of the mournful procession, stood several yards away from the crowd assembled at the graveside. Andrew had been left at the Ponds' house in the care of Jenny Tasker.

'Forasmuch as it hath pleased Almighty God to take unto Himself the soul of our dear brother here departed, we therefore commit his body to the ground; earth to earth, ashes to ashes, dust to dust . . .'

Herbert Pond could hardly read the words aloud without emotion. Meg Lennox wept and Noah Reeve gave a loud sob as the coffin was lowered. Many of the company, both men and women, shed tears, as did the senior Mrs Siggery; the young widow remained blank-faced and dry-eyed.

At the end of the proceedings the Miss Buxtons had provided refreshments to be served in the porch as was customary. Sir John had donated game pies and rich fruit cake, on which the poorer families feasted gratefully, but it was noticed that the two Mrs Siggerys ate nothing and left without exchanging a word with anybody.

Elizabeth's mind had reeled away from the horror of William's death. She could not and would not accept the unbelievable calamity that had fallen upon her, the fact that she would never see her beloved husband again. She took refuge in her memories, especially of April and May the previous year when they had declared their mutual love: a love he had kept hidden for years. In her memory she walked again with William on those beautiful spring and summer evenings. She lived again those first kisses, those whispered promises that had seemed like a dream, but a dream which had come to pass in truth.

'I couldn't believe it then, Papa, and I can't believe it now,' she said to her father on one of his daily visits.

'My dear child, you can't live for ever in the past,' he said gently, saddened by her flat, toneless voice. 'Remember the words of the Burial Service, taken from the Book of Job, a man of many sorrows. "The Lord gave, and the Lord hath taken away." You must give thanks for that precious time you spent together and—'

'Don't talk to me of the Lord, Papa, for I can't accept that He has taken Will away. I question whether there is in fact a God or, if there is, how He could be so cruel.'

'My dearest Lizzie,' her father said, sighing, for he had heard such words before from the lately bereaved. He knew that it was useless to argue with grief, but he needed to try to point out what still remained in life.

'My dearest Lizzie, you have your son, my grandson Andrew. He needs you as much as ever – more than ever before.'

'I know, Papa, but I fear I have nothing to give him in place of his father – and such a father! I have nothing to put in his place.'

'Hush, my child, you have your love to give him, the greatest gift a parent can offer.'

She fell silent and he decided to talk of practical matters.

'You know that you and Andrew are welcome to come back home to your mother and me, my dear, and the life you lived before your marriage.'

Slowly and sorrowfully she shook her head. 'No, Papa, I couldn't go back to the life I lived then. I shall stay here in my own home with Andrew.'

'Will Mary – will Mrs Siggery come back to live with you?' he enquired.

'I don't know, Papa,' she answered wearily. 'She seems to be settled with her sister at Flaxford and enjoys her work at the manor. I don't think she would care to go back to Oak Hall.'

He noticed that she had difficulty in pronouncing the very name of de Boville and so he decided to put forward another suggestion.

'But you cannot live here alone, my dear. If William's mother decides not to return, I shall send Jenny Tasker to be a companion for you and Andrew. She is a sensible, good-hearted girl.' It would be good for Andrew, he added silently to himself, for he feared that the boy would suffer if his mother fell into melancholy.

'It will be as you please, Papa,' she said, without any obvious interest.

'Er – mention of the de Bovilles brings me to another matter, Lizzie,' he continued, uncertain as to what her reaction might be. 'Sir John has been to see me, to talk about Andrew's future.'

She looked up quickly and answered in a much sharper tone. 'If the de Bovilles have got their eyes on Andrew, they can think again, for they shall not have him.'

'No, no, my dear, that's not what he said. Please listen to me, for we must be practical. He wishes to help you by paying a regular sum of money for the boy's needs.'

'William never wanted the de Boville's money and neither do I, Papa!'

'But if that allowance was paid to *me*, Lizzie, to give you as the need arose or to be saved for Andrew's future – wouldn't that be acceptable?' He did not repeat Sir John's actual words. *'Richard and I are determined that Mrs Siggery and the boy shall want for nothing.'*

'I suppose so, Papa – only it would have to come through you. I couldn't receive money from their hands.'

'Very well, my child, we will leave it at that.' He sighed heavily. 'You must know that Sir John and his son are filled with regret over the tragic accident.'

'Oh, enough of the de Bovilles and their regrets, Papa,' she said impatiently. 'The next time a de Boville talks to you of regret, you may assure him that I am thankful for the deception, for it led me to a far better man – one whose bootlaces they were not fit to tie up! Pray speak to me no more of them!'

'As you wish, Lizzie.' Pond was pleased to see a flash of her former spirit, but judged it not the right time to mention the father and grandfather's wish to take Andrew for tea at Oak Hall, one afternoon in each month.

Elizabeth spoke frankly to her mother-in-law. 'If you would prefer to stay here with Andrew and me at the cottage and see your grandson every day you would be very welcome,' she said. 'But if you would rather live with your sister-in-law and continue to work at Flaxford Manor with her, I will understand. My father has offered the housemaid Jenny Tasker to come and keep us company here if you'd rather live at Flaxford. Whatever you choose will content me.'

Mary Siggery burst into tears and put her arms around her daughter-in-law. 'Dear Lizzie,' she sobbed. ''Twill be a sacrifice for Mr Pond to part with that good girl, but I'll accept his offer, dear. I'd be mournful in this cottage where I lived so long with Billy. Jenny'll be a ray o' sunshine, though your mother'll have somethin' to say, I don't doubt!'

To the parson's satisfaction it was decided, if not to his wife's, who'd begun to discover all sorts of virtues in Jenny to which she had previously been blind. Jenny herself was delighted and Elizabeth had to admit that her mother-in-law had been right about Jenny bringing sunshine with her. Andrew benefited by her willingness to play games with him and take him for walks when his mother was tired and low-spirited. She seemed unable to rouse herself to take an interest in anything. Parson Pond told Jenny that was not to be wondered at in the sad circumstances.

'But 'ow long is she goin' to take to come back to the land o' the livin', Mr Pond?' asked the maid with a worried look.

She had tried to get Elizabeth to confide in her, to talk about William, but the young widow fended off her questions.

'We must give her time, Jenny, it's early days yet,' replied the parson, which did not altogether satisfy the sharp-eyed girl. She frowned and privately muttered to herself that there might not be as much time as the good man reckoned.

'I'm deeply grateful to you, Jenny, for your kindness to my poor girl,' he said. Although he sorely missed the girl's cheerful presence at home, he gladly gave her up for the sake of Elizabeth and Andrew.

Sir John was as good as his word, and entrusted the parson with a generous monthly allowance for Andrew when the need arose. Nothing had been said about Andrew visiting Oak Hall and there came a day towards the end of May when Richard accompanied his father to the Ponds' home, where they were shown into the small parlour by a new, sulky-looking maid.

'Yer got two gen'lemen visitin' from Oak 'All, Parson!' she shouted out of the window to Pond who was hoeing in the vegetable garden. Mrs Pond winced at the voice.

'Good morning to you, Pond,' said Sir John. 'To come straight to the point, Richard and I would like to come to a definite arrangement to see our . . . to see Andrew from time to time. There seems to be no good reason for not allowing this.'

Herbert Pond looked at the two men; he noted Richard's troubled eyes. While he felt some sympathy because of these two men's blood relationship to the boy, Elizabeth's unhappiness was uppermost in his mind.

'At present my daughter is still suffering melancholy and weakness,' he replied, 'and I do not want her to be upset further. God knows she has grief enough to bear.'

While Sir John was considering how best to reply, Richard broke in. 'We understand how she . . . how you feel about your daughter, Mr Pond. If she only knew how much I want to help her and my son. I want to compensate.'

'Mere money is no compensation for a loss such as hers,' snapped Pond. ''Tis the love of a good husband that she misses.'

'But I have loved her and love her still. I always shall!'

cried Richard, not able to contain himself longer. 'I'd protect her, I'd do anything for her if she'd only grant me a few words and let me see my son.'

Sir John and Parson Pond exchanged a startled glance at this outburst. Pond wondered how best to react to it; he did not want to refuse absolutely to grant Richard's request.

'My daughter has no great love for your family,' he began bluntly.

'And I certainly do not blame her for that,' said Richard. 'But if you would only give me a chance to explain to her how I too have suffered, Mr Pond, then if she refused to hear me out, I would not trouble her again. Only let me speak once to her, I beg you.'

There was silence for a moment before Herbert Pond replied. 'I'm afraid it isn't in my power to grant you such a meeting, Mr de Boville. I can only say –' he hesitated and went on – 'that my daughter's close friend Mrs Lennox usually drives over to the cottage on Wednesday afternoons, and if you could engage *her* sympathy she might use her influence in a way that I cannot do. In other words, you may ask Meg Venn, daughter of the man you so ill-used, Sir John, and drove from his patch of common land. You may ask Meg if she will consent to be a go-between. And now, gentlemen, I have visits to make and parish business to attend to. I wish you good morning.'

'By God, Pond has got the upper hand over us now, Richard!' exclaimed Sir John when they were out in the lane. 'No other man, clergyman or not, would dare to speak to me in that fashion!'

'The thing about Pond, Father, is that he is a man of integrity. He only sees himself answerable to God,' said Richard. 'He won't compromise his principles, either through fear or for favours.'

'That's all very fine, Richard, but he takes my money willingly enough.'

'But not for himself, Father. He won't be bribed by it. He has dropped me a hint and I shall follow it.'

'You mean Mrs Lennox?'

'Yes, Father. I will endeavour to get her cooperation if I can. And I must do it alone, Father, and succeed or fail.'

There was a finality in his words that forbade further

comments or questions. Sir John was left to wonder what on earth Lady de Boville would say if she knew that Richard was to beg a favour of the girl who had once been Meg Venn.

Richard at first decided to ride up to the Common the following Wednesday and waylay Mrs Lennox on her way to the Siggery cottage. But which route would she take? he wondered. If she rode her pony she would come across the Common, but if she drove her pony trap she would have to come by the winding lane between Flaxford and Wollaston. How could he know what she would do? He could be left dawdling around on the Common if she came by the lane, or vice versa if she came by the Common. In the end he decided to ride over to Flaxford at midday and do his dawdling near to the manor, so as to waylay Mrs Lennox as she left.

On Wednesday Richard rode over to Flaxford and tethered his horse behind a coppice of young elms and alder bushes. He then settled himself to spy on the house. But to his dismay he had been seen.

'Hello there, Richard! What a pleasant surprise!' said Charles Lennox. 'I've spent the morning inspecting all the gates and fences on the estate for I'm determined to prove myself a farmer! Are you going on to the village or can you stay here for an hour or so? My wife goes over to Wollaston on Wednesdays to visit her poor friend –' a shadow passed over Charles's face as he uttered the words – 'so if you have a mind to look over the estate, I'd be glad of any advice you can give me.'

Here was a quandary: having just ridden over from Wollaston, Richard could hardly say he needed to go back straight away and if he stayed for an hour or two, he would have little or no opportunity to speak to Mrs Lennox alone. He had more or less decided to give up the idea of talking with her on this occasion, but fate played into his hands. As soon as she saw him, Mrs Lennox herself suggested that he should ride back with her to Wollaston. With engaging frankness she said that she wanted to consult him on a matter concerning Mrs Siggery and her child. Richard glanced at Charles to see how he responded to this and saw it met with willing consent.

'Meg has been fretting about Elizabeth for some time, Richard, and has actually talked of approaching you about her. Now that a happy chance has sent you here today, I shall have to postpone our exploration of the farm for another time. It's a splendid day for riding over the Common, and Meg may talk with you as much as she pleases!'

Richard smiled his gratitude and let them go on believing in the happy chance, though it was with some apprehension that he set out with Mrs Lennox. As soon as they were out of the lane and approaching the Common, she suggested that they dismount and walk with their steeds, the better to talk easily.

'Now, then, Richard de Boville, d'you recall where you first met me?'

'It was . . . it was at your mother's funeral, Mrs Lennox,' he said uneasily, for it was on that occasion that Zack Venn attacked him at the lychgate. 'You were there, and Elizabeth was trying to comfort you, and then . . .' He stopped speaking for sheer embarrassment.

'Yes, Richard, my poor father tried to throttle you. His mind was already becoming unhinged through poverty and hardship – but let us leave that for now. Can you remember when we next met and exchanged a few words?'

'It was at that coaching inn at Ipswich, wasn't it?'

'Yes, I was a serving maid at the Sun in St Stephen's Street, and you and your sister were at table. You recognized me, and asked if I knew how Lizzie was. You were so anxious for news of her and I couldn't help you because I'd lost touch with her. Your sister got quite cross with you for talking to me!'

'Ah, yes, poor Frederica,' he said with a sigh. 'But I remember you well, Meg – er, Mrs Lennox. We were interrupted by—'

'By my father attempting to kill yours, Mr de Boville. Happily he did not succeed, but in spite of all the trouble my poor pa and I were going through at that time, I remember thinking to myself, "Now there's a man in love."'

'And you were right, Meg, I was in love with Elizabeth Pond, but my parents had sent me away to London to forget her – I was but seventeen – and deceived me into thinking that she had taken up again with . . . with another. If I'd only known –! Oh, Meg, if I'd known that she was with child! I'll never forgive my mother and father for that, never! Through it I lost both wife and son!'

He stopped, overcome by emotion. Meg said nothing, her face gravely sympathetic as she waited for him to go on; their two horses appeared to be waiting also. Richard wiped his eyes.

Meg said softly, 'That was five years ago, Richard. Since then Lizzie has had a child – your child – and married the best of men, but now she's a widow. I lost my poor father who died in an insane asylum, but I've been sent a good husband, and been reunited with my brothers.'

'And I have been to America and back to fight in a stupid war – and I returned to find the girl I loved married to another. But I haven't been able to love any other woman – I've not even considered it.'

'Not even Miss Mulholland?' asked Meg, a mischievous little gleam in her dark eyes.

'Oh, hang Miss Mulholland,' he said irritably, and then recollected himself. 'I'm sorry, I shouldn't have said that, I only meant—'

He stopped when he saw that Meg was laughing at his brusque dismissal of the young lady.

'Come, Richard, you have told me a great deal, and most of it is what I wanted to hear. Come with me now to the Siggery cottage, and I will speak for you to my friend, for 'tis only fair and right that you should see your son and that he should see you. He needs the benefit of a father's love as well as his money. Will you come to the cottage with me?'

'I cannot refuse, Meg – but will she order me out? Her father says she is melancholy,' he said, though his heart leaped at the thought of seeing Elizabeth again.

'Even if she does order you out – which I don't think she will with me there – I shan't give up hope, Richard,' Meg replied with conviction. 'These situations need only time, and we have plenty of time ahead of us yet.'

They remounted their steeds, and when the cottage came into view Meg dismounted and tethered her pony to the iron ring set in the wall; Richard did likewise.

'Come, Richard, let us go in.'

So with love and hope and also fear, Richard de Boville followed Meg Lennox into the little living room where Elizabeth sat sewing, Jenny Tasker stood ironing and Andrew was playing on the carpet with his alphabet bricks.

'Lizzie *dear!*' exclaimed Meg with a beaming smile. 'I declare you're looking better today. And just *see* who I met on the Common!'

Elizabeth put her hand to her mouth and stared at the man who faced her with such emotion in his eyes – and who held out his hand to her. She took it, only to draw it back again when he would have raised it to his lips.

Meg spoke quickly. 'Lizzie, I have promised to put this man's case before you, and plead like a lawyer for him. And any lawyer would say that – well, you know, that Andrew should see and know his own father.'

Hearing this word, Andrew looked up, his eyes wide. 'Farver?' he repeated uncertainly. 'I had a papa, but he died, with Ladyfox. Are *you* a farver?'

Richard went down on his knees to be on a level with the child. 'I am *your* father, Andrew,' he said. 'You had a very good papa who loved and looked after you and your mother while I was away. But now I've come back to love you and look after you. Oh, come to me, Andrew!'

He and Meg and Jenny were silent and completely still, hardly daring to breathe until Andrew gave his answer. Everything seemed to depend on the child's reception of this declaration. The little boy stared hard at Richard, then said solemnly, 'Good day to you, Farver. How do you do?' And was gathered into Richard's arms.

Meg and Jenny exchanged a look, and each saw that the other had tears in her eyes. Meg cleared her throat.

'Now, Lizzie, I have promised to speak for Richard so you must listen,' she said, but Richard interrupted her.

'*No*, Meg, I must speak for myself, for it's about time. Elizabeth, you have to know, in front of these witnesses, that I have loved you for five years. I did not know about Andrew until I returned from America, when I found you married to a good man who cared for my son as if he was his own. I shall always be grateful to him for that – no, Elizabeth, hear me out, I implore you! I love you still, and always shall, and I offer you my hand and my heart, for it has been yours since I first set eyes on you outside St Bede's.'

Elizabeth had risen from her chair, but now sat down again. Richard remained kneeling on the carpet, his left arm around Andrew. He held his right hand out to her.

'Speak to me, dear Elizabeth, and give me leave to hope. Answer me.'

Elizabeth gave him a long and intent look, as if trying to see into his soul. The others waited, and Jenny sent up a silent prayer.

Elizabeth finally spoke. 'If you're asking me to marry you, Richard de Boville, it is only right that I should warn you of what your commitment would be,' she told him without smiling. 'As you have said, William Siggery looked after your son as if he'd been his own. He could not have had a better father. And if you marry me, Richard, you'll be taking on *his* child in the same way.'

Meg's jaw dropped open. '*His* child?' she gasped.

Jenny nodded frantically, laying a finger on her lips.

'Yes, I'm carrying Will's child,' said Elizabeth. 'At first I thought 'twas the shock of his death that caused my body to stop its natural course, but now I know that William has blessed me with his child. What do you say to *that*, Richard de Boville?'

For answer, Richard stood up, and still holding Andrew by the hand, he made a solemn avowal before them all.

'My dear Elizabeth, if you will accept me, I promise to love you and care for you as your husband. And I also promise to look after William's child as if it were my own, just as he cared for Andrew.'

'But will your parents accept me?' Elizabeth asked. 'And William's child?'

'I know my father and Georgina and Edward will, and as for my mother, if she wants the best for me, she too will accept you as my chosen wife. What the rest of the world thinks or says is of no importance to me. Dearest Elizabeth, take me and make me the happiest man on earth.'

And she, seeing that he was as open and honest as William Siggery had always been, silently gave him her hand and let him raise it to his lips.

'Thank the Lord for that!' exclaimed Jenny Tasker happily. 'She's come back to the land o' the livin'!'

'And we'll have a wedding before the summer's out!' cried Meg.

'The sooner the better!' said Jenny with a wink.

Epilogue
Changes Ahead

July 1786

L ady de Boville's funeral at St Bede's had been a subdued
affair, with only family members attending; Sir John, who
had noticeably aged in recent years, followed the coffin,
flanked on either side by his sons, Richard and Edward, the
latter in his army officer cadet's uniform. Mr and Mrs Felix
Wilborough followed, having left their little daughter Clarissa
at home in Beccles. Elizabeth de Boville walked with the
squire and Mrs Horrocks, followed by Mr and Mrs Adam
Horrocks. A few faithful family retainers brought up the rear
as Dr Webb, the rector, assisted by Parson Pond, led them to
the graveside. Dr Webb had judged that he should make the
journey from Ipswich to Wollaston for the obsequies of Lady
de Boville, which may have explained why the parishioners
stayed away, the rector being as unfamiliar to them as Lady
de Boville had become, shutting herself away in Oak Hall,
refusing to visit or receive visitors. She had never recovered
from the shock of Frederica's death, coming so soon after the
death of her own mother at Diss. After hearing of Frederica's
illness Sir John had at once journeyed to London, intending
to bring her home; but he had found her at the point of death
in a charity hospital, having contracted a fatal disease which
he described to his wife as a putrid fever. He had been the
sole mourner at her funeral in Marylebone and returned to
Wollaston where his chief consolation was his adored grand-
children. Andrew was now eight, he would be going away
to school next year, and little Mary would be four in
December; another baby was expected in October, in just
three months.

Sir John planned a handsome brass memorial plaque to be set up on the south wall of St Bede's, with a weeping stone angel on each side.

'I'll leave enough space for you to put my name underneath, Richard,' he said with a sigh. 'It won't be as much remarked on as the headstone you put up over the grave of young Siggery and his father. Many's the time I've seen visitors stop to read the inscription, though they must think it strange.'

Richard smiled. 'I owed him that much, Father.'

Two days after the funeral Sir John came to a decision. 'I've been thinking about you and Elizabeth in that cottage, with two children, soon to be three, and I've decided that you should move into Oak Hall, and I'll move out to the estate cottage. You might as well start learning to be Sir Richard.'

Since Richard had given up hunting and taken to horse racing with notable success at Newmarket, Sir John had given up as master of the Wollaston Hunt, though he occasionally rode on his remaining favourite hunter.

Richard saw no reason to disagree with his father. The idea appealed to him, though he was not sure how Elizabeth would take it.

'*Richard!* Oak Hall is so big, and with all those rooms and so many servants, I shan't know what to do!' she cried in dismay.

'You'll be just as capable as you are now, Lizzie my love,' he assured her, smiling. 'My mother didn't do much in recent years, but you'll bring the old place to life again, especially when our third child is born. You'll have an excellent house-keeper to instruct you in your duties. Life will be much better for us and the children, you'll see!'

Elizabeth was far from reassured at the prospect of this big change. She had enjoyed the domesticity of the well-appointed cottage on the estate – the same cottage that had been offered to William Siggery and declined – and being with child again, she did not welcome such an upheaval so soon.

At her earliest opportunity she confided in her friend Mrs Lennox.

'I'm just not ready to be mistress of Oak Hall, Meg! And I shall have to be hostess when Richard comes home from Newmarket with his friends! I'll just feel like the parson's daughter all over again!'

'And what's wrong with that?' asked the mistress of Flaxford Manor, mother of two lively little boys. 'If I can manage with a houseful of servants and a nursemaid, I'm sure that you can do just as well. And think of all the good you'll be able to do for the Oak Hall tenants.'

Elizabeth knew that the future Viscountess Lennox was very much liked, even revered in Flaxford, a poor parish with the gloomy House of Industry. Meg knew all the cottagers by name and gave tea parties at the manor for the orphaned and deserted children from the House and summer picnics for them in the fields. Elizabeth could not help comparing her deeds with Lady de Boville's superior attitude to their tenants in the past. Charles Lennox encouraged his wife in good works; he only kept working horses and was involved in trying out the latest methods of agriculture.

'I'm sure the outdoor servants take unfair advantage of his easy-going ways!' Meg said, laughing. 'But he looks upon himself as a farmer and a countryman and is as happy as a lark!'

Elizabeth began to be persuaded. She thought of her father and his endless parish visiting; she would look upon her new duties as a challenge and give them her best.

'What does Mary think?' asked Meg, smiling at the little girl who had accompanied her mother. Mary, named for her grandmother Siggery, was a happy child, beloved by both her grandfathers, who loved to listen to her merry prattle.

'Yes, we'll do it, won't we, Mary?' said her mother, and on an impulse picked up the child and looked into her little face. Her wide eyes and sweet rosy mouth that always brought back to mind a wise and honest man, a man whom the people of Wollaston in their blindness had once called Silly Billy Siggery.